zombies in CONTEMPORARY CULTURE

HORROR STUDIES

Preface

Horror Studies is the first book series exclusively dedicated to the study of the genre in its various manifestations – from fiction to cinema and television, magazines to comics, and extending to other forms of narrative texts such as video games and music. Horror Studies aims to raise the profile of Horror and to further its academic institutionalisation by providing a publishing home for cutting-edge research. As an exciting new venture within the established Cultural Studies and Literary Criticism programme, Horror Studies will expand the field in innovative and student-friendly ways.

Zombies in CONTEMPORARY CULTURE

JOURNEYS, BODIES, PANDEMICS AND POLITICS

EDITED BY LINDA FLORES, EMMA TONKIN
AND CONOR HEFFERNAN

UNIVERSITY OF WALES PRESS
2025

www.uwp.co.uk

British Library Cataloguing-in-Publication Data

A catalogue record for this book is available from the British Library.

ISBN 978-1-83772-303-4
eISBN 978-1-83772-304-1

For GPSR enquiries please contact:
Easy Access System Europe Oü, 16879218
Mustamäe tee 50, 10621, Tallinn, Estonia.
gpsr.requests@easproject.com

Typeset by Chris Bell, cbdesign

MIX
Paper | Supporting responsible forestry
FSC® C013604

Printed and bound by CPI Group (UK) Ltd, Croydon, CR0 4YY

Contents

Abstract

IN THE WAKE of a global pandemic and political upheaval, *Zombies in Contemporary Culture: Journeys, Bodies, Pandemics and Politics* offers a timely and innovative exploration of the zombie figure in contemporary culture. This interdisciplinary collection examines zombies through three key lenses: the materiality of the zombie body; the COVID-19 pandemic; and the recent political shifts. Drawing together an international group of scholars, the volume provides fresh insights on topics ranging from zombie sex toys to suburban zombies, from pandemic trauma to race and class tensions in French zombie cinema. Several chapters engage directly with how zombies reflect anxieties surrounding the coronavirus pandemic and its societal impacts. Others explore how zombie narratives intersect with current political concerns, including rising extremism and geopolitical shifts. By applying the framework of *zombiism* to analyse contemporary issues, this collection demonstrates the continuing relevance of the zombie as a cultural metaphor. It offers new perspectives on how zombies embody current fears about contagion, social breakdown and loss of individual agency, while revealing how zombie narratives can be used to work through trauma, reimagine social structures and explore alternative modes of being. This timely volume provides both a state-of-the-field overview and a roadmap for future directions in zombie studies.

Particular chapters contain material that some readers may find sensitive or potentially offensive. This content is included for critical and scholarly purposes and reflects the subject matter under discussion; reader discretion is advised.

List of Contributors

Conor Heffernan is lecturer in the sociology of sport at Ulster University. His primary research interest is the history and sociology of health, fitness and gym cultures. Somehow, Conor marries his study of the living and muscular body with those of the dead and decaying zombie. Conor is still unsure why this is.

Emma Tonkin is a research fellow in digital health at the University of Bristol. Her work spans information science, digital humanities and health technologies.

Linda Flores Ohlson works as an assistant professor of Spanish linguistics at the University of Gothenburg. She has conducted research on Spanish-English codeswitching in music lyrics and on how zombies are pronominalised and why. She has recently been working on a book project about the Spanish language in the Nordic countries. She is also the creator and host of a Spanish language true crime podcast, *Entre tinieblas nórdicas*, that takes on cases from the Nordic countries.

Scott Eric Hamilton is an English lecturer at California Polytechnic State University (Cal Poly), San Luis Obispo, California. He co-founded the Zombie Studies Network and Theorizing Zombiism conference series. He has published on zombiism and Irish literature and co-edited several volumes of collected essays in these fields, including on the Irish authors Samuel Beckett and Flann O'Brien and the first volume from the inaugural Theorizing Zombiism conference. His current research project is examining how the zombie functions in various medias and the public sphere as a monster of the era of neoliberalism.

Robert Curran earned his master's degree in English at Florida Atlantic University and is currently a PhD candidate at Florida State University. His love for horror began at a young age after watching *Night of the Living Dead* for the first time. Little did his family know that this viewing would spark a lifelong obsession with all things horror. Robert has taught zombie-film classes for several years and is currently writing his dissertation on the protean nature of the zombie. One of Robert's pastimes is alcohol-friendly ghost hunting at spooky locals. To date, he has not found anything except for a good time.

Caroline West is a sexual violence and harassment prevention and response manager based in Cork, Ireland. In 2020, She completed her PhD at Dublin City University on the experiences of women working in the American pornography industry. Her thesis also looked at stigma, violence and feminist discourses on pornography. In addition, she holds an MA in sexuality studies. Caroline is the host of the Glow West podcast, which focuses on sexual wellness, and she is also a relationship columnist with the Irish Independent. She has spent over two decades working and volunteering in social care and has been a media commentator about consent, pornography, feminism and sexual wellness since 2016. Caroline is interested in the relationship between sex, power and knowledge, as well as the weird and wonderful world of sex.

En-Chi Chiou is an academic examining posthumanism and transhumanism in zombie narratives.

Addy Berry is a senior research fellow at the University of Huddersfield. They are an avid horror fan whose research interests focus on intersex, transgender, sex work, health care, mental health care, gerontology and epistemic injustice. Addy teaches art classes to the intersex community internationally and regularly speaks about their research interests at conferences and elsewhere. Like Bram Stoker, Addy has debated at the Trinity College Historical Society. Their intersex illustrations have been included in *Mercury Rising* in the Berlin Schwulesmuseum's first ever intersex-themed art show and their poetry has been included in *Pride in Print* by the Small Trans Library at Smock Alley Theatre, Dublin. Addy hopes to one day follow in the footsteps of fellow Dubliners Joseph Sheridan Le Fanu and Bram Stoker by writing a vampire novel before they die. If not, they'll come back as a zombie and write it.

Violeta Alarcón Zayas holds a PhD in audiovisual communication. She is a research fellow at the Universidad a Distancia de Madrid. She teaches in the fields of communication and philosophy and is part of the research group Communicational, Audiovisual and Artistic Narratives in the Digital Society. Violeta has multiple publications in indexed journals in the areas of communication, film, gender studies and cultural studies. Her research focuses on discursive analysis of hegemonic and counter-hegemonic narratives through verbal-visual texts. Her interests include the grotesque, the monstrous, humour, the fantastic, sexuality, sexual dissidence, female representation in literature and film, horror, queer cinema and theory and feminist art and performance. Her passion for the dark and the fantastic fuels her work as a performer and actress, where she explores themes of monstrosity, the construction of identity and the subversion of gender norms.

Catherine Pugh completed her PhD at the University of Essex, and is now a writer and independent scholar. Primarily writing about horror and science fiction across theatre and screen media, her research interests concern disability, mental illness, animals, metamorphic monsters and horror landscapes. She has contributed to various collections including: American Horror Story *and Cult Television*; *Female Identity in Contemporary Fictional Purgatorial Worlds*; and *The Undead in the 21st Century: A Companion*, as well as online journals including *Studies in Gothic Fiction*, *Cinergie Il Cinema E Le Altre Arti* and the *Journal for Cultural Research*.

Madeline Becker is a senior lecturer at the cultural studies department at Rostock University. She studied English and American culture and literature at Magdeburg University and Bath Spa University. Her dissertation, which she defended in June 2024, provides a critical study of how nature documentaries mediate environmental crises and their particular materialities. Her research and publications focus on post-apocalyptic literature, film, video games, fungal zombies and reproductive technologies, all examined within the broader context of anthropogenic environmental crises and their challenges.

Hossein Mohammadzade began his academic research in game studies with the thesis for his master's degree in English language and literature at the University of Guilan. Since graduation, he has been an independent researcher studying video games, zombies, television, education and the representations of scientific research in the media. His main area of interest is the relationship between ideology, narrative and video games.

Grace Jung is the author of *K-Drama School: A Pop Culture Inquiry into Why We Love Korean Television*, published by Running Press/Hachette Book Group. She earned her PhD in cinema and media studies from the University of California, Los Angeles and is a former Fulbright scholar. Grace's academic publications appear in *Media, Culture & Society*, *New Review of Film and Television Studies*, *Jump Cut: A Review of Contemporary Media* and *Acta Koreana*. She is also featured in NPR, *Time* and *Literary Hub*. She is a visiting assistant professor of Korean studies at the University of Wisconsin-Madison, where she teaches Korean TV, film and literature.

Rodrigo Gonsalves is a practising psychoanalyst, teacher, writer and translator. Having graduated in philosophy and psychology, he recently earned his PhD in philosophy, critical theory and the arts at the European Graduate School, and is currently a PhD candidate in clinical psychology at the University of São Paulo. Rodrigo is author of *Monstrosity and the Psychoanalytic Dimensions of the Uncanny* (unpublished, Routledge). He has co-edited the books *Essays on the Undead: A Critical Review* (2018) and *Essays on Vampires and Zombies: Psychoanalysis, Philosophy and the Arts* (2021). He also authored numerous chapters and articles about Lacanian psychoanalysis and new directions in Marxist theory. He is currently a researcher for Latesfip (the Interdepartamental Laboratory of Social Theory, Philosophy and Psychoanalysis/USP) and a member of SIPP-ISPP (the International Society of Psychoanalysis and Philosophy). Rodrigo is a member of the editorial committee of Jacobin Brazil and an editor-member for the publisher Lavra Palavra.

Reece Goodall is a director of student experience at the University of Warwick, where he completed a PhD thesis comprising an industrial and theoretical analysis of contemporary French horror cinema. His research interests include horror and other genres in French cinema, film music and the interplay between media, news and politics. He has previously written for *French Screen Studies*, *Horror Studies* and *Animation Studies*.

1

Introduction: Theorising Zombiism

Conor Heffernan, Linda Flores and Emma Tonkin

LIKE MANY OTHER works conceptualised during the COVID-19 pandemic, this is a work intimately related to death, pandemics and political breakdowns, not to mention travel and the ability to restrict travel. In that sense, this is a work reflective of a unique moment in modern history, hopefully one never to be repeated. What differentiates this work from others is, of course, the subject matter. Wary of the dangers in being too direct, or indeed, blunt, zombies appeared to be well positioned when it came to explaining the COVID-19 phenomenon. The idea of virality in popular culture was used with reference to zombie outbreaks, anti-mask and anti-vaccine campaigners used zombie memes and lore to make their arguments and many 'zombie' institutions were critiqued for their inaction. Likewise, scenes from zombie films and television shows of emptied streets and quarantined cities now suddenly seemed to echo modern life. *Zombies in Contemporary Culture: Journeys, Bodies, Pandemics and Politics*, however, is a collection about far more than a multi-year pandemic that many would prefer to forget. Instead, this collection is simultaneously a call to arms and an example of how meaningful zombie work can be conducted. It is both a companion piece and a distinct split from the previous *Theorising the Contemporary Zombie* volume published in 2022.[1]

Since then, zombies have continued to proliferate in popular culture, with some astute commentators now noting that we are at risk of over-exposure to zombies. It is telling that what was once an object of abject terror has now been transformed into something that appears in romantic novels, children's cartoons and collectible toys.

How then should we treat the zombie at a high moment in zombie pop culture? While excellent research has been conducted on the Disneyfication of the undead, this volume approaches a more Romeroesque approach; that is, to refer to the doyen of zombie film, George Romero, who insightfully noted that his movies did not point the finger at zombies, but rather at humans – how they react, fail to react, or react stupidly. The zombies themselves, Romero attempted to treat with respect and sympathy. And so too does this volume focus on humans as opposed to zombies. The previous volume offered the term *zombiism* to add a theoretical impetus to the study of zombies. In effect, zombiism as a theory seeks to understand how zombies are both a reflection of, and contributor to, broader social anxieties and issues. To understand the zombie phenomenon, it is thus not enough to explain how zombies reflect social anxieties, it is pivotal to explore how zombies contribute to these anxieties themselves. In this collection the authors have stressed the social impact of the zombie in discourses, as well as the symbolism of the zombie figure. This approach adds a nuance and richness to the study of the undead.

The field of zombie studies, mimicking its subjects, continues to grow unopposed. Multiple readers exist, for student, scholar and fan alike. New zombie media has cast a critical lens of racial, gendered and political fissures that have lay dormant for far too long. Most importantly, the zombie remains one of the most obvious, yet unappreciated, interdisciplinary areas in academia. Intellectually our collection owes a great debt to previous handbooks produced by Sarah Juliet Lauro, Laura Hubner, Marcus Leaning, Paul Manning and Murali Balaji among others.[2] Likewise, monographs by Kyle William Bishop, Aaron Clayton, Steven Kirsh, T. May Stone, Gary Rhodes and countless others have inspired and pushed this field, and by default this collection, to new depths.[3] A common occurrence for many 'outsiders' to this field is the surprise at the scholarly depth and rigour accompanying zombie studies. As the above names and others have shown, zombies are not only a serious topic, but a vital one in dealing with some of the most pressing issues in the humanities and beyond.

Zombies have been used by both those in the humanities and the sciences as a useful category of analysis. The background to this collection is testament to that. In 2019 University College Dublin hosted the inaugural Theorising Zombiism conference, which sought to bring together those studying the undead under the auspices of the zombie research network. Since that time, two more conferences have been hosted, the latter during Europe's largest Halloween festival in Derry, Northern Ireland. What has become clear is that the undead have never been more lively. What then does the current collection provide in an admittedly rich field? Owing to the moment in history when this collection was envisioned, travel, pandemics and politics have taken our sole attention. Outside of the obvious, the reasons for this are twofold.

First, the collection introduces new voices and approaches into the field of zombie studies. Zombie media continues to proliferate, so too does the ability to use the zombie as metaphor and allegory in new and exciting ways. Thus, attention is given to currently existing areas such as ecology, pornography, pandemics and materiality, as well as recent zombie books and film. The introduction of new voices, and in some instances, relatively unresearched disciplines, provides a critical platform for future works. Here you will find true interdisciplinarity as scholars from different fields come together to tackle the undead. Second, the collection provides new insight into how the zombie figure can be understood in the aftermath of the COVID-19 pandemic, the rise of far-right politics in the West and the growing importance of race and 'culture wars' in zombie media. Even during the COVID-19 pandemic, the zombie was being deployed in a political context by opposing sides. This collection offers the opportunity to take stock of where we are as a field and, even more importantly, where the study of the undead should explore. Our hope is that this collection enlivens in readers the same tenacity for knowledge as the undead have for us. It is the diversity of this volume that we believe is its success.

Structure

Our collection is divided across four distinct but, nevertheless, interrelated strands: journeys; bodies; pandemics; and politics. Beginning with journeys, the collection opens with Emma Tonkin's study of place and space in zombie literature. Studying a wide variety of settings from city to countryside, fields of war, oil rigs and even outer space, Tonkin challenges the idea of zombie literature as derivative of other better-known works, and in doing so examines the author's deeper meanings of place. As Tonkin's makes clear, localised journeys, although they may present familiar thematic elements and plot beats, may also contain an afterlife of their own: illustrating elements of the author's world and experience to the reader. Regardless of the often-familiar nature of the destination, the reader may enjoy the glimpses into other worlds afforded by the journey.

Whereas Tonkin studies zombie journeys and literature from a macro perspective, Scott Hamilton's chapter focuses solely on hit AMC television show *Fear the Walking Dead*. Studying the drive for power and privilege among the show's protagonists, Hamilton explores the show's backdrop from Los Angeles to Mexico and back again to the United States. In this way, the places that characters flee to or traverse are not mere stage pieces, but rather physical manifestations of broader cultural debates concerning immigration, border violence and exclusion. Furthermore, through a study of elitism within American society, and the show itself, Hamilton plays with ideas of race and class as crucial settings for zombie lore. Tonkin and Hamilton both explore the thematic elements within the zombie genre but where Tonkin's chapter delves into the literary aspects, emphasising the use of place and space in zombie narratives, Hamilton's chapter examines the sociopolitical critique embedded within place and space. While Tonkin discusses the journey aspect of zombie narratives, Hamilton explores the implications of elitism and privilege through the lens of movements.

Furthering this focus is Robert Curran's study of media in George R. Romero's early zombie movies. Critically, Curran examines Romero's commentary on humanity's overreliance on media such as television and radio. Such media serve to offer both despair and chaos for zombie survivors. Much like the present age, these devices serve to bring individuals closer together, linking disparate communities in a time of great upheaval. The fight for who controls these devices is, however, rarely peaceful. Romero's films emphasise the limitations of media and warn against excessive dependence on it lest we forget the reality of our current situations. Curran's analysis prompts reflection on the potential consequences of our reliance on media in contemporary society.

Moving from place to persons, Caroline West explores a unique and provocative aspect of the zombie genre: zombie sex toys. West notes that while zombies are generally depicted as asexual in mainstream media, there has been a recent rise in the popularity of sex toys designed to resemble zombie genitalia. West delves into the phenomenon of these toys and their role in exploring abject sexuality, where disgust becomes a source of arousal rather than repulsion. The chapter questions how the acceptance of decay and putrescence as desirable attributes in these sex toys influences our understanding of taboo sex, necrophilia and desire. West connects this intersection of horror and pleasure with broader discussions of zombiism and its relevance to sexual borders.

En-Chi Chiou's chapter focuses on the Netflix series *Santa Clarita Diet*, which presents a unique take on the zombie comedy genre. Instead of a traditional apocalyptic setting, the series portrays the mundane problems of a suburban couple, Joel and Sheila Hammond, dealing with Sheila's sudden transformation into a zombie. Chiou explores how the series raises questions about what it means to be a decent human being in the face of such a transformation. She draws on the insights of scholars such as Ashley Knox and Dale Knickerbocker, who see zombies as symbols of anti-humanism and posthumanism. Chiou's analysis offers a fresh perspective on the zombie genre by highlighting the series' exploration of posthuman and transhuman themes within the context of suburban life. In distinct ways West and Chiou explore the commercialisation embedded within the neoliberal and how it changes our understandings of ourselves as well as others.

Addy Berry's chapter delves into the unsettling theme of zombie sex, which has made its way into popular entertainment through independent movies and erotic short stories. Berry explores the concept of incels ('involuntary celibates'), a misogynistic subculture that obsesses over their inability to attract conventionally attractive women. Berry connects this incel ideology with the idea of 'trophy wives', women considered status symbols that enhance the worth of their male partners. This chapter suggests that zombies offer incels a way to live out their fantasies of dominance by trapping less attractive women as 'corpusculent Carrie' in the absence of competition from more attractive partners. Berry examines the cultural implications of this phenomenon and explores potential mitigations, such as artificial intelligence, robotics, live action role play (known as 'LARPing') and therapy.

Our final chapter that is concerned with bodies is Violeta Alarcón Zayas's study of the Mexican film *Halley* and its exploration of the zombie as a metaphor for postmodern malaise. The film challenges the conventional boundary between life and death, offering insights into the existential and political condition of humanity. Zayas connects this to the broader theme of zombies serving as vehicles for sociopolitical critique in literature and cinema. In *Halley*, becoming a zombie signifies a physical rather than a mental death, trapping the character's mind in a decaying body. Zayas argues that this grotesque portrayal reflects the emptiness and discomfort of postmodern individualism and narcissism in the context of transnational capitalism. The chapter draws on concepts of post-existentialism and narcissism to analyse how the film conveys the contemporary sense of malaise and loss of freedom.

Moving to pandemics and the zombie, Catherine Pugh and Nikki Foster-Kruczek explore the lasting traumatic consequences of a zombie apocalypse on survivors. They emphasise that the trauma does not cease with the initial outbreak; instead, survivors grapple with its effects for months and years afterwards. This prolonged trauma creates a state of *historical trauma*, altering how survivors perceive both the undead and other humans. The chapter applies psychological defence theories such as 'terror management' to analyse the psychological impact on survivors in post-apocalyptic worlds. It highlights the perpetual cycle of trauma and its consequences, including disassociation from reality, existential angst and the search for meaning. Moreover, it distinguishes between adult survivors and children in coping with the new, brutal reality where the primary threat shifts from the undead to other humans. The loss of the old world and nostalgia compound the challenges to survival.

Madeline Becker's chapter delves into the contrasting narratives surrounding the COVID-19 pandemic and the zombie genre. It explores how the pandemic has generated discourses depicting the virus as malevolent, imagining heroes as saviours who conquer death. In contrast, zombies in popular culture, such as *28 Days Later* and *The Walking Dead*, highlight the fragility of human bodies and the impossibility of overcoming death. The chapter examines how these narratives conceptualise humanity, corporality and notions of order and stability. Becker suggests that in times of crisis, such as the pandemic or environmental challenges, the zombie narrative may offer a unique perspective by revealing the vulnerability of human systems and bodies. This, Becker argues, prompts us to rethink what it means to be human in the twenty-first century.

Hossein Mohammadzade's study delves into the recurring theme of human survivors in post-apocalyptic zombie worlds and their ideological significance. It questions whether these survivors represent individualism that is crucial for individual and societal well-being or an extreme form of hyper-individualism, often encouraged by capitalism, that endangers communities. The study analyses how protagonists in universes like *The Walking Dead* embody individualism, blurring or reinforcing the distinction between individuals and antagonistic zombie masses. It scrutinises the potential implications of this portrayal for contemporary society's values and social contradictions. In doing so, Mohammadzade builds on Becker's work to again challenge our understanding of how to treat survivors, be they victims of trauma, acts of nature or violent attacks.

The collection's final section concerns zombie politics. Grace Jung's chapter focuses on the South Korean zombie film *The Wailing* and its political and cultural significance in the context of modern Korean history. The film serves as a unique platform to examine the Korean zombie's role in addressing decomposing national memory and trauma, particularly related to the Korean War and the suppression of memories. Jung argues that the deranged zombies in the film represent Korea's unresolved war trauma and its cultural decomposition due to political fearmongering during the Cold War. By connecting these zombies to the concept of decomposing memories, the chapter highlights how they embody the unexcavated post-war Korean trauma, shedding light on local perceptions and experiences during the Cold War era. More importantly, this chapter, along with those by Rodrigo Gonsalves and Reece Goodall, remind us that the zombie is a truly transnational phenomenon and not one rooted in American-British concerns.

Indeed, Gonsalves's chapter explores the symbolism of zombies in global culture and academia. It references Slavoj Žižek's interpretation of undeadness as inspired by Marx's capitalist vampires and examines how zombies have been reinvented over time, such as in George Romero's *Dawn of the Dead* and Max Brooks's *World War Z*. Gonsalves ponders whether zombies can still be a meaningful theoretical tool to address contemporary societal contradictions, particularly those stemming from late capitalism. The chapter considers how zombies, with their dialectics between life and death, challenge the prevailing norms of capitalist realism and pose questions about our current societal structures. More so, Gonsalves's work highlights the malleability of the zombie figure, which acted as our original rallying point for a deeper engagement with zombiism itself.

Finally, Goodall's chapter explores the emergence of French zombie cinema over the past two decades and its relevance to French society. The analysis focuses on films like *La Horde* and *Goal of the Dead* to argue that French zombie cinema serves as a lens for discussing racial and class tensions within the French Republic. Zombies, stripped of identity, are used to articulate anxieties about national identity in an increasingly globalised world. The chapter considers how these films reflect France's struggle to define itself in a changing society and global landscape.

Zombies are ephemeral figures. They signify rebirth and death simultaneously. The goal of this collection – and one we believe that it achieves – is to continue previous work on the undead and explore new boundaries while deepening existing ones.

Notes

1. Scott Hamilton and Conor Heffernan (eds), *Theorising the Contemporary Zombie: Contextual Pasts, Presents, and Futures* (Cardiff: University of Wales Press, 2022).
2. Influential works include Shawn McIntosh and Marc Leverette (eds), *Zombie Culture: Autopsies of the Living Dead* (Lanham MD: Scarecrow Press, 2008); Kyle William Bishop and Angela Tenga (eds), *The Written Dead: Essays on the Literary Zombie* (Jefferson NC: McFarland, 2017); Deborah Christie and Sarah Juliet Lauro (eds), *Better Off Dead: The Evolution of the Zombie as Post-human* (New York: Fordham University Press, 2011); Stephanie Boluk and Wylie Lenz (eds), *Generation Zombie: Essays on the Living Dead in Modern Culture* (Jefferson: McFarland, 2011); Laura Hubner, Marcus Leaning and Paul Manning (eds), *The Zombie Renaissance in Popular Culture* (Basingstoke: Palgrave Macmillan, 2014).
3. Kyle William Bishop, *American Zombie Gothic: The Rise and Fall (and Rise) of the Walking Dead in Popular Culture* (Jefferson NC: McFarland, 2010); Aaron Clayton, *Dead, White and Blue: The Zombie and American National Identity* (Jefferson NC: McFarland, 2023); Steven J. Kirsh, *Parenting in the Zombie Apocalypse: The Psychology of Raising Children in a Time of Horror* (Jefferson NC: McFarland, 2019); T. May Stone, *Reading the Great American Zombie: The Living Dead in Literature* (Jefferson NC: McFarland, 2022); Gary D. Rhodes, *White Zombie: Anatomy of a Horror Film* (Jefferson NC: McFarland, 2015).

PART ONE

THE ZOMBIE JOURNEY

2

Place, Space and the Localised Apocalypse

A Data-Led Exploration of The Zombie Novel as a Road Trip

Emma L. Tonkin

THROUGH A DATA-LED exploration of a selected corpus of geo-tagged self-published and formally published zombie novels, this chapter explores the selection and use of location in this dataset, evaluating quantitatively the extent to which self-published and formally published novels vary in narrative scope, finding an indication of an association (p = 0.08), and in the proximity of the events of the novel to the authors' own biographies (weak association of p = 0.25), and qualitatively, how the narrative is adapted for the geographical context in which it is told and, finally, questioning in what ways these works make use of the structure of the 'American road trip'. This is a decidedly different type of zombie scholarship. Inspired by work in the humanities, this chapter attempts to use data science to provide an alternative means of studying the 'road trip' within zombie media. In doing so, the chapter examines a wide array of zombie novels from different geographic regions to both map and unpack the meanings of travel within zombie lore. The subject of study is, of course, well-worn within zombie scholarship. Kyle Bishop used the road trip to scrutinise deeper fears about globalisation.[1] From a different perspective Toivanen as well as Ferhle looked at zombie travel to deconstruct migration and refugee discourses, while May examined broader geographical landscapes through zombie travel.[2] Inspired by such works, the chapter provides a deeper, geographically critical meaning of what travel represents within zombie worlds.

I explore the proposition that a large subset of zombie survival narratives can be viewed as the confluence of the zombie narrative with another established genre: the American road trip. This observation was made by Bishop in the context of *World War Z* as 'an international kind of road trip movie', by many reviewers of recent zombie movies (e.g., The News Wheel, 2014), forms the basis of a tabletop board game (*Zombie Road Trip*) and is subverted by Miller's 2011 self-published novel titled *Zombie Road Trip*, which humorously re-imagines the story of survival from the perspective of a zombie. The connection is intuitive. Zombie survival narratives often take the form of a journey.[3] The archetypal zombie narrative relies heavily on a progression of events following the instigating event: a new peril, an ongoing search for something such as a safe haven, a cure, a decisive weapon or for remnants of a world that has been lost. Consider the first season of *The Walking Dead*, in which the protagonists travel to the CDC facility in Atlanta to seek help, a cure or answers, and *Z Nation*'s journey across America, to enable the development of a cure or, later, to seek out what America has become. *The Girl with All the Gifts* and *Zombieland* (2009) explicitly present a road trip through a post-apocalyptic landscape as a process of coming of age – the last glimpse of an old world and the beginning of the new.[4]

Methodologically, this chapter is data-led and will primarily explore the genre through methods drawn from the digital humanities. Hence, I explore this proposition first through literature review, develop a series of hypotheses and explore them through text mining of a subsample of zombie texts including self-published and commercially published works. This wide net reflects Boon's observation that many zombie novels are 'self-published fan fiction', and that these tend to reflect Romero's vision, relying heavily on the tropes emerging from Romero's works.[5] Here it is argued that a distinction exists between the narrative scope of zombie road trips between self-published and formal novels. More formally, it appears that many writers 'write what they know' and, more importantly, that authors tend to adapt the zombie narrative to local conditions within a grand framework of zombie invasions. This argument, which helps provide a more conclusive base for further study, used a scientific method that in addition to the above conclusion furthers the manner in which zombies can be studied.

The Road Trip

The road trip, McWilliams Barndt suggests, is the embodiment of being brave, young and free.[6] The possession of a mission of sorts and the means and opportunity to carry it out is a powerful differentiator from those tied to a more mundane daily routine, a 'great American romance'. There is an intersection with American politics, too – post-presidency, Harry Truman embarked on an 'excellent adventure' journeying from Missouri to the East Coast, describing himself and his wife as 'plain American citizens'.[7] Such a journey is difficult to imagine today, but it encapsulates very well the idea of a road trip as transformational, at least temporarily. For others, as for Truman, a road trip may be symbolic of freedom, offering the potential for reinvention.[8] In juxtaposition to the security of home, the road represents the potential for change, and the journey often takes on an intellectual or spiritual dimension, which McWilliams Barndt summarises as 'a journey … in search of meaning'.[9] Where the open road confers freedom, it also divorces the traveller from lasting human connection, giving rise to new anxieties – the loosening of social ties, loss of family, community membership and recognition. It is an isolationist form of freedom. The road, Walt Whitman wrote, is 'freedom! … I ordain myself loos'd of limits and imaginary lines'.[10] It presents choice, and, in Whitman's telling, acceptance, openness to all. D. H. Lawrence spoke of 'American democracy / where all journey down the open road'. This is a vision that may be viewed as idealised, viewed with a diversity of perspectives in mind. For example, 10 per cent of white households in the United States do not own a car, versus 27 per cent of African-American households. Against this objection, we might note, as McWilliams Barndt does, that the car is not indispensable to the road trip. There is the motorcycle, which McWilliams Barndt views as a symbol of individualism and independence, and what Pirsig refers to in *Zen and the Art of Motorcycle Maintenance* as freedom from 'social authority'.[11]

In summary, the protagonist embarking on a road trip is joining a new community of a sort, one typically made up of brief encounters with fellow travellers. The traveller's choice of transport mediates their experience of the road: insulated by the glass and metal of a car; negotiating the power and roar of a motorcycle behind a Kevlar-lined jacket and helmet; walking or cycling, vulnerable to the weather, aware of every sound and motion around them. And, in general, the traveller undertakes a spiritual journey – a hero's journey from the known to the open road, undergoing trials, experiencing loss and, as Lowe remarks, coming to terms with the inevitable unworthiness of the 'road movie macguffin' motivating their search before returning home. In the context of the zombie novel, such 'macguffins' typically motivate an exploration of the question: is there room for the protagonist(s) in this new world?

In zombie media, location is often key: consider the shopping mall in Romero's *Dawn of the Dead* and its centrality in drawing out the movie's overt critique of consumerism; the journey towards central London in *Girl with All the Gifts* that leads to the denouement that changes the world, and so forth.[13] This study grew in part from an informal observation that while formally published novels tended to select location to such allegorical ends, self-published novels in particular seemed to be more closely linked to the lived experience of the author. Self-representation is a significant aspect of fan fiction: if the origin of the self-published zombie novel is representative of the author's own experience of the world, this paints a picture of the self-published zombie novel as a form of remix or participatory culture, a partial self-insertion, perhaps not of the author's self, but of their environment.

In part, we might view the hypothesis that self-published authors draw heavily on their own experiences as an illustration of that most venerable writing advice, 'write what you know', but there is more to it than that. There is an extensive literature surrounding the adaptation of stories, such as urban legends, to new contexts via new variants. Similarly, regional variation is common in folklore. Storytelling layers narrative over location, places 'acquir[ing] meanings, both personal and shared, through lives, experiences and narratives'.[14] Through a remix of existing zombie narratives applied to the locations in which a writer spends their own lives, they might hope both to explore their role in that imagined world, and to recontextualise what to them is ordinarily the mundane, and hence of little interest, for other readers' eyes. In other words, to paraphrase Pratchett, self-published authors may be 'trying to gift-wrap a city'.[15]

Another reason to extend exploration of zombie literature into the realm of self-publication is that it is increasingly commonplace. In 2017–18, nearly half of paid US e-book unit sales fell into this category.[16] Yet it is worth noting that self-publication and formal publication is a continuum rather than a binary, with the complex publication ecosystem comprising individual self-publication, small press and major publishers, international translation and audiobook and performance rights. In particular, it is not unusual for self-published works to be picked up by publishers. In this study, we include several books in our dataset that began as self-published works and were later traditionally published, often in translation (such a pathway is also possible for certain fan fiction works). It is also possible for formally published works later to be republished through self-publication as they fall out of print. In this study we employ a simplifying definition of 'self-published' that depends only on the publication status of the original edition, rather than any later developments. Works published through a small press are viewed as examples of traditional publishing.

Method

It is at this point that we depart, somewhat, from a 'traditional' humanities paper and move into more data science/hard science methods. To address our interests, we make use of text mining to explore the properties of the text, initially by employing text mining to enable a distant read of the corpus.[12] We begin by developing a dataset consisting of a series of locations named within each work. Since the second question explores the similarity between the author's work and what we know about their biography, we also collect their biographies, either from the works themselves, from any websites that they may curate, or from interviews. We also mark these up with locations. The method by which the dataset is generated, geolocated using spaCy and Mordecai, analysed and mapped in Cartopy, is briefly summarised in Figure 1.[18]

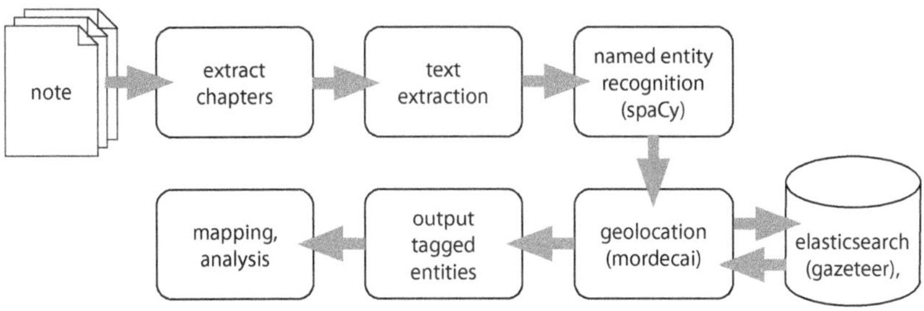

Figure 1: Methodological Framework

This geolocation method has certain shortcomings. Some map points are too vague to be interesting, such as when an author refers to the planet Earth. Sometimes the system wrongly identifies names as places (Georgia,

Meridian), and hence it is necessary to perform checks on the entity type and, potentially, to manually review matches.

Several parameters are set in generating the dataset. First, we note that self-published works are often in permanent draft. The copy used was current as of July 2021. Egregious gazetteer errors are corrected through manual review. In this study, historical novels are excluded (such as *The Viking Dead*, *Deathless Divide*, and so forth) as a consequence of the observed difficulty of effectively geolocating such works using a modern gazetteer. In this study, only works available in English translation are considered, although in principle the method could be adapted to other languages. Graphic novel text is not currently accessible for this type of text mining. Finally, anthologies were excluded. Overall, a corpus containing twenty-six works, of which fourteen were formally published and twelve self-published – a total of 2,486,746 words – was developed and geotagged. Works were selected for a broad geographical distribution, rather than by a formal ranking (e.g., popularity, bestseller list placement, review ranking).

The Zombie Novel as a Road Trip

The geographical 'footprints' of the novels in this dataset vary extensively. At one extreme is Carrie Ryan's *Forest of Hands and Teeth*, which is written in the style of a fantasy novel and contains almost no geographical indicators at all. At the opposite extreme is Max Brooks's *World War Z*, which narrates events from all over the globe. The journey in *Forest* is divorced from the geography of the present day, relying primarily on broad concepts such as the choice of the ocean as a destination. Brooks's work, by contrast, is thoroughly grounded in contemporary geographical and political history. The road trip, however, is a widely represented subgenre within this dataset. Logan's *Apocalypse Cow* presents a journey across the United Kingdom. In Cline's *Ex-Patriots*, superheroes journey to Los Angeles in a non-linear narrative in which safety is to be found in a Hollywood studio. The journey is sometimes explicitly freeing: in *Zombies in Saudi Arabia*, the female protagonists find themselves empowered to do things that their conservative society ordinarily denies them. A character remarks at the beginning of the novel, 'I can't wait until we get to drive our own cars', the narrator reflecting '[t]hough we were legally allowed to drive, no arrangements have been made to pave the way for that new lifestyle'. In this scenario, the breakdown of society becomes an emancipating event.

In practice, novels often feature a diversity of forms of transport. Their use appears to be surprisingly geographically uniform, which is likely to reflect the consensus around the zombie and its capabilities, particularly the idea that the zombie's hearing remains sharp, as in Bourne's *Day by Day Armageddon*, in which it is explained that 'the creatures are primarily attracted to loud noises'. One might expect that authors from regions with a greater reliance on the car would reflect that preference for car culture, for example. In practice, the choice of transport is typically described in strategic terms, on the basis of reasoning about the capabilities of the adversary, and is hence defined more by the author's worldbuilding and narrative influences than by local preferences. As Talluto's Chicago protagonist remarks, '[s]ure, [my car] could go further faster, but it was also a magnet for zombies and others. If I used my bicycle and child trailer, I should be able to move relatively undetected'. This attitude is a relatively widespread piece of lore, often expressed in self-published zombie novels. Vohs's Indiana-based novel *Zombie Crusade* expresses a similar view: 'noise-concerns would probably soon reduce them to bicycles … Two Hummers were stored nearby in a neighbor's barn, giving them the option of using vehicles to actually fight from if they found themselves in situations where they didn't have to worry about noise control.' The protagonist in Tyrell's London-based *Surviving the Evacuation* summarises his view as, 'the bike is fast, zombies are slow, and most importantly They don't hear me coming'.

Beyond the road, boats are also a popular choice of transport mechanism, although motorboats attract similar caveats regarding noise. In Bourne's novel, a Texas-based protagonist observes 'there are numerous small boats in the marina … I want to check them all at once to avoid starting the engines at different times, making too much noise.' Vohs's *Zombie Crusade* series makes heavy use of river travel via small boat or canoe, making use of portage and wading where necessary. This, however, is a localised tradition: the decision to make use of this method is explicitly described as being linked to the history of the land, being attributed to 'a class in Fort Wayne history' that taught the protagonist that 'tribes from all over eastern North America could connect with the Mississippi Valley through the headwaters. They'd just pick up their canoes and portage … then follow the river'. In another reference to neglected forms of transit, Vohs's protagonists come to rely on the train for contact and trade across states, reflecting the historically transformative nature of the American railway.

Certain works also feature the use of aircraft, as in Bourne's *Day by Day Armageddon* and Brooks' *World War Z*, and it is noticeable that where a human antagonist is present, helicopters, such as the Black Hawk in Maberry's *Dead of Night*, may be employed. It is possible that this reflects historical uses of the aircraft (e.g., association with special forces) or the impracticality of the vehicle in post-apocalyptic scenarios. A key distinction between the concept of the open road as expressed by Whitman and that portrayed in these works is that on this road, human travellers are not equal participants. Rather, the survivors and the zombies are competitors. A survivor who fails to remain undetected or to outpace the undead is harshly punished for their transgression. If, as Farmer's restauranteur remarks, 'adventure's kind of a controlled world', the monoculture of the undead is usually the limiting factor. In general, survivors find little joy in the journey. As Bourne's protagonist remarks, 'We have agreed it is time to move. I have come to realize that if you do not move, you die'. This restlessness is mirrored by the zombies themselves: during one journey, the protagonist has a close encounter with 'the lone corpse of a drifter that still wore a pack on his back. It couldn't see us. It wasn't long before the drifter moved on, into the darkness of the Texas night to the next stop'. Neither human nor zombie have chosen this path and the change that it may bring.

In this sense, Lowe's 'inevitable unworthiness of the "road movie macguffin"' ordinarily holds true.[19] One arguable exception to this rule is in the sequence of novels that make up Talluto's *White Flag Rising* series, which dramatises the popular theme of the search for a new America in the ruins of the old in a very literal manner. In these novels, a sympathetically portrayed protagonist finds himself in direct conflict with a ruthless antagonist who travels to Washington to destroy the documents on which America was founded: the Bill of Rights, the Constitution and the Declaration of Independence (with the antagonist snarling, 'I figure if we get rid of the source of rights, then these idiots will finally shut up'). The rescuing of the documents operates as a none-too-subtle analogy for the defence of the principles on which the nation is built, which the protagonist views as fundamental and essential. The journey dramatises a struggle between political ideologies as a contest of will and skill: the group that successfully completes the journey first, mastering the challenges of post-apocalyptic travel, is portrayed as capable of setting the conditions under which the nation is to be reconstructed.

Returning to Fehrle, the zombie does not recognise borders, but it imposes limitations on human protagonists' movements and way of life

– at its extreme, telescoping the protagonists' experiences down to a single 'besieged, fixed location'.[20] In these examples, we see journeys that rely on modes of travel unfamiliar to the twenty-first-century American lifestyle, or those that are seen as unconventional or even transgressive (e.g., seeing the use of bicycles as a technology that brings a freedom that car journeys no longer can, returning to the use of small watercraft and portage, or walking and wild camping). The hubris of seeking to return to an established way of life – the car or the camper van, perhaps – may be the error in judgement that leads to tragedy. The process of overcoming these barriers is, arguably, the crux to survival, and the recognition and development of strategy to overcome of the limitations imposed by the horde a crucial moment of anagnorisis, new knowledge on which the story turns. As Bishop remarks, such narratives carry a note of optimism.[21] Whatever the destination, there is catharsis to be found in the ritual of the journey and in its completion.

Limitations

This study has several evident limitations. The dataset reported in this study is small, and hence cannot easily support statistically significant conclusions, and the selection of works was made with diversity of geolocation and author biography in mind, rather than as a true random sampling. The performance of the geotagging software, while reasonable, requires some level of manual oversight and therefore scales poorly to very large datasets. Non-linear narratives such as Cline's *Ex-Patriots* present the additional challenge of timeline parsing and reconstruction, which we have not handled here. Interpretation of non-linear narratives is a complex task. Willemsen *et al.* require the reconstruction of a chronological account from a series of propositions that may not be clearly labelled – indeed, a successful reconstruction may be in some instances be the climax of the narrative.[22] Despite the complexity, there exist approaches to the reconstruction and visualisation of timelines, although the temporal reconstruction of such data is relatively difficult, which Kim *et al.* attribute to the fact that this information is difficult to infer from a narrative.[23] This problem can be related to the reconstruction of timelines in film scripts and news articles.[24] We leave the temporal reconstruction aspect of this work to future work, and have limited ourselves here to evaluation metrics that do not rely on correct temporal reconstruction. Finally, a key limitation as it stands is the lack of formal classification of subgenres in zombie narratives. Some narratives do not follow the physical road trip format, taking place almost entirely in one location. Some, as with the epistolary novel *World War Z*, have a large cast of characters, several of whom undertake journeys of their own. A useful improvement in modelling the geographic structure of the work would therefore be to chart the movements of individual characters. The extension of the method to languages other than English would also be helpful in permitting a broader study: for example, an extension to the French language would permit the inclusion of works such as Berrouka's remarkable *Le Club des Punks Contre L'apocalypse Zombie*, a delirious search for meaning that travels through key tourist and media destinations in Paris, culminating at the Disneyland Paris theme park.

While there is considerable variation within these works, there is also significant intertextuality – for example, in the selection of signals, the choice of viral origin and in other aspects undiscussed in this work, such as the characteristics of the malaise, its progression and the weapons, tactics and solutions used by the living. This is beyond the scope of this study. However, its further study with a larger corpus might permit the identification of influence networks within the genre; that is, how do ideas spread between works and become prevalent within zombie literature? And, returning to the question of self-publication versus formal publication, do we find, as we might expect, that their spread is mostly limited to self-publication, with greater originality in the formally published works?

Despite these limitations and the challenges identified here, there is significant potential for data-driven approaches to zombie narrative and media to provide new insights. A corpus-based approach, whether a large textual or multimedia corpus, provides the opportunity to render accessible to the reader aspects of narrative, text and performance that are not ordinarily compared, and hence to explore aspects of the broader corpus and the relationships between the works through a data-driven lens. The capabilities of such approaches continue to improve with the increasing availability of novel tools. For textual corpora, as well as masked-language models such as BERT, we might consider large language models (e.g., GPT4) for tasks dealing with textual corpora, although there is a pressing need to validate these tools with practical tasks to establish their applicability.

Conclusion

As a framework for analysis of the zombie novel, the road trip is often applicable. More broadly, however, this characterisation may also cast new light on the relevance and draw of the self-published zombie novel to its readers. While each individual novel focuses on a relatively narrow area, as a collective corpus of works the self-published zombie genre contains significant diversity of location, alongside corresponding reinterpretation and recontextualisation of the mythos. The zombie lore may be unoriginal, often openly borrowed from other works with a knowing nod and a wink to the audience, but the placement of the familiar tale into a new environment and cultural context is an opportunity for the reader to experience a world that may well be unfamiliar to them. In these works we experience the zombie apocalypse as a travelogue, a glimpse into other people's mundane worlds, and we are given the chance to view their workings as the apocalyptic scenario picks the depicted society apart at the seams.

Notes

1. Kyle William Bishop, 'The New American Zombie Gothic: Road Trips, Globalisation, and the War on Terror', *Gothic Studies*, 17/2 (2015), 42–56.
2. Anna-Leena Toivanen, 'Zombie Travels', in Birgit Englert, Barbara Gföllner and Sigrid Thomsen (eds), *Cultural Mobilities Between Africa and the Caribbean* (London: Routldge, 2021), pp. 156–70; Johannes Fehrle, '"Zombies Don't Recognize Borders": Capitalism, Ecology, and Mobility in the Zombie Outbreak Narrative', *Amerikastudien/American Studies*, 61/4 (2016), 527–44; Jeff May, 'Zombie Geographies and the Undead City', *Social & Cultural Geography*, 11/3 (2010), 285–98.
3. Bishop, 'The New American Zombie Gothic', 42–56.
4. For a fascinating paper see Gerry Canavan, 'We are the Walking Dead: Race, Time, and Survival in Zombie Narrative', *Extrapolation (pre-2012)*, 51/3 (2010), 431–50; Ruzbeh Babaee, Sue Yen Lee and Siamak Babaee, 'Ecocritical Survival through Psychological Defense Mechanisms in MR Carey's *The Girl with All the Gifts*', *Journal of Science Fiction*, 1/2 (2016), 47–55.
5. K. A. Boon, 'Ontological Anxiety Made Flesh: The Zombie in Literature, Film and Culture', in Niall Scott (ed.), *Monsters and the Monstrous: Myths and Metaphors of Enduring Evil* (Leiden: Brill, 2007), pp. 33–43.

6. S. McWilliams Barndt, *The American Road Trip and American Political Thought* (London: Rowman & Littlefield, 2018).
7. M. Algeo, *Harry Truman's Excellent Adventure: The True Story of a Great American Road Trip* (New York: Simon & Schuster, 2011).
8. Barndt, *The American Road Trip*, p. 45.
9. Barndt, *The American Road Trip*, p. 45.
10. Walt Whitman, *Leaves of Grass* (New York: Open Publications, 1856), p. 5.
11. Barndt, *The American Road Trip*, p. 78.
12. K. Lowe, 'The Hero's Road Trip', *Paste Magazine*, 5/9 (2016), 33–8.
13. M. Bailey, 'Memory, Place and the Mall: George Romero on Consumerism', *Studies in Popular Culture*, 35/2 (2013), 95–110.
14. Ü. Valk, and D. Sävborg, *Storied and Supernatural Places: Studies in Spatial and Social Dimensions of Folklore and Sagas* (Helsinki: Finnish Literature, 2018).
15. T. Pratchett, *Men at Arms* (London: Discworld, 1993), p. 21.
16. A. Semuels, 'The Authors who love Amazon', *The Atlantic* (12 July 2018), *www.theatlantic.com/technology/archive/2018/07/amazon-kindle-unlimited-self-publishing/565664/* (last accessed 24 February 2025).
17. J. Drouin, 'Close- and Distant-Reading Modernism: Network Analysis, Text Mining, and Teaching the Little Review', *The Journal of Modern Periodical Studies*, 5/1 (2014), 110–35.
18. B. Srinivasa-Desikan, *Natural Language Processing and Computational Linguistics: A Practical Guide to Text Analysis with Python, Gensim, spaCy, and Keras* (London: Packt Publishing Ltd, 2018); A. Halterman, 'Mordecai: Full Text Geoparsing and Event Geocoding', *The Journal of Open Source Software*, 2 (2017); Met Office, *Cartopy: A Cartographic Python Library with a Matplotlib Interface 2010–2015* (Exeter: Met Office, 2015).
19. Lowe, 'The Hero's Road Trip'.
20. Fehrle, 'Zombies Don't Recognize Borders'; Bishop, 'The New American Zombie Gothic'.
21. Bishop, 'The New American Zombie Gothic'.
22. S. Willemsen and M. Kiss, 'Keeping Track of Time: The Role of Spatial and Embodied Cognition in the Comprehension of Nonlinear Storyworlds', *Style*, 54/2 (2020), 172–98.
23. N. W. Kim *et al.*, 'Visualizing Nonlinear Narratives with Story Curves', *IEEE Transactions on Visualization and Computer Graphics*, 24/1 (2018), 595–604.
24. Kim *et al.*, 'Visualizing Nonlinear Narratives', 595–604; I. Mani, B. Schiffman and J. Zhang, 'Inferring Temporal Ordering of Events in News', *Companion Volume of the Proceedings of HLT-NAACL 2003-Short Papers* (2022), 55–7.

3

Fear the Walking Dead

Elitism, Privilege and Zombie Americana

Scott Eric Hamilton

THE ZOMBIE – simultaneously dead and alive, human and non-human – is a literal walking (dead) contradiction that dissolves parameters of sameness and difference. Jeff May posits that the zombie destabilises 'the ambiguous distinctions between "living" and "dead" and "us" and "them"'.[1] Consequently, the zombie, 'us' and 'them', signifies any detrimental action that humans inflict on themselves. The universe of *The Walking Dead* (*TWD*), then, confronts the undead self-inflicted social contaminants that plague society.[2] Part of the *TWD* universe, *Fear the Walking Dead* (*FTWD*) begins, prior to *TWD*, on the US west coast and confronts social issues specific to that region. Beginning in Los Angeles, season 2 concerns Madison Clarke and her family and other survivors as they attempt to survive the outbreak: son, Nick (middle-class privileged heroin addict); daughter, Alicia (naive, idealistic teenager); and a cohort of survivors including Daniel Salazar (ex-El Salvador military),[3] his daughter Ofelia, and Victor Strand, a self-(en)titled businessman. The narrative for the first four seasons begins in Los Angeles, migrates to Mexico, then relocates to Texas. Through the geographical trajectory, *FTWD* confronts specific US issues, including immigration, racism, border cultures and environmental concerns, all exacerbated by the crisis of detrimental privilege.

The confined spaces in zombie narratives examine specific issues through speculative ethics in a context of anxiety-laden isolation. In *FTWD* those anxieties reflect, in part, the conservative mentality of migration and free movement as a threat to elitist privilege. Although inclusive of gender, race, sexual orientation and disability, *FTWD* explicitly portrays elitism as detrimental to survival and inclusivity. Privileged individuals in apocalyptic narratives often expect not only survival but success because of their previous social status.[4] Stefanie Fishel and Lauren Wilcox argue that *TWD* 'offers more than a superficial state of exception; narrative of survival in a state of nature under white male leadership'.[5] However, *FTWD* departs from this model as exceptionalism is not determined by gender or race but the American tendency towards expectation of privilege and the potentially deplorable means by which that dominance is maintained. Such elitism includes the indifferent expenditure of life and resources to propagate continued self-entitlement. Subsequently, privilege is imbued with the expectation of the sacrifice of others to maintain advantages. In *FTWD* forms of elitism are subjected to the destabilising crisis of zombiism to confront notions of inherent privilege within the context of survival justification. Expectations of privilege threaten sympathetic community, and *FTWD*, like the rest of the *TWD* universe,[6] testifies to the potential zombification of American culture through privilege and access to mobility. Mobility and privilege perpetuate each other undermining healthy moral communities and decreasing empathy that erodes interpersonal and inter-communal relations. Concerned primarily with seasons 1–4,[7] this chapter presents the argument that *FTWD* portrays the expectation of privilege, which promotes anti-empathetic and isolationist tendencies, as increasingly detrimental to social well-being: *FTWD* represents the mindless advancement of the culture of privilege, which produces zombie elitism that consumes genuine intra-communal benefit.

Mobility, Elitism and Zombies

May argues that 'Zombie geographies offer a worldview that suggests that the polarization of real world spaces into rigid rich/poor and public/private divides is ideological and dangerous' (291). This worldview relates to places that threaten to blur those clear divides, especially as the number of displaced people increase, along with more globally mobile lifestyles and work forces. As mobility privilege is enhanced, the elite increasingly perceive others as competition. The attempt at maintaining ideological divides to weaken competition often occur along conservative lines, which, intentionally or not, is a tendency towards authoritarianism shared by comparable ideologies responsible for perpetuating dehumanising rhetoric, politics and policies.

Although initially released in 2015, season 1 of *FTWD* is a precursor to the post-2016 political and cultural sphere of conservative populism. Not predicting future events, *FTWD* indicates specific unresolved social issues within American culture persisting prior to their increased public attention since 2016. Those issues include a culture of increasing expectation of elitism resulting in emboldening conservative republican discourse; intensifying divisive rhetoric and diminishing sympathetic communal bonds resulting in dehumanising public rhetoric and policies; and promoting an increasingly unethical and indifferent border culture. Kenneth Hansen contends US border security policy has been 'hijacked by nativist … fears … [of a] "vast sea" of illegal immigrants streaming into the United States from Mexico'.[8] The impoverished border communities generated by the refugee 'crisis', reflects the necropolitics of Achille Mbembé, which he claims creates 'death-worlds' where "vast populations … [obtain a] status of living dead'.[9] The zombiism of *FTWD*, then, is imbued with necropower and the paradoxically unstoppable mobility that requires no privilege.

'Fear' the Walking Dead

Heide Crawford indicates that the title *Fear the Walking Dead* reflects how the narrative induces fear: 'Feelings of fear and existential terror, then, are directly connected with the act of seeing and understanding that which is being seen as a threat.'[10] The mobile dead (signifying zombies and humans in the *TWD* universe), therefore, defy structures of social privilege while paradoxically embodying the dehumanising consequences of being rejected by that same social privilege. The 'fear' is the loss of privilege and the loss of the ideology of an autonomous individualistic self, because of increasingly isolationist and elitist culture. The experience of 'fear' is primarily generated by the gruesome zombie but also the realisation that in extreme conditions human nature is inherently, and detrimentally, callous and unsympathetic. *FTWD* emphasises the necessity to fear both zombies and humans equally to survive the apocalypse of self-entitled individualism.

Self-entitlement is a result of the increasing elitist mentality of contemporary society. This kind of elitism generates unsympathetic responses to those perceived as undeserving of privilege further diminishing communal inclusivity. Elitism accepts that privileged individuals should maintain a select number of advantageous associations. These exclusive, and always temporary, associations reinforce elitism by directly confronting others who threaten perceived inherent privilege. Most alliances in *FTWD* are initially advantageous associations intent on maintaining degrees of authority. Challenging typical race and gender portrayals as they are not heroes, Madison and Victor may technically be protagonists of the narrative, but they are also antagonists to those within the various contexts that they occupy who challenge or threaten their power. For Madison and Victor, especially, their sustained alliance and continued self-entitlement contributes to the eventual deterioration of any established sense of safety or community. Consequently, the deterioration of inclusive, sympathetic community and inter-community relations, is mirrored by the monstrously mobile corpses populating the *TWD* universe.

Privilege, Exclusion and Zombies

Fear causes the privileged to expose the detrimental aspect of elitism.[11] In the examination of the zombie as representational of political fear-based self-defence, Steven Pokornowski indicates that *TWD* 'demonstrates how the logic of self-defence provokes … an autoimmune reaction, which destroys the very life it sets out to protect'.[12] The destructive nature of self-defence is exacerbated when extended to maintaining threatened elitism. Season 1, episode 4 begins with Victor and Nick detained in a facility that resembles 'temporary' Immigration and Customs Enforcement (ICE) detention centres. A fearful Nick, in the throes of detoxification, is misidentified by the guards as potentially infected. Victor trades an expensive cuff link for the guard to ignore the situation. When asked why Victor saved him, Victor replies: 'I didn't save you, I obligated you' (season 1, episode 4). Victor clearly expects that those to whom he extends his privilege are obliged to return the investment. Victor views people not as potential relationships but potential resources. Eventually, Nick and Victor escape and meet with Nick's family establishing an advantageous association. Consequently, Victor leads the group to his oceanside luxury house and reveals his plan to survive, a $10 million yacht named 'The Abigail'.[13] He offers them passage and safety, but more for the need of a crew than any moral virtue.[14] The lack of human resources would undoubtedly instil the fear of failure in an elite individual like Victor.

Season 2 begins with the Clarke cohort departing south on Victor's yacht (its extravagant value emphasised repeatedly), which provides the group privileged means of circumventing the Mexico-US border. Although not without hardships, the group bypasses the physical border, which allows them the vantage point to witness incendiary bombs decimate southern California.[15] This vantage point indicates that if crossing the border had been attempted by conventional means (through the physical land border) the unprivileged limitation of movement would have resulted in their demise. Southern Californian culture, synonymous with excessive consumption and superficial relationships, is dramatised through the initial zombie infestation and the subsequent bombing to portray a social geography that consumes genuine relationships.

Victor's priorities often lie with asserting authority and maintaining status. One morning they pass a sinking boat with the occupants pleading for assistance:

> Madison: 'Strand, stop the boat.'
> Victor: 'That's funny.'
> Madison: 'There are people out there…'
> Victor: 'Then they should return to land.'
> …
> Madison: 'There's nothing to go back to.'
> Victor: 'I filled my mercy quota. Seven people saved to date'
> (season 2, episode 1)

Victor's callousness grants the power either to deny or grant others mobility and by extension the most remedial privilege: life. The violent inaction of Victor results in the same small boat later found capsized without survivors: his privilege, manifested by the yacht, affords him the ability to disavow the deaths that he caused. In the episode 'Monster', Victor's inaction indicates that the real monsters of the world are not necessarily zombies, but self-entitled humans with the means to exert necropower.

In crisis contexts, unsympathetic passivity can result directly in violence. Thom Davies *et al.* examine a neglected refugee camp in Calais as result of inaction, arguing, 'the conditions to which all of these forced migrants are abandoned to, have violent, bodily consequences'.[16] They explain that:

> The active state practices and biopolitical experiences of pan-EU migration … can be compared with the deliberately inactive, violently forsaking forms of desertion that allow such squalid conditions to continue. Together, these form a tapestry of 'bio' and 'necro' forms of governance. The camp's grave environmental conditions were regulated with deliberate indifference by French authorities who intentionally withheld care. (1276)

Refugee camps, such as 'The Jungle' in Calais,[17] force asylum seekers into apocalyptic-like existence. Similarly, season 2, episode 4, 'Blood in the Streets', opens with Nick swimming ashore at night where he encounters an example of such inaction. The abandonment of survivors, as a form of violent inaction by governments and other agencies with responsibility of care is a recurring theme in the first two seasons of *FTWD*. At the end of season 1 the military, which had established a safe zone around El Sereno, revealed to the Clarke group by a soldier, abruptly abandoned the area without any warning or contingency for the survivors. Whereas, in 'Blood in the Streets', the beach encampment, the lack of survivors and the minimal number of zombies roaming the encampment reflect the existence of refugees in similar grievous conditions.

Zombiism, as a theory of crisis, adapts to the fears of the given era.[18] Correspondingly, the mass migration of refugees in the twenty-first century has brought the speculative ethics of zombiism closer to reality. The designation of remote locations for encampments and asylum accommodation functions as a type of internment from social consciousness – where the host society disavows the existence of the 'grotesque outsider' through the justification of obliging them to a society merely to perpetuate their existence.[19] Carceral refugee encampments, like in Calais, enact the minimum functions of life, verging close to being undead. Survival narratives, and especially zombie apocalypse narratives, are in part refugee allegories of the hardships of asylum-seeker existence for an audience that would otherwise not have access to that experience. *FTWD* season 2 presents the potentially devastating human cost that refugee existence can exact if left unaddressed. *FTWD* theorises that human cost through zombiism to an American audience largely isolated from experiencing, or even aware of, large refugee camps.

After navigating the zombified refugee camp, Nick enters an almost pristine 'gated' community to meet Victor's associate, Luis. The unfinished housing community represents the privilege of resources that contributed to the 2008 economic crisis. Lisa Sun Park and David Naguib Pellow argue that 'those with the greatest privilege … have created privatized refuges … These spaces of seclusion not only maintain but also increase inequality, which exacerbates the impact of climate change … these structures require considerable resources and generate economic growth – central cause of climate change in the first place'.[20] Luis prearranged Victor's rendezvous and payment to authorities, allowing unimpeded entry into Mexico. Consequently, Victor's privilege allows him unprecedented mobility across national borders, as in the actual world. Luis, however, is concerned about the extra people that Victor had on the yacht. Nick asks Luis, rather naively, about transit for everyone into Mexico: 'so how difficult is just a few extra people?' Luis responds: 'We got to go through the flotilla. I secured transit for two. I got money for two. Adding seven more, it's a problem' (season 2, episode 4). They return to the yacht besieged by pirates, but Luis, somehow, while on a moving boat, shoots two of the captors and reclaims the ship. However, prior to Luis's arrival, Victor selfishly abandons the ship on the only life raft. Luis indicates 'Without Strand we don't get into Mexico' (season 2, episode 4), which associates Victor's privilege with their mobility. Victor returns and, after some drama with the Mexican military, they enter Mexico freely.

Through the north-to-south trajectory, *FTWD* exposes the crisis of isolationism on everyday citizens, highlighting contentious Mexico-US relations. Isolationist policy does not affect the privileged: anyone with the means can obtain access to, and often residency in, most countries. Victor's romantic, advantageous association with his wealthy partner Thomas Abigail, and their international business success, ensured free movement through borders. Being both black and homosexual, Victor disrupts typical depictions of privilege, especially compared to *TWD*, in which most of the principal characters with power are white and male (although this does change somewhat as the series progresses). In Mexico, Victor and company arrive at Thomas's fortified Hacienda (a stronghold of family and communal values). Eventually, and typically, the American outsiders destabilise the already fragile sanctity of the Hacienda. Daniel, haunted by his immoral acts during the El Salvadoran civil war of the 1980s and 1990s, mistrusts the spiritual matriarchal figure and sets fire to a room containing zombies because he cannot accept the local spiritual outlook.

As the Hacienda burns in the background, Nick leaves his group to exist among the walkers. Madison asks why he is leaving, and he exclaims 'We destroy everything' (season 2, episode 7); Nick means that both the Clarke cohort and humans in general are ultimately a destructive force.

Mobility results in the capability of acquiring stable and fortified accommodation. In the next episode, Madison and company find themselves refuge in a luxury hotel. Victor and Madison again insert themselves as leaders. On arrival, the manager of the hotel controls the situation, but the addition of Madison and company increases the amount of influence that the Americans could exert, even if at odds with themselves. When Madison arrives, the hotel manager controls the master set of keys, and the Americans have sequestered themselves to the specific part of the hotel in which they occupy rooms. Eventually, Madison obtains the keys and initiates her own rules. She bestows the other Americans the privilege of moving more freely through the hotel and engaging socially (having meals with the other occupants, for example). As in the Hacienda, the forceful and invasive American influence in the hotel is palpable. Madison clearly expects to dominate any situation. The results almost always culminate in destruction, such as the reservoir at the end of season 3. Nonetheless, the Madison cohort tends to 'destroy everything'. Thus, the seemingly inevitable human inclination towards destruction is the ultimate crisis at the core of zombiism.

Meanwhile, Nick, unable to survive alone, is offered shelter in a *colonia* in Tia Juana. *Colonias*, a type of slum, have become more prominent in recent decades. Hansen reports that at the Mexico border, as of 2009, '400,000 people live in *colonias*, or slums, where living conditions are substandard at best', and '[t]hese *colonias* are almost completely lawless, with state, local, and federal police unable to keep control of the population or even provide basic infrastructure. For them it is easier to encourage people to cross the border into the United States' (347). These communities, as Hansen indicates, act as stages for illegal border crossings, attracting people trying to gain entrance into the United States illegally, often risking lives. Border militarisation contributes to the increased prevalence of *colonias*: the situation that punitive border policies are supposed to end, lawlessness and immigration, also perpetuates that situation. This self-perpetuating issue began decades before 2016, but *FTWD* forces the frightful reality of border culture into confrontation with the fearful, often inattentive, gaze of a post-2016 American audience exposing the passive compliance of a potentially uniformed populace.

The *colonia*, like refugee encampments, lacks basic sanitation and water facilities with a near dilapidated pharmacy and triage hospital. The isolated *colonia* may provide physical protection from the dangers outside the walls, but the standard of life inside is encroaching on destitution. The health of the inhabitants is clearly an issue: the pharmacy has numerous people waiting for treatment from Alejandro Nuñez, the acting doctor to the *colonia*. The lack of basic facilities is confirmed by the numerous makeshift water tanks that Nick is shocked to find mostly empty. Water must be obtained from the local cartel, a task with which Nick volunteers to assist Luciana. Therefore, except for Nick and Luciana, the *colonia* is as much place of internment as means for survival. The *colonia* resembles necropower posited by Mbembé:

> First is the dynamics of territorial fragmentation, the sealing off and expansion of settlements. The objective of this process is twofold: to render any movement impossible and to implement separation along the model of the apartheid state. The occupied territories are therefore divided into a web of intricate internal borders and various cells. (28)

The *colonia* only survived the onset of the apocalypse because it already existed in an isolated state of 'internal borders and various cells'. The *colonia*, a type of colonialism through exclusion, is not intended to be exploited for economic gain, but controlled as a threat to privilege. The isolation of the *colonia* represents an excess of necropower through erasure of social access.

In season 2, episode 8, Nick quickly obtains a prominent position, like Madison, and becomes romantically involved with Luciana, literally the only attractive female resident (another indicator of privilege). His middle-class drug-addict background allows him to assist Nuñez, the leader of the *colonia*, to trade OxyContin with a nearby cartel in exchange for water and supplies. Even his unsavoury past attests to his privilege as he assists Nuñez to cut the OxyContin and profit more from each trade with the cartel. Eventually, the cartel, lacking supplies, attacks the colonia to acquire their supply of OxyContin, suggesting that the 'opioid crisis' plagues Mexico as much as, if not more than, the United States, although the former receives considerably less mainstream media attention.[21]

Nick, although attempting to integrate, superficially engages with Mexican spirituality. Nuñez asks Nick, 'Why come all this way?', to which he replies, 'I want to be where the dead aren't monsters' (season 2, episode 9).

Wanting to believe that the living are more than monsters, Nick accepts the convenient myth that Nuñez was bitten but did not become a zombie, which serves to maintain community survival. However, Nick's naive idealism emphasises his privilege. The protective 'wall', a type of zombie mote, to the *colonia* on the surface is an extension of the spiritualism that he tries to accept. The *colonia* is located atop a hill where the only point of access is through the wall of zombies. Individuals volunteer to enter, get bitten and thus maintain the zombie defence. The spiritual divide between living and dead dissolving, like during *Dia de los Muertos*, influences both the residents of the Hacienda and the *colonia* who accept the apocalypse as a physical manifestation of their beliefs. Unlike Nick's naive search for redemption, spiritualism for the two communities serves as both a means of maintaining sympathetic, spiritual community and as a mechanism for sympathetic communal survival.

Although based in spirituality, maintaining zombies for the wall is not so much a sacrifice for the greater good as it is a deterrent for the living. The zombie 'wall' represents, in part, what Jason De Léon deems the 'necroviolence' of Mexico. By displaying corpses, usually by the cartels, De Léon claims a 'manipulated dead body can also be a vector for violent messages directed at the living' (70). The displaying of manipulated corpses demonstrates the power of necroviolence. Maintaining the zombie wall is a message of deterrent to the living as much as a means of communing with deceased. Nick's scepticism of Mexican culture highlights US elitism in relation to different spiritual beliefs. Eventually, the cartel exhausts its supplies and attacks the *colonia*. Although the need for food and refuge initiates the attack, the leader of the cartel is more interested in acquiring the supply of opioids. Nonetheless, before the attack begins, Nick witnesses a helicopter land at a military facility just over the border, and, Moses-like, leads the *colonia* towards salvation. His saviour status is thus established, but only temporarily.

Nick and Luciana, in 'North' (season 2, episode 15), lead the faithful *colonia* residents, camouflaged with blood of the dead, towards safety, which resonates with Gilberto Rosas's 'Necro-Subjection' that concerns the 'the politics of death … representing those who are made – and who make themselves – dead – in order to live'.[22] Trapping the cartel in the *colonia* with zombies, making them actually dead, Nick and the residents then make themselves appear dead, for a chance at living. For the *colonia* residents seeking potential safety is not an exodus but, to invoke Mbembé, a 'procession of the condemned through the streets prior to execution' (19). Militia guards, occupying the border, fire on the group, either killing or dispersing the entire caravan. Nick and a wounded Luciana are imprisoned and what remains of the caravan retreats unprotected into Mexico. Johannes Fehrle argues that:

> *World War Z*, and other films like it nevertheless hint at America's realization of the porosity of its borders – national borders as well as the personal, biological borders of the human body. They tie this realization in with anxieties over the global movement of "unwanted" human and undetectable non-human agents.[23]

The US southern border is a representation and means of enforcing American racial and economic dominance by denying mobility of the underserving other. Zombies may not recognise borders, but humans are especially conditioned to fear them.

The border scenes of *FTWD* contain uncanny parallels with the migrant caravans inhumanely detained at the border in 2018–19 resulting in separation of families, thrusting individuals backward into uncertainty, destitution and, in far too many cases, death. The 'crisis', however, is not exclusively the transgression of any one US administration but has been escalating since the 1990s.[24] Raymen, discussing *TWD*, accentuates 'the resemblance between Trump's [presidential] campaign on immigration and the depiction of the terrorist Other, and marauding sub-human walkers who threaten destruction and chaos' (434). Season 2, episode 15 portrays US border policy as violently dismissive of the loss of humanity, and sympathy for others, in the service of national security.[25] As such, *FTWD* reflects the contemporary fear-based border culture that promotes rejecting sympathy for others in need.

This episode echoes the unsympathetic fear-mongering rhetoric that dominated Mexico-US border relations in 2018–19. The distinct metal-slatted fence of the southern US border is a symbol of the privilege of mobility denied to a specific underprivileged demographic. Randall McGuire explains that the 'materialized border' replaced the 'picket fence' neighbourly relationship that Mexico and the US maintained for decades.[26] The metal fencing and increased border patrol is not solely the materialisation of US border policy, but the militarisation of the geographical region both sides of the border. As McGuire indicates, the beginning of the twenty-first century intensified the militarisation of the border (471–2). The militarisation of borders establishes violent privilege by enforcing population stagnation through limited or restricted mobility.

The increasing restrictions at the main border crossing forces desperate individuals further into the Sonoran Desert, risking almost certain death. The Sonoran Desert has been labelled 'The Killing Desert' by Gilberto Rosas, who claimed, 'The U.S.-Mexico border has become a zone of sacrifice' (304). Sacrifices in this area do not necessarily go unnoticed but are silenced by the indifference of modern surveillance. The indifference to life is a common feature of US border surveillance. McGuire notes that around Ambos Nogales:

> Over five thousand people have died on the militarized border since 1998 … Their decomposing bodies and bones tragically materialize the contradiction between the commerce in their labor and the enclosure to keep them out. … Agents patrol a dirt road along the north side of the wall. Helicopters routinely buzz the wall and the countryside north of the wall. A few yards from the road stands a series of remote video-surveillance system towers with cameras and motion sensors. (472)

The border scenes in *FTWD* demonstrate the 'fear' produced in the act of witnessing border related violence. In season 3, Ofelia arrives alone at the border with the only option of return to the United States being to follow the fence into the Sonoran Desert. Eventually she finds a gap in the fence but is met with a militia soldier patrolling for illegal immigrants, even after the apocalypse. In an episode poignantly titled 'Welcome to America', Jeremiah Otto, the owner of the Broke Jaw Ranch and an example of the *TWD* universe cowboy 'post-frontier' figure,[27] refrains from killing her because she is American. However, on account of not being white he leaves her without water to die. Jeremiah, agent of unsympathetic surveillance, ignores the possible consequences of his violent inaction. The combination of criminalising undocumented border crossing and enhancing punitive surveillance measures promotes the disavowal of suffering to maintain space that relentlessly, and often violently, denies mobility. Therefore, border enforcement that operates without any humanitarian mandates is an act of unsympathetic elitism and necropower.

The inhumane treatment of migrants is commonly associated with nativist notions of 'border security'. Linda Green indicates that illegality on the border 'fosters a climate where hate crime flourishes. The rise in armed militias like the famous Minuteman Project and the American Border Patrol in southern Arizona illuminate this'.[28] Season 3, episode 8 represents the disturbing history of state and militia border violence through Ofelia's ordeal. Militarised borders establish privilege by enforcing population stagnation through limited or restricted mobility. The harsh desert landscape, with the potential brutality of militaristic patrols, ceases to be natural terrain and becomes a racially charged, weaponised geographical space.

Environmental Privilege and Zombies

In *FTWD* environmental privilege is cultural privilege as much as racial privilege. Park and Pellow argue that 'environmental privilege is accrued through the exercise of economic, political, and cultural power', which

> reveals how *mobilities* of power and nonhuman actants function to inflict and reproduce environmental racism and injustice on vulnerable communities through mechanisms that simultaneously, consciously, and deliberately preserve the health and security of wealthier, and more politically connected, and usually whiter communities' (395–6).

Season 3 is located on the Broke Jaw Ranch, owned by Jeremiah Otto (a white survivalist and the same individual that confronted Ofelia) and inhabited by mostly white occupants that enjoy relative seclusion, security and resources.

Prior to arriving at the ranch, Madison and family converge, albeit through different means, at the same militarised border facility in which Nick and Luciana were detained at the end of season 2. The facility is overrun by zombies, and they escape with the occupying militia. Troy Otto is in command and his lack of empathy results in him killing anyone from across the border he deems 'sick or infirm', which tends to be anyone of colour or anyone who may threaten his authority. At the facility his men murder detainees and then time the zombification process after death under the pretence of conducting 'science'. However, Troy provides Madison and Alicia preferential treatment due to their gender and race. Relocating north of the border, season 3 is located primarily on the Otto farm, which is a survivalist stronghold from before the apocalypse. Madison and family assert themselves in leadership roles early into their residence: Madison assumes a pseudo-maternal role for Troy; Nick becomes a kind of confidant for Jeremiah Otto; and Alicia becomes romantically involved with Jake Otto. All three members of the Clarke family obtain a privileged position within the ranks of the Broke Jaw Ranch and the advantage of available natural resources. During this time, Victor and Daniel are still in Mexico and become involved in the operation of a dam, a symbol of power in the region. The two locations, north and south of the border, establish the crux of season 3 as within the environmental crisis of the apocalypse where access to water is the new wealth, and that wealth is controlled primarily by white, male privilege.

Jeremiah, as pre-apocalypse legal owner of the land, is embroiled in a long-standing feud with the Indigenous community that once resided there, the contention between the two groups being legal occupation versus legitimate heritage. Jeremiah owned the land prior to the outbreak and as a result feels entitled to retain ownership.[29] Whereas the Hopi 'Black Hat' tribe intends to reclaim the land since laws no longer exist to enforce legal ownership. Qaletaq Walker, the tribal leader, invokes ancestral connections combined with allegations of injustices by the Ottos as just cause. Pokornowski indicates that *TWD* as Western presents 'colonial ideologies echoing the annihilation of Native Americans in the U.S. West'.[30] *FTWD* extends this colonial ideology into the modern context to include landscape management and environmental resource, the Dakota Pipeline being one such example where the sovereignty of Indigenous nations are breached in the name of US national interests.[31] Furthermore, positioning the militia and the Otto family in opposition to the Indigenous community reflects the long history of the forceful occupation of land to obtaining privilege. The forceful occupation of land, legal or otherwise, by the Otto family exposes environmental privilege as the foundation of the cultural (and racial) history of the United States.

Water access is a pressing issue on the precipice of a potential real-world environmental crisis.[32] Reflecting an impending real-world crisis, Jake, near a dilapidated aquifer, explains to Alicia that although the ranch has benefitted from a substantial water supply, that resource is dwindling faster than expected. The detriment to the local environment suggested here indicates how *FTWD*, in season 3 at least, reflects the concerns of the Anthropocene. Park and Pellow contend that

> those with the greatest privilege … have created privatized refuges … These spaces of seclusion not only maintain but also increase inequality, which exacerbates the impacts of climate change … In effect, these actions create greater vulnerabilities for everyone, including themselves' (398).

Eventually, Walker and Madison, through an advantageous association, coordinate a deal after Jeremiah's death for both groups to share the resources of the ranch. The long political history of water ownership in the region lurks behind season 3.[33] Madison and Walker transport water to Mexico in exchange for much-needed supplies. The black market where Madison and Walker trade water portrays a disadvantaged, near-lawless, destitute Mexico, dependent on the United States for resources. Meanwhile, back at the ranch, the co-occupation of the ranch is unsustainable. Troy, banished from the ranch, weaponises a horde of walkers to destroy the ranch because his elite status was revoked in place of inclusive community structure. Troy would rather eradicate the ranch than relinquish the privilege of power. In season 3, the destruction of the means of environmental privilege reflects the elite mentality of refusing to relinquish positions of power over access to resource consumption.[34] The zombie is a threat to the living, as the zombie has no dependence on resources nor the need to control those resources to maintain elitist privilege.

Conclusion

FTWD demonstrates the contradictory aspect of the zombie in the US context, as a figure of both unyielding mobility and immovable occupation. The infallibility of the necropolitical force of the mobile zombie dissolves the difference between the mundane and the elite. The zombie also disrupts carceral spaces of refuge intent on stagnating non-elite movement. The elitist mentality is ceaseless in the acquisition of privilege, of which the means of mobility is of primary importance. Privileged individualism is, therefore, undead elitism devouring genuine, sympathetic community. Unless the elitist mentality is confronted, the living will continue to claim: 'We destroy everything.'

Notes

1. Jeff May, 'Zombie Geographies and the Undead City', *Social & Cultural Geography*, 11/3 (2010), 289.
2. For issues of American identity, especially violence and masculinity, see Jeffrey A. Sartain 'Days Gone Bye: Robert Kirkman's Reenvisioned Western *The Walking Dead*', in Cynthia Miller and A. Bowdoin Van Riper (eds), *Undead*

in the West II: They Just Keep Coming (Lanham MD: Scarecrow Press, 2016), pp. 249–68.

3. Daniel reveals in season 3, episode 4 that he was a member of 'Sombra Negra', trained by the CIA during the El Salvadorian civil war 1980–92, largely caused by resistance to the country's land reform proposals. As a child, Daniel was forced into one of the Salvadoran Junta death squads after witnessing a massacre on a river, most likely the *Sumpul River* massacre of 1980. Although he eventually reconciles with his past atrocities, in the earlier seasons his presence suggests immigration that resulted from US involvement in the region during the civil war.
4. The Kaufman character in *Land of the Dead* (2005), for example, embodies the corporate mentality of capitalising on any situation regardless of the cost to others.
5. Stefanie Fishel and Lauren Wilcox, 'Politics of the Living Dead: Race and Exceptionalism in the Apocalypse', *Millennium: Journal of International Studies*, 45/3 (2017), 338.
6. Including *TWD*, *FTWD*, *The Walking Dead* graphic novel and *The World Beyond*.
7. Although season 5 is interesting, seasons 1–4 are more overt in their engagement with certain aspects of American culture and society. Season 5, for example, portrays the mythologised history of the American West as a performative facade with the fictitious 'Humbug's Gulch' culture park setting. The fictitious Humbug's Gulch re-enactment parks suggests that the maintaining of the 'wild west' aspect of American history is primarily for entertainment more than curating authentic cultural identity. Nonetheless, season 5 posing as a mock-western (in the second half at least) would not add much more to the current discussion except for added examples. Therefore, to examine the elitism of *FTWD* within the space provided seasons 1–4 will be of primary concern.
8. Kenneth Hansen, 'Postmodern Border Insecurity', *Administrative Theory & Praxis*, 31/3 (2009), 348.
9. Achille Mbembé, 'Necropolitics', *Public Culture*, 15/1 (2003), 40.
10. Heide Crawford, 'Peering Through the Blinds: Gothic Gaze in *Fear the Walking Dead*', in Phillip L. Simpson and Marcus Mallard (eds), *The Walking Dead Live! Essays on the Television Show* (Lanham MD: Rowman & Littlefield, 2016), p. 83.
11. As this chapter examines the detriment of elitism portrayed in *FTWD*, similarly detrimental masculinity is one of the central crises in *TWD*, as Katherine Sugg claims the male characters 'are so often shown to be questionable, if not

awful, people who make horrific, if not stupid, decisions': '*The Walking Dead*: Late Liberalism and Masculine Subjects in Apocalypse Fictions', *Journal of American Studies*, 49/4 (2015), 803. Equally horrific decisions in *FTWD* result from the attempt to establish privilege.

12. Steven Pokornowski, 'Burying the Living with the Dead: Security, Survival and the Sanction of Violence', in Dawn Keetley (ed.), '*We're all infected': Essays on AMC's The Walking Dead and the Fate of the Human* (Jefferson NC: McFarland, 2014), p. 42.
13. The elite being able to prepare for catastrophe echoes Victor's privileged contingency plan. Thomas Raymen refers to 'doomsday consumption' in relation to *TWD* as a dystopian critique of late capitalism: 'Living in the End Times through Popular Culture: An Ultra-Realist Analysis of *The Walking Dead* as Popular Criminology', *Crime, Media, Culture*, 14/3 (2018), 443. Furthermore, the COVID-19 pandemic exposed an increasing amount of ultra-rich individuals retreating to million-dollar bunkers in New Zealand and other locations. Numerous publications showcased wealthy people in luxurious bunkers aggrandising individualistic preservation.
14. Suzanne Woolley and Devon Pendleton provide an exposé on how the 'ultra-rich' can access their yachts through 'sanitised' travel packages from VistaJet and avoid the 'germ-ridden' masses: 'Quandary for High Flyers: How to Travel Safely to Your Yacht', *Bloomberg Wealth*, 22 May 2020.
15. This reflects Nicholas Beuret and Gareth Brown's assertion, in 'The Walking Dead: The Anthropocene as a Ruined Earth', *Science as Culture*, 26/3 (2017), 330–54, that *TWD*, and by extension the *TWD* universe, 'offers a fictional meditation on the political conditions of the Anthropocene as a ruined earth' (332). However, in *FTWD*, and especially this scene, a ruined earth is less devastating to those with the means to avoid the ramifications of that ruinance.
16. Thom Davies, Arshad Isakjee and Surindar Dhesi, 'Violent Inaction: The Necropolitical Experience of Refugees in Europe', *Antipode*, 49/5 (2017), 1247.
17. The Jungle refugee camp in Calais was established in the early 2000s and demolished by French authorities in October 2016. See Oli Mould, 'The Not-So-Concrete Jungle: Material Precarity in the Calais Refugee Camp', *Cultural Geographies*, 25/3 (2017), 393–409, and Elisa Sandri, '"Volunteer Humanitarianism": Volunteers and Humanitarian Aid in the Jungle Refugee Camp of Calais', *Journal of Ethnic and Migration Studies*, 44/1 (2018), 65–80, for scholarship addressing the complex humanitarian and political context of the Calais refugee camp. Likewise, see Fishel and Wilcox on *TWD* and international relations.

18. For a history of the origins of the zombie in Haitian culture see Roger Luckhurst, *Zombies: A Cultural History* (London: Reaktion Books, 2015).
19. Viet Thanh Nguyen, in the op-ed 'The Sympathizer' for *The New York Times*, 6 September 2016, highlights that 'refugees are the zombies of the world, the undead who rise up from dying states to march or swim toward our borders in endless waves'.
20. Lisa Sun-Hee Park and David Naguib Pellow, 'Forum 4: The Environmental Privilege of Borders in the Anthropocene', *Mobilities*, 14/3 (2019), 398.
21. Although scholarship has begun to examine the increasing opioid addiction in Mexico, see Lawrence A. Palinkas, 'Opioid Use Epidemic in Mexico: Global Solutions to a Global Problem', *American Journal of Public Health*, 109/1 (2019), 26–7. *FTWD* season 3, of course, was produced before the current addiction increase in Mexico, but the cross-border opioid relationship is clearly represented in season.
22. Gilberto Rosas, 'Necro-Subjection: On Borders, Asylums, and Making Dead to Let Live', *Theory & Event*, 22/2 (2019), 304–5.
23. Johannes Fehrle, '"Zombie Don't Recognize Borders": Capitalism, Ecology, and Mobility in the Zombie Outbreak Narrative', *Amerikastudien/American Studies*, 61/4 (2016), 543.
24. See Kristina Campbell, 'A Dry Hate: White Supremacy and the Anti-Immigration Rhetoric in the Humanitarian Crisis on the U.S.-Mexico Border', *West Virginia Law Review*, 117/3 (2015), 1081–130, for an overview of this issue.
25. Kyle William Bishop, *American Zombie Gothic: The Rise and Fall (and Rise) of the Walking Dead in Popular Culture* (Jefferson NC: MacFarland., 2010), argues *Land of the Dead* is a critique of American immigration policy under Bush (30); and Stella Gaynor, 'A Braindead Nation: *Black Summer* and Trump's America', *Revenant*, 7 (2021), 246–71, argues that the Netflix series *Black Summer* is indicative of immigration policies under President Donald Trump.
26. Randall McGuire, 'Steel Walls and Picket Fences: Rematerializing the U.S.-Mexico Border in Ambos Nogales', *American Anthropologist*, 115/3 (2013), 468.
27. The Morgan character (one of the cross-over characters from *TWD*) will embody the 'post-frontier' cowboy figure later in *FTWD*; see Amanda R. Keeler, 'A Postapocalyptic Return to The Frontier: The Walking Dead as Post-Western', *Critical Studies in Television*, 13/4 (2018), 422–37.
28. Linda Green, 'The Nobodies: Neoliberalism, Violence, and Migration', *Medical Anthropology*, 30/4 (2011), 378.

29. The Broke Jaw ranch and Hopi tribe feud is most likely a fictionalisation of US Senator Barry Goldwater's (R-Ariz), and others', intervention in the Navajo-Hopi decades-long land dispute. See Rhiannon M. Koehler, 'Two Nations, Indivisible: Unity, Discord, and the Cartoon of the Navajo-Hopi Land Dispute, 1973–1974', *Journal of Arizona History*, 60/2 (2019), 183–216.
30. Steven Pokornowski, 'Vulnerable Life: Zombies, Global Biopolitics, and the Reproduction of Structural Violence', *Humanities*, 5/71 (2016), 6. See also, David Callahan, 'Rotting, Blistered, Staggering Bodies and the Last of Ethnicity', in David Callahan and Anthony Barker (eds), *Body and Text: Cultural Transformations in New Media Environments* (Cham: Springer, 2019), discussing commodified ethnicity in zombie narratives regarding the depiction of the Hopi tribe in *FTWD*.
31. See Nick Estes and Jaskiran Dhillon, 'The Black Snake, #NoDAPL, and the Rise of a People's Movement', in Nick Estes and Jaskiran Dhillon (eds), *Standing with Standing Rock: Voice from the #NoDAPL Movement* (Minneapolis MN: University of Minnesota Press, 2019), pp. 1–10, regarding the threat to the water supply of the resident Indigenous nations. Likewise, see Katie M. Grote and Jay T. Johnson, 'Pipeline, Protectors, and Settle Colonialism: Media Representation of the Dakota Pipeline Protest', *Settler Colonial Studies* (November 2021), 1–25, regarding the disregard on Indigenous sovereignty.
32. Peter Leigh and David A. Sonnenfeld, 'Water Crises and Institutions: Inventing and Reinventing Governance in an Era of Uncertainty', *Society & Natural Resources*, 30/4 (2017), 395–403.
33. The 1944 Water Treaty mandates that the United States provide Mexico with a designated amount of water from the Colorado River, which clearly establishes the United States in a position of power over Mexico. See Nicole Carter, Stephen Mulligan and Clare Seelke, 'U.S.-Mexican Water Sharing: Background and Recent Developments', *Congressional Research Service Report*, 2 March 2017.
34. Thomas Wiedmann *et al.*, 'Scientists' Warning on Affluence', *Nature Communications*, 11 (2020), claim that 'affluent citizens are responsible for most environmental impact' through overconsumption and a disregard for societal well-being (1, 5). In other words, the mindless disregard for environmental impact is creating a form of zombified elite consumption.

4

The Zombie Revolution Will Not Be Televised

Examining the Importance of Media in George R. Romero's Early Zombie Movies

Robert Curran

DESPITE THE EMPHASIS given to director and author George Romero's work in zombie studies, relatively few scholars have focused on the importance of media in early his early zombie films.[1] One exception is Allen Cameron's excellent work, 'Zombie Media: Transmission Reproduction and the Digital Dead'.[2] Cameron opens his essay noting, 'The modern zombie is a media zombie. Beginning with George A. Romero's *Night of the Living Dead*, zombie films have drawn attention with insistent frequency to the role of broadcast media'.[3] Throughout Romero's and later zombie films, either by technical issues or human duplicity, media is never the lifeline that the living need. In Romero's zombie films, mass media reflects the ongoing turmoil that society is experiencing.

Eric Bohman's text, 'Zombie Media' is another important work focused on how media is represented in Romero's *Dead* trilogy (*Night of the Living Dead*, *Dawn of the Dead* and *Day of the Dead*).[4] Bohman claims that 'Tracing the zombie event and media coverage of it over Romero's career unearths a fraught nexus – one that bring together our relations to history, social institutions, ethics and our present mediated state'.[5] This passage shows the importance of media in the trilogy, as media can be viewed as a nerve centre throughout the body of his work, starting with *Night of the Living Dead*.

More attention has been given to the overall themes and societal commentary of the films. *Night of the Living Dead* is seen by many critics as a commentary on civil rights and racist attitudes, *Dawn of the Dead* is traditionally seen as an indictment of capitalism and commercialism, while *Day of the Dead* is frequently viewed as a critique of the military-industrial complex. While these views are not wrong, a focus on how media and communication devices impact on survivors in Romero's early zombie films will provide an alternative understanding of the individual films and their overall synergy with each other. While many of these themes are seen in the remakes of Romero's films, this article focuses on Romero's original versions of the films. In each case that a film is referred to, the reference is relating to the original, not its remake. This chapter focuses on Romero's ambivalent relationship with media during the zombie apocalypse. On the one hand, it appears to offer salvation and connectivity but, as Romero cleverly reveals, such technology often proves more isolating and destructive. Thus, it is argued here that Romero depicts media as a sort of false friend for humanity – a device that divides more than it binds.

The Use and Failure of Media in Romero's Films

Why claim in the title that the zombie revolution will not be televised? This is a reference to the multiple failings of media seen throughout Romero's first three zombie films more so than actually claiming television plays no role in reporting on the zombie outbreak. The title is also a reference to Gil Scott-Heron's 1971 poem and song 'The Revolution Will Not Be Televised'.[6] Similarly, to Scott-Heron's revolution, the zombie revolution is one found on the streets, not on a small screen in one's living room. *Night of the Living Dead* has a scene where Sheriff McClelland is interviewed on camera by a news reporter. The sheriff states that his group has killed nineteen ghouls that day,[7] yet during this interview, we never see the cameraman film any ghouls. Sheriff McClelland tells his men to, 'Put that thing all the way in the fire! We don't want it getting up again'.[8] The fire and the burning ghoul are not filmed by the cameraman, likely due to being considered too graphic to show on a news broadcast. All the scenes of the survivors watching the televised reports in *Night of the Living Dead* clearly frame the broadcast with the television on screen, making sure to keep the broadcasts detached from how the rest of the film is shot. *Dawn of the Dead* has even more scenes featuring televised broadcasts than *Night*, but like *Night*, we never directly see zombies shown in a broadcast. These programmes focus more on informing the public of the zombie menace, but ultimately document the fracturing of society, and how even so-called experts cannot agree on a solution.

Jovanka Vuckovic and Jennifer Eiss praise *Night of the Living Dead*, but largely gloss over the role that media plays in the film, merely stating, 'According to newscasts the dead have been rising up all over the eastern seaboard and consuming the flesh of the living, but no one has any idea why or what can be done about it'.[9] Much of their focus on the film is that 'Whether or not the filmmakers had deliberately planned it, the result was a contemporary horror film that was subversive on many levels, but chiefly as a critique of American authority and its involvement in the Vietnam War'.[10] To be fair, their work encompasses the history of the zombie from its folkloric inception hundreds of years ago, to the present-day depiction of zombies, they likely did not have the space in their text to delve further into how media is portrayed in Romero's *Dead* trilogy. This is brought up because like many other critics, Vuckovic and Eiss focus on the social commentary of Romero's *Dead* trilogy. While this aspect should not be overlooked, other important concepts such as how mass media is represented in the trilogy are worthy of more consideration.

Romero's 1968 film, *Night of the Living Dead*, is rife with examples of how media influences characters' actions. At the beginning of the film, just before Johnny exits his car to follow Barbra, his radio broadcasts the following: 'Ladies and Gentlemen, we're coming back on the air after an interruption due to technical problems.' After turning off the radio, Johnny tells Barbra about this, saying, 'There's nothing wrong with the radio, it must have been the station'.[11] This shows that sometime before the start of the film, Johnny and Barbra were trying to listen to the radio during their trip. Had Johnny continued to listen to the broadcast, he would likely have been warned about the seemingly random acts of murder and violence occurring in the area. This technical difficulty foreshadows how media directly impacts on the plot of the film. Again and again, the media is rendered useless through technical issues, or ineffective in providing the survivors with needed information.

Shortly after this, Barbra is attacked by a zombie and Johnny is killed while defending her. After seeing her brother fall, Barbra retreats to a nearby farmhouse. While in pursuit of Barbra, the zombie incidentally tears down the telephone line connected to the farmhouse, severing Barbra's ability to call the authorities for assistance. After trying to use the telephone and finding that she is unable to do so, Barbra becomes mute, not speaking for a long time to another survivor, Ben, who joins her in the farmhouse. Like Barbra, Ben is unable to use the telephone and tells her, 'I suppose you tried this'.[12] The first actions of both Barbra and Ben are to reach out for help using the farmhouse's telephone. Romero shows us how much people have come to rely on such technology.

Ben soon discovers a radio in the farmhouse and immediately tunes in to a broadcast. With the telephone inoperative, the survivors are dependent on non-interactive media, limiting their ability to communicate with the outside world. Despite this, the radio provides both Ben and the film's viewers with important details regarding the zombie threat. The radio broadcast informs Ben – and the audience – that the undead encounters are not limited to his local surroundings. The newscaster informs listeners, 'There is an epidemic of mass murder being committed by a virtual army of unidentified assassins'. We see the ambiguous nature of the broadcast when the reporter states, 'So at this point, there is no really authentic way for us to say who or what to look out for and guard yourself against'. The radio describes the zombies as both 'ordinary looking people' and 'misshapen monsters' leading to further uncertainty.[13] It advises people to remain in their homes and not go outside for any reason. While this broadcast provides Ben and the viewers with some exposition, it is hydra-like. Nothing is certain, for every question answered, two more take its place.

As Ben is further exploring the farmhouse, the newscaster provides background regarding the zombie outbreak, reporting: 'This whole ghastly story began two days ago with a report of the slaying of a family of seven in their rural home.'[14] The broadcast follows up, noting that the day before it became clear that they were facing a national emergency. The delay in informing the public served to endanger people and increased the number of undead. The media failed the public by pondering over what was happening and searching for a reason. Theories of the cause of the situation that are reported by the media vary from a conspiracy to creatures from outer space, or even radiation from a recently destroyed Venus space probe.[15] Throughout all Romero's zombie films, we never learn why the dead return to life.

While Ben searches the upstairs of the farmhouse, a second group of survivors, ones sheltering in the cellar, emerge. Immediately, one of these members, Harry Cooper, exclaims 'A radio!', largely ignoring Ben and Barbra to focus on the broadcast.[16] We learn that there are five survivors who have been sheltering in the cellar: Harry, his wife (Helen Cooper), his daughter (Karen Cooper) and a young couple named Tom and Judy. Ben and Harry immediately argue over the best course of action, with Harry wanting everyone to go into the cellar, and Ben wanting to defend the floor-level. Harry goes back into the cellar after Tom and Judy stay upstairs. While talking with his wife, Harry mentions that there is a radio upstairs, to which Helen replies, 'Radio? There's a radio upstairs and you boarded us in down here?' Helen clearly sees the importance of the radio and questions her husband's rash action. After hearing that the group upstairs has also found a television, Helen convinces her husband that the two of them should leave the cellar. Access to the radio and television is important enough for Harry and Helen to unbarricade the cellar and join the group upstairs.

Desperate for news, the group surrounds the television and learns that people should no longer remain sheltered in one place but attempt to reach a nearby rescue station. The earlier radio broadcast's recommendations of sheltering in place are now obsolete. We see that the group's viewpoint has been influenced by the telecast when Tom tells Judy, 'The television says that's the right thing to do'.[17] This broadcast spurs the group to leave the farmhouse. Tragedy strikes during their attempt to refuel the truck – both Tom and Judy are killed. *Night of the Living Dead* is set more than a decade before the advent of the twenty-four-hour news cycle, the broadcast regularly stops, leaving the survivors waiting for the next update, increasing their uncertainty of the situation. The omnipresence of the television in American households at the time *Night of the Living Dead* was released is shocking compared to just fifteen years earlier. Madie Ward notes that: 'From 1950 to 1966, the percentage of Americans who owned a television skyrocketed from "9 per cent" to "93 per cent" as televisions became essential for everyday life.'[18] Americans came to depend on the television rather than radio and newsprint during this era, not only for entertainment, but also to learn about what was going on in the world. Despite regular television broadcasts, we see that the survivors in *Night of the Living Dead* still face a large degree of uncertainty regarding how to cope with the undead menace. Elizabeth Aiossa writes about this, stating that media and law enforcement agencies are revealed as incompetent and ignorant, if not wholly important, in dire times.[19] The ever-changing narrative of the news broadcasts leave the survivors with doubts on how to proceed.

A later news report serves to further divide the remaining survivors. In a pre-recorded interview, a reporter asks Sheriff McClelland, 'Chief, if I were surrounded by six or eight of these things, would I stand a chance with them?' The sheriff responds, 'Well there's no problem, if you had a gun, shoot them in the head, that's a sure way to kill them'. After hearing Sheriff McClelland's interview, Harry is convinced that he needs to take Ben's rifle, telling his wife 'Helen, I have to get that gun'.[20] We see here the chaos depicted on the television acted out in real life. Rather than help Ben fight the ghouls attempting to gain entry to the farmhouse, Harry uses the opportunity to take Ben's gun. Ben regains control of the rifle and, in turn, shoots Harry for his betrayal. Harry is directly motivated to take the gun after hearing Sheriff McClelland's interview where he states how useful firearms are against ghouls.

At the end of the film, Ben finds himself the lone survivor of the group barricaded in the cellar, with no radio or television. After being roused in the morning by the sound of gunshots, Ben leaves the cellar and is mistaken for a zombie and killed. *Night of the Living Dead* closes with a notably grainy photo montage of a posse disposing of dead bodies, along with Ben, taken by media journalists. These media images depict Ben as just another undead, erasing both his humanity and heroism.

Breakdowns and Isolation

George Romero's second zombie film, *Dawn of the Dead*, opens *in medias res*. We follow Fran, who works for a television station. We see the newsroom in chaos, mirroring the situation occurring on the streets. Throughout a prolonged scene, we see the newsroom crew bickering and on edge. Fran learns that the station has been providing the public with a news crawl that is listing out-of-date rescue stations and that they have been doing so for the past twelve hours. Fran orders that the list be removed, which upsets her boss. She asks her boss if he is willing to cause people to die by sending them to overrun stations, and he tells her that without the lists people will tune out, clearly showing he is more concerned about ratings than lives. Tony Williams writes, 'Romero again provides another devastating critique of the television apparatus. He depicts it as dishonest and emotionally unstable'.[21] Williams focuses on how Romero's films (not only his *Dead* trilogy, but other films such as *Martin*, *The Crazies* and *There's Always Vanilla*) cynically present mass media. Romero's critique of the media is consistent throughout the films he directed. Gloria Pastorino states that Romero's penultimate zombie film, *Diary of the Dead*, 'Documents the obsession with rouge media reporting and broadcasting everything, editing and manipulating information in reality-TV mode'.[22] *Diary of the Dead* is yet another example of Romero's focus on media, which occurs time and time again in his work.

As we have seen in this chapter's title, the zombie revolution will not be televised; no footage of the zombies is broadcast in *Dawn of the Dead*. Instead, the station is broadcasting an interview with an expert doctor who asks the sceptical host if he believes that the dead are returning to life. The host responds that he is unsure what to believe. We learn that this phenomenon has been going on for three weeks. The doctor continues, 'Every dead body that is not exterminated gets up and kills, the people it kills get up and kill'.[23] He stresses that there is a state of martial law in all major cities and the public can no longer remain in their homes and will be moved into central areas of cities and that all dead bodies must be turned over to the National Guard. The host responds, saying 'People aren't willing to accept your solutions doctor, and I for one don't blame them'.[24] This early television interview provides viewers with a look into the major issue of public reluctance to deal with the zombie outbreak. Many people value the tradition of treating the dead with respect and are unable to adapt to this new crisis, despite the media telling them otherwise.

As social order breaks down, we see the media and other institutions also fracturing in lockstep. Christopher Paul Wagenheim writes, 'Without commitment from subordinate institutions, however, power cannot be consolidated into a dominant hegemony which causes massive social instabilities such as a breakdown in mass media, police enforcement, and long held social values'.[25] Shortly after seeing the breakdown in the newsroom, we are shown the impact on the government's draconian policies in a disastrous police raid on a low-income housing project, whose residents refuse to turn over their dead. After the raid, *Dawn* cuts to Fran and Stephen refuelling the helicopter at the city's police boat dock. While searching the building, Stephen finds that the dock's radio operator has committed suicide, likely due to listening to the constant unfolding madness. This shows a further fracturing of society as its pillars of order collapse. Stephen informs police headquarters of the operator's death and after meeting with Roger and Peter the four fly off in their helicopter.

While in flight, the group discovers a modern shopping mall, a somewhat new concept in 1978. Irwin Landau writes that 'Air-conditioned, sanitized, standardized' shopping malls became 'the new Main Streets of America'.[26] It is these qualities that lead the group to use the shopping mecca as a place for their pilot Stephen to rest, while Peter and Roger gather much-needed supplies there. While exploring the mall, Roger and Peter encounter a control room and find a pair of walkie talkies and blueprints showing the layout of the shops. Roger also finds a power console, which, among other things, broadcasts music and helps to cover any noise that they will make. These radios help the survivors communicate with each other and better understand their location.

While in a department store, Roger proclaims, 'Watches, watches!' Peter responds 'Hey, hey, hey, let's get the stuff we need. I'll get a television and a radio'.[27] Clearly, these items are considered of great importance, along with the walkie talkies. Communication is key. Stephen meets up with Roger and Peter, having found a binder that shows a series of passageways above the shops that allow them to avoid the zombies following them back to their saferoom. As a form of media, the binder is critical in allowing the group to remain in the mall without being besieged by zombies. Also of note, throughout their stay in the mall the survivors regularly hear announcements of sales and special events, which speaks to the film's influence of capitalism and its narcotic-like effects.

Back in the saferoom, the group set up the television and radio, and while the television only displays a standby signal, the radio informs them that communications have been knocked out in Detroit, Atlanta, Boston and parts of Philadelphia. This update notifies the survivors that things are not improving but rather becoming worse. During the first television broadcast that the survivors receive, they are told that the zombies are not cannibals since they do not consume each other. The expert being interviewed, Dr Millard Rausch, states, 'We must not be lulled by the concept that these (the zombies) our are family members or our friends, they are not. They will not respond to such emotions'. Someone in the crowd interjects, yelling: 'They are!' to which Dr Rausch responds, 'They must be destroyed on sight!'[28] Here we see the breakdown between the experts and the general populace. In this scene, Dr Rausch further extolls the importance of dispassionately dealing with the zombie menace. While he is speaking, the audience argues against his viewpoint. Due to the live aspect of the programme, survivors, along with the audience, have no certainty of how best to handle the situation. During their occupation of the mall, broadcast media enables our group of survivors to remain engaged with the outside world, similarly as it does in *Night of the Living Dead.*

The survivors decide that the first step to making the mall safe is to stop the zombies from being able to enter it. To do this, they plan to use nearby articulated lorries to block the entrances. With Stephen dropping them to ground level and observing them using the helicopter, Roger and Peter drive the lorries. They communicate using the lorries' radios, but they should have maintained contact with Stephen using the walkie talkies or other means. Stephen's aerial view allows him to see the zombies approach Roger, but he is unable to communicate this. Roger is nearly bitten, and the encounter causes him to become unhinged. This ultimately leads to Roger taking greater risks and he is bitten while parking a lorry. Better communication would likely have prevented this.

During their occupation of the mall, we see the interviewed experts offer increasingly absurd solutions to the zombie menace, such as feeding them or dropping nuclear weapons on large cities, as seen in 2021's *Army of the Dead.*[29] During the last television broadcast we see in *Dawn*, Dr Rausch admonishes his audience and viewers saying, 'We are down to the line folks! We are down to the line … We've got to remain unemotional', to which Fran says to Stephen, 'It's really all over isn't it?'[30] This scene is crosscut with Roger returning as a zombie and we hear Peter shoot him. While we see Stephen and Fran looking at each other, knowing Roger has just been shot, Dr Rausch exhorts, 'We've got to remain rational, logical … There's no choice, it's that or the end'. This is a fitting message considering that Roger's death was caused by arrogance and acting irrationally and illogically.

While the group is still living in the mall, the television broadcasts eventually stop. Eating dinner, Stephen walks to the television and changes channels, hoping to find an update, which causes Fran to tell him, 'There hasn't been a broadcast in three days, why don't you give it up?' Stephen responds, 'They might come back on'.[31] After Stephen sits down, Fran angrily gets up and turns off the television. Stephen now gets up and turns the television back on. He holds out hope that the broadcasts will return, but Fran is more pessimistic. Media divides them.

Soon after this exchange, a large group of scavengers attempt to contact the survivors via radio, but Peter and the group do not respond, despite receiving their calls. This prompts the raiders to invade the mall. Peter and Stephen close the gates to prevent the group, and they stay in touch with each other using their walkie talkies. While seeing the raiders loot 'their' mall, Stephen becomes enraged and starts to shoot at the interlopers. Peter desperately attempts to contact Stephen via radio, but because of his ire, Stephen does not contact him until he is seriously injured. Peter hears Stephen fall victim to zombies and is powerless to save him. The film ends with Fran and Peter flying away from the mall, with little fuel. Earlier in the film, we saw the group loading supplies onto the helicopter; hopefully they included a radio.

The Limits of Media

In Romero's third zombie film, *Day of the Dead*, released in 1984, we find a new group of survivors using a helicopter in the hope of finding living allies. They set down in Fort Myers, Florida, and attempt to contact other people using a bullhorn and a radio broadcast from the helicopter. During the scene, a newspaper page blows by that reads 'THE DEAD WALK'.[32] This is perhaps the first time that we see print media in a Romero zombie film. Interestingly, copies of this newspaper page are frequently sold at horror conventions, showing the importance of physical media, even in today's age.

The survivors shelter in an underground storage facility. The group is made up of two technicians, three scientists and seven army soldiers. While discussing their precarious situation in a meeting, the radio operator Bill McDermott tells the group, 'Not a peep, long range or short, high band or low, I can't raise anybody'.[33] He goes on to say that he is sure that there are other groups, but due to their location and the age of their equipment, they are unable to send a strong signal. Not being able to contact other groups increases the tension among the survivors due to their sense of isolation.

Day's major protagonist, Sarah, is a scientist hoping to find a way to eradicate the zombie problem. She goes to visit McDermott and John, the group's helicopter pilot. While discussing their predicament, John tells Sarah that their shelter contains film negatives, books and historical records. He then asks Sarah what good this media is to him in their dilemma. He tells her that he sees a possible future for humanity, but that future generations should start afresh and never dig up the old historical records and media. John continues:

> We've been punished by the creator. He visited a curse on us. So we might get a look at what Hell was like. Maybe he didn't want to see us blow ourselves up and put a big hole in his sky. Maybe his just

> wanted to show us he was still the boss man. Maybe he figure, we was getting to big in our britches, trying to figure his shit out.[34]

To John, the knowledge contained in the media archives in their base is a threat to future generations, as he believes that mankind's hubris has led to their current situation.

Dr Logan's views on physical media stand in stark contrast to those of John. The doctor hopes to civilise the zombies and we see him introduce his zombie test-subject named Bub to common items such as a toothbrush and a razor to spark memories of the zombie's earlier life. Dr Logan also gives Bub several media items to accomplish this. We see him give Bub a copy of Stephen King's novel *Salem's Lot*, which Bub flicks through. Bub is also given a disconnected telephone; he holds the receiver to his ear and, with Dr Logan's prodding, rasps out 'Hello Aunt Alicia'. Finally, Dr Logan provides Bub with a tape recorder and teaches him how to start the player. Bub is awestruck when he hears Beethoven's 'Ode to Joy'. During this lesson, while Dr Logan is adjusting Bub's headphones, Bub grabs hold of Dr Logan's arm, but only out of curiosity, he does not try to bite him. It seems as though Dr Logan has at least partially civilised Bub and that the media objects have played a role in awakening Bub's memories.

Ultimately, things fall apart for the group, and Sarah, John and McDermott are the only survivors. They take their helicopter to a small, seemingly uninhabited island. It appears that John's wish to abandon the past's records and media has happened, but there is now nothing to stop future generations from obtaining these sources.

Conclusion

Media in Romero's first three zombie films is far-reaching and provides viewers with 'big picture' understanding of the scope of the problem that the different groups face. Despite media's helpfulness throughout the films, we also see its limitations. In *Night of the Living Dead*, technical issues prevent Johnny and Barbra from receiving radio warnings of the danger. In *Dawn of the Dead*, media broadcasts frequently reflect ongoing societal chaos. Finally, in *Day of the Dead* we see that without contact with other groups, feelings of isolation lead to a pressure-cooker situation. In *Night of the Living Dead*, we see that the televised advice leads to the survivors doing rash things, such as confronting dozens of ghouls outside the farmhouse, or Harry's coveting of Ben's rifle. In *Dawn of the Dead*, the survivors decide not to communicate with the motorcycle gang, despite their ability to do so, leading to the zombies reclaiming the mall. In each film, media and communication are a direct cause of the groups' downfall. Diem-My T. Bui quotes from an interview where Romero states that '*Night of the Living Dead* is specifically saying that you're not talking to each other, electronic media doesn't work, people don't communicate'.[35] Examining how media and communication are portrayed in these films provides us with valuable insight. Throughout the *Dead* trilogy, we see that on both the personal and societal level people are unable to adapt to the new paradigm of the dead returning to (un)life. In these films, media mirrors the divisions that we see in people and fails to provide the living with any sure path forward. In fact, it echoes humanity's downfall. Romero's *Dead* trilogy serves to caution the viewer, showing us that despite its seeming omnipresence, media is fallible.

Notes

1. Colin Tait, '(Zombie) Revolution at the Gates: The Dead, The "Multitude" and George A. Romero', *Cinephile: The University of British Columbia's Film Journal*, 3/1 (2007), 61–70; Matthew Bailey, 'Memory, Place and the Mall: George Romero on Consumerism', *Studies in Popular Culture*, 35/2 (2013), 95–110; Tony Williams, *The Cinema of George A. Romero: Knight of the Living Dead* (New York: Columbia University Press, 2015).
2. Allan Cameron, 'Zombie Media: Transmission, Reproduction, and the Digital Dead', *Cinema Journal*, 52/1 (2012), 68–89.
3. Cameron, 'Zombie Media: Transmission', 68.
4. Erick Bohman, 'Zombie Media', in Edward P. Comentale and Aaron Jaffe (eds), *The Year's Work at the Zombie Research Center* (Bloomington IN: Indiana University Press, 2014), pp. 150–92.
5. Bohman, 'Zombie Media', p. 151.
6. Gil Scott-Heron, 'The Revolution Will Not Be Televised', track 1 on *Small Talk and Lenox*, Flying Dutchman Records (1971), compact disc.
7. George A. Romero (dir.), *Night of the Living Dead* (United States: Image Ten, 1968).
8. Romero, *Night of the Living Dead.*
9. Jovanka Vuckovic and Jennifer Eiss, *Zombies! An Illustrated History of the Undead* (New York: St. Martin's Griffin, 2011), p. 60.

10. Vuckovic and Eiss, *Zombies*, p. 65.
11. Romero, *Night of the Living Dead.* This is a critical part of the film where Romero shows the limits of radio and how media is not failproof, much to the chagrin of the survivors.
12. Romero, *Night of the Living Dead.*
13. Romero, *Night of the Living Dead.* Again, media fails to adequately inform the survivors about the situation, offering them two vastly different descriptions of the undead.
14. Romero, *Night of the Living Dead.*
15. Romero, *Night of the Living Dead.* In this instance, Romero again shows how media is unable to accurately describe the cause of the outbreak, fomenting public panic.
16. Romero, *Night of the Living Dead.* Cooper seemingly values the radio above other survivors.
17. Romero, *Night of the Living Dead.* Tom's viewpoint is obviously shaped by the reporting, despite the station's contradictory advice to its viewers.
18. Madie Ward, 'Vietnam: The First Television War', *Pieces of History, U.S. National Archives* (2018), *https://prologue.blogs.archives.gov/2018/01/25/vietnam-the-first-television-war/* (last accessed 22 January 2023).
19. Elizabeth Aiossa, *The Subversive Zombie: Social Protest and Gender in Undead Cinema and Television* (Jefferson NC: McFarland, 2018). p. 25.
20. Romero, *Night of the Living Dead.*
21. Tony Williams, *The Cinema of George A. Romero: Knight of the Living Dead* (New York: Wallflower Press, 2015), p. 94.
22. Gloria Pastorino, 'Zombie Films as Allegorical Westerns', in Bruce Peabody and Gloria Pastorino (eds), *Beyond the Living Dead: Essays on the Romero Legacy* (Jefferson NC: McFarland, 2021), p. 73. For those interested in further scholarship on *Diary of the Dead*, consider Randy Laist's 'Soft Murders: Motion Pictures and Living Death in *Diary of the Dead*', in Stephanie Boluk and Wylie Lenz (eds), *Generation Zombie: Essays on the Living Dead in Popular Culture* (Jefferson NC: McFarland, 2011). pp. 101–12.
23. George A. Romero (dir.), *Dawn of the Dead* (United States: Laurel Group Inc, 1978).
24. Romero, *Dawn of the Dead.*
25. Christopher Paul Wagenheim, *From Night to Dawn: The Cultural Criticism of George A. Romero* (MA thesis, University of South Florida, 2010), *https://digitalcommons.usf.edu/cgi/viewcontent.cgi?article=5019&context=etd* (last accessed 12 January 2023).

26. Irwin Landau, *I'll Buy That! 50 Small Wonders and Big Deals That Revolutionized the Lives of Consumers: A 50-Year Retrospective by the Editors of Consumer Reports* (Mount Vernon WA: Consumers Union, 1986).
27. Romero, *Dawn of the Dead.* Interestingly, both these items were of high importance to the survivors in *Night of the Living Dead.*
28. Romero, *Dawn of the Dead.*
29. Zack Snyder (dir.), *Army of the Dead* (United States: The Stone Quarry, 2021).
30. Romero, *Dawn of the Dead.* In this scene we see a media representation of societal collapse, while the survivors deal with a similar collapse of their own (that of Roger's downfall and upcoming demise).
31. Romero, *Dawn of the Dead.*
32. George A. Romero (dir.), *Day of the Dead* (United States: United Film Distributing Company, 1985).
33. Romero, *Day of the Dead.* Here, once again, Romero shows us the limits of media.
34. Romero, *Day of the Dead.*
35. Diem-My T. Bui, 'Communications in a Zombie Apocalypse: Usage, Control and Collapse of Mass Media', in Amy L. Thompson and Antonio S. Thompson (eds), *... But If a Zombie Apocalypse Did Occur: Essays on Medical, Military, Governmental, Ethical, Economic and Other Implications* (Jefferson NC: McFarland, 2015), p. 99.

PART TWO

DISSECTING THE ZOMBIE BODY

5

Decaying Dicks and Putrid Pussies

Zombie Sex Toys and Pleasure

Caroline West

THE ZOMBIE IS OFTEN positioned as asexual in mainstream depictions; however, the existence of zombie sex toys alongside zombie porn shows that there is space for sexuality within zombie discourse. These sex toys claim to resemble 'realistic' zombie genitalia and receive reviews such as this intriguing example from reviewer Amber on Amazon: 'for those of you out there with secret zombie sex fantasies, this is for you! Finally a zombie cock that won't rot and fall off' – from a user who rated it five out of five stars and noted that it satisfied a 'horror fetish'.[1] Zombiism interrogates borders that are geopolitical or economic, but we cannot build a complete theory of zombiism without looking at sexual borders and how the zombified orgasm challenges notions of sexual pleasure.

Sex should be firmly situated within zombie semiotics to explore what transgressive sexual activity means for zombie epistemology. This chapter looks at the phenomenon of zombie sex toys and how they fit into explorations of abject sexuality, where disgust is a turn on instead of a turn off. If decay is a selling point instead of a disgust elicitor, how does this affect our comprehension of sex? When pustules and exposed testicles are promoted features on dildos, and grey, rotting flesh is used as the skin tone for vagina replicas, what does this say about the nature of taboo sex and the abject?

Thus, this chapter explores this intersection of horror and pleasure, and asks how the sexualised zombie can contribute to our understanding of both zombiism and desire. Clasen suggests that 'the emotional response to the ontological breach represented by the zombie can fall on a continuum from religious awe to full-blown terror'.[2] Further to this positioning, this chapter will examine how arousal is part of this spectrum.

Masturbation

Before we can discuss zombie sex toys, we must look back in history to see the connections between masturbation and the fear of infectious, rotting bodies. The history of masturbation is as gory as zombie lore. Tales of leaking bodies and stupefied droolers have dominated masturbation literature as much as George A. Romero has dominated the Hollywood zombie-film genre with his grisly zombies. The semiotics used in these dual discourses of anti-masturbation and zombies point to a semiotics of corporeality where the body is the locus of the abject, particularly the genitals and sexualised body. When sexology began to establish itself as a discipline in the seventeenth and eighteenth centuries, masturbation was not viewed as the sexual wellness practice it is today in sex-positive circles.[3] Mutilation of the genitals was seen as an appropriate treatment for masturbation, leaving children disfigured and presumably also traumatised. The link between masturbation and disease was popularised by Dr Samuel-Auguste Tissot in his 1758 book *Onanism: A Treatise on the Maladies Produced by Masturbation*,[4] in which he described in graphic detail the damage that masturbation was presumed to do to the body. The fear of masturbation arose from literature such as Tissot's that described masturbation as the source of disease of the mind and body, leaving a victim lifeless, drooling and stupefied. The focus in many descriptions was on damage to the brain, which was alleged to shrink with masturbation, and the descriptions used for victims recall the zombified body: 'with flesh rotting away', 'weak', 'lifeless', 'death', 'wasting bodies', 'loss of flesh', 'convulsions' and resembling a 'cadaver'.[5] The semiotics here suggest a connection between sex and death, which is as ever-present as the fear around sex that has dominated Western culture for centuries. Masturbation was regarded as unnatural sex, murder, a diabolical practice and the cause of two-thirds of all diseases and disorders, including insanity, neurosis and neurasthenia.[6]

Bodies can harbour disease and can present as disgusting, and Jones outlines how sex intertwines with the fear of the leaky body: 'because sex commonly entails the exchange of various bodily fluids (such as saliva, sweat, vaginal juices, semen), sex can provoke fears about interpersonal pollution and pathogenic infection'.[7] The zombie represents these locums of disgust in its decaying corporality, and the idea that sex can and will corrupt not only a person, but wider society is represented in anti-masturbation literature. A woman enjoying sexual agency and masturbation was as monstrous as their leaky bodies, and Screats warns of the devastating effects of women corrupted by desire:

> if a woman is infected with desire, she ... ceases to be [a] passive recipient of kiss and penetration and becomes active and penetrative herself ... [G]ive a woman a taste of the vampire/erotic, and she will become depraved and may even run riot, infecting the whole of society.[8]

The corrupting infectious nature of desire was manifested in anxious narratives around pleasure, particularly self-pleasure.

The preventative step against mutilation via masturbation was mutilation via medicine. The clitoris became a removable object, a sacrifice to make in the quest to prevent masturbation and moral decay, often called 'onanism' in these texts. Rubin details how masturbation in girls was horrifically treated:

> Asked his advice, Dr. J. Guerin affirmed that, after all other treatments had failed, he had succeeded in curing young girls affected by the vice of onanism by burning the clitoris with a hot iron ... 'I apply the hot point three times to each of the large labia and another on the clitoris ... After the first operation, from forty to fifty times a day, the number of voluptuous spasms was reduced to three or four.[9]

This viewpoint was not to be short lived. While Dr John Harvey Kellogg may be most known for inventing cornflakes, it was his fear of sex and disease that made him justify mutilating children in the name of preventing self-pollution through masturbation. Kellogg believed that female masturbation was especially corrupting and argued that the best way to 'treat' it was to pour carbolic acid on a clitoris to solve the 'abnormal' desire.[10] He also carried out clitoridectomies (surgical removal of the clitoris) on girls as young as ten and pronounced this a success as masturbation ceased; hardly surprisingly when forced to undergo such surgery. The masturbator is consumed by lust instead of a virus, but the effect is the same – they are no longer safe for themselves or others nor agents of their own destiny; condemned to suffer mindlessly. The zombie becomes the abject when infected by a virus, and the genitals become abject when touched through one's own hands. The resulting physical and moral decay that violates societal norms has been now eroticised in the form of zombie sex toys, which transform the rotting zombified genitalia into a source of pleasure.

Zombie Sex Toys

While many zombie films focus on relationships between humans, zombie-human relationships have not historically been part of the mainstream zombie oeuvre, although this is changing with 'millennial zombie narratives'.[11] Zombie porn does cross this life-and-death boundary, showing graphic zombie-human sex that, while transgressive in appearance, follows mainstream porn scripts. Sex with zombies represents an apocalyptic state for sexuality and society, one that threatens everyone with moral decay. The zombie represents an insatiable hunger that evokes the uncontrollable nature of sex and lust. Ward argues that 'sexualizing the zombie breaches the last barriers against a floodtide of excess that threatens to swamp us all'.[12] By framing the abject body as erotic, zombie sex toys offer a space to reflect on narratives of disgust, necrophilia, corrupting sex and gendered iterations of the monstrous.

Zombies are a visual assault. There is no hiding from the open wounds and body fluids of a zombie, nor the startling loss of their humanity and sense of self. Mainstream films enjoy the squick factor from close-ups of wounds and the moment of biting which is used as a selling point for films such as *Dawn of the Dead* (1978), *World War Z* (2013) and *Army of the Dead* (2022). Pulliam lists extreme gore as an essential part of zombie iconography, especially post Romero.[13] Building on this sense of grotesque carnival, zombie sex toys revel in the gore, the visceral, the excess, the unapologetic nature of fucking. The sexualisation of disgust and the abject defilement of the body is the explicit selling point of zombie sex toys. It is perhaps not surprising that horror would be a theme for a sex toy since these self-pleasure devices come in a diverse range of sizes and colours. Tentacles, aliens and dragons have been replicated in dildo form, and given that zombie porn is a genre of pornography, it is no surprise that zombie sex toys exist in the world. While zombie porn offers a space for viewers to engage with the abject safely via a screen,[14] zombie sex toys remove that barrier and allow for physical contact with the abject. In this case, silicone replaces flesh to allow for a safe space to explore the border between pleasure and death. Zombie sex toys expose the ontological borders between sexuality and death as porous, intermingling disgust and desire in zombified masturbatory bliss.

When it comes to choosing the right toy for satisfying necrophiliac desires, zombie sex toys predominately come in two forms – one for a penis and one for a vagina/anus. For the penis, there are two options: the Zombie Lady Fleshlight and the Zombie Mouth Fleshlight, and for the vagina/anus the Zombie Dildo offers some gruesome delights.

The Zombie Lady Fleshlight

Released in 2011, the Zombie Lady Fleshlight was made by the company Fleshlight. Fleshlights are sex toys described by sex toy reviewers Sex Toy Collective as:

> A portable masturbation aid also known as an artificial vagina or a pocket pussy. Typically, it's a narrow tube about the size and shape of a flashlight (hence the name), that a guy can stick his penis in to masturbate. The inner sleeve is made of silicone or other materials designed to feel as realistic as possible.[15]

The Fleshlight anus and mouth simulators are often made to resemble famous porn stars' genitalia, catering to straight and queer men. The zombie version of the Fleshlight is called the Zombie Lady Fleshlight and stands out to some reviewers for its choice of internal texture: 'The Zombie uses the "Necro Feelya" texture, which is a combination of an intensely textured and ridged first few inches, followed by the wavy "Forbidden" texture for the remaining length of the sleeve' (edensfantasys.com). Labelling the material used as 'Necro Feelya' sets the tone that is present in other zombie sex toys – necrophilia is overtly framed as attractive and an acceptable desire to indulge.

In this case, the reviewer acknowledges that it might not appeal to all users' tastes:

> Admittedly, the design of the Zombie is probably polarising. The idea of sex with a zombie doesn't leave much middle ground; looking directly and the opening, you are either turned on by torn labia and wrinkled flesh or repulsed by it. However, this concern dissipates quickly once you're inside, as the Zombie's distinguishing features are not really visible during use.[16]

The external genitals being framed as surplus to requirements has been reflected in anti-masturbation narratives and heterosexist sexual scripts seen in mainstream and zombie porn and is noted across several reviews of this product. The grotesque nature of this device is highlighted as a selling point by another reviewer who uses the name 'Casquetero', the owner of fifty-six Fleshlight toys and an active reviewer on fleshassist.com, where he reviews Fleshlights in detail for the benefit of other consumers:

> If there is an ugly entrance for a masturbation sleeve is the one for the FL Zombie. It has a design of rotten meat, just like the sickest man in [*sic*] Earth could imagine the pussy of a degrading corpse … Good thing I never pay too much attention to the orifice look because the Zombie is a boner killer.[17]

Casquetero acknowledges the desexualised zombie as the standard zombie in mainstream zombie content but personally embraces the sexualised zombie as a source for pleasure. He navigates its monstrous appearance by avoiding looking at the 'rotten pussy' and the 'ugliest and sickest orifice'. In many modern mainstream zombie narratives, the grotesque nature of zombie genitalia and zombie sexuality is sanitised for a wider audience than who the Fleshlight may appeal to. Streaming shows such as *iZombie* (2015) and *Santa Clarita Diet* (2017) depict characters who fit Western celebrity beauty standards – beautiful, white, thin and looking very much alive. Drew Barrymore's character in *Santa Clarita Diet* is bubbly and beautiful, and enjoys an active sex life with her husband, despite his knowledge of her body beginning to rot. Indeed, her rotting body and need to eat humans is sanctified through humour and framed as a couple's date-night activity for supportive partners. In *Warm Bodies* (2013), there is human-zombie kissing, but this occurs after the undead R is on the cusp of subjectivity and humanness as he comes back to life. The zombie sex toy challenges this framing of the undead body by refusing to sanitise its appearance, returning the focus to the abject by highlighting the grotesque nature of the product. Even if the user cannot look at it, it is still overtly positioned as a replica of a corpse to be used for penetration. The graphic depictions of the rotten body are reminiscent of how, since the zombie is ontological anxiety made into flesh, the zombie sex toy is the same anxiety made into silicone.

Zombie Mouth

In addition to the Zombie Lady Fleshlight toy, the range includes the Zombie Mouth Fleshlight which was released in 2016. Similar to the Zombie Lady, this masturbation device is made to resemble a rotting zombie part, specifically the mouth, complete with bared teeth. Christensen suggests that what makes the Zombie Mouth even more disturbing is that:

> aside from the synthetic 'skin' around it, which is dyed green and designed to look like rotting flesh … the mouth opens to receive the sexual organs of its owner, it bares a set of pronounced, sharp-looking teeth that create the illusion that those who place their genitals inside this mouth risk having them bitten off in the process.[18]

While the human body is subject to beauty standards that insist on being blemish free, the zombie mouth and vagina explicitly reject this pressure and instead revel in the zombie's 'unsteady corporeality' and the decay of the once perfect body.[19] Zombie sex-toy user 'Casquetero', who previously reviewed the Zombie Lady, documents his experience using the Zombie Mouth on thecasqueterofiles.com. He highlights how the appearance of the toy is off-putting for many, but desirable if zombies are a turn on for the user:

> If the Zombie vagina was ugly, its mouth is even uglier! The face of this toy is simply haunting … A rotten corpse mouth with perfect teeth that demands cock no matter what! It is difficult to describe how much of a bone killer this toy is for those of us not attracted to necrophiliac models.[20]

The reference to the insatiable mouth here recalls the heterosexism present in zombie pornography, where women's mouths are to do sex *to* in their framing as passive and ever receptive. The overt acknowledgement of necrophilia in these reviews positions the abject as erotic and highlights the supremacy of desire over the death drive or social norms.

Liminal Space

The zombie mouth is the locus for infection in traditional zombie films, yet with this toy it is positioned as the ultimate pathway to pleasure. The Zombie mouth and the Zombie Lady sex toys can therefore function as liminal spaces, dancing on the thresholds of life, sex and death. The zombie mouth and vagina offer a space at the moment of orgasm, where the ejaculate meets plastic, to connect with death. It is a horrifying liminal space as it can hold the potential to flow into the real world – the corruption of necrophilia and zombie attraction can sully an individual and society, breaching the borders of acceptable sexuality. Cooper suggests that 'the ultimate liminal space between life and death should not be permeable in both directions',[21] and the potentially infectious body fluids from both human and zombie combining evokes the fear of these liminal spaces leeching into the world of 'good' sex.

Zombie sex toys propel the user into a psychological liminal space that mimics the trajectory of mainstream zombie narratives that keep the user in a state of tension before a resolution. In zombie films, this is a cure; with zombie sex toys, it is an orgasm. These toys provide an emotional liminal space between disgust and desire, arousal and fear. This living/dead threshold interrogation reflects mainstream zombie narratives who explore the 'fragile life–death boundary' between humans and zombies, as Jones suggests.[22] Jones describes a dialectical tension between the horrific side to sex and the sexual side to horror,[23] and this tension can be located in the zombified orgasm, which allows us to reconsider the nature of human sexuality and our relationship with the abject. The 'deliciously disgusting'[24] encounter with the abject delves into the liminal space of violence and pleasure, solidifying Christensen's identification of the 'monstrous orality' present in the Zombie Mouth and highlighting ontological anxiety about the body and death.[25] This 'subversive liminality'[26] adds to the sense of horror at zombie sex toys for their potential to infect society with unruly sexuality.

Castration

Christensen posits that the metaphorical castration of the toy holds the potential to be reparative:

> the Zombie Mouth co-opts the bite of castrating horror and then reinstates it as a bite of impure bliss. In effect, it illuminates the possibility that bad objects deemed nothing more than sexist tools of male gratification may also rethink, distort, and queer the dividing lines often imposed, in the name of good *taste*, between moments of violation and eroticization.[27]

This impure bliss subverts the zombified body part to become a vehicle for orgasm despite *and* because of its decaying appearance. The violent-erotic tension present on penetration of these toys evokes established fears of deathly contamination through sex, especially through sexual body fluids, *vagina dentata* and moral decay. Rather than this fear being ignored, it is subverted into an erotic impulse to be satisfied via masturbation with a zombie sex toy. Queering the nuances of the potential castration fantasy present in these toys leads to understanding the eroticisation of the abject as a way to reflect on the subversive liminality inherent in these toys.

Christensen focuses on phallic castration in his analysis of the Zombie Lady and Zombie Mouth, but clitoral castration is also present in zombie sex toys, with the clitoris being surplus to the male orgasm in the Zombie Lady. The zombie sex toy highlights how mutilation and monstrous sexual desire destroyed the place of the clitoris in society, upholding its erasure through heteronormality and heterosexism. What zombie sex toys and the clitoris have in common is the clitoridectomy on not only the clitoris itself, but also on its place in society, Freudian psychoanalysis and in zombie porn. The clitoris serves no function on the Zombie Lady Fleshlight, and it is rarely prioritised in zombie porn, which instead focuses on the vagina and penile penetration. The clitoris is sacrificed to uphold dominant heterosexual scripts that prioritise male pleasure, penetration and the phallus. It reaffirms the vagina as the centre of female sexual pleasure and upholds the female body as passive and to be penetrated, while the penis is active. The vagina and mouth are also frozen in everlasting reception for the penis to penetrate. A zombie does not need a brain; sexual subjectivity, the clitoris and consent are not needed during the use of zombie sex toys. *Deadgirl* (2008) applies this framing to its depiction of zombie rape – consent is not needed for sex with zombies given their undead status, and female zombies are reduced to sexual objects devoid of subjectivity and respectability. The zombie is kept as a prisoner to be penetrated with no mutual pleasure permitted or considered.

The Zombie Lady and Zombie Mouth both function as a metaphor for lack, and the Lacanian *objet petit a*. Lacan defines the *objet petit a* as the empty place of desire that can never be attained and, thus, never satisfied.[28] This starts in childhood as the child realises that they cannot be the sole source of desire for their mother and must look outwards to find attainable objects of desire. The horror unleashed if the infant is to succeed in their attempt to figuratively consume the mother is reflected in the BBC3 series *The Baby* (2022). The undead baby protagonist is relentless in his quest for a loving mother, but once he finds one, he cannot help but destroy her as he subsumes her. Lack and unquenchable monstrous orality in the undead is also depicted in *Coraline* (2009), as the protagonist tries to embrace her maturing sexuality amidst the fight to break free from the undead Other mother who wants to sustain the impossible mother-child desire. The relentless nature of the zombie and the everlasting frozen-in-time zombie mouth and vagina also represents this all-consuming lack, and the fear of never breaking free. Sex becomes monstrous and abject, and all consuming. Consumption is often commented on with regard to capitalism and food in mainstream zombie films, but all-consuming sexuality is another element of zombiism that can aid our understanding of sexuality.

Zombie Dildo

Completing the Fleshlight zombie range in 2011 is the zombie dildo, which is part of the Fleshlight Freaks series of sex toys. Although several versions of the zombie dildo can be found on sites such as etsy.com, the Zombie dildo from Fleshlight is the dominant version of this putrid, plastic penis. Similar to the reviewers for the Zombie Mouth and the Zombie Lady, the undead hyperbole is strong in reviews. Reviewers note the graphic decay of the toy as a positive feature, even if it does provoke a visceral reaction for reviewer Kelvin Sparks:

> There's little tears of flesh and skin missing, and one testis is visible through skin tears on the balls. There's a slight texture all over the dildo – which is actually little boils and spots on closer

> inspection – and there appears to be a pulled back but rotted foreskin. It's an amazing piece of art, and you can tell a ton of work went into designing the dildo, but it does make the stomach churn a little bit.[29]

Reviews for the Zombie Lady and Zombie Mouth highlight how the visceral reaction these toys evoke is one of disgust tinged with arousal. Users note the 'exposed testicle, gross little pistales'[30] and the enmeshment of disgust with desire is seen in the graphic depiction of rotting skin being listed as a selling point:

> The Zombie dick is incredibly detailed. No bit was overlooked, even the stringy-ness of the muscle as it slid down the zombie penis. There are layers upon layers of muscle and skin that drip off the dildo (of course, that's just the effect). It's beautiful, in a disgusting sort of way.[31]

A reviewer at hotmoviesforher.com labels the texture of exposed skin as a conduit for pleasure: 'How fitting that what makes it especially undead is exactly what makes it come alive in your vag, butt, or wherever else you are playing with the awakened dead.'[32] The disgust associated with decay, death and the body becomes a selling point for the zombie sex toy and positioned as a source of pleasure instead of a depiction of the abject that should be avoided.

Queering the Zombie Sex Toy

The use of the zombie dildo by lesbians and gay men challenges this heterosexism connected with the Zombie Mouth and Zombie Lady and inserts queerness into zombie discourse. Queer zombies have been rare, both in Hollywood films and pornographic films. The queer subtext in *Girl with all the Gifts* (2014) is often minimised,[33] and explicitly queer films such as *Otto, or Up with Dead People* (2008) challenge mainstream zombie narratives and the zombified dildo offers the space to explore these implications of queer theory on zombiism.

Day suggests that using a dildo and strap-on can challenges societal notions of domination, pleasure and the meaning of phallic signifiers. While Day writes about women, her words can be applied to all genders:

> Portraying a woman wearing a strap-on receiving pleasure from penetration is likewise ambiguous. In what way precisely is she receiving pleasure? To what extent is this pleasure physical? What about the portrayal of fellatio on a strap-on? Here, we question whether sexual pleasure need be directly associated with physical sensation. Where is pleasure situated in an encounter with a strap-on? Is the woman wearing a strap-on taking pleasure in giving pleasure to the woman she penetrates? Force pleasure on her? Is the pleasure in the performance of masculine dominance we recognize from mainstream porn? Or in the queering of that masculinity?[34]

These questions provoke an examination of how the zombie dildo raises questions around pleasure, consent and mental pleasure at the expense of physical disgust. Paraphilias such as necrophilia complicate our understanding of mental and physical pleasure and queering our understanding of the dildo can trouble the concept of castration. If domination and patriarchal heterosexism are removed from the sexual act, does the zombie dildo also provide reparative castration? Can it be viewed as a cure for heterosexism in the same way that a cure is sought for zombies in mainstream narratives? If the dildo has queer potential, then lesbians and gay men using it are subverting the heterosexism in mainstream films, but they are also digressing from pornographic lesbian zombies who still cater to the male gaze and participate in heterosexual acts. Thus, the woman or man using the zombie dildo to penetrate themselves or others is overtly challenging this gender norm of the passive woman penetrated by a phallus and therefore imbuing the zombie dildo with the power to challenge heterosexism. Using a zombie dildo as a strap-on may allow for queer liberation from what sex should look like and who it should be done with.

Jenzen suggests that the queered dildo contains the potential to challenge the borders between life and death, heteronormality and queerness.[35] She argues that the queer uncanny critiques heteronormativity, and zombie sex toys also produce a sense of the uncanny. The zombie is uncanny because it is familiar, yet strange. Our loved ones, but not our loved ones; our genitals, but zombified. Laue posits that the abject is inextricably linked to the uncanny, outlining how Kristeva draws a monstrous line between the abject and the uncanny: 'the uncanny represents the establishment of abjection – the forceful casting out of the strange in a system of ethics and aesthetics centred on facing familiarity and turning away from difference.'[36] Cooper suggests that the zombie revenge narratives that challenged hypermasculinity in post-9/11 society is part of a 'zombie renaissance' that uses liminality as a subversive counter-discourse to heterosexism.[37]

The uncanny may be a response to stimuli that are resistant to strict categorisation in nature, and the attempts to build an impermeable border between acceptable sexuality and zombies is doomed to fail.[38] The meanings provoked by zombie sex toys can be ambiguous, frustrating those who wish for sexuality to be stable. Pulliam describes the zombie as 'quite literally a *memento mori*, reminding us that our belief that we can completely control our destiny, and perhaps through the right medical technology, even cheat death, is mere hubris'.[39] Sexuality proves itself to be no more controllable than death, and the zombie sex toy provides a sexual aesthetic for the abject.

Perhaps the real joy of zombie sex toys is that they resist meaning. When asked why lesbians would enjoy giving fellatio to a dildo, queer porn star Jiz Lee resists a simplified answer: 'Why do lesbians suck fake cocks? Because they like it.'[40] Lee's refusal to define the pleasure of a dildo frames it as queer, resisting meaning and traditional sexual and gendered scripts about dominance and pleasure. Cooper's identification of the 'malleable zombie'[41] trope in mainstream zombiism can be applied to the multiplicity of meanings produced by the zombie sex toy. Is the meaning of the zombie sex toy malleable, or is their meaning as rigid as their plastic casing? What do zombie sex toys really tell us about humans? Do they tell us that, really, a lot of humans are necrophiliacs? That our desire is too scary to really explore and because it is too grotesque, we should stick to socially acceptable sex? Or do they tell us that we are afraid – afraid of death, so we explore death through sex in order to manage our feelings? After all, the French do call the orgasm *le petit mort* ('the little death'). These toys offer a pathway into the borderless lands of sexuality; the area that is undefined, murky and therefore liberatory and free from restriction. The zombie sex toy is truly a liminal space, one that allows for any meaning to be transposed onto its pustules.

Millennial zombie narratives and the zombie renaissance include both queer zombie discourse and zombie sex toy discourse. These discourses reject simplified meanings and metanarratives and expand on previous zombie epistemologies to create new ways to use the zombie to understand sexuality and society. New ways to coexist with the zombie and its underlying anxieties include creating space for living with zombies – not attempting to cure them, but to use them for sexual pleasure. Szander and Ashley note that zombie narratives had previously usually ended with either the elimination of humans or a cure and a way to live in peace with the zombie,[42] which is reflected in *Warm Bodies* (2013), *iZombie* (2015) and *Shaun of the Dead* (2004). In *Shaun of the Dead*, the zombified Ed is kept in a shed by Shaun, who spends quality time with him post-death. The emotional intimacy depicted between the two friends is framed as funny and caring, showing potential for peaceful and intimate zombie-human relationships.

The option of zombie assimilation into human culture has begun to enjoy a sexual element. Jones posits that the zombie has become increasingly sexualised since the 1990s through films such as *Zombie Strippers!* (2008), *Zombies! Zombies! Zombies!* (2008), *Big Tits Zombie* (2010) and *Zombies Vs Strippers* (2012), and this zombified sexuality is further developed through zombie porn such as *The Evil Head* (2012). Before this shift towards sexualising the zombie, zombies were viewed as no longer being our loved ones; not to be in proximity with nor desired. What then, of zombie sex toys? The rise of sexualised millennial zombie narratives allows for the existence and consumption of zombie sex toys. Consumer capitalism is often critiqued through zombiism and metaphors for excessive consumption, and zombie sex toys represent a literal consumption of excess in relation to sexuality, making masturbation even more grotesque than described by anti-masturbation literature.

Conclusion

The zombie has neither ontological stability nor corporeal stability, and nor do zombie sex toys. When sexuality refuses to conform to social norms, the meanings suggested by zombie sex toys are fluid and plastic. The abject is designed to repel, but it beckons through the zombie sex toy, imploring the user to juxtapose disgust with their orgasm. The zombified orgasm then becomes a multiplicity of liminal spaces where life is affirmed through the medium of decay and death. 'Unusual erotic targets', as termed by Bering,[43] such as zombie sex toys, expose zombie horr/orality as having an element of arousal that is often missing from older mainstream zombie narratives.

Clitoridectomies done via medicine and society are reflected in zombie porn and zombie sex toys. The disintegrated corporeality of the mutilated child and the zombie sex toy expand on discourse around 'good' sex and what is considered taboo. However, sexual desire continues to prove to be as unruly as the zombie and both anti-masturbation and zombie narratives place priority on a cure that is often violent. In zombie sex toys, the fear of death has become enmeshed with the fear of uncontrolled sexual desire and the orgasmic nature of the depiction of rotting flesh. Zombie sex toys as sexualised silicone aesthetic objects of the abject offer a space to critique heterosexism in zombie discourse, and their queer uncanniness offers an insight into how monstrous sexuality is defined. Liminal spaces can invoke this sense of the uncanny, and zombie sex toys produce a multiplicity of challenges to attempts to reinforce corporeal and ontological borders between the human/zombie, life/death and the sexual/abject. Szanter and Richards's suggestion of 'millennial zombie narratives',[44] such as *Warm Bodies* and *iZombie*, are now giving way to Gen Z narratives such as *Santa Clarita Diet*. The zombie is further cleansed through the Disneyfication of zombies in *Zombies* (2018), which continues the humanisation of the zombie while fusing comedy and sex with horror. Through this process, the ontological border with the abject is being transformed via human-zombie intimacy.

Thus, zombie sex toys offer a glimpse at the sexualised abject though the liminal spaces it provokes, using this subversive liminality to challenge heterosexism, definitions of pleasure, zombie-human relationships, and consumption in zombie narratives. The zombie sex toy builds on our understanding of zombified desire by enmeshing horror and desire in graphic capitalistic reality. By firmly situating zombified orgasms and desire within zombiism, the erotic abject becomes as malleable and transgressive as the zombie itself.

Notes

1. See *www.amazon.com/Fleshlight-FL6753-Freaks-Zombie-Dildo/product-reviews/B006JMDUTG* (last accessed 25 February 2025).
2. Mathias Clasen, 'The Anatomy of the Zombie: A Bio-Psychological Look at the Undead Other', *Otherness: Essays and Studies*, 1/1 (2010), 13.
3. Betty Dodson, *Liberating Masturbation, A Meditation on Self Love* (New York: Betty Dodson, 1976).
4. Samuel. A. Tissot, *Diseases Caused by Masturbation: Onanism* (New York: Gottfried & Fritz, 2015).
5. Tissot, *Diseases Caused by Masturbation.*
6. Michael. S. Patton, 'Masturbation from Judaism to Victorianism', *Journal of Religion and Health*, 24 (1985), 133–46.

7. Steve Jones, 'Sex and Horror', in *The Routledge Companion to Media, Sex and Sexuality* (New York: Routledge, 2017), p. 293.
8. Steve Jones, 'Porn of the Dead', in C. M. Moreman and C. J. Rushton (eds), *Zombies Are Us: Essays on the Humanity of the Walking Dead* (Jefferson NC: McFarland, 2011), p. 45.
9. D. Zambaco, 'Onanism and Nervous Disorders in Two Little Girls', in G. Rubin (ed.) *Deviations* (London: Routledge, 2011), p. 3.
10. John Harvey Kellogg, *Plain Facts for Old and Young* (Battle Creek MI: Battle Creek Sanitarium, 1888), pp. 294–6.
11. Ashley Szander and Jessica K. Richards, 'The Sexy Millennial Reinvention of the Undead in *Warm Bodies* and *iZombie*', in Ashley Szander and Jessica K. Richards (eds), *Romancing the Zombie: Essays on the Undead as Significant 'Other'* (Jefferson NC: McFarland, 2017), pp. 68–75.
12. James J. Ward, 'What Happened to the Money Shot?', in Karen A. Ritzenhoff and Catriona McAvoy (eds), *Selling Sex on Screen: From Weimar Cinema to Zombie Porn* (Lanham MD: Rowman & Littlefield, 2015), pp. 78–90.
13. June Pulliam, 'The Zombie', in S. T. Joshi (ed.), *Icons of Horror and the Supernatural 2* (Westport CT: Greenwood Press, 2007), pp. 723–53.
14. Caroline West, 'Abject Bodies and Borders: What Zombies and Porn Indicate About Sex, Stigma, and Society', in Conor Heffernan and Scott E. Hamilton, *Theorising the Contemporary Zombie* (Cardiff: University of Wales Press, 2022), pp. 14–30.
15. 'Best Male Sex Toys', *Sex Toy Collective*, *https://sextoycollective.com/best-male-sex-toys/fleshlights/#tab-con-6* (last accessed 12 April 2023).
16. 'Male Sex Toys', *Eden Fantasys*, *www.edenfantasys.com/sex-toy-reviews/male-sextoys/treat-yourself-to-the-undead-this-halloween?tag=cb08e927-ce39-f072-b92d-5940ab362374&pnid=110650378* (last accessed 25 February 2025).
17. 'Zombie Review', *Flesh Assist*, *https://fleshassist.com/en/texture/zombie/review/DGKNQJj8* (last accessed 25 February 2025).
18. Kyle Christensen, 'The Reparative Bite of the Zombie Mouth', *The Velvet Light Trap*, 85 (2020), 4–15.
19. Steve Jones, 'Gender Monstrosity Deadgirl and the Sexual Politics of Zombie-Rape', *Feminist Media Studies*, 6/2 (2012), 1–15.
20. 'Rubber Pussy Project', *The Casquetero Files*, *https://thecasqueterofiles.com/rubber-pussy-project-178-fleshlight-freaks-zombie-mouth/* (last accessed 25 February 2025).
21. Veronica, L. Cooper, 'Subversive Liminality and Ideological Warfare: The Zombie Mash-Up as Resistance to Hypermasculine Revenge Narratives Post-9/11' (unpublished PhD dissertation, Eastern Kentucky University, 2012).

22. Jones, 'Gender Monstrosity', 3.
23. Kobi Kabalek, 'Ghosts, Vampires, Zombies', in *Handbuch Sozialwissenschaftliche Gedächtnisforschung* (New York: Springer, 2022), pp. 13–19.
24. 'Fleshlight Freaks', *Hot Movies for Her*, *www.hotmoviesforher.com/sex-blog/lesbian-blog/fleshlight-freaks-the-zombie/* (last accessed 25 February 2025).
25. Christensen, 'The Reparative Bite of the Zombie Mouth', 9.
26. Cooper, 'Subversive Liminality and Ideological Warfare'.
27. Christensen, 'The Reparative Bite of the Zombie Mouth', 13.
28. Lewis. A. Kirshner, 'Rethinking Desire: The Objet Petit A in Lacanian Theory', *Journal of the American Psychoanalytic Association*, 53/1, (2005), 83–102.
29. 'Review: Fleshlight Freaks', *Kelvin Sparks*, *https://kelvinsparks.com/2017/11/08/review-fleshlight-freaks-zombie-dildo/* (last accessed 25 February 2025).
30. 'Fleshlight Freaks Zombie', *Reddit*, *www.reddit.com/r/SexToys/comments/7aka9t/fleshlight_freaks_zombie_sex_toy_review/* (last accessed 25 February 2025).
31. 'Fleshlight Zombie Dildo', *On Her Back*, *www.onherback.com/2015/03/12/review-fleshlight-zombie-dildo/* (last accessed 12 April 2023).
32. 'Fleshlight Freaks', *Hot Movies for Her*.
33. R. J. Renner, 'Zombie Desire, Queerness, and Race in The Girl with All the Gifts', *Revenant Journal*, 55/3 (2021), 165–89.
34. Allison Day, *Feminism and Pornography after the Sex Wars: Diversifying Pornography* (Berkely CA: University of California, 2009), pp. 3–4.
35. Olu Jenzen, 'The Queer Uncanny', *Gender: Power and Authority*, 9 (2007), 9.
36. Cheyenne Laue, 'Familiar and Strange: Gender, Sex, and Love in the Uncanny Valley', *Multimodal Technologies and Interaction*, 1/1 (2017), 2.
37. Cooper, 'Subversive Liminality and Ideological Warfare', 6.
38. West, 'Abject Bodies and Borders'.
39. Pulliam, 'The Zombie', 724.
40. Sarah Schaschek, *Pornography and Seriality: The Culture of Producing Pleasure* (New York: Springer, 2013), p. 65.
41. Cooper, 'Subversive Liminality and Ideological Warfare', 6.
42. Szander and Richards, 'The Sexy Millennial Reinvention'.
43. Jesse Bering, 'Perv: The Sexual Deviant in All of Us', *Scientific American*, 66/12 (2013), 155.
44. Szander and Richards, 'The Sexy Millennial Reinvention'.

6

The Suburban Zombie

Exploring Posthumanism and Transhumanism in Netflix's *Santa Clarita Diet*

En-chi Chiou

FOR THE PAST FEW DECADES, zombies have become a prominent cultural trope, making their entrances into movies, novels, video games and other popular media. When it comes to the zombie imagery in films and television series, the shambling growling undead yearning for human brains is the first that comes to mind. Yet director George A. Romero's 1985 film *Day of the Dead* complicates this tradition with the contradiction between inhumane humans and humane monsters, encouraging us to question the presumed evil nature of zombies. Netflix's *Santa Clarita Diet* is a refreshing zombie comedy, distinguished from other zombie films or television series as it depicts the life of an ordinary realtor (estate agent) couple, Joel and Sheila Hammond. The only slight inconvenience in their daily lives is that Sheila is, in fact, a zombie, due to unknown reasons.[1] In the series, the couple must come up with ways to cope with Sheila's new diet preference for fresh human flesh without disturbing their normal life and alarming their daughter Abby. Forgoing the conventional apocalyptic setting of the zombie genre, the series depicts the almost laughably mundane problems of a zombie's daily life. While other zombie films often discuss the blurred line between inhumane humans and humane monsters, this series asks what it takes to be a decent human, whether day to day or through an ordeal.

While *Santa Clarita Diet* offers fresh perspectives on zombie comedy, it builds on a rich tradition dating back to the 1940s. Abbott and Costello's encounters with Universal Monsters helped establish horror-comedy as a viable genre, and by the 1980s, films like *Return of the Living Dead* (1985) and *Re-Animator* (1985) were demonstrating how humour could enhance rather than diminish zombie narratives. The 1990s saw this tradition expand with *Dead Alive* (1992) and *Army of Darkness* (1993) using comedy to explore themes of family, identity and heroism. This comedic approach to zombies allows creators to examine serious themes – such as humanity, consumption and social decay – through a lens that makes such commentary more accessible and, often, more incisive. *Santa Clarita Diet* continues this tradition, using suburban domesticity and situational comedy to explore posthuman themes in ways that more serious zombie narratives cannot achieve.

Scholars like Ashley Knox and Dale Knickerbocker have pointed out that the zombie can be seen as a symbol of antihumanism and posthumanism.[2] Others have turned to the rotting yet undead characteristics of the zombie, using it to discuss its posthumanistic nature.[3] I wish to focus on posthumanism's main idea of decentring the human. In *Santa Clarita Diet* the human is no longer the focus of attention but, at the same time, the series teasingly questions what it means to be human and non-human. Transhumanism is another aspect that this chapter considers, as I discuss the ever-evolving human beings within the series. Without mortal or moral constraints, what does it take for humans to be human? Here, I argue that the zombie figure, as depicted in *Santa Clarita Diet*, challenges what it takes to be human in a posthumanist era. Put another way, the zombie challenges the binary between human and non-human.

Santa Clarity Diet

Released on Netflix in 2017, *Santa Clarita Diet* is one of the online streaming platform's most popular zombie pieces. The series revolves around the daily life of a realtor couple in Santa Clarita, high-school sweethearts Joel and Sheila Hammond, played by Timothy Olyphant and Drew Barrymore. Their life as real estate agents, and as parents, raising their daughter Abby (Liv Hewson) in a middle-class suburban neighbourhood, is presented to viewers as mundane and uneventful. One day, when Joel and Sheila are showing a house to their clients, Sheila suddenly feels ill, and throws up a tremendous amount of vomit. Soon after, her heart stops beating. After Sheila's miraculous reanimation, Joel realises that his wife no longer has a heartbeat yet is somehow still alive. Sheila then throws up an organ, and an unidentified bloody red orb. This orb later grows legs and turns into a spider-like creature, endearingly called 'Mr Ball Legs' by Sheila. After Abby discovers that her mother no longer has a heartbeat but is alive, she advises her parents to consult the only person who may have some knowledge of zombies, their friendly neighbour Eric (Skyler Gisondo). Being the only other person with knowledge of Sheila's condition, Eric later becomes close friends with Abby and helps her through several difficult situations. At first, Sheila can eat raw animal meat to satiate her thirst for flesh. But after she accidentally kills her new colleague, Gary (Nathan Fillion), she finds it impossible to go back to eating raw animals. Although disturbed by the fact that Sheila must eat people, Joel decides to stay her and help her survive. Eventually the couple compromise on killing and eating only bad people – Joel even joins Sheila in choosing the 'target' and planning the kill.

When taking a cursory look back at classic zombies portrayed in films, Romero's depictions cannot be omitted. Extolled as the 'Shakespeare of zombie' by Peter Dendle, Romero opened a new chapter in zombie depiction.[4] Kyle Bishop states that, 'Romero took a rather insipid, two-dimensional creature, married it to an established apocalyptic storyline, and invented an entirely new genre'. Continuing, Bishop opined that since Romero, zombies have surpassed the feared boundary that straddles the living and the dead, and has simultaneously tied the zombie genre to the classical apocalyptic setting.[5] The fear of zombies in such texts comes from the fact that they are the 'ultimate foreign Other', and they are uncanny because they serve as a 'grotesque metaphor for humanity itself'.[6] The ultimate fear of zombies is summed up succinctly by Bishop when he states that 'The one-time protagonists of the movie become its eventual antagonists'.[7] However, the varied types of fear of zombies in these texts is incompatible with that of the zombies in *Santa Clarita Diet*, an indication that Sheila is fundamentally different from the 'classic' zombie.

Zombies in Suburbia

Santa Clarita Diet stands out from the many other zombie films and series not only because of Sheila's identity as an uncanonical zombie, but also because of the series' unique categorisation as a zombie comedy. According to Katie Garrett, the subgenre of zombie comedy 'makes fun of established zombie tropes but, as a whole, refuses to contemplate the original critique of modern society that movies like *Night of the Living Dead* presented'.[8] While I agree with Garrett's viewpoint that zombie comedy challenges the classic zombie texts, I argue that *Santa Clarita Diet* nonetheless discusses and confronts aspects that at times went unnoticed in these classic texts. Lorna Jowett and Stacey Abbott push the point further by stating that 'horror unsettles and destabilizes; on TV it plays with pleasure and transgression in terms of content and the televisual, often by juxtaposing genres'.[9] With this statement, Jowett and Abbott emphasise the contradictory nature ingrained in zombie comedy as a genre. Sheila's identity, as the leading character of *Santa Clarita Diet*, proves problematic in the analysis of zombies and discussion of related themes. Amanda Howell and Lucy Baker point out that the series 'blends two routinely denigrated genres of screen entertainment: the nuclear family sitcom and gore-based horror', and on this basis 'explores the transgressive potential of its monstrous-female protagonist' after Sheila's 'zombie makeover'.[10] Roxanne Douglas instead examines Sheila through neoliberalist feministic perspectives.[11]

The definition of a zombie in the series is found in Eric's explanation. When being consulted about zombies, Eric explains, 'I don't like that word, I think it's inherently negative'. His statement sets the fundamental tone of how the family comes to perceive Sheila's new identity.[12] Although still critical at times, Joel tries his best to keep an open mind when it comes to Sheila and her new need to kill and eat people. Aside from the lack of a heartbeat, Sheila's personality undergoes a huge change after she becomes a zombie, or one of the 'undead'. Before her change, Sheila tells Joel that she would like to be bolder and more courageous. And after becoming undead, she is no longer timid and does not hesitate to speak her mind or express her opinions. Sheila's capability of rational and reasonable thinking – albeit following her logic as undead – makes her vastly different from the mindless walkers or ramblers in other films and television series. However, she is not immune to some of the basic framework of zombies. Eric further explains that 'one thing we know about the undead is they're completely driven by their id' and that 'impulse control, the dead do not have it'.[13] In addition to her altered personality, Sheila also becomes more impulsive and sexually active. Sheila herself says that 'I don't feel dead and undead, I feel the opposite. Totally alive'.[14] Yet she did not escape the fate of deteriorating. She is spared the doom of falling apart only when the family enlists the help of a scientist, and Sheila receives a specially developed serum to stop the deterioration.

In addition to Sheila being a rational-by-choice zombie, one of the reasons why *Santa Clarita Diet* stands out from other zombie-themed films and TV series is its location, Santa Clarita. The fact that Sheila, Joel and Abby live in a suburban neighbourhood plays an important role throughout the series. While other zombie texts often have an apocalyptic setting and discuss the solemn issue of survival, the setting of Santa Clarita, a peaceful suburban neighbourhood where the biggest concern is bickering neighbours, cannot be more different.

An antecedent with a similar suburban setting is the zombie comedy film *Fido*, released in 2006. In its suburban setting, zombies are used as labourers in the neighbourhood. As Bernice Murphy states, the film 'resurrects the folkloric origins of the Caribbean zombie [and] seeks to recreate an idealized vision of 1950s suburbia'.[15] Murphy further points out that the suburban setting in Fido functions as 'a stage on which a drama of perfect family life should ideally be played out'.[16] Therefore, while different from an apocalyptic setting, the suburban setting is still a major element in the zombie story. Murphy's viewpoint is intriguing, as I believe that the suburban setting in *Santa Clarita Diet* functions in a very similar way. Being a couple with stable jobs and a daughter, living in a middle-class suburban neighbourhood, Joel and Sheila lead an almost mundane life, their biggest troubles are problems with their boss at work, bickering with neighbours, and, of course, friction with their daughter Abby. This further emphasises the point that they are just like any ordinary suburban American family. Joel brings home this point by saying that beside from Sheila being undead, 'the rest of the time, and believe me when I tell you … We're just like any other Santa Clarita family'.[17] Obviously, everything changes when Sheila becomes an undead zombie.

Murphy further indicates that the suburban is also 'a recognition that for many people buying into the suburban dream, they are purchasing not just a home, but hopefully an entire way of life'.[18] This perspective finds particular irony through Joel and Sheila's profession as a real estate agent, where they repeatedly emphasise that they sell dreams, not just houses. They simultaneously embody and market the ideal American family lifestyle, at least until Sheila's transformation shatters their own perfect suburban existence. The ultimate irony lies in their continued sale of this dream even as their own lives deviate dramatically from it.

Transhuman Zombies

Because of their undead nature, zombies have been analysed a great deal in recent years by those interested in posthumanism. Given both the depth and breadth of this field – which does not always have a compatible set of beliefs – this chapter focuses on the core posthumanism concepts found in the *Santa Clarita Diet*. To begin, posthumanism concerns the decentring of the human species. As Francesca Ferrando points out, it is the 'decentering of the "human" from the privileged place that classical theology and the long philosophical history handed down from Plato has traditionally positioned it', indicating that the human has now stepped away from the centre and focus of discussion, allowing others to enter.[19] However, although the human is no longer the centre of discussion in posthumanism, it does not mean it is omitted completely. This is a radical shift in the typical nature of history that tends to privilege human movements over those of other species. It opens a space for non-humans, including, perhaps, zombies. Basak Agin Dönmez states that 'the posthumanist discussions in our current era involve humans and nonhumans alike … a horizontal, rather than a hierarchical, alignment of the human and the nonhuman'.[20] Ferrando likewise agrees that 'posthumanism does not stand on a hierarchical system'.[21] More specifically, Dönmez points out that 'posthuman challenges the dichotomies of self/Other … human/nonhuman'.[22] Likewise, Rosi Braidotti is also of the opinion that the emergence of a new posthuman subjectivity lies at the heart of the intermingling of human/non-human.[23]

From the abovementioned viewpoints, we can conclude that zombies can be viewed as posthuman, as Sarah Lauro and Karen Embry state that the zombie's 'symbolic duality' makes it a 'boundary figure' between the living and the dead.[24] The dual nature of the zombie makes it the perfect representation of posthumanism. Ashley Knox observes how traditional zombie narratives typically enforce a strict binary between humans and zombies, positioning them as irreconcilable opposites. However, when zombie stories begin humanising their undead characters, they create space to explore the tensions between humanist and posthumanist philosophies. *Santa Clarita Diet* takes this concept further by presenting a zombie protagonist who actively maintains her human relationships and social roles while embracing her transformed state.[25] Pramod K. Nayar pushes this further as he questions what it means to be human in posthumanism.[26]

Viewed through the lens of posthumanism, there are moments in the series when the boundary between the human and the undead is questioned. At the very beginning, when the family comes to Eric to ask him the reason behind Sheila turning undead, he offers a very engaging point of view:

> Well, many new viruses come from animals, like bats. As humans destroy their habitats we're exposed to all kinds of unfamiliar diseases. We're the real so-called zombies, aren't we? Consuming everything we want without regard for consequences. As we destroy the Earth so too, do we destroy ourselves.

Although Sheila, Joel and Abby were too preoccupied at that time to give this statement any thought, I believe it merits further deliberation as it completely blurs the boundary between human and zombie, and especially from the posthuman point of view, it is possible that humans do more harm to each other and to the environment than zombies do.

In addition, both Sheila and Joel are aware that the line between human and the undead is unexpectedly thin. After an event that leads him to be arrested by the police, Joel tells a psychiatrist, 'When I look back at my life just three weeks ago I think maybe I was the dead one'.[27] His statement proves interesting, as although he struggles to came to terms with his new life of helping his wife murder people and overcoming various difficulties, he somehow realises that these experiences make him more alive and, in some ways, more human.

Being undead, Sheila herself refuses to be defined only by her 'undeadness'. Her outright refusal comes when she considers the word zombie, saying, 'No, it just perpetuates stereotypes. That the undead are nothing more than B-movie killing machines. Some of them might be very nice'.[28]

As Sheila says, she is more than a nice zombie, she is also very human. In one episode, when she is hungry and she and Joel are planning to kill someone for Sheila's dinner, the couple finds that their daughter Abby is having a hard time adjusting to her mother's undeadness. Joel suggests that Abby's problem can wait until after the killing, but Sheila reminds him, 'I know we have to kill somebody today, but we have to be parents every day'.[29] Beside her need to consume human flesh, Sheila makes it clear that she is also a mother, and being a mother means having to take care of her child.

In addition to her role as a parent, Sheila is also an employee to her boss in a real estate company. During an especially stressful meeting with a new housing development firm and her overbearing boss, Sheila accidentally chews off her own finger, and is so stressed out that her eye falls out of its socket. Sheila's role as both a caring mother and a nervous employee shows us that she is worlds apart from other zombies. As Sheila herself insists, she refuses to be defined by her new identity. Her new identity as the undead leads to another prevalent theory in examining zombies: transhumanism. Can the undead can be viewed as a transhuman?

The first two points of the revised Transhumanist Declaration released in 2012 are:

1. Humanity stands to be profoundly affected by science and technology in the future. We envision the possibility of broadening human potential by overcoming aging, cognitive shortcomings, involuntary suffering, and our confinement to planet Earth.
2. We believe that humanity's potential is still mostly unrealized. There are possible scenarios that lead to wonderful and exceedingly worthwhile enhanced human conditions.[30]

To perceive the undead in this TV series as transhuman, a closer examination of the transformation that the undead go through is required. From the very beginning Sheila makes it clear that she actually enjoys being undead, although Joel has difficulty processing this reality. Sheila describes her transformation as an amplification of her entire being, particularly celebrating her newfound confidence and fearlessness. She captures the profound nature of this change by comparing it to Dorothy's transition from Kansas to Oz – the moment when her monochrome world erupts into vibrant colour. Through this metaphor, Sheila frames her undead state not as a diminishment of life but as an awakening to a more vivid and authentic existence.[31]

Seeing that Sheila is so energetic and fearless after becoming undead, Joel's new friend Ron asks Sheila to bite him. After experiencing the transformation himself, Ron describes the undead state not as an imposition of new traits but as a kind of liberation. His use of the term 'unlocks' suggests that becoming undead removes inhibitions and social constraints, allowing one's authentic desires and personality to emerge. Rather than forcing specific changes, the transformation acts as a catalyst for self-actualisation, enabling each person to become their truest self.[32] Turning undead does not make everyone bolder and more fearless, but it allows you to become who you want to be. When Joel confronts Sheila on her new personality as an undead, she counters that she did not really change, saying 'maybe it's who I've always wanted to be' and '[b]y dying, we get to be the people we've always wanted to be'.[33]

The series extends its exploration of posthuman transformation beyond Sheila through Gary – or, rather, through his disembodied head. As Sheila's first victim, Gary offers a radically different perspective on what it means to exist beyond traditional human form. Gary is Sheila's initial victim, and since she didn't know that she had to kill the brain of her victims, Gary is accidentally turned into a zombie. Since Sheila ate the rest of Gary, only his head remains. Although being a mere head in a vase and previously having asked to be killed, Gary later says that 'I feel like my life could still have meaning', as he realises, through a notepad put in front of him and with the help of Alexa, that he can still accomplish many things through the internet.[34] He even hosts the opening party for Joel and Sheila's new real estate company. Just like Sheila says, 'There's no better time in history to not have a body'.[35]

Gary's unique condition introduces a crucial technological dimension to the series' exploration of transhumanism. While Sheila's transformation raises questions about humanity through her newfound need to consume human flesh, Gary presents a different paradigm entirely. His continued existence as a conscious, interactive head, sustained without the need to feed like other undead, demonstrates how technology can enable new forms of posthuman existence. Through tools like Alexa and written communication, Gary maintains his personality and social connections despite his radical physical limitations. His adaptation challenges both traditional zombie narratives and conventional notions of what constitutes meaningful human existence. And, through the help of technology, he can still find meaning to his existence in his state. Garrett argues that the zombie comedy genre transcends its initially dismissed status to become an effective vehicle for social commentary. Rather than diminishing the zombie narrative's critical potential, humour enables these stories to engage with political and philosophical ideas in uniquely accessible ways. *Santa Clarita Diet* exemplifies this potential, using its suburban setting and family dynamics to explore complex questions about identity, consumption and human nature, while maintaining an engaging and comedic tone. The series demonstrates how zombie comedy can tackle serious themes without sacrificing entertainment value, validating Garrett's observation about the genre's capacity for meaningful cultural critique.[36] As a refreshing addition to the genre, *Santa Clarita Diet* undoubtedly still holds a special place among its peers, as Garrett points out that the series 'takes a different approach to the zombie comedy', and

Knox highlights that zombie films 'indicate that our conceptions of human identity are more complex than previously imagined, and that previous humanist philosophy does not sufficiently engage with this complexity'.[37] Knickerbocker states that the zombie has 'changed so radically while still being recognizable, and lent itself to so many cultural uses and interpretations demonstrates that, despite the rigidity of its limbs, it is a very flexible figure indeed'.[38] I believe that these two quotes sum up my argument precisely, that the zombie challenges what it takes to be human in a posthumanist era, and that itself is an incredibly flexible medium for us to imbue meaning in it or run discussions through it.

Notes

1. K. Macfarlane, 'Where Have All the Monsters Gone?', *The Australasian Journal of Popular Culture*, 12/2 (2023), 113–26.
2. A. Knox, 'Resurrecting the Humanity of the Undead: Humanism and Posthumanism in Zombie Films' (thesis, Regis University, 2015); D. Knickerbocker, 'Why Zombies Matter: The Undead as Critical Posthumanist', *Bohemica litteraria*, 18/2 (2015), 59–82.
3. The connection between zombies and posthumanism is brilliantly explored in D. Christie, and S. J. Lauro (eds), *Better Off Dead: The Evolution of the Zombie as Post-human* (New York: Fordham University Press, 2011).
4. K. Bishop, 'Raising the Dead', *Journal of Popular Film and Television*, 33/4 (2006), 198.
5. Bishop, 'Raising the Dead', 201.
6. Bishop, 'Raising the Dead', 201.
7. Bishop, 'Raising the Dead', 203.
8. K. Garrett, 'The Evolution of Modern Zombie Comedies', *Digital Literature Review*, 5 (2018), 99.
9. Lorna Jowett and Stacey Abbott, 'Victor Fresco's *Santa Clarita Diet*: Television Horror', in Simon Bacon (ed.), *Horror: A Companion* (New York: Peter Lang, 2019), pp. 45–52.
10. A. Howell and L. Baker, 'Hungry, Unruly and Bold: A Sitcom Mom's Zombie Makeover in Santa Clarita Diet', in *Monstrous Possibilities: The Female Monster in 21st Century Screen Horror* (Cham: Springer International Publishing, 2022), pp. 45–62.
11. Roxanne Douglas, '"It Feels Like I'm Giving My Body Something It Needs in an Intense and Powerful Way": Netflix, Santa Clarita Diet, and the Neoliberal

Feminist Encounter with Pleasure Politics', in S. Shapiro, G. Champion and R. Douglas (eds), *Decolonizing the Undead: Rethinking Zombies in World-Literature, Film, and Media* (London: Bloomsbury Publishing Plc, 2023), p. 121.

12. 'So Then a Bat or a Monkey', *Santa Clarita Diet*, season 1, episode 1, 2017.
13. 'So Then a Bat or a Monkey', *Santa Clarita Diet*, season 1, episode 1, 2017.
14. 'So Then a Bat or a Monkey', *Santa Clarita Diet*, season 1, episode 1, 2017.
15. B. Murphy, 'Imitations of Life: Zombies and the Suburban Gothic', in Christie and Lauro (eds), *Better Off Dead*, p. 117.
16. Murphy, 'Imitations of Life', p. 132.
17. 'So Then a Bat or a Monkey', *Santa Clarita Diet*, season 1, episode 1, 2017.
18. Murphy, Imitations of Life', p. 132.
19. F. Ferrando, 'Towards a Posthumanist Methodology: A Statement', *Frame Journal for Literary Studies*, 25/1 (2012), 18.
20. B. A. Dönmez, 'Recent Approaches in the Posthuman Turn: Braidotti, Herbrechter, and Nayar', *Relations. Beyond Anthropocentrism*, 4/1 (2016), 106.
21. Ferrando, 'Towards a Posthumanist Methodology', 30.
22. Dönmez, 'Recent Approaches in the posthuman Turn', 107.
23. Dönmez, 'Recent Approaches in the posthuman Turn', 107.
24. S. J. Lauro and K. Embry, 'A Zombie Manifesto: The Nonhuman Condition in the Era of Advanced Capitalism', *boundary* 2, 35/1 (2008), 90–1.
25. Knox, 'Resurrecting the Humanity'.
26. Dönmez, 'Recent Approaches in the posthuman Turn', 107.
27. 'So Then a Bat or a Monkey', *Santa Clarita Diet*, season 1, episode 1, 2017.
28. 'Zombody', *Santa Clarita Diet*, season 3, episode 9, 2019.
29. 'We Can't Kill People', *Santa Clarita Diet*, season 1, episode 3, 2017.
30. M. Sand and K. Jongsma, 'Towards an Ageless Society: Assessing a Transhumanist Programme', *Ageing and Technology*, 291 (2016).
31. 'Knighttime', *Santa Clarita Diet*, season 3, episode 2, 2019.
32. 'Zombody', *Santa Clarita Diet*, season 3, episode 9, 2019.
33. 'The Queen of England', *Santa Clarita Diet*, season 2, episode 4, 2018.
34. 'The Queen of England,' *Santa Clarita Diet*, season 2, episode 4, 2018.
35. 'Belle and Sebastian Protect the Head', *Santa Clarita Diet*, season 3, episode 5, 2019.
36. K. Garrett, 'The Evolution of Modern Zombie Comedies', *Digital Literature Review*, 5 (2018), 100.
37. Knox, 'Resurrecting the Humanity', p. 41.
38. D. Knickerbocker, 'Why Zombies Matter: The Undead as Critical Posthumanist', *Bohemica litteraria*, 18/2 (2015), 71.

7

Incel Zombie Sex

Trophy Wives of the Damned

Adeline Berry

SCENES OF SEXUAL encounters with zombies are crawling out from the subconscious and slithering into popular entertainment. This chapter asks who is the intended customer base, and should we be worried? Without suggesting that all zombie-sex afficionados are of the same mindset, this chapter examines overlaps between lotharios of the living dead and incel culture. Incel – short for 'involuntary celibate' – is a misogynistic subculture found primarily online whose members obsess over their inability to attract beautiful women, or 'Stacys' who incels believe are drawn to attractive men, or 'Chads'. 'Trophy wife' is a term applied to a woman that is considered a status symbol that elevates the worth of her male partner in the eyes of other men. Hegemonic masculinity theory illustrates ways that men buy into unhealthy representations of masculinity that perpetuate ideas of alpha males, subordinate females and inferior, feminine males. Zombies, even if fictionally, present an opportunity for incels to emulate 'Chads' by trapping their own 'Corpusculent Carries' in the absence of the possibility of attracting a living 'Stacy'. This allows the incel to remain complicit in his own subjugation through fantasies of possessing the reanimated corpse of a beautiful woman. Explored solutions to putrescent obsessions include sex robots and therapy. This chapter concludes that comprehensive sex education might prevent future incel radicalisation and perhaps the zombie apocalypse.

Zombie rape scenes have, in recent years, crept and writhed their way into popular entertainment through independent films such as *Deadgirl* and *Fido*.[1] Zombie sex toys exist for the aficionado that wants to move their fantasy off the screen and into the privacy of their bedrooms. Fleshlights, sleeve-shaped sex toys for men that are usually modelled after well-known adult performers, are available for purchase in designs modelled to resemble the rotting vulva of a corpse.[2] One reviewer writes, 'Alright, I finally did the unthinkable: I fucked a dead body. Well, not really … I just fucked the Fleshlight Freaks: Zombie pussy'.[3] A review by the same author of a sex toy designed to resemble the mouth of a zombie, reads:

> If the Zombie vagina was ugly, its mouth is even uglier! The face of this toy is simply haunting … A rotten corpse mouth with perfect teeth that demands cock no matter what! It is difficult to describe how much of a bone killer this toy is for those of us not attracted to necrophiliac models.[4]

> What would it be like to screw a zombie? Would it be exciting, gross, or something in between? Would it be dry or slippery with pus? Think about it, the zombie apocalypse has arrived and is in full swing, and a year later, you still haven't been laid. What's a person to do? How about going out and getting yourself a piece of undead ass. Remember that little honey at work you had your eye on before the dead began to walk, and thought was out of your league? Well, now she's one of the walking dead, and I bet if you ask her out, she won't say no. How could she? She can't talk or think anymore! So, get dressed in your best clothes, put on some smooth make-out music, and prepare to get busy, because your undead date is about to arrive, and I promise you … she will put out![5]

Zombies as portrayed in the films of George Romero do not yet exist outside entertainment, so this chapter explores a phenomenon that is relegated to fantasy but is nonetheless worthy of examination. The US Department of Justice defines 'rape' as 'The penetration, no matter how slight, of the vagina or anus with any body part or object, or oral penetration by a sex organ of another person, without the consent of the victim'.[6] Zombies in popular culture typically have diminished mental capacities, which would therefore make them incapable of consenting to engage in sexual relations. The zombie in *Deadgirl* is raped while bound to a medical trolley, while the zombie character Tammy in *Fido* is fitted with an electronic neck collar that makes her controllable enough to be manacled to a wall in order to be raped.[7] While rape fantasies are of course less harmful than physical rape, and while not all rape fantasists become rapists, there are nonetheless those whose careers as rapists began with fantasies of rape and there are rapists that indulge in rape fantasies.[8] For those whose rape fantasies are confined to zombies, there is perhaps less risk of fantasies crossing over into acts of actual rape. It could be that the diminished faculties and personhood of the zombie absolve the zombie-rape fantasist of guilt that might trouble them if indulging in non-zombie rape fantasies. Similarly, necrophiliacs have been described as having poor self-esteem, being fearful of rejection by women and desirous of a sexual object that is incapable of rejecting them.[9] This chapter asks who these would-be lotharios of the living dead are that provide the market for zombie rape scenes, how they came to be, and whether we should be concerned.

Incels

Incels are a misogynistic subculture found primarily online whose male members obsess over their inability to attract beautiful women.[10] The incel movement, begun by a woman struggling to find love, was co-opted by frustrated members of the pick-up artist movement, where tips proliferated for tricking women into having sex with men, as a basic human right pick-up artists believed they were being denied.[11] Many of the movement's members became enraged at women for denying them the sex that they felt entitled to, which they saw as a crime worthy of punishment. In recent years the incel movement has come to be seen as a part of the larger far-right movement whose misogyny and belief in male supremacy aligns with their own belief system.[12] In 2014, Elliot Rodger, the twenty-two-year-old son of a British filmmaker, stabbed his three male roommates to death and then made his way to a nearby sorority house. When he was unable to gain access to the building, he drove around in his car shooting at women and men that symbolised to him those he felt he had been wronged by. By the time his rampage had ended, ten people were dead, including himself by suicide. Afterwards, his manifesto was discovered online in which he had written, 'I am an intelligent gentleman, and I deserve the love of girls more than the other obnoxious boys of my age, and yet they get girls, and I don't'.[13] Four years later in Toronto, twenty-eight-year-old Alek Minassian drove a van into pedestrians killing ten and injuring sixteen. Before beginning his spree, he posted online referencing incel murderer Elliot Rodger, 'Private (Recruit) Minassian Infantry 00010, wishing to speak to Sgt 4chan please, C23249161. The Incel Rebellion has already begun! We will overthrow all the Chads and Stacys! All hail the Supreme Gentleman Elliot Rodger!' (BBC, 2018). School shooters Christopher Harper-Mercer, William Atchison and Nikolas Cruz have all expressed admiration online for Elliot Rodgers and a fascination with incel ideology.[14]

Chad

'Chad' to the incel is the supreme male archetype who through sheer luck has been gifted the bone structure, features and physique that attracts 'Stacys', the women that incels are both attracted to and feel entitled to. Self-depreciating memes abound online where incels compare exaggerated, and often digitally manipulated versions of themselves with equally exaggerated or manipulated versions of Chads. Incels distort photographs of themselves to match their own distorted self-images.[15] Rather than acknowledging misogyny and an inflated sense of entitlement as barriers to relationships with beautiful women, incels blame a 'few millimetres of bone'.[16] The 'few millimetres of bone' refers to their sloping foreheads, imagined or otherwise, which they convince themselves they are powerless to remedy without access to plastic surgery.[17]

Stacy

'Stacy', the beautiful female countertype of 'Chad', is also the subject of memes, and is described on *Incels Wiki* as:

> a woman able to secure sexual intimacy with Chad. Stacy is vain and obsessed with jewellery, makeup, and clothes. She is an entitled whore whose rich daddy funds her Caribbean vacations to go 'find herself'. A typical Stacy entertains a flock of orbiters who shower her with attention and validation, only to open her legs for Chad or Tyrone (a Black 'Chad') instead.[18]

In addition to the evident racism on display, this quote illustrates the incel misogyny central to the conflict within incel desire. 'Stacy' is *what* incels want rather than *who*, as there is no evidence that incels are interested in who 'Stacy' is as a person. In 'Stacy', incels simultaneously see the coveted object of their desires; their tormentor, denying them their human right to reproduce, and a dehumanised creature that is intellectually inferior to them and unworthy of the incel's companionship.

> All I ever wanted was to love women, and in turn to be loved by them back. Their behaviour towards me has only earned my hatred, and rightfully so! I am the true victim in all of this. I am the good guy. Humanity struck at me first by condemning me to experience so much suffering. I didn't ask for this. I didn't want this. I didn't start this war … I wasn't the one who struck first … But I will finish it by striking back. I will punish everyone. And it will be beautiful. Finally, at long last, I can show the world my true worth.[19]

Incels resign themselves to being forever taunted by 'Stacy' who remains hopelessly out of their reach. Incels believe if they can't have 'Stacy' then they will seek revenge on both 'Stacy' and 'Chad'.

Trophy wives

'Trophy wives' are beautiful young women married to older, wealthy men, signifying the man's position in society while validating his masculinity. 'Trophy wives' are often expected to assume a subservient role in the relationship, remaining glamourous while cooking and cleaning, and supplying sex to their spouses in exchange for access to a lavish lifestyle.[20] The term 'trophy' implies that the trophy wife's husband is the trophy winner, reducing his wife to a conquest, a glittery object whose physical appearance takes precedence over her personality. In the films *Deadgirl* and *Fido* male characters use beautiful captive zombies to elevate their status among other men. Thus, 'trophy wife' is an appropriate analogy for the amorous focus of the zombie-attracted incel's attentions.

The Zombie Apocalypse

We live in unprecedented times at the intersection of late-stage capitalism and global warming. None of us know what will finally bring about the zombie apocalypse, if anything; however, an incel that feels at home in a biochemistry career may find themselves presented with opportunities to bring about the sort of outbreak seen in the film *Resident Evil.* An incel biologist, dreaming of creating an obedient girlfriend through cordyceps fungi, may dream of initiating the type of apocalypse seen in the television show *The Last of Us.* Recently, scientists have discovered previously unknown viruses, some more than 48,000 years old, as the permafrost in Siberia melts (Bressan, 2021; Waters and Loffhagen, 2023) echoing the television show *Fortitude*, where a defrosted mammoth carcass unleashes a virus that causes its victims to feed on their fellow townspeople, as well as bestowing them with superhuman strength.[21]

In the beginning of *Return of the Living Dead Part II* vibrations cause a barrel to break free of its tethers and fall out of a military truck, sparking a zombie outbreak. In early 2023, the vibrations of a truck carrying radioactive material caused a capsule to fall out, sparking a frantic search across Western Australia.[22] Radiation leaks and pollution are responsible for zombie outbreaks in films such as *C.H.U.D.* and *City of the Walking Dead.* A month following the radioactive capsule incident, a train carrying dangerous chemicals derailed in Palestine, Ohio, causing a large explosion and a leak that reportedly polluted rainwater and the local water supply, resulting in animals acting strangely before dying.[23] A military response, such as that seen in the *Return of the Living Dead Part II* and *Shaun of the Dead*, followed. At least one reporter was arrested, giving rise to speculations of a government cover up.[24]

Acts of sabotage by incels angry at a society they feel excluded from could potentially contribute to spelling the end of humanity as we know it. The future may bring with it increasing opportunities for a zombie-apocalypse-minded incel to attempt bringing about such a calamity. In an attempt to prevent such a situation, it may be prudent to try and understand such an incel's motivation.

Analysis

Antonio Gramsci (1891–1937) developed the theory of cultural hegemony to describe how a ruling class might maintain order, through ideology and manufactured consent rather than through physical violence (although not precluding the use of physical violence) by manipulation of that society's culture via its educational systems, its cultural mediums and religion, to establish the ideology as common sense.[25] Hegemonic masculinity theory was developed by Raewyn Connell to describe and account for male patterns of behaviour that facilitate men's continued dominance over women in society.[26] Connell's theory detailed how scripts that govern male behaviour are internalised, with certain traits considered masculine and therefore acceptable, such as competitiveness, violence, aggression and risk-taking. Although hardly normative, exaggeratedly male stereotypes personified by actors such as John Wayne or Sylvester Stallone are exalted within hegemonic masculinity, while behaviours that are seen as less masculine, and therefore more feminine and a betrayal of masculinity, are punished. Hegemonic masculine behaviour is enforced early in the schoolyard through bullying and peer pressure, sometimes manifesting as 'gay bashing' later on.[27] Hegemonic masculine stereotypes and lifestyles are promoted in men's magazines and advertisements for products ranging from meat to cars.[28]

It is from these stereotypes that the 'Chad' takes form in the mind of the incel. 'Simply defined, in any culture, hegemonic masculinity is the idealized form of masculinity in a given historical setting. It is culturally honoured, glorified, and extolled.'[29] As previously noted, the unattainability of 'Chad' status justifies the incel's resignation and acceptance of their incel status, deterring them from engaging in any work on themselves or their misogynistic worldviews that act as barriers to their having dates, friendships or relationships with women. Incels and other men who fail to exhibit stereotypically male behaviour nonetheless benefit from a patriarchal system, demonstrating what has been termed complicit masculinity by Connell and Messerschmidt.[30] While some questions relating to women's work have been taken up – notably sex segregation in the labour market and equal pay – women are generally treated as a special case in that men are still assumed to be the universal standard against which women are measured. It is women who are marked as 'gendered', the ones who are different.

Hegemonic masculinity dictates not just male behaviour but also men's treatment of women. Demetriou, in a critique of Connell's original theory, explains that hegemonic masculinity consists of two halves, internal and external hegemonic masculinity. Internal hegemonic masculinity refers to the system of masculine governance where one type of male, even if they exist only in media, advertisements or the imagination, rule over all other men. External hegemonic masculinity refers to the system of male dominance over everyone else including women. In the workplace women are evaluated against masculine standards, while in dating and relationships the treatment of women by men is guided by hegemonic masculine codes.[31] Competitiveness facilitates hierarchy in relationships and encourages conquest or trophy thinking. Expressing feelings is considered feminine, so emotional detachment, control and objectification of women are encouraged under hegemonic masculinity.

The concept of the 'trophy wife' is a product of hegemonic masculinity. The objectified 'trophy wife' exists primarily as a conquest that elevates her husband in the eyes of other men rather than as a partner, simultaneously exalted and devalued. Incels use dehumanising language for women such as 'femoid', a combination of female and humanoid to suggest that women are humanlike but not fully human.[32] Incels meanwhile, become radicalised through their longing for the attractive women that they have in their minds devalued.

It is perhaps here that for some, fantasies involving sexual relations with the living dead are born, with the deceased and reanimated corpse of a beautiful woman detached from her personality through death and subsequent reanimation.

The zombie rape-slave fantasy takes the form of a hegemonic masculine loop in which the incel finds themselves raising their own status to that of a 'Chad' by being in possession of a 'Stacy'; however, in their fantasy their 'Stacy' is a rotting corpse, or a 'Corpulescent Carrie'. This simultaneously justifies both the incel's self-loathing and their place at the bottom of the male hierarchy. As their fantasy zombie captive is a dehumanised, rotting corpse, this also helps justify the incel's misogyny. Separated from her personality and with only enough brain power to teeter around and eat people, 'Corpulescent Carrie' is incapable of challenging the incel's misogynistic worldviews. While 'Carrie' is capable of killing and devouring her captive, she is not likely to reject him, making the incel – at least in his own mind – a type of 'Chad' contender, starting this fantasy cycle over again.

In the incel's fantasies they may dream about a world crawling with the living dead where the reanimated corpse of a beautiful woman could be subdued and captured, as portrayed in a DVD extra for the 2004 film *Dawn of the Dead*. In this scene, a group of young men have created a chicken-wire enclosure in the basement of a house where they attempt to wrestle a captive, scantily clad, beautiful female zombie. This short clip ends with a wrestler being subdued and bitten to the shock and dismay of his acquaintances. Fantasies of capturing zombie trophy wives play into hegemonic masculine traits of risk-taking and conquest. 'Corpulescent

Carrie' might be chosen in this scenario over a living female survivor of the zombie apocalypse that might challenge or reject them. The skills needed to survive a zombie apocalypse suggest that a female survivor may have the ability to easily overpower the incel both mentally and physically. This defeat would challenge and potentially unravel the incel's belief system, which positions the incel at the bottom of the male hierarchy but still above women. This factor may make the female zombie preferable to capable, tough and quick-witted female survivors during apocalypse-themed fantasies.

'Fantasy offers a system of symbols every one of every age understands; it enriches and simplifies our lives and makes them bearable.'[33] Zombie film scenes and sex toys might benefit both the zombie incel and society by presenting the incel with safe, convenient and legal outlets for their fantasies, while sparing others from murderous incel rampages. Zombie Fleshlights and zombie fantasies may allow the incel to entertain and enact his fantasy in a limited capacity without intrusive realities such as fears of being overpowered by potential victims and laws intended to discourage rape and kidnapping. Other benefits to the incel might include avoiding the realities of necrophilia such as laws that discourage the practice and 'the stench of rotting meat'.[34] Benefits to society may include the absence of an actual zombie apocalypse.

Solutions and Prevention

Not all zombie-sex afficionados are incels, nor do most zombie-sex afficionados pose any level of real-life threat. It is, however, important to pay attention to the threat that incels pose, and perhaps with it, the possibility of a threat posed by zombie-attracted incels who may have woven either fantasies of literal zombie girlfriends or approximations of such into their yet-to-be-discovered manifestos. As shown, incels have proven themselves on more than one occasion to be murderous. While not all incels have or will commit mass murder, there are many comments by incels online celebrating the murders committed by Rodger and Minassian, while supporting both murderers expressed sentiments. Following Minassian's spree, one incel Reddit user wrote:

> it just needs to be strategic and punish normies in some way, they need to be in constant fear for EVERY ASPECT OF THEIR LIFE,

> killing normies from my perspective is kinda pointless but this is still good, I prefer acid attacks to mass killings though, wonder who is going to do a 'mass acid attack'.[35]

While 'mass acid attacks' may be a far cry from a literal zombie apocalypse, incel fantasies of disfigurement are likely linked to a desire to dehumanise, and perhaps, therefore, reducing their intended victims to something subhuman and monstrous. If this were the case, it would not be the first time that a young man with social and mental difficulties has attempted to create a real zombie. Serial killer Jeffrey Dahmer displayed traits common among incels, such as a disregard for the lives of others and a sense of entitlement to their bodies. He had tried to turn four of his last victims into zombies with crude attempts at trepanning and lobotomies. At Dahmer's trial, a psychiatrist for the prosecution suggested that Dahmer might have stopped killing if he had succeeded in making a zombie, 'unless he wanted two zombies'.[36] Articles online ask whether Ted Kaczynski, the Unabomber, might have been the 'first incel', due to his frustration at his lack of romantic success and his history of harassment and abuse towards women he was attracted to and felt rejected by.[37] At forty-four, he reportedly expressed fury at his brother for breaking the bond between them by marrying and losing his virginity with his wife. Kaczynski gained notoriety by killing three and injuring twenty-three with at least sixteen sophisticated bombs that he had built. While perhaps slim, there nonetheless exists the possibility that there are incels in the world with a background in biology or chemistry who are dedicating their time and energy to attempts at engineering their own approximations of a zombie apocalypse.

This section, while not exhaustive, will suggest some solutions to the problems that Zombie-attracted incels might pose. Live action role play (LARPing) is a roleplaying game where each player develops a character whose behaviour and abilities are governed by pre-established rules.[38] During a LARP, players interact with other live LARPers while adhering to an agreed upon encompassing story or script. While many LARPers enact a blend of medieval or fantasy characters and worlds, companies such as Dystopia Rising in Oklahoma give those brave enough an opportunity to see how they might survive a three-day zombie apocalypse.[39] LARPing might satisfy aspects of the zombie-attracted incel's desire to live during a zombie apocalypse but perhaps not their desire for sexual conquest.

Real Dolls are lifelike, posable sex dolls available through the Real Doll website for $7,000 or under.[40] The dolls are customisable for an additional fee, so it may be possible to arrange with the company for a doll to be customised so that it resembles a 'Corpulescent Carrie'. Sex robots, however, could be an option for some. While the $5,000–$15,000 price tag might put them out of the reach of some incels, they may provide some therapeutic relief. Alternatively, there is a possibility that Real Dolls or sex robots might exacerbate existing feelings of isolation.[41] Applying free time to learning to build robots, however, may prove a healthier use of the incel's time than fraternising in online incel communities, and may improve the incel's prospects by giving him a marketable skill. This may, however, lead to the possibility of some incels purposefully working to bring us closer to a robot-style apocalypse like the one represented in the *Terminator* films rather than a zombie apocalypse.

A cheaper and more practical option for the incel might be taking the time to challenge their own world view, as it tends to lead them inevitably towards despair. The word despair is mentioned eighteen times in Rodger's manuscript in reference to his own mental state.[42] Rodger's worldview failed to bring him peace, instead bringing pain and suffering to his victims and their friends and families. Incels prove repeatedly that the wormhole of incel culture does little to address their feelings of loneliness, rejection or isolation, instead amplifying them. Listening to the voices of the women that incels both covet and hate might be the start of a road to recovery. There are a multitude of books on feminism that should prove beneficial even for those that see themselves as self-professed enemies of it. In an *Ms. Magazine* article, Ben Atherton-Zeman (2018) writes:

> Instead of staying angry at my female friends, I chose to listen to them … Joining the feminist movement is one of the best decisions I've made. It's given my life a sense of purpose that it didn't have previously – and deepened my relationships with women and men.[43]

In her introduction to feminism primer, *Feminism is for Everybody: Passionate Politics*, bell hooks relays that common misconceptions such as the belief that feminism is anti-man come third-hand rather than from first-hand feminist sources.[44] For incels that are initially opposed to dedicating money and time to feminist literature, there are podcasts and social media. A popular TikTok account, Herspective, run by gender scholar and Harvard graduate Evelyn Koh offers feminist perspectives and wisdom in the form of short, entertaining videos that are available to most people with access to social media.

A relationship with a good therapist could prove beneficial for incels. Maxwell *et al.* have suggested incel-specific group therapy as an option.[46] Men are statistically less likely to seek help with mental illness and are more likely to kill themselves.[47] One study with 778 male respondents suffering mental illness found that masculine hegemonic beliefs that men need to solve their own problems was one of several barriers to men seeking treatment from a psychotherapist.[48] Elliot Rodger had attended sessions with a therapist but, tragically, it had not been enough to prevent his murder spree. Aspects of hegemonic masculinity that discourage expressing feelings or emotion outside of rage and anger may prove themselves to be barriers to progress, but barriers that could potentially be addressed with a good therapist.[49]

Pornography, it could be argued, reflects the culture in which it is created. In a more misogynistic society, rape pornography might be more prevalent. Ethical feminist or fair-trade pornography is pornography that features a wide variety of diverse natural bodies, ages, races and abilities.[50] Pornography of this type is more likely to show more realistic depictions of sex and is created with the consent of all involved. Ethical feminist zombie pornography could provide a path away from fantasies of zombie rape by portraying zombies that, while still a reanimated rotting corpse, retain their faculties and agency. The film *Teeth*, for example, utilises the folk device of *vagina dentata* in a cautionary tale for would-be rapists.[51] Pornography of this nature could perhaps provide an opportunity for zombie-attracted incels to learn about consent, healthy approaches to sex and why a sense of entitlement to women's bodies, whether living or undead, is unlikely to manifest in satisfaction for either party. Comprehensive education that introduces children to helpful concepts such as digital literacy and consent that breaks down harmful barriers to understanding and relationships between sexes and genders may provide the best alternative for dispelling incel-type belief systems before they take hold. Conservative and patriarchal agents, however, are reluctant to allow education that promotes sex.[52] In 2022, there has been a wave of attacks across the United States, from attempted book bans in Texas to a successful ban of the teaching of subjects such as racism in Georgia that might be considered by some to be 'divisive'.[53] It is crucial that these efforts are resisted. In addition to dissuading developing minds from misogynistic and racist ways of thinking, comprehensive sex education may also reduce the likelihood of future incel mass murders and perhaps even a zombie apocalypse.

Conclusions and Future Work

For incels, fantasies of zombie-rape may play into hegemonic masculine ideas that allow them to emulate envied and loathed Chads by finding in their captive zombie women their own desired and devalued Stacy, or trophy wife. Within their fantasies, their Stacy is a reanimated and rotting corpse, which may serve to confirm their subordinate place among men. This fantasy may form a cycle of elevation and self-oppression whereby the zombie-attracted incel continuously attempts to be elevated among men only to be plunged repeatedly into accepting his status as worthless and hopeless. Zombie sex toys, rape scenes and fiction, while aiding the zombie-attracted incel in their fantasies, may also fuel and encourage them. Ethical feminist zombie pornography could provide a path to healthy sex education and recovery for incel zombie-rape fantasists. Although under attack from conservative groups and politicians, comprehensive sex education that teaches the concept of consent may provide preventative measures that deter incel mindsets and help prevent an incel-engineered zombie apocalypse. Future research could include qualitative research with zombie attracted incels and quantitative or mixed-methods research that explores related therapeutic options including ethical feminist zombie pornography.

Notes

1. A. Currie (dir.), *Fido* (Anagram Pictures; British Columbia; Film Commission; Telefilm Canada, 2006); G. Harel and M. Sarmiento (dirs), *Deadgirl* (Hollywoodmade, 2008).
2. K. Christensen, 'The Reparative Bite of the Zombie Mouth', *The Velvet Light Trap*, 85 (2020), 4–15.
3. Casquetero, 'Flesh Assist, Fleshlight zombies review: Zombie NECRO-FEELYA', *Flesh Assist* (11 May 2012), *https://fleshassist.com/en/texture/zombie/review/Nqjm5Aj8* (last accessed 26 February 2025).
4. Casquetero, 'The Casquetero Files, Fleshlight zombies review: Fleshlight Freaks Zombie Mouth', *The Casquetero Files*, 27 October 2016, *https://thecasqueterofiles.com/rubber-pussy-project-178-fleshlight-freaks-zombie-mouth/* (last accessed 26 February 2025).
5. A. Giangregorio, 'Zombie Erotica: An Undead Anthology about Sex' (2011), *www.amazon.com/Zombie-Erotica-Undead-Anthology-about/dp/161199005X* (last accessed 26 February 2025).

6. US Department of Justice, 'An updated definition of rape', *Justice.gov* (6 January 2012), *www.justice.gov/archives/opa/blog/updated-definition-rape* (last accessed 15 July 2022).
7. Currie, *Fido*.
8. V. Baić, O. Lajić and Z. Ivanović, 'Sexual Fantasies of the Rapists', *Trames: A Journal of the Humanities and Social Sciences*, 23/4 (2019), 439–54.
9. J. P. Rosman and P. J. Resnick, 'Sexual Attraction to Corpses: A Psychiatric Review of Necrophilia', *Journal of the American Academy of Psychiatry and the Law Online*, 17/2 (1989), 153–63.
10. D. Maxwell, S. R. Robinson, J. R. Williams and C. Keaton, 'A Short Story of a Lonely Guy: A Qualitative Thematic Analysis of Involuntary Celibacy Using Reddit', *Sexuality & Culture*, 24/6 (2020), 1852–74.
11. J. Taylor, 'The Woman who Founded the 'Incel' Movement', *BBC* (30 August 2018), *www.bbc.co.uk/news/world-us-canada-45284455* (last accessed 26 February 2025).
12. R. Janek, '"I laugh at the death of normies": How Incels are Celebrating the Toronto Mass Killing', *SPLC* (24 April 2018), *www.splcenter.org/hatewatch/2018/04/24/i-laugh-death-normies-how-incels-are-celebrating-toronto-mass-killing* (last accessed 26 February 2025).
13. Elliot Rodger, 'Elliot Rodger Manifesto: My Twisted World', *Documentcloud* (2014), *www.documentcloud.org/documents/1173808-elliot-rodger-manifesto.html* (last accessed 25 July 2022).
14. N. Jensen, 'Understanding and Addressing "The Incel Rebellion"', *Pubpoli* (17 September 2020), *www.pubpoli.com/posts/2020/9/17/understanding-and-addressing-the-incel-rebellion* (last accessed 4 February 2023).
15. C. Cauterucci, 'Incel Memes Aren't a Joke', *Slate* (19 July 2018), *https://slate.com/human-interest/2018/07/incel-memes-like-millimeters-of-bone-and-virgin-vs-chad-mask-a-dangerous-and-toxic-culture.html* (last accessed 26 February 2025).
16. T. Squirrell, 'Don't Make the Mistake of Thinking Incels are Men's Rights Activists – They Are So Much More Dangerous', *Independent* (26 April 2018), *www.independent.co.uk/voices/incels-alek-minassian-mra-mens-rights-terrorism-toronto-van-attack-a8323166.html* (last accessed 26 February 2025).
17. O. Petter, 'Incels Undergoing Plastic Surgery in Desperate Attempt to Attract Women', *Independent* (31 May 2019), *www.independent.co.uk/life-style/incel-plastic-surgery-chad-cut-article-new-york-magazine-a8934306.html* (last accessed 26 February 2025).
18. 'Stacy', *Incels wiki* (19 December 2020), *https://incels.wiki/w/Stacy* (last accessed 26 February 2025).

19. Rodger, 'Elliot Rodger Manifesto', 137.
20. J. Meszaros, 'American Men and Romance Tourism: Searching for Traditional Trophy Wives as Status Symbols of Masculinity', *Women's Studies Quarterly* (2017), 225–42.
21. D. Bressan, 'Glacier Ice Reveals Previously Unknown Viruses', *Forbes* (21 July 2021), *www.forbes.com/sites/davidbressan/2021/07/21/melting-glaciers-reveal-previously-unknown-viruses/?sh=826104816042* (last accessed 26 February 2025); L. Waters and E. Loffhagen, 'What is the 50,000-year-old "Zombie Virus" Uncovered in Siberia?', *Evening Standard* (3 January 2023), *www.standard.co.uk/news/world/zombie-virus-siberia-what-permafrost-fortitude-pathogen-microbes-b1043528.html* (last accessed 26 February 2025).
22. 'Radioactive Capsule that Fell Off Truck Found in Australia'. Associated Press (1 February 2023), https://apnews.com/article/australia-radioactive-capsule-f02bfceb67639fbd0244873bebd9f888 (last accessed 26 February 2025).
23. B. Knox 'Toxic Chemicals Leave Health Concerns for Ohio residents Returning After Train Crash', *Washington Examiner* (10 February 2023), *www.washingtonexaminer.com/policy/energy-environment/toxic-chemicals-leave-health-concerns-ohio-residents-returning-train-crash* (last accessed 26 February 2025).
24. 'Reporter Arrested During News Event on Ohio Train Derailment', *Toronto Sun* (9 February 2023), *https://torontosun.com/news/world/reporter-arrested-during-news-event-on-ohio-train-derailment* (last accessed 26 February 2025).
25. A. Gramsci, Q. Hoare and G. Nowell-Smith, *Selections from Prison Notebooks* (London: Lawrence & Wishart, 1971).
26. R. W. Connell, *Gender and Power: The Person and Sexual Politics* (Stanford CA: Stanford University Press, 1987).
27. D. Bhana and E. Mayeza, 'We don't play with gays, they're not real boys … they can't fight: Hegemonic Masculinity and (Homophobic) Violence in the Primary Years of Schooling'. *International Journal of Educational Development*, 51 (2016), 36–42; T. Van Der Meer, 'Gay Bashing: A Rite of Passage?', *Culture, Health & Sexuality*, 5/2 (2003), 153–65.
28. R. A. Rogers, 'Beasts, Burgers, and Hummers: Meat and the Crisis of Masculinity in Contemporary Television Advertisements', *Environmental Communication*, 2/3 (2008), 281–301.
29. J. W. Messerschmidt, 'Men, Masculinities, and Crime', in Michael S. Kimmel, Jeff Hearn and R. W. Connell (eds), *Handbook of Studies on Men and Masculinities* (Thousand Oaks CA: SAGE Publications, 2005), p. 193.
30. R. W. Connell and J. W. Messerschmidt, 'Hegemonic Masculinity: Rethinking the Concept', *Gender & Society*, 19/6 (2005), 829–59.

31. D. Z. Demetriou, 'Connell's Concept of Hegemonic Masculinity: A Critique', *Theory and Society*, 30/3 (2001), 337–61.
32. R. Janek, 'I laugh at the death of normies'.
33. N. Babbitt, 'The Purposes of Fantasy', *Children's Literature Association Quarterly*, 1 (1982), 29.
34. Casquetero, 'The Casquetero Files, Fleshlight zombies review: Fleshlight Freaks Zombie Mouth', *The Casquetero Files* (27 October 2016), *https://thecasqueterofiles.com/rubber-pussy-project-178-fleshlight-freaks-zombie-mouth/* (last accessed 26 February 2025).
35. R. Janek, 'I laugh at the death of normies'.
36. R. Worthington, 'Dahmer may have stopped killing if he had a zombie, Doctor says'. *Chicago Tribune* (11 February 1992), *www.chicagotribune.com/news/ct-xpm-1992-02-11-9201130508-story.html* (accessible to US residents only).
37. G Tron, 'Was the Unabomber the Original Incel? Unpacking Ted Kaczynski's Relationships with Women', *Oxygen* (28 February 2020), *www.oxygen.com/true-crime-buzz/what-was-unabomber-ted-kaczynskis-relationship-with-women* (last accessed 26 February 2025).
38. R. Bienia, 'Why Do Players LARP? Motivations for LARPing in Germany', *Wyrd Con Companion* (2012), 99–105.
39. Dystopia Rising, 'Dystopia Rising Oklahoma' (n.d.). *www.dystopiarisingok.com/* (last accessed 26 February 2025).
40. Abyss Creations, 'Real Doll' (2021), *www.realdoll.com/* (last accessed 16 July 2022).
41. C. Cox-George and S. Bewley, 'I, Sex Robot: The Health Implications of the Sex Robot Industry', BMJ *Sexual & Reproductive Health*, 44/3 (2018), 161–4.
42. Rodger, 'Elliot Rodger Manifesto'.
43. B. Atherton-Zeman, 'Dear "Incel" Guys: Try Feminism for a Change', *Ms. Magazine* (30 April 2018), *https://msmagazine.com/2018/04/30/dear-incel-guys-try-feminism-change/* (last accessed 26 February 2025).
44. bell hooks, *Feminism is for Everybody: Passionate Politics* (London: Pluto Press, 2000).
45. E. Koh, [@herspective], 'It's not women's job to acquire men's respect', #greenscreenvideo #MyColoredHair #stitch #feminism #feminist #intersectionalfeminism #intersectionalfeminist #radicalfeminism #radicalfeminist #fypシ, TikTok (25 June 2021), *www.tiktok.com/@herspective/video/6977810977790184710?lang=en&is_copy_url=0&is_from_webapp=v1&sender_device=pc&sender_web_id=6919467120967714310* (last accessed 26 February 2025).

46. D. Maxwell, S. R. Robinson, J. R. Williams and C. Keaton, 'A Short Story of a Lonely Guy: A Qualitative Thematic Analysis of Involuntary Celibacy Using Reddit', *Sexuality & Culture*, 24/6 (2020), 1852–74.
47. A. Chandler, 'Masculinities and Suicide: Unsettling 'Talk' as a Response to Suicide in Men', *Critical Public Health*, 32/4 (2022), 499–508.
48. Z. E. Seidler, S. M. Rice, D. Kealy, J. L. Oliffe and J. S. Ogrodniczuk, 'What Gets in the Way? Men's Perspectives of Barriers to Mental Health Services', *International Journal of Social Psychiatry*, 66/2 (2020), 105–10.
49. T. A. Kupers, 'Toxic Masculinity as a Barrier to Mental Health Treatment in Prison', *Journal of Clinical Psychology*, 61/6 (2005), 713–24.
50. A. Chatel and G. Wynne, '12 Places to Watch Ethical Porn that Focuses on Female Pleasure', *Bustle* (9 September 2021), *www.bustle.com/wellness/places-watch-ethical-porn-female-pleasure* (last accessed 26 February 2025).
51. M. Lichtenstein (dir.), *Teeth* (Roadside Attractions, 2007).
52. S. K. Rosa and N. Archer, 'UK Christian conservatives Join "Disastrous" Global Backlash Against Sex Education', *Open Democracy* (12 September 2019), *www.opendemocracy.net/en/5050/uk-christian-conservatives-join-disastrous-global-backlash-against-sex-education/* (last accessed 26 February 2025).
53. O. Laughland, 'Georgia Passes Bill Restricting Discussion of Race in Schools', *The Guardian* (5 April 2022), *www.theguardian.com/education/2022/apr/05/georgia-passes-bill-restricting-discussion-race-schools* (last accessed 26 February 2025).

8

The Zombie as a Metaphor of Postmodern Malaise in *Halley*

Surviving the Zombie Pandemic

Violeta Alarcón Zayas

THE MEXICAN FILM *HALLEY* deals with the intrinsic paradox of being a zombie; specifically, it addresses the transgression of a basic boundary in Western rationality: the one that separates life from death. Grotesque creatures, such as monsters and ghosts in literature and cinema, have served as reflections on the existential and political conditions of human beings. In the same vein, there are vast numbers of studies on how zombies function as devices for sociopolitical criticism in the arts, social sciences and humanities. Zombie narratives have expressed not only the fear of death, but also the fear of losing will and freedom. Traditionally, becoming a zombie implies losing will and human reason. On the contrary, in *Halley* the most terrifying fact is that the main character's death is physical, not mental; in other words, his mind is forever trapped in a putrefied body.

This chapter studies the zombie in cinema and literature, but specifically those found in Mexican media. Studying Sebastián Hofmann's wonderful *Halley*, the chapter argues that the work redefines the zombie archetype to explore the grotesque metaphor of postmodern malaise, where the protagonist's physical decay contrasts with his mental clarity, embodying the existential and narcissistic crisis within transnational capitalism. Through the lens of post-existentialism and narcissism, the film critiques the alienation and consumption-driven identity crisis, portraying the zombie's struggle as a reflection of the individual's battle against the dehumanising forces of contemporary society. Beginning with the analysis of the peculiar characteristics of Hofmann's zombie, I will show how the discomfort and emptiness produced by its grotesque nature reveals the current malaise condition of the postmodern individualism and narcissism in the transnational capitalism, relying mainly on Gerard Imbert's concept of 'post-existentialism' and Gilles Lipovetsky's concept of 'narcissism'.

Zombies and Cinema: Social Imaginaries

The main zombie cinematographic vision can be summarised generally as one of slaves and plagues.[1] On the one hand, the first films about zombies are based on Ethnological research about zombiism and voodoo in Haiti. *White Zombie* (United States, 1932) by Víctor Halperin and the horror film masterpiece *I Walked with a Zombie* (United States, 1943) by Jacques Tourneur, established the canonical characteristics of the genre. In these films 'the zombies dragged their feet, with hieratic gestures and bodies, which in many ways evoked a nightmarish vision of starving queues'.[2] These zombies, the Haitian Voodoo characters, represent the consequences of the colonial historical process that Depestre identifies with *zombification*, replacing the Marxist concept of alienation, which he defines as the 'sterilization that threatened the cultural personality of the colonized black'.[3] These zombies are the victims of colonialism. The white master, manipulating the culture of the Afro-descendant population cancels their minds and will (or spirit) to achieve his own interests.[4] Therefore, this first type of cinematographic zombie reproduces the master/slave domination process based on a control that goes beyond the subjugation of the body.

On the other hand, George Romero popularised the second canonical figure of the zombie with films such as *Night of the Living Dead* (1968), *Dawn of the Dead* (1978) and *Day of the Dead* (1985). It is about a new form of representation, which speaks of a different reality: 'After the Vietnam War, Romero's Dawn of the Dead settled a shopping center, with meat-eating undead, an indelible image of maddened consumerism.'[5] These undead are insatiable cannibals, highly contagious, victims either of a kind of curse of undetermined origin or of an uncontrollable pandemic disease. It goes from an ultra-dominated world to an ineffable chaos. As L. X. Brito and D. Segovia argued, zombies developed from a subjugation by a voodoo master-priest to a domination by the drive to devour.[6] Romero's zombies no longer embodied subjects enslaved by the old colonialism, but rather monsters that emerged in the maelstrom of capitalist consumption. Luis Pérez put it thus: 'Romero's cinema judges its time ... We wince as the zombie rips through the flesh; but, before and after, Romero tells us about the really scary monsters, about soldiers, tycoons and fanatics, in short, about us who have surrendered to barbarism'.[7] These zombies – increasingly fast and voracious – reflect consumerism and pandemic paranoias, already announcing the beginning of the crises of the capitalist system. Since then, zombies 'are white and Western' to quote Ian Olney, thereby showing western society as predatory and pandemic.[8] This character constitutes the classical canon of the capitalist zombie, as it appears in the famous video clip by Michael Jackson, *Thriller* (Landis, 1983) or in *The Return of the Living Dead* (Dan O'Bannon, 1985). This idea of the pandemic zombie endures throughout the twenty-first century in the apocalyptic horror genre such as Danny Boyle's *28 Days Later* (2002) or Robert Rodríguez's *Planet Terror* (2007), or in comedies like *Zombieland* (Fleischer, 2009).[9] In these productions, the narrative presents a pessimistic vision of capitalist society and its future, proclaiming an imminent apocalyptic end, in which rotten and insatiable bodies will spread fear, death and destruction all over the planet.[10] Pointing towards the synthesis between these two canonical figures in cinema, in Romero's latest film production *Survival of the Dead* (2009), the characters question whether the undead can be tamed and coexist with humans. The pandemic-zombies appear again in chains, and they are treated like farm animals. Thus, zombies continue to represent the most extreme helpless beings in the global neo-colonial context. This ultra-capitalist perspective appears in the famous German saga *Resident Evil* (P. W. S. Anderson, A. Witt, R. Mulcahy, 2002–16) based on the homonymous video game, in which the zombie pandemic has been caused by the Umbrella corporation, which experiments with zombies to exploit them. Another example is the Canadian production

Fido (Currie, 2006) where the Zomcon Company uses zombies as domestic slaves thanks to a collar that inhibits them from killing and devouring humans, until a meteor shower frees them, and the rebellion-carnage begins.

In recent times, along with the growing success of zombies in mainstream culture, a new category of zombie appears in which we can include the undead of the Mexican film that concerns us here, *Halley* (2012) by Sebastián Hofmann. In classical canons, zombies represent lack of will, that is, the idea of a body without a 'soul', and for this reason, they are denied the moral capacity to distinguish between good and evil. Zombies are not evil, but they are potentially harmful, like a disease or a plague of locusts, and therefore destroying them doesn't pose any moral dilemma.[11] Nobody can reason with traditional zombies, and without reason morals are impossible, therefore we cannot call them evil. On the other hand, we cannot have pity on them, because they lack feelings, so it is difficult to empathise with them, and in any case, empathy pushes to eliminate them. On the contrary, *Halley* shows Beto as a zombie who hasn't lost his rational and moral capacities. We can find other rare examples in the twentieth century, such as Robert Zemeckis's comedy *Death Becomes Her* (1992), where the main characters are rational zombies. They remain conscious after death, they only want to be eternally young and beautiful, so they fight desperately, and they do everything against decomposition and ugliness. As they are rational, we can say that these frivolous and selfish zombies are evil, and they reflect capitalist obsessions with the perfect female body.

From the turn of the century, these creatures began to be the main characters of the stories and to have feelings and the ability to reflect on their own existence and their moral acts. The zombies have recovered 'the soul', managing to arouse the empathy of the spectator. This re-humanisation is observed in films such as Romero's *Land of the Dead* (2005), or in the independent British film *Colin* (Price, 2008), which is based on zombies' feelings. In *Infected* (Pastor, 2009), the zombie virus is a pandemic, but those who are infected do not transform or lose consciousness immediately after being infected, so the zombie can decide to end his or her life in order to avoid being a danger to the rest. This twist even encourages the reconversion of the zombies, a deepening of their emotions, desires, pain and anguish, and even starring in love stories in the mainstream romantic comedy (such as ghosts and vampires), as in *Life After Beth* (2014) by J. Baena, or *Warm Bodies* (2013) by J. Levine, where romantic love re-humanises and saves them. This narrative is based on 'the idea that zombification doesn't have to be permanent – especially if one is a young white American'.[12]

Zombiism in Mexican Cinema

Zombiism does not appear much in Mexican cinema, but the most widespread idea of the zombie in its imaginary is the original stereotype of undead slaves. Most of them are found in classical B series, such as *Santo contra los Zombis* (Alazraki, 1961) or *Santo contra la magia negra* (Crevenna, 1972). El Santo is a popular iconic figure, famous for Mexican wrestling, whose character, played by himself (Rodolfo Guzmán Huerta), was the protagonist in many films from the late 1950s to the 1980s. El Santo faced and defeated all kinds of characters: vampires, zombies, spectres, mummies and even aliens. The appearance of zombies in these films is not terrifying, they are not violent by themselves, they only move like automata obeying their master's commands. These zombies are submissive and alienated beings. Therefore, this representation emphasises racist and imperialist discourses:

> zombies of *El Santo*'s cinema have to obey the oppressor for the oppressor benefit. This is especially notable in *Santo contra la magia negra*, where a white witch, played by Sasha Montenegro, conjures up black zombies against the fighter to sabotage his mission with Interpol. Here the dynamic power between the zombie and his master reflects racial privilege, as the zombies in this film are the products of an exotic representation of voodoo.[13]

The film *Thieves of Souls* (Riba, 2015), set in the Mexican War of Independence, also follows this perspective. The Cordero sisters spawn a zombie the way they learned from Haitian bokores, in order to fight back the monarchists.

On the other hand, the animated film *El Santos vs la Tetona Mendoza* (Lozano; Couturier, 2012) partially reproduces this imagery with the Sahuayo zombies. These zombies have bluish skin and walk with a blank stare. They move mainly in groups and do not speak. Sahuayo's zombies are neither cannibalistic nor aggressive. They are docile like the first zombies of the slave imaginary, although they lack a specific master, so any human can command them, mistreat them and even kill them without them complaining or resisting. The main character of this film, El Santos, is a parody of El Santo. He is an anti-hero, marginal, rude, failed, alcoholic and polydrug addict dwarf. In the movie, El Santos confronts his ex-girlfriend, Tetona Mendoza, an evil businesswoman who hates and exploits zombies. He starts a campaign to help the zombies because he is resentful of Tetona Mendoza, but he pretends to be a hero, so he argues that he cares about zombie life conditions, and he asserts that the hunger suffered by Mexican zombies is the country's main problem:

> in many movies, zombies represent … a distorted image of the masses, especially the working class that has been deceived by capitalism and in the process has lost its humanity … Historically, the subaltern classes have been represented as a disorderly mass of physically unpleasant individuals, depraved, insane, bloodthirsty, and, in short, outside of all civilization.[14]

The Sahuayo zombies are not aggressive, nor do they try to infect anyone; their undead existence is peaceful like *Halley*'s protagonist. Society does not fear zombies, but they are considered as abject beings denoting how racist and classist colonialism endure in the hegemonic imaginary. In this way, the zombies symbolised the lower class as a dirty, ugly, sick, stupid and passive crowd. Therefore, Ladrón de Guevara associates these zombies with Mexican indigenous people. He sees them as a metaphor for Mexico's paradoxical relationship with its indigenous roots.[15] On one hand, natives are used to glorify the national past. At the same time, indigenous peoples and its traditions are conceived as an obstacle to the development of the Mexican country. Nevertheless, it seems that their relationship with the most exploited classes in general goes beyond their ethnicity. This is made evident within the film by emphasising that the zombie virus spreads during tax payment (because they are the only ones who do not cheat on their taxes). The infection may also be produced by listening to the music of Juan Porres, a parody of a popular traditional musician. Honesty and popular tastes, as attributes of the impoverished classes, are identified with stupidity and submission. These two aspects prove that zombies are the economic base of the country; in fact, when they die out, the country's economy sinks. That is, neoliberal capitalism despises and disgusts zombies/working class, but at the same time, it needs them.

The Hyper-Consciousness of Oneself as a New Zombie Model

Halley's zombie functions as a grotesque metaphor and, at the same time, as a macabre satire of the global process of capitalist individualisation, consumerism and narcissism. Beto, the main character, reflects, from the abjection of grotesque, the nightmare of the contradictions that the postmodern condition causes within the individual, a gap that opens between being and desire, causing such tiredness that death occurs in life. Although the film takes place in Mexico City, it could have taken place in any other modern capital city.

Halley does not develop the traditional perspective of zombiism; in fact, the viewer must discover the harm that the protagonist suffers through his gloomy and claustrophobic daily life. Beto, like millions of people, creeps alone around a colossal city. He wanders the streets carrying unspeakable secrets, dragging an execrable body through blurred and impersonal spaces, aimlessly observing life around him. As a liminal creature who is trying to survive, this zombie epitomises postmodern monstrosity.[16] He is a middle-aged man who works as a night security guard at a gym. One day, he goes to his boss's office, Silvia, and presents his resignation, arguing that he is tired. Throughout the film, we discover that Beto is not sick, but rather a zombie. Beto is not a conventional zombie, he is not controlled by voodoo, and despite being the grotesque reflection of the capitalist worker, he is not a voracious and irrational zombie, a product of consumerism. Beto is not a cannibal, he does not move by irrational instincts, in fact, he lacks appetite and seems to lack desires, but he has an excessive self-awareness. Furthermore, there is no allusion to the fact that his disease of unknown origin is contagious. Above all, he is defined by his rational capacity and self-control and that is why he coexists with the living, hiding his posthuman condition. He is a zombie with shyness, will and self-awareness, but without passions.

Control the Uncontrollable: When Abjection Overflows Every Limit

Empathy towards the undead puts the viewer in an awkward position. From the opening sequence and through the self-care of a sick body, the film goes through the grotesque, traumatic and abject sphere, where putrefaction and insects associated with death flood quotidian life. The film starts from the minuscule, with a detailed shot of some flies on an indefinite background through dirty glass, which we will later discover is a jar where Beto puts the flies after extracting them from his body. The trapped flies struggle to live, just like him: a detailed shot shows how two of them couple for a few seconds and then fall into the void together. This occurs accompanied by a sound resource of 'dissonance' or 'audiovisual counterpoint' that consists of the disproportionate amplification and distortion of sounds almost imperceptible to the human ear in normal situations; this case, the flapping wings of flies. These counterpoints challenge 'the conventional code' of realism, they are surprising, they are not what is expected to be heard and therefore they generate a feeling of strangeness and uneasiness.[17] Hofmann, in an interview, calls these counterpoints 'sound zooms', which he says he uses to increase the feeling of anguish. Indeed, by exaggerating sounds that normally are unnoticed, or are heard at a very low intensity, it is not easy to recognise them. This alteration of sound generates a grotesque atmosphere and disorientates the viewer before a reality that escapes the usual dimensions of perception and cinematographic conventions. Familiar objects and actions become strange, sordid and scary, especially when Beto is alone.

After a fade to black with the title of the film, the audiovisual counterpoint continues with the buzzing of flying insects, which increases in volume and speed. This sound introduces us to the territory of the abjection, by linking these flying insects with faeces and with decomposing matter in general. Beto appears in the foreground looking at himself in a mirror, in profile, divided in two by his reflection. This duality indicates a creature divided between the mind and the body, which inhabits the indeterminacy between life and death. In this shot, a small sponge is passed over his face, and then he tries insistently and unsuccessfully to capture something in his nasal cavity. This activity reveals Beto's obsession with controlling and cleaning his own body.

This sequence advances and synthesises the storyline of the film: Beto's useless fight against the corruption of his body, to save something incurable; the absurd and desperate gesture of a cursed monster to avoid his inevitable destiny. The film shows – with almost microscopic detail – through long, slow and parsimonious sequences, the same as the protagonist's own movements, how he extracts the larvae and insects that infest his body, closes all his orifices with plugs, puts on makeup, cleans the pus from the sores, injects himself with formalin and covers the always open wounds with adhesive tape.

Abject Posthuman Narcissism

The monotonous existence of the zombie revolves exclusively around the Ego, the self, concerned only with combating and disguising the corruption of its cadaveric state. He treats his body as another object of his possessions, but it is an 'expired' body, it is weak, it stinks, it rots and it harbours vermin. Beto's body is unusable waste for the system, in its inorganic and abject condition. Beto shows his 'abjection of self' by being hidden and ashamed. We understand here the abjection as 'absence or lack', in this case, absence of life.[18] Beto's body, despite not being dangerous, is rejected because it no longer fulfils any vital or social function. Beto, in his posthuman condition, finds himself divided from himself, so his 'soul' or 'mind' and his body confront each other. It is a grotesque paradox that the dead body keeps moving and conscious: Beto seems alive, but he is not. Beto takes care of his own corpse, which at the same time he repudiates, but which implies his only possibility of existing. Beto strives to fight against the absence that affirms his body, because to maintain the fiction of being human he must preserve it, he must cohabit with his own death in order to appear alive. This split causes the distancing of the abjection and influences the anthropological dualism: it is his body, but it is not him.

Beto's condition offers a grotesque vision of today's transnational reality: a capitalism that has stopped focusing on productivity to focus on consumerism. Beto's narcissism transgresses the limit of death, in a neurotic self-awareness: 'Narcissism, a new technology of flexible and self-managed control, socializes by dissocializing, puts individuals in accordance with a pulverized social system, while glorifying the kingdom of expansion of the pure Ego.'[19] All Beto's efforts are focused on taking care of himself, but also of what surrounds him, to the extent that he conceives it as an extension of himself, his property, his reified and alienated Ego. This fetishism of subjectivity, as well as the expansion of the Ego, seems to be confirmed in the accumulation of live flies and worms in jars, caring for them as an extension of himself, his putrid flesh, his being. In this way it seems to establish a link with the only living thing that inhabits his body. Beto's abjection suggests that desperate effort to stay connected to life by expanding his Ego, even if it is through the conservation of what is socially despicable, such as the insects that his corpse engenders.

According to the French philosopher Lipovetsky, narcissism has become the symbol of the 'second individualist revolution' that postmodernity brings, where a 'total individualism' based on the absolute 'privatisation' of experiences, in 'psychologism' has triumphed. That is imposed on collective projects: 'self-consciousness has replaced class consciousness, narcissistic consciousness replaces political consciousness.'[20] The malaise of *Halley*'s zombie is the result of this hedonistic, individualistic and alienated culture, obsessed and frustrated in its quest to fulfil unattainable ideals. Beto is a product and a reflection of the exclusion caused by this context of individualistic narcissism of capitalism, so the zombie functions as an expression of contemporary malaise. So far, what Imbert considers the typical characterisation of the international postmodern cinematographic imaginary is fulfilled, through 'an absent body that only offers its surfaces … prey to an existential vacuum, or rather post-existentialist'.[21]

Consciousness and Putrefaction: The Curse of Infinity

Towards the middle of the film, the protagonist walks through a long and lonely underground subway corridor, in one of the characteristic non-places of dim light through which *Halley* takes place: spaces of transit, without memory, without the possibility of communication where often the individual cannot get in touch 'except with another image of himself'.[22] Beto is exhausted, he moves with difficulty, he finally loses his strength and falls to the ground unconscious. In the following sequence, Beto lies naked on a stretcher surrounded by corpses. He is in the morgue. No one has come looking for him because he has no friends or family. Beto is a forgotten individual. He is a complete outsider. While the embalmer (Hugo Albores) soaps him up, Beto suddenly wakes up and opens his eyes. The following is a general shot where the embalmer, sitting in a chair, looks straight ahead at Beto, who is still naked, sitting on the stretcher with his head bowed on his knees, in an attitude of introspection. The embalmer is not scared or especially surprised, but he feels a great interest in Beto and his strange condition. It is a sequence in which a macabre humorous tone prevails, playing with the absurdity and uncomfortableness of a situation close to an Edgar Allan Poe nightmare. In fact, the scene takes place in an atmosphere of tension that causes the introversion of the zombie in front of the tranquillity of the embalmer who eats noodles while speaking to Beto and confesses that he is a misfit being who has never known how to relate well in society. However, he is passionate about corpses. In fact, he calls them by invented nicknames and watches with fascination the different colours they acquire, which he finds beautiful. The character, a worshipper of dead bodies, naturalises Beto's situation. He expresses that he was certain that something like this was possible and that Beto seems very lucky to him, although Beto, on the contrary, suffers.

A transformation takes place here in the viewer's perception of Beto. The main character faints and wakes in a morgue, so Beto goes from sick to dead, and from dead to not-dead and not-alive at the same time. Beto provokes a mixture of ambivalent feelings, ranging from compassion to disgust and horror; compassion as well as horror, because his death in life has not yet made him lose his humanity, but we, the audience, feel that he is about to lose it – and it is this abyss that indicates the grotesque trauma. This sequence establishes several key ideas to define the type of zombie that the film presents: Beto's shyness, his forgetfulness, consciousness, loneliness, vulnerability and immortality. In this zombie, three characteristics that Imbert attributes to the cinematographic expression of current postmodern malaise are evidenced through the grotesque trauma. On the one hand, it presents the 'forgetfulness', which accentuates the feeling of overwhelm of the protagonist in a situation whose origin is unknown. On the other hand, the decomposition of the body and infinite consciousness generates a 'feeling of emptiness' that is revealed in the absence of projects, goals and links. Finally, the constitutive 'ambivalence' of the contradictory and indefinite nature that characterises the undead.[23] The embalmer asks Beto how long he has been like that. He replies that he has been like this for so long that it seems to him as though he has always been this way. Beto is in an amnesic spiral that has erased everything prior to his death in life. The forgetfulness displaces him referentially, erases his links with the past, blurs his relationships and affections, and therefore undermines his identity. Beto suffers from the amnesia characteristic of zombies, so he cannot explain when and how he died for the first time. Nor can he explain the reason for his immortality, for which there is no scientific or supernatural explanation. The dissociation of the immortal mind from the dead body in inevitable decomposition generates a categorical clash that shows how terrifying and aberrant the daily routine of his cleaning and self-care are. 'The grotesque image is revealed through its changes, in the interstitial moments in which the familiar becomes strange or unexpectedly changes towards something else.'[24]

The eternity to which he is condemned snatches the past and the future from him, which makes it impossible for him to write a story, to build an identity that is diluted along with memory. His compulsive routines of cleaning his house and his corpse suppose the narcissistic struggle to maintain a reference, to maintain the unity of the Ego, but his body is diluted together with his memory and his identity.

When the embalmer asks whether he feels cold Beto does not answer. He only asks for his clothes. This attitude shows that what he still preserves is shyness, the shyness of showing his naked, dead body; that is, conscience and self-abjection. The embalmer acts naturally. He likes the presence of the zombie, so he suggests that Beto stay with him; he wants to protect him, and he warns the zombie of the dangers that he will be exposed to when returning outside. The typical zombie keeps moving, even if it is mutilated. They do not feel, but they move by irrational and impersonal instinct; they want, but they do not think. However, if Beto were to burn, he would be 'thinking ash', he would be pure Cartesian *Cogito* tied to his pulverised *res extensa*. His immortality means intellectual perception, rationality, morality, affection; he is a 'soul' or a mind trapped indefinitely in a body in a state of decomposition, always tired and vulnerable. This shows another difference between Beto and the stereotypical zombie; he cannot be a slave. Although his character is docile and peaceful, his body is weak and fragile, in the face of the superhuman strength and energy of the canonical zombies – this makes him useless for the productive system, but also for subversion or any collective project.

Zombie Onanism, an Oxymoron?

In the following sequence, Beto arrives home after a long date with Silvia, his ex-boss. She has tried to be kind and loving to the zombie: she danced with him and invited him to her house. Nevertheless, Beto has remained passive in front of Silvia, watching her drinking, eating and talking without daring to approach her. It seems that something in him wakes up when she hugs him while they are dancing very close at a disco. For the first time, he lets himself go and caresses her back. Then, she whispers to him that he smells like an 'old lady' (we know that is because of the formaldehyde), so he turns away from her because of his shyness, because self-abjection prevents him from enjoying the otherness.

Beto sits on his laminated bed. He stares into space and lies down slowly, with an almost stony stiffness. It is already daylight. The light passes through the window curtain, producing a dim, sad scene. Beto lies down in a characteristic movie plane in which he appears against the light, intensifying the gloom of his distorted figure and in contrast to the highly luminous background, as if the external reality has burned and forced him to protect himself in the gloom of his home, accentuating the feeling of loneliness and unreality. Once lying on the bed, staring at the ceiling, his hand slides down his legs to his crotch and he begins to caress himself.

Next, the sequence continues with a frontal chopped close-up of Beto's impassive face. Everything that happens off screen must be reconstructed by his face gestures and sounds. Also, by the audiovisual counterpoint effect of the 'sonorous zooms', we can hear in an intensified way how he undoes his belt buckle, the zip of his trousers, or the agitation of his body and the force and rhythm of his breathing, which is progressively increasing. The grotesque traumatic emerges here with the taboo of masturbation, although the visual representation of the sexual organ is euphemistically avoided, everything that happens is made explicit. Therefore, the sequence has explicit, sordid and disturbing content. The second grotesque aspect emerges because of something more conflicting than showing a taboo act, it is due to the philosophical questions that arise regarding the ambiguous nature of the zombie: does a zombie have sexual desire? Can an undead masturbate satisfactorily? Hofmann claims that this question was the germ idea of the film. The director wanted to make a movie about a masturbating zombie. In other words, the director had an explicit interest in capturing the zombie's conflict regarding sexuality and autoeroticism.

The viewer does not know whether the protagonist can feel pain or pleasure because it is never made explicit. Nor has he made any gesture of joy or sadness, or reaction to physical stimulus, except when he hugged and caressed Silvia and she commented on his smell. On the other hand, at a physiological level, blood had never been seen in the zombie's body, only pus, dry open wounds and insects. He was taken to the morgue because he lacked vital signs. But, since Beto thinks, moves, listens, sees and speaks without blood circulating his body, and although he does not heal or digest, it is plausible – if we do without scientific explanations – that if his 'spiritual' desire achieves this, he may also get some kind of sensual physical pleasure. As with other spectra, custom can keep the undead moving, cleaning and healing. It is possible that a metaphysical inertia drags the body of the zombie to continue its routines, including onanism. It is evident that the motor principle of the movement of his body and his thought does not respond to physiological explanations without a functioning nervous and circulatory system, so it is confirmed that the body is conceived as an automaton or avatar directed by the 'soul'. That is, the brain doesn't move the body, because there is no circulation, there are no fluids, there are no electrical impulses, the heart no longer beats, his body does not breathe, but it moves.

So, ignoring that his body is dead, and relying solely on his gestural and acoustic expressions, it seems indeed that it responds to physical pleasure. However, we can think that both excitement and pleasure come from his imagination and from the memory of Silvia, while masturbation is a mere mechanical movement reflecting the eroticism that arose and was satisfied in fantasy. This would establish that the hand moves out of habit, but without erogenous effectiveness, only as an empty gesture that reflects habit. This erotic unleashing could be read as Freud's description of a negative narcissism. According to Freudian theory, physical discomfort supposes a translation of the libidinal desire towards oneself, and from there comes the narcissistic withdrawal of the patient, incapable of satisfying and being satisfied, which is linked at the same time to the abject narcissism that reflects his obsession with hygiene and the meticulous care and control of his body.[25]

We could also venture an inverted platonic explanation, as in the film *Warm Bodies*, where intellectual pleasure and loving feeling revive the dead body; that is, erotic attraction and love come from the spiritual and breathe life into the body. In other words, Silvia could have made Beto recover the soul-body bond through erotic and/or love attraction. From a romantic perspective, we could interpret that Silvia arouses emotions and feelings in Beto that make the zombie revive through his penis; that is, through onanistic desire. As happens in the hegemonic stories of romantic love, we could think that Beto recovers life through this passionate love, but we aren't in a romantic comedy, and the sequence returns us to a very different reality. Beto's face expresses pleasure for the first time in the film. At the same time, it is perceived that the arm movement accelerates by his breathing. Due the vibration of his body we can deduce that the speed and intensity of the action increases. We get to know that he reaches climax when he twists and moans. Then, just as his hand stops, we hear a crack of something that falls apart off screen. His eyes widen in surprise. Pleasure is suddenly replaced by bewilderment, denial and finally horror. Incredulous, he tilts his head and looks at his crotch and then immediately he sits up and leaves the shot.

The zombie appears with his back to the camera, in front of the sink mirror. His agitation leaves no room for doubt. He wants to repair something: he turns on the tap and opens the cupboard, he rummages around and we hear him unrolling tape. The uselessness of the hustle causes a sordid and ridiculous situation, which becomes tragic when Beto accepts the loss. Then he stops and sobs. His crying, or whining – because we don't know if he sheds tears – occurs with his back to the camera and results in the following general shot, where he appears from the front, sitting on the bathroom floor, naked from the waist down, exposing his mutilated crotch. The literal castration shows Beto's body final defeat. He has not only lost his humanity, but this supposes the breakdown of his masculinity, he has lost the last possible connection with his body. The penis here becomes something more than the sexual organ, its amputation represents the failure of all heterosexual desire and physical pleasure, but it also implies a breakdown of its essence, of its subjectivity as a male: 'the phallus would be nothing without the penis. And in that sense in which the phallus requires the penis for its own constitution, the identity of the phallus includes the penis, that is, a relation of identity holds between them.'[26] The phallus is the basis of all meaning, and it is evident how the anatomical is confused with the symbolic here, because if the phallus symbolises the penis, and at the same time serves as a synecdoche of the male body, physical castration supposes the disappearance of the identity of the male. His body is instituted as the ultimate abjection, as the absence and loss of his sexual condition. The relationship with his body has been definitively broken. The importance of the penis, a narcissistically imbued organ, comes from its symbolic rise in the construction of male identity, which turns it into the symbolic order as a 'structuring principle which forms and gives access to all knowable objects'.[27] The seriousness of this amputation, which leads the zombie into total disorientation, is highlighted when Beto breaks down crying, since until that point he had been an almost impassive character. After castration, he loses self-control, he despairs and collapses. At this crucial moment, the identification with heterosexual male pleasure is no longer possible for him. His body rebels against all physical desire and pleasure. Crying is the expression of his powerlessness, helplessness and ultimate failure, the ironic response to the hedonistic insistence of the consumer society, where people are also objects of consumption, as conceptualised by Bauman.[28] The zombie can no longer fulfil any of the imperatives of society: he can neither produce nor consume, neither desire nor be desired, and, ultimately, he cannot enjoy anything. Beto's narcissism emphasises the body-mind duality creating a grotesque monstrosity, a posthuman disorientated in the absolute becoming of infinity. If masturbation is satisfactory, this means that Beto still feels or thinks something, so he pretends to participate in the courtship ritual. Beto only had that last trace of pleasure related to life, that ghost of desire, of fantasising in solitude about being desired. Then the lie reveals itself when he loses the phallus, which evoked its ability to give pleasure and receive it. The absent phallus, reduced to a piece of putrid flesh, denies the fiction of subjectivity, denies the last possibility of connecting with life. It is here where absurdity and despair reach the climax of the castrated self-abjection through ostracism, culminating in an ascetic exile to a hidden glacier.

Conclusion

Halley meets all the symptoms that Imbert attributes to the discomfort of the body shown in postmodern cinema. On the one hand, Beto epitomises passivity and docility, both attributes of the colonialist zombie model. However, he also shares with the capitalist zombie archetype the critique of postmodern alienation and depoliticisation. He denounces the weakness, loneliness and emptiness caused by the individualising devices of capitalism. He also denounces a society of isolated monads, where one's own body turns into an object of consumption. This self-obsession transforms subjects into narcissistic and consumerist zombies. The finite body of the posthuman reveals incompleteness. The body always rebels against the narcissistic imperative of the ego device, the body will never submit to the ideal of the soul. Beto, a humble security guard of a small gym, does not reach the ideals of society, neither as a worker nor as a man. The postmodern subject clings more and more to a body that fails to respond to his desires, increasingly volatile and ephemeral, but also more frequent and urgent. The zombie, isolated and lost, wanders through a world without footholds, without strong referents, without lasting ties.

Halley's zombie reflects a solipsistic and cadaverous society in disagreement with its own body, which has lost all affective, political and temporal references. Consumerism and hyper-control of the body have destroyed the possibility of a community that guarantees any social project. The obsession with the construction of an individual identity makes this same subjectivity impossible, since it eliminates otherness, desire and recognition. The final apocalypse does not appear as a violent, irrational and voracious plague, but as a world full of narcissistic Sisyphi, who crawl their putrefaction up an ice mountain looking only for themselves, while their bodies crumble infinitely.

Notes

1. James McFarland, 'Philosophy of the Living Dead: At the Origin of the Zombie-Image', *Cultural Critique*, 90 (2015), 22–63.
2. David John Skal, *Monster Show: Una historia cultural del horror* (Madrid: Valdemar, 2008), p. 206.
3. René Depestre, *Buenos días y adiós a la negritud* (La Habana: Casa de las Américas, 1986), p. 208.
4. Depestre, *Buenos días y adiós a la negritud*, p. 209.
5. Skal, *Monster Show*, p. 387.
6. L. X. Brito and D. Segovia, 'Las Metáforas sociales del zombi romeriano', *Antropología Experimental*, 21 (2021), 527.
7. Luis Pérez, *George A. Romero: Cuando no quede sitio en el infierno* (Madrid: Akal, 2013), p. 73.
8. Ian Olney, *Zombie Cinema* (New Brunswick NJ: Rutgers University Press, 2017), p. 19.
9. Robert Wonser and David Boyns, 'Between the Living and Undead: How Zombie Cinema Reflects the Social Construction of Risk, the Anxious Self, and Disease Pandemic', *The Sociological Quarterly*, 57/4 (2016), 628–53.
10. P. McReynolds, 'Zombie Cinema and the Anthropocene: Posthuman Agency and Embodiment at the End of the World', *Cinema: Journal of Philosophy and the Moving Image*, 7 (2015), 149–68.
11. Robert Kirk, *Zombies and Consciousness* (Hounslow: Clarendon Press, 2005).
12. Chera Kee. *Not your Average Zombie: Rehumanizing the Undead from Voodoo to ZombieWalks* (Austin TX: University of Texas Press, 2017), p.26.
13. D. S. Dalton, 'Intenciones enmascaradas en la pantalla plateada. El Santo y el mimetismo imperial', *Alambique: Revista Académica de Ciencia Ficción y Fantasía*, 4/1 (2016), 1–15.
14. A. Ferrero and S. Roas, 'El Zombi como metáfora contracultural. Nómadas', *Critical Journal of Social and Juridical Sciences*, 32 (2011), 97–220.
15. V. Ladrón de Guevara, 'Once upon a time, Santos was reading about the Sahuayo zombies when …': Performances of (Post) Modernity and Nationalism by Mexican Zombies', *Studies in Theatre and Performance*, 34/3 (2014), 211–18.
16. E. Vossen, 'Laid to Rest: Romance, End of the World Sexuality and Apocalyptic Anticipation in Robert Kirkman's *The Walking Dead*', in S. McGlotten and S. Jones (eds), *Zombies and Sexuality: Essays on Desire and the Living Dead* (Jefferson NC: McFarland, 2014), p. 95.
17. Michel Chion, *La audiovisión* (Barcelona: Paidós, 1990), pp. 36–7.

18. Julia Kristeva, *Powers of Horror: An Essay on Abjection* (New York: Columbia University Press, 1984).
19. Gilles Lipovetsky, *La era del vacío* (Barcelona: Anagrama, 1983), p. 55.
20. Lipovetsky, *La era del vacío*, p. 55.
21. Gerard Imbert, *Cine e imaginarios sociales* (Madrid: Ediciones Cátedra, 2017), p. 37.
22. Marc Augé, *Non-places: Introduction to an Anthropology of Supermodernity* (New York: Verso, 1992), p. 85.
23. Imbert, *Cine e imaginarios sociales.*
24. Frances. S. Connelly, *The Grotesque in Western Art and Culture* (Cambridge: Cambridge University Press, 2012), p. 26.
25. Sigmund Freud, *On Narcissism: An Introduction* (Bristol: Read & Co., 2014).
26. Judith Butler, *Bodies That Matter: On the Discursive Limits of Sex* (London: Routledge Classics, 1993), p. 84.
27. Butler, *Bodies That Matter*, p. 78.
28. Zygmunt Bauman, *Consuming life* (Cambridge: Polity Press, 2007).

9

Hear the Dead, Bite the Living

Beyond Post-Apocalyptic Trauma

Nikki Foster-Kruczek and Catherine Pugh

WHETHER CONSIDERED as symbols of trauma, indications of individual or societal moral corruption, or as simply a mindless monster, zombies are insidious, tenacious and unrelenting. These creatures are an ever-present reminder of physical and psychological death, with their destruction obliterating reminders of human mortality. Witnessing a deceased loved one reanimate as a member of the undead is particularly traumatic for a survivor; the individual and treasured subject becomes a corrupted, polluted object. This facsimile of the victim represents a physical and psychological danger, threatening to destabilise the binaries of human/monster as well as life/death. 'Putting down' an infected loved one is therefore not only a key survival tactic, but a responsibility and duty of care; an act of mercy that also completes the death ritual and in doing so encourages emotional healing in the mourners. However, the destruction of these once-human creatures is rarely clean or complete. The end of the story does not necessarily mean the end of the undead, even in narratives that do not rely on sequels or spin-offs. The immediate threat of the zombies may have been neutralised, but large numbers of them inevitably remain, with their complete destruction becoming an impossible task. As an increasing number of zombie texts focus on a post-apocalyptic world, survivors undergo a constant bombardment of emotional trauma, alongside constant fear of attack and struggle for survival. Post-apocalyptic narratives do not simply look at the ongoing battle between humans and the undead, but how humans must learn to live alongside them, keeping themselves safe both practically and psychologically. Some characters ultimately adapt psychologically to post-apocalyptic worlds, though many inevitably suffer from a variety of traumatic and/or anxiety disorders. However, this work focuses specifically on post-traumatic stress disorder (PTSD) within the post-apocalyptic environment of *The Walking Dead* (2010–22), both in the more general sense of survivors attempting to thrive in a traumatised world, and as a clinical framework for various characters.

Trauma is defined as an event that is life threatening or that severely compromises physical and emotional well-being.[1] Many people who experience trauma work to make sense of it, successfully integrating it into their memory, which enables them to move forward in life. Untreated traumatic experiences can become increasingly difficult to live with; the memory of the event can feel incredibly real as it is flashed into consciousness, causing emotions experienced at the time to resurface alongside anxiety at reliving events. When an individual is unable to process what they have gone through over a period of time, this can be diagnosed as post-traumatic stress.[2] In addition, complex post-traumatic stress disorder (C-PTSD) can be diagnosed by assessing persistent, repeated trauma that in addition to PTSD has a major impact on the individual's ability to relate to other people and regulate their emotional state. Symptoms of both conditions include nightmares or flashbacks of the traumatic event, a state of high alert known as hyper-vigilance, an increased startle reflex in response to stimuli (e.g., loud noises), and avoidance of both the places and emotional states associated with the source of trauma.[3] Both PTSD and C-PTSD are treatable with a combination of medication and talking therapy. The use of emotional regulation techniques such as cognitive behavioural therapy[4] and eye movement desensitisation reprogramming[5] are possible interventions. For most people, the prognosis is good, and recovery is possible, although what this potential recovery looks like can vary. An individual managing to navigate flashbacks as they happen is deemed to be in the process of recovery. On the other hand, a person who develops enough psychological tools and abilities to allow them a sense of persistent safety in terms of physical space and relationships might be experiencing considerable recovery. Most treatment is lengthy and arduous, although recent studies offer evidence that short, intensive, trauma-focused treatment can dramatically reduce symptoms, allowing for quicker recuperation.[6] Whatever form treatment takes, the goal is the same: to reset the trauma-triggered thoughts, actions and behaviours in favour of those that assist in physical and psychological well-being. However, is this dynamic possible in a post-apocalyptic text, where not only are the preferred therapeutic avenues obliterated, but the world itself is in a constant state of re-traumatisation?

The Walking Dead is set some time after a worldwide infection has resulted in the existence of slow-moving, mindless zombies known as 'walkers'. Furthermore, the virus itself is only activated after death, meaning that every remaining human will inevitably transform into a walker irrespective of whether they are bitten. The series tells the story of those who remain and how they learn to survive in a world among the dead. There are three main areas of psychological theory that can be applied to the survivors of *The Walking Dead*: post-traumatic stress, terror management theory and stages of grief. The series itself begins with three different but interlinking moments of trauma surrounding deputy Sheriff Rick Grimes; finding a zombified little girl; followed by a flashback to Rick being shot by an armed suspect resulting in a coma; and finally, with Rick waking up to discover the post-infection world overtaken by walkers.

The world that Rick emerges into has very few doctors and increasingly limited resources, particularly in terms of technology, food or medication. Survivors live in a continuing state of trauma to one degree or another for the rest of their lives, ultimately leading to a change in their natural trauma responses in order to be able to function. First, they must come to accept that things have changed, and that the world is radically, permanently transformed. Only then will they be able to learn what it takes for long-term survival in this dead world. However, there is no opportunity for survivors to recover from the initial traumatic (world-ending) event; not only is the world still dominated by walkers, but the survivors themselves must live with the knowledge that they are already infected and will reanimate after death unless certain measures are taken. There is no therapy, no medication and the potential for reducing fear of both place and people is low. If the goal of psychological recovery is to be able to navigate life 'normally' in healthy, non-trauma-inducing ways (as far as possible, at least), the survivors are at a disadvantage from the beginning. The 'new normal' offers no stability, no respite and no official or sanctioned treatment.

Fear of Death and Terror Management Theory

Adjusting to a post-apocalyptic world means learning to survive, developing tools and strategies for coping with new and insidious dangers. The threat of the walkers not only lies in their desire to kill and consume, but their ability to transform the victim into the very thing that they fear. Death by walker is essentially *undeath* by walker, a fate psychologically devastating, not just to the one who dies, but to all potential witnesses. For instance, in an early episode of season 1, Andrea is not only forced to watch her sister die, but waits beside her until she begins to change before 'putting her down' ('Wildfire', 1.5). Andrea must not only accept the reality of her sister's imminent death and the memory of that trauma, but she must also reconcile with her own actions. Witnessing the death of a member of the community after a walker attack is psychologically difficult, but, initially, survivors take comfort in the belief that only those bitten will turn. However, it is revealed in 'TS-19' (1.6) that every human being is infected and will transform into a walker after death. Trauma triggered by sudden bereavement and the subsequent knowledge that no one is immune to becoming a walker is multilayered and complex, tapping into the human need to protect one another, to face difficulty together and, most importantly, to belong.[7]

In the initial stages of the apocalypse, the biggest fear for the living is death by walker. The primary facet of survival in both the apocalypse and post-apocalypse is therefore learning to deal with walkers; becoming so used to seeing them and putting them down that it becomes a skill that even the youngest members of the group learn how to do. Carol, for example, teaches the children at the prison settlement how to handle weapons and kill walkers as a life skill ('30 Days Without an Accident', 4.1). Pragmatism is also a key defence tool for Michonne who uses two mutilated walkers on chains to protect herself as she moves around ('Beside the Dying Fire', 2.13). Furthermore, characters frequently employ zombie fluids and entrails to allow freedom of movement through the walkers.

Terror management theory explains that humans experience death anxiety, which drives people to adopt beliefs, opinions, practices and views that protect their sense of self and allow them to believe they play an important role in the world.[8] In seasons 5 and 6 of *The Walking Dead*, the original leader of the settlement Alexandria, Deanna, attempts to cling to a sense of normality through social structure and the resurrection of meaningful roles for people. She encourages Rick to don his uniform again, asking both Rick and Michonne to police the community ('Forget', 5.13). Morgan, in turn, upholds his value that life is sacred by refusing to kill walkers ('Here's Not Here', 6.4). Establishing new communities like Hilltop, the Kingdom and Oceanside with leadership, defences and social roles offer adjusted but valid means of pushing away the presence of death. The vast majority of humans fear death, and one way of combating this involves individuals completing achievements or undertaking tasks in order to leave a legacy of some kind, some signal or symbol that they matter.

This sometimes-destructive compulsion to survive through the formation of groups takes on increased significance when considering the leaders of the different communities within *The Walking Dead*. More benevolent leaders, such as Rick, Maggie, Jesus, Tara, Ezekiel and Deanna ultimately advocate cooperation and good relations between different groups, allowing for trade, travel, shared resources and protection. Malevolent leaders, however, such as Negan or the Governor (see below) manipulate people's need for community to bolster their own sense of security. Negan, having experienced the death of his wife, transforms himself into a violent but charismatic larger-than-life persona, a brutal antithesis to Ezekiel's cult of personality. Along with his constant companion, a barbed-wire-covered baseball bat called Lucille, Negan rules through an indoctrination of fear and unquestioning obedience. Negan successfully cements his own status as a leader while ensuring that those who join the Saviours fear him enough to obey him. The followers' repeated declaration that 'I am Negan' demonstrates both submission and solidarity; while a group (or an idea) cannot be fought as easily as a person, it equally erodes individuality and free will. Furthermore, the Saviours are scavengers and extortionists, demanding a regular tariff from nearby communities, willing to maim and murder (within the boundaries of Negan's 'rules') in order to get it. Despite their violence and displays of power, they are intrinsically reliant on other people. With this in mind, it becomes clear that although everyone in the post-apocalyptic world is under stress and experiencing trauma as well as facing their own mortality, they are also connected with other people in deep and fundamental ways, sometimes by being reunited with loved ones and at other times, by meeting others who join the group.

For two seasons *The Walking Dead* focused on the human need to belong to one another, meet their basic needs for shelter and food and learning all-important skills for survival. The group's shared historical trauma[9] binds its members together, while individual traumatic experiences allow for empathy under intense conditions; at some point every character has seen horrific events, committed atrocities, experienced personal loss and (at best) made morally ambiguous decisions. As people adjust, the memory of trauma helps to keep them safe by reminding them of danger not just from the walkers but people and places.

There comes a moment where *The Walking Dead*'s protagonists stop being victims of circumstance and face the reality of life in a world where they are forced to co-exist with the dead. Gradually, fear of the Other is transferred from the walkers to the living. Conflict over resources, places, leadership, weapons and who is allowed in and who is not, all become priorities as the world turns upside down once more and the living become the enemy, while the ever-constant threat of the walkers is reduced to background noise.

Treatment, Coping Strategies and Suicide

In *The Walking Dead*, nobody has the means or the time to treat their trauma symptoms. There is no medication, very few doctors and, crucially, the absence of stability, causing characters to be thrown from crisis to crisis with very little time to process in between. The medically trained are just as vulnerable to psychological discomfort as everyone else; psychiatrist Denise is an able practitioner but initially struggles as she is in far more demand as a surgeon, a position that terrifies her ('Now', 6.5).[10] There are occasions throughout the series where characters take positive or constructive steps to addressing trauma, such as intimate and honest conversations, ritualistic or symbolic destruction, creative arts such as singing or music, the creation of graves or memorials and so on (a notable example of therapeutic actions occurs during the season 4 episode 'Still', 4.12). However, those who offer to listen or advise tend to become affected further by witnessing the emotional fallout of others. Even Gabriel, with the experience of Priestly training is likely to experience some level of additional, secondary or vicarious trauma[11] as a result of hearing from others. In pre-apocalyptic systems a mental health professional would have had supervision and probably their own therapist as places to process secondary trauma, but post-apocalypse these options are unlikely to be available, leaving people with increasing traumatic burdens and fewer places to take them.

There are many examples where coping strategies become dangerous or destructive, including violent outbursts ('Say the Word', 3.5; 'A', 4.16), self-harm (Daryl, 'Them', 5.10); isolation (Carol, 'Twice as Far', 6.14), reckless revenge missions (Rosita and Sasha, 'The Other Side', 7.14); obsessive quests (Morgan, 'Clear', 3.12); preservation of the undead (The Governor, 'Say the Word') as well as nihilism, dissociation and depression ('Them'). Hallucinations by traumatised characters occur throughout the series and can be framed as either positive or negative: Rick and Michonne's hallucinations are unwanted and upsetting, yet nevertheless allow them to confront their grief and guilt; Daryl's experiences in 'Chupacabra' (2.5) motivate him to survive despite being severely wounded; and Tyreese and Sasha are comforted by images of loved ones as they die ('What Happened and What's Going On', 5.9; 'The First Day of the Rest of Your Life', 7.16).

As well as the constant threat of being killed by walkers, other survivors or even by accident, *The Walking Dead* involves many examples of suicide, either as self-sacrifice to protect others or to prevent further suffering. The issue of suicide is introduced into the series as early as the first season and while self-sacrifice is seen as virtuous, any other kind of self-harm tends to be portrayed critically. At the end of the first season, Jenner and Jacqui remain in the CDC as it explodes and while Andrea originally stays with them, Dale manipulates her into leaving by insisting that he stays with her no matter her decision ('TS-19', 1.6). She confronts him about taking away her choice, rejecting his suggestion that she should be grateful that he saved her life ('What Lies Ahead', 2.1). Similarly, when Beth Greene becomes catatonic and later attempts to end her life, Andrea encourages it rather than attempting to stop her, pleased that the experience ultimately proves Beth's willingness to live. She advises Beth that, 'The pain doesn't go away. You just make room for it', while dismissing the attempt itself when confronted ('18 Miles Out', 2.10). In comparison, at the climax of 'Thank You' (6.3), Nicholas chooses to shoot himself in the head to avoid being eaten alive when he becomes trapped by a herd of walkers. This moment is framed as an act of cowardice and selfishness from the terminally self-centred and unpleasant Nicholas (whose actions have already caused the death of Noah), even more so as he accidentally knocks Glenn into the crowd of ravenous walkers. Ezekiel considers suicide after losing his Kingdom but is dissuaded by Michonne ('Silence the Whisperers', 10.4), while Daryl is repeatedly derisive when coming across bodies of suicide victims ('Save the Last One', 2.3; 'Indifference', 4.4). With the exception of characters who sacrifice themselves defending the group (T-Dog, 'Killer

Within', 3.4; Sasha, 'The First Day of the Rest of Your Life', 7.16), suicide of the uninfected tends to be seen as a selfish or foolish act, done without consideration for those left behind.[12]

Grief and Mourning

Although virtually any character in *The Walking Dead* can be examined in the context of trauma and grief, this work focuses on Rick, Carol and Carl. With repeated trauma feeding the fear of death and reinforcing the terror of undeath in an unending cycle, the survivors could be forgiven for never leaving the safety of their walled communities. However, resources are needed, whether that is wood for fuel, searching for food or scavenging useful items from deserted homes. There are discussions to be had with other communities, the transportation of skilled people from place to place and information to be shared. It is simply unrealistic for these survivors to stay put. But to brave the outside world is also to add traumatic experiences, recognising a walker as someone once known, coming across a walker horde, being stopped and intimidated by another group in the middle of a journey, even being attacked and taken prisoner are all devastating to the individual and exacerbate the fear of those left behind.

Elizabeth Kübler-Ross composed and analysed a number of studies about grief and grieving.[13] She worked directly with patients who were adjusting to terminal illness, and she identified five stages to the process observed: denial, anger, bargaining, depression and acceptance. Her research has since been used as a framework for bereavement and, while that approach has merit, for the purpose of this text, it is most usefully seen through the lens of those facing their own mortality. Every apocalypse survivor lives with a sense of borrowed time, whether they acknowledge it or not. Although the stages of an individual facing their own death are clear, they are not linear; there is no smooth straight line from stage to stage, starting with denial and ending with acceptance. Rather, they are to use an image, more like a bowl of noodles, each being twisted around, looping through and connecting with each of the others in a random, pattern-less, unidentifiable fashion, and each individual's bowl of noodles is unique to them. Denial can be mixed in with acceptance, depression can result in disbelief, acceptance can be part of a bargain, as each person works their way towards their own demise, the risk becoming greater with each journey outside the walls.

From the beginning, Rick Grimes is forged from trauma; victim of a traumatic event (the shooting and his resulting coma) even before the world becomes overrun by the dead. From the moment that Rick stumbles out of his hospital room and into the world, he is bombarded by distressing and psychologically damaging experiences. What he sees before him is a world transformed, unrecognisable from his pre-hospitalisation life. There is no escaping the fact that something world-changing has occurred: the eerily quiet hospital is littered with signs of battle and degradation, while hundreds of bodies line Rick's exit, some organised in rows, many simply left where they fell ('Days Gone Bye', 1.1). Rick is left alone in this seemingly abandoned world, temporarily disconnected and with only sinister environmental clues as to what has happened. With no people to help him, no provisions, weapons or even clothes, Rick is exceptionally vulnerable to this dangerous and virtually unrecognisable uncanny environment.

Still wounded from the gunshot that put him in a coma, physically weakened and without context for the chaos before him, Rick is alone, confused, anxious and unable to make sense of what he sees, with no people or information to offer guidance. When Rick meets Morgan and his son, they fill in some of the details and Rick then embarks on his quest, first to find his family, then to keep them alive. He becomes so hyper-focused on his quest that he distances himself from the violence around him. This dissociation from the reality of the experience allows him to function in stressful environments but postpones the onset of his trauma response. Once Rick reunites with his family ('Tell It to the Frogs', 1.3), he almost immediately leaves to start another mission (rescuing Merle), resulting in an almost compulsive series of quests in order to solve the most pressing danger or traumatic event at the time, whether this is searching for Sophia, rescuing Carl, leading the group to the Center for Disease Control (CDC) in Atlanta and so on. Although Rick does not necessarily see himself as a hero, he does see himself as responsible for the group and an authority figure, adopting a leadership position almost straight away. He may have to make difficult and unpopular decisions, but putting himself into these leadership and quest roles acts as a way for him to avoid and deny the extremely vulnerable and powerless position he originally found himself in. It is these quests that are at the root of how Rick copes with his own fear of mortality and the persistent trauma he is forced to undergo; an attempt to regain control after his traumatic introduction in a world where his helplessness was amplified.

Carol already shows signs of PTSD from her first appearance in 'Tell It to the Frogs', with it quickly becoming clear that her husband Ed is abusive. Her response is to become quiet and do what he asks out of self-preservation and most importantly, to avoid him turning his attention to their daughter. It is only when he dies that Carol can begin to recover from what has passed, and we begin to see her strength, only for her daughter Sophia to go missing and for the search to lead the group to Hershel Greene's farm, where the child is discovered among the walkers being tended to in his barn ('Pretty Much Dead Already', 2.7). In this scene, Carol is confronted with a series of traumas over a very short space of time: grief and guilt over Sophia's death (along with anger that she had been close by the entire time they had been searching for her); Sophia's transformation into a walker and finally witnessing the zombified Sophia being 'put down'.

Unlike characters such as Rick, who, in pre-apocalypse life had a relatively quiet existence, Carol's past experience of domestic violence and rapid succession of traumas as the series begins eventually causes a level of PTSD-related dissociation that numbs her to the compassion and empathy that Rick feels; she learns to match the brutal events around her with ruthless pragmatism.[14] She teaches the children to take down walkers, but she still demonstrates her traumatised self in how she is able to manipulate others and act on her own authority. She uses cookies to manipulate a child into keeping a secret, and when there is a deadly illness at the prison it is Carol who decides to burn the first people to die, going against the rule that walkers are burned, people are buried.

Characters continually accuse each other of not giving voice to their trauma, with some using this silence as a show of strength or to establish an emotional distance. Carol, for example, while still considering Lizzie and Mica to be 'her girls', sometimes treats them very coldly, chastising Lizzie when she accidentally calls her 'mom'. Rick asks her why she never uses Sophia's name, to which Carol replies, 'She's dead, Rick. Sophia. Dead', simultaneously demonstrating acceptance and the detachment from emotions, places and physical self, known as dissociation.[15] Rick, still clinging on to pre-apocalypse ideas of grief and loss, expects Carol to publicly perform the role of grieving mother, even though she has managed to compartmentalise her complex emotions, for better or worse ('Indifference', 4.4). Rick finds Carol's detachment disturbing, yet, at this point, it is a source of strength for her, helping her to cope with the multiple traumas she has suffered. She attempts to impart this outlook to Lizzie, advising the girl that she 'can't' feel fear (as opposed to 'shouldn't'), telling her to 'fight it. And fight it. You don't give up. And then, one day, you just change. We all change' ('Indifference'). However, *The Walking Dead* is critical of those who dissociate or isolate themselves from the group; characters such as Rick, Carol, Michonne and Daryl become vicious, cold and animalistic when separated for too long. To regain their humanity, they must be reintegrated into the community, usually by helping the group or through acts of empathy.

Laura Kremmel writes that:

> Mourning rituals, like all rituals, provide a sense of structure and duty during a time when emotion clouds reason and judgment. The anticipation of the body returning to life, however, disrupts the peace and comfort of traditional mourning rituals as the state of becoming a zombie complicates what death is, provoking ever more conflicted reactions of love, loss, fear, devastation, hatred, and repulsion.[16]

There can be no healthy recovery from grief without mourning, meaning that the survivors must establish new rituals in order to psychologically manage the fallout. However, while Lori sees this process as a way of asserting humanity ('We haven't had a minute to hold on to anything of our old selves. We need time to mourn, and we need to bury our dead. It's what people do'), the rules of death and post-death ritual have changed and must be adapted accordingly. Kremmel suggests that in 'Wildfire' (1.5), following the first major walker attack, it is Andrea and Daryl who begin to explore these new ways of managing mourning, with Andrea using the opportunity of her sister's reanimation to gain closure: to do and say what she could not when she was alive (namely, protection and acknowledgement).[17] Simultaneously, Daryl begins his new role as 'the zombie apocalypse's equivalent of the grave-digger, replacing emotion, reflection, and kind words with the sheer labor – sweat and blood and guts – of putting the dead to rest in their many pieces'. In doing so, he 'illustrates exactly what mourning has become: a hostile battle against the zombie and, for him, the black-and-white duty of destruction, ranging from burial to burning, both after a sharp blow to the brain'.[18]

Survivors in *The Walking Dead*, whether consciously or not are all engaged in Kubla-Ross's stages of grief, which are denial, anger, bargaining, depression and acceptance.[20] Movement through these stages is not linear, they overlap and repeat, sometimes for prolonged periods: Carol's response to Rick when Sophia goes missing (anger); facing her daughter as a walker (denial); witnessing her being 'put down' (bargaining and depression) and eventually finding her place (acceptance). Michonne's journey from bereaved mother and loner to Rick's partner and mother of his children places Michonne as navigating grief multiple times in overlapping stages. As each of these women move to face their trauma, they begin to use it as an agent of transformation and each becomes a warrior who has their trauma to face, their fear of death to conquer and their grief to process. These stages are embodied by the Grimes family as they face the death of Lori and the birth of Judith, Sasha who decides to die and allow herself to turn to attack Negan and Carl Grimes in facing his own death after being bitten ('How It's Gotta Be', 8.8).

When Rick discovers his wife has died, he shows signs of shock and begins to act strangely, starting with a series of telephone calls in which Rick hallucinates several voices, finally speaking to Lori with an expression of deep grief and despair:

> I loved you. I loved you. I couldn't put it back together, I couldn't put it back together. I made a deal with myself. I will keep you alive, I will find you a place, I will fix that. I couldn't open that door, I couldn't risk it. I was going to keep you alive; Carl; the baby. And then I thought there'd be time. There's never time. I loved you. I love you. I couldn't put it back together. I should've said it, should've said it. ('Hounded', 3.6)

Rick goes on to see visions of Lori as he learns to live with his grief, giving other members of the group reason to question his mental health. Rick does appear to process his grief enough to be able to continue with life, although the viewer never knows for certain whether he is accepting of his loss or if he must go on by necessity, placing Rick in a situation reflected by all bereaved people, asking the question 'when does life continue?' In addition, Rick's widowhood may have acted as a trigger for his trauma response, potentially setting back any recovery. As for Judith, a child of the apocalypse knows only a world of walkers and she learns very early in life to deal with them. But it is Carl who ensures that she knows who her mother was and what she did so that Judith would live.

Carl Grimes is a survivor. He survives the apocalypse as a child, is shot twice and loses an eye, assists in the birth of his sister while being forced to kill his mother. Carl makes friends only to lose them to death and undeath, he protects his sister Judith at all costs and makes a point of doing the right thing because that is how he was raised. Carl is also a fighter, used to putting down walkers and standing his ground against people. But he is also vulnerable, initially believing that his father was dead, becoming close to Shane and then playing a part in Shane's death. Carl goes through cycles of trauma responses, each one leading him to become more focused, aggressive and engage in risk-taking behaviour. Carl is forced to toughen up too quickly and is given adult responsibilities as a child; for example, learning to shoot a gun and then being allowed to carry one for protection. Psychologically, the viewer is never really sure how old Carl is, he looks like a child or a teenager, acts like a warrior and is given leadership responsibilities, but at his core Carl is a traumatised boy. He is not always able to keep the veneer of adult toughness stable though, at times he shows frustration to the point of tantrum, misplaced aggression and at times becomes upset and tearful.

When Carl is bitten while rescuing a stranger from walkers, his first instinct is to ignore it, save the man and get them and everyone else safely evacuated into the sewers beneath Alexandria ('Honor', 8.9). Carl says nothing about his bite, tending to it himself and covering it with a dressing. For a while he is able to continue life as normal but soon begins to show signs of illness and in one of the most devastating revelations, the truth comes out. Carl begins facing his mortality long before this event, in the zombie apocalypse, but when it becomes clear that his life is now in danger, Carl demonstrates almost classic denial. He makes no reference to it at all, preferring to introduce the new member of the group and get on as normal. The truth comes out only after the people of Alexandria are safely hidden in the sewers. Facing the truth means allowing others into his trauma, putting away denial and allowing those who love him to begin to grieve with him for his lost future. Like Sasha, Carl also ends his own life. But, also like Sasha, Carl's decision is about control rather than acting out of a traumatised place. Controlling the end of his life allows Carl to reclaim some of the agency that the bite denied him, to the point that he insists on being alone at the final moment of his life. Carl acts in the only way he knows how in order to save his family and friends from the trauma of euthanising him or having to confront his undead form. His memory of his mother's death plays a significant role in his choice to not put others in that position. Carl tries to limit the trauma experienced by others, he keeps his outward expression generally positive, spends time making memories with Judith and he writes letters to all his friends. It seems that Carl Grimes comes to an acceptance of his own impending death at least enough to try to help those who love him to accept it too.

'It's About Facing Reality': Beyond Post-Trauma

In the post-apocalyptic world of *The Walking Dead*, there is no 'getting beyond' trauma. Carol reminds Rick that, 'It's not about what you say. It's about facing reality. It always comes for us over and over again. We face it so we can live' ('Indifference'). Later, at the sheltered community of Alexandria, Jessie bluntly tells the Alexandrians, 'I used to not want to see the way things are. It's not that I couldn't, it's that I – I didn't want to. But this is what life looks like now. We have to see it. We have to fight it. If we don't fight, we die' ('Now'). Trauma cannot be avoided or denied; despite some people's delayed response or inability to acknowledge a traumatic event the effects always make themselves known in the end. Although not everyone who experiences traumatic events within the series gets PTSD, this does not mean that they are unaffected by the trauma. Virtually every encounter with either the living or the undead can result in a trauma, with no time for recovery in between. Resources to establish appropriate psychological processing to move individuals through layers of traumatic experience to the beginnings of recovery are absent. Furthermore, it is more necessary and urgent for survivors to confront their own mortality, particularly in cases where they have been bitten and know they will soon transform into the undead. However, there is opportunity and hope for psychological balance. In 'Save the Last One', Lori wonders whether it would be better for Carl to die from his injuries rather than having to endure the brutality of the post-apocalyptic world, worrying that if he survives the dangers, the suffering will inevitably turn into 'another animal who doesn't know anything except survival' (a foreshadowing of how several characters become later in the series). Carl, however, ultimately proves her wrong; although he suffers and eventually dies, he remains compassionate, brave and ultimately human, able to work through the periods of emotional detachment that occur as he develops psychologically. His final acts – writing letters, making mementos with Judith[21] and his decision to die from suicide rather than turn – ultimately prove him to be level-headed and caring, attributes that are also found in his sister. Despite the next generation growing up in a savage world, the majority of them do not become the monsters that trauma can create. As the post-apocalyptic world continues, psychological responses evolve in turn, with grief and grieving playing a much more significant role in how survivors live with trauma. With little to no chance of full psychological recovery (only acceptance), the world of the zombie post-apocalypse not only becomes a world beyond trauma, but a world beyond post-trauma.

Notes

1. American Psychiatric Association, *Diagnostic and Statistical Manual of Mental Disorders*, 5th edn, DSM-5-TR™ (Washington DC: American Psychiatric Association, 2022).
2. *Diagnostic and Statistical Manual of Mental Disorders.*
3. J. L. Walton *et al.*, 'Sometimes Less is More: Establishing the Core Symptoms of PTSD', *Journal of Traumatic Stress*, 30/3 (2017), 254–8.
4. L. J. Harvey *et al.*, 'Dialectical Behaviour Therapy for Emotion Regulation Difficulties: A Systematic Review', *Behaviour Change*, 36/3 (2019), 143–64; 'Cognitive Behavioral Therapy (CBT) for Treatment of PTSD' (Washington DC: American Psychological Association, 2017).
5. F. Shapiro and L. Maxfield, *Eye Movement Desensitization and Reprocessing (EMDR) Therapy* (Washington DC: American Psychological Association, 2017).
6. E. M. Voorendonk *et al.*, 'Trauma-Focused Treatment Outcome For Complex PTSD Patients: Results of an Intensive Treatment Programme', *European Journal of Psychotraumatology*, 11/1 (2020), 178.
7. R. F. Baumeister and M. R. Leary, 'The Need to Belong: Desire for Interpersonal Attachments as a Fundamental Human Motivation', *Psychological Bulletin* (Washington DC: American Psychological Association, 1995).
8. Clay Routledge and Matthew Vess, *Handbook of Terror Management Theory* (London: Academic Press, 2018) p. 24.
9. Historical trauma refers to the emotional harm experienced by a group or generation caused by a traumatic event and the manifestation of subsequent actions. This is not just trauma from the past but is trauma still happening. See Michael O'Loughlin and Marilyn Charles (eds), *Fragments of Trauma and the Social Production of Suffering: Trauma, History, and Memory* (Lanham MD: Rowman & Littlefield Publishers, 2014), p. 38.
10. Doctors in general appear to have a particularly short lifespan on *The Walking Dead* and Denise is no exception.

11. Natalie McNeillie and John Rose, 'Vicarious Trauma in Therapists: A Meta-Ethnographic Review', *Behavioural and Cognitive Psychotherapy*, 49/4 (2021), 426–40; Amelia van der Merwe and Xanthe Hunt, 'Secondary Trauma Among Trauma Researchers: Lessons from the Field', *Psychological Trauma: Theory, Research, Practice, and Policy*, 11 (2019), 10–18.
12. On coming across a woman who could have shot herself rather than turning into a walker, Carol notes that, 'Some people can't give up. Like us' ('Them', 5.10).
13. Elisabeth Kübler-Ross, *On Death and Dying: What the Dying Have to Teach Doctors, Nurses, Clergy & Their Own Families* (New York: Scribner, 2011).
14. J. Machorrinho *et al.*, 'Embodiment-Related Risk Factors for Posttraumatic Stress, Anxiety and Depression in Female Victims of Intimate Partner Violence', *Journal of Trauma & Dissociation*, 23/3 (2022), 212–28.
15. A. V. Seligowski *et al.*, 'Autonomic Responses to Fear Conditioning among Women with PTSD and Dissociation', *Depression and Anxiety*, 36/7 (2019), 625–34.
16. Laura Kremmel, 'Rest in Pieces: Violence in Mourning the (Un)dead', in Dawn Keetley, *'We're All Infected': Essays on AMC's* The Walking Dead *and the Fate of the Human* (Jefferson NC: McFarland, 2014), p. 84.
17. Kremmel, 'Rest in Pieces', pp. 86–7.
18. Kremmel, 'Rest in Pieces', p. 87.
19. Kremmel, 'Rest in Pieces', p. 87.
20. Elisabeth Kübler-Ross and David Kessler, *On Grief and Grieving: Finding the Meaning of Grief Through the Five Stages of Loss* (New York: Simon and Schuster, 2005), pp. 2–5.
21. Incidentally, objects such as photographs, heirlooms (notably watches), drawings and the handprints that Carl makes with Judith ultimately become *memento mori* rather than fond memories.

10

Abject Body of the Zombie as a Counter-narrative to the Pandemic Hero

Madeline Becker

Zombies and Heroes in the Twenty-First Century

DURING THE COVID-19 pandemic, two imaginary figures gained particular prominence: the hero and the zombie. Throughout the pandemic narratives about noble heroes featured physicians, nurses and supermarket personnel as pandemic heroes. At the same time, the pandemic evokes contemporary zombie films in which ultra-contagious viruses cause the collapse of our social, cultural and political world. While both the hero and the zombie tend to emerge in times crisis (pandemics and other), they could not be any more different. The hero is strong and powerful, in many cases even invincible, offering us comfort and assurance in times of uncertainty. The zombie, on the other hand, constitutes an imaginary manifestation of our deepest fears and anxieties; it unsettles and frightens rather than reassures. This chapter compares the hero and the zombie and asks how these two figures invite us to think about what is means to be human; how they prompt us to think about the (in)stability of our social, cultural, political and bodily borders; and, finally, which ways of dealing with crises they suggest. Ultimately, I argue that in a time in which we are facing various, often human-made, crises, we may need the zombie more than we need the hero.

Since the emergence of the COVID-19 pandemic, I have often heard people say that they feel as if they were in a zombie movie. Indeed, many of the films and series featuring zombies that were produced and released since the turn of the century do have an eerily prophetic quality: a virus unexpectedly emerges and rapidly spreads throughout the entire planet; our ways of life, social, cultural and political structures are disrupted; and people need to protect themselves as they are constantly on the verge of infection. What we have seen played out in countless zombie films has become our reality with the beginning of the COVID-19 pandemic. Even though the recent pandemic took many of us by surprise, the prominence of representations of fictional viral outbreaks in zombie films suggests that fears and anxieties related to such outbreaks must have haunted the cultures that produced those films for longer.

Since the beginning of the twenty-first century zombies have increasingly often been imagined as being contagious; as a being brought about by a viral pandemic rather than voodoo magic (e.g., *White Zombie*, 1932; *I Walked with a Zombie*, 1943), or through alien invasions (e.g., *Plan Nine from Outer Space*, 1959). In Danny Boyle's *28 Days Later* (2003) and its sequel *28 Weeks Later* (2007) a rage-virus transmitted by chimpanzees turns people into super-aggressive, flesh-eating zombies. In Zack Snyder's remake of *Dawn of the Dead* (2004), zombiism is also highly contagious. Everyone who is bitten by a zombie rapidly becomes one themselves. The television series *The Walking Dead* (2010–present) takes this notion of the hyper-contagious virus a step further as every human being is already infected, so that after their death they will eventually rise again as zombies. Zombies no longer move slowly and arrive in small groups, as they did in the films of the twentieth century but appear in great hordes and sometimes move with superhuman speed. While in films such as *White Zombie* and *I Walked with a Zombie*, the zombie does not kill (unless ordered to do so by the voodoo master), contemporary zombies seem to be driven by nothing but an instinct to kill and eat the yet uninfected.

The highly contagious, fast-moving, flesh-eating zombie horde combines a number of twenty-first-century fears. Lars Schmeink, for instance, points out that since the turn of the century we have become increasingly aware of our corporality and the frailty of the human body. According to Schmeink, this is due to the increasing amount of research on human genomes and developments in genetic engineering.[1] Similarly, Mark

Honigsbaum observes that the increasing number of epidemic and pandemic outbreaks over the past twenty-one years – including Ebola, swine flu, bird flu and COVID-19 – makes us 'hyperaware'[2] of viral threats. As a result of this awareness zombie apocalypses are imagined as being brought about by a virus pandemic rather than voodoo magic. In addition, the fast-moving zombie mirrors anxieties concerning a rapidly and constantly changing world that is characterised by an international mobility that allows viruses to spread globally within a short period. In short, the recent COVID-19 pandemic has touched a sore spot and seems to have instantiated a number of fears and anxieties concerning the stability of our cultural, social and political structures and institutions, about globalisation and global mobility, and the integrity of the human body. These anxieties have been negotiated in the zombie imagination in the past twenty years. At the same time, another, but very different, imaginative figure has featured prominently in our cultural imagination, which, just like the zombie, tends to emerge in times of crises.

The hero has featured in our cultural imagination even longer than the zombie has. Ancient mythology has brought forth countless heroes, the most prominent of which include Herakles, Achilles, Odysseus, Siegfried, and so forth. Their stories are well known, have been retold and adapted countless times, and have inspired the invention of even more heroes. Like zombies, heroes emerge when cultures are experiencing a crisis or trauma. The first superhero comics, for example, emerged in the United States in the late 1930s and early 1940s when the country was battered by the Great Depression and experienced the early years of the Second World War. They experienced a resurgence after the terrorist attacks on the World Trade Center and the Pentagon in 2001. Unlike the zombie, the hero does not place a finger onto the sore spot but rather re-contain our fears and anxieties. Heroes provide a sense of stability; they safeguard the *status quo*, our social and cultural structures, values and worldviews. More recently, stories about heroes reflect a trend of an growing awareness of human vulnerability and mortality, as increasingly often heroes die, sometimes from mundane illnesses, and do not return from the dead. Captain Marvel (Mar-vell), for instance, dies of cancer in the 1982 comic *The Death of Captain Marvel* by Jim Starlin, and the title passes on to a new Captain Marvel (Carol Danvers). Nonetheless, as this example illustrates, although specific heroes do not live on as individuals, they pass their heroic identities on to new characters and in so doing, despite their mortality, safeguard a sense of continuity and stability.

As the COVID-19 pandemic probed contemporary fears and anxieties, both the zombie and the hero (re-)gained prominence and, hence, must be regarded in terms of how each of these figures asks us to make sense of this pandemic, and the fears and anxieties connected to it. I argue, while the figure of the hero aims at re-establishing a sense of human invulnerability, power and control, that the rotting, disintegrating body of the zombie and the ultra-vulnerable body of the survivor of the apocalypse remind us that we are in fact vulnerable, mortal and material bodies. They remind us that our ways of life, our social, cultural and political institutions are fragile.

Worldviews at Crisis: Viruses, Borders and the Human

When a virus emerges and – ignoring national borders – rapidly spreads globally, when it enters and sickens countless human bodies and brings our social life to a halt, that virus not only has an impact on our health but, as Dahlia Schweitzer notes, it also profoundly impacts on our understanding of the world.[3] In particular, viruses destabilise worldviews that are based on binary distinctions by ignoring national, social, cultural and bodily borders; worldviews that are based on the idea of borders that separate what we believe does not belong together. Peter Schuck points out that as viruses take possession of our bodies, the border between self and other, between inside and outside, blur.[4] What is more viruses disregard social and cultural categories constructed around gender, class, age, 'race' and sometimes species,[5] as they sicken the poor and the rich, young and old, humans and non-humans, and so forth. In particular, the COVID-19 virus further revealed the porosity of national borders: within a few weeks the virus had spread globally, putting much of the world in a state of emergency.

Furthermore, as a virus enters our bodies, it calls into questions what we believe it means to be human. In particular, it challenges our idea of the human body.[6] We commonly understand the human body as an integral whole, protected by bodily barriers. Viruses, on the other hand, reveal that we are porous, open to disease and other intruders from the outside world. As Alessandra Boller points out, 'mankind is commonly imagined and discursively produced as a stable being'.[7] Referring to Sherryl Vint, she states that 'the human body is perceived in terms of dichotomies and boundaries such as the body and the outside world'.[8] But not only do we tend to think of the human body as an integral whole, we also think of the human being as a possessor of reason, of an immortal soul, of agency. We generally understand the human in terms of its mental facilities rather than as a body. Viruses, however, remind us that we are in fact vulnerable, mortal bodies that are open to disease. The coronavirus threatens this mind-body division, as it not only affects our respiratory organs, assigned to the body, but also wanders into and sickens the neurological system, understood as part of the mind.

Hence, as Schweitzer concludes, the threat of a highly contagious disease reinforces the concern that all boundaries, bodily ones in particular, but social and cultural ones by extension, are porous and that there is no real protection against microbial (and other) invasions.[9] As the real and conceptual barriers that pre-empt borders are being breached and become ineffective, the threat of disease is increasingly difficult to contain. As a result, we feel powerless, exposed to a threat that we find difficult to control. Both the awareness of the corporality of the human and the human body's vulnerability to disease call into question the ways in which we have so far commonly conceptualised the human being. While for a long time we might have perceived the human being as a possessor of a soul together with a rational mind, we are now confronted with idea that we are, after all, material bodies.

During the COVID-19 pandemic, the public discourse responded in ways that re-affirm and stabilise our sense of control and invulnerability. As Steve Hinchliffe and his fellow authors point out, '[i]n the first instance, approaches to infectious disease management or control … involve constructing and maintaining real as well as metaphorical walls'.[10] A US public-health poster, reprinted in Hinchliffe's book, illustrates this argument. The image on the poster shows diseases taking the form of wild, vicious dogs, which are separated from playing children. There is a wall that separates the children from disease, not only physically but also metaphorically, as it also upholds the idea of the nature/culture binary.[11] Such images render pathogens part of the non-human world, which must be kept separate, managed and controlled in order to prevent diseases from emerging and 'crossing' into the human world. Similar attempts at re-instating real and conceptual borders have been made during the COVID-19 pandemic: the language used when talking about the virus contained various conceptual metaphors such as the notion of a 'lockdown', 'quarantine' or 'isolation', alluding to the idea of containment, physical barriers such as masks and protective suits were used, and international mobility was restricted, giving a sense of national borders as protection. While these examples illustrate attempts to re-institute borders in times when our sense of stability and integrity are endangered, I find one narrative that has been created in response to the COVID-19 pandemic particularly interesting: the hero.

Guardians of the *Status Quo*: Heroes of the Pandemic

Since the beginning of the pandemic, different texts and institutions have collaborated in creating pandemic-heroes. These attempts have focused in particular on medical personnel, nursing staff and supermarket staff. Many local and governmental campaigns and events contributed to the heroisation of human individuals during the COVID-19 pandemic. For instance, photos of heroes were hung up in public spaces in the United Kingdom,[12] and there were public events and parades to thank pandemic-heroes, clapping on balconies and from front doorsteps.[13] A UK comic artist drew images of 'NHS superheroes' using a visual vocabulary that is reminiscent of actual superhero-comics.[14] In one of those images, the SARS-CoV-2 virus is depicted as a monster (much like the healthcare poster that I referred to earlier). In doing so, the virus is rendered a non-human intruder, which needs to be warded off the human world by a hero. *The Australian Post* has released a collection of stamps with illustrations of 'frontline heroes'.[15] The heroes on the stamps are depicted wearing masks and protective suits, picking up on the idea of re-instituting borders protecting the body when our bodily borders do not suffice. As countless texts have taken up the hero motif, it has become an omnipresent feature of the public discourse on the COVID-19 pandemic.

As Jeffrey A. Brown highlights, heroes emerge in times of crises to help us re-write traumatic events such as the Second World War, 9/11[16] or the recent pandemic. When we feel weakened, Brown continues, heroes maintain an image of strength.[17] In the same vein, Sidney Hook observes that our need for a hero grows when we experience social or political crisis from which we want to be saved.[18] In addition, Joseph Campbell suggests that we seek heroes in times of crisis because we look to them as guardians of our systems of order and the *status quo*.[19] Accordingly, the prominence of the hero during the coronavirus pandemic is hardly surprising considering that one of the main cultural functions of the hero is to re-establish a sense of power, agency and security in times of crisis.

Indeed, the notion of stability is ingrained in the narratives that are usually employed when telling the story of a hero. As Campbell notes, most stories about heroes follow a universal plot pattern and employ a number of recurring tropes. Hence, Campbell refers to stories about heroes as 'monomyths'.[20] Likewise, Umberto Eco observes that the hero narrative is defined by its stasis. He writes that the plot is characterised by 'a need to forbid the release of excessive and irretrievable developments'.[21] Eco further explains that 'the mythic character embodies a law, or a universal demand, and, therefore, must be in part predictable and cannot hold surprises for us'.[22] When the ways in which we understand the world are challenged and everything seems uncertain and uncontrollable, these well-established, and hence predictable, stories offer us comfort and a sense of stability.

Campbell has pointed out that one defining moment in the hero-narrative is that of the hero returning from the dead and in doing so conquering death.[23] At some stage of their journey, most heroes must climb into an abyss where they face and overcome trauma. Often the hero dies a metaphorical or literal death in the abyss but is then reborn and becomes even more powerful than before[24] – hence, the abyss has been read by Campbell as a metaphor for the maternal womb.[25] Campbell writes, '[t]he hero has died as a modern man; but as eternal man – perfected, unspecific, universal man – he has been reborn'.[26] In so doing, the hero narrative reassures us that threats and dangers can be contained, that man is invulnerable – even immortal. After his rebirth, heroes are finally able to ward off the threat that has endangered his world and to re-establish order and the *status quo*.[27] Therefore, the hero narrative seems to suggest that trauma and crisis can be overcome if we prove resilient and strong. They take times of crisis not as turning points that herald social, cultural or political change, but rather understand crises as an opportunity to protect, maintain and prove the resilience of our established systems of order.

Representations of the hero's and, particularly, the superhero's body work in a similarly ensuring way. The (super)hero's body is usually represented as extraordinarily strong and invulnerable. Sometimes the hero's body has a weak spot, such as Achilles' heel, the spot between Siegfried's shoulder blades or Superman's vulnerability to Kryptonite, but these only work to highlight that the rest of the hero's body as impenetrable. Therefore, for instance, Steve Roger's transformation into Captain America is, first and foremost, a physical transformation: using genetic experimentation his frail and weak body – a metaphor for the United States after the

Great Depression – transforms into a super-strong, muscular and invulnerable body that symbolises America's strength. As Yen-Lian Liu adds, the strength of the hero is often associated with the masculine body. She writes, 'The image of many American superheroes is always represented as being "phallic" [original emphasis] in their costumes'.[28] Accordingly, the heroic male body comes to stand in for endurance and stability.[29] Liu further emphasises the importance of the costumed body, which she reads as referring to the performativity of gender identity,[30] but which may also be read in terms of its capacity to protect the hero. The superhero's costume constitutes a protective suit, which shields the hero from various threats: it safeguards the hero's identity as well as its body from injuries (e.g., Iron Man's metal armour or Captain America's shield). In so doing, the hero's body is often metaphorical for the strength and resilience of the culture that created it; the body re-installs the notion of the human body being protected by its own and created borders.

Last Wo/Men and Zombies

While the public discourse on the COVID-19 pandemic revolves around narratives of immortal, powerful heroes and the protection of the *status quo*, the zombie imagination draws a contrasting image. The rapid global spread of an ultra-contagious virus, visual representations of human bodies turned into rotting, walking corpses, the collapse of all social and political institutions, and last wo/men fighting for their survival constitute recurring tropes of the zombie imagination of the twenty-first century. While the hero narrative is concerned with re-establishing a sense of order and human agency, the zombie narrative confronts its audience with a world of collapse and chaos, in which the human is represented as either a walking corpse or as an ultra-vulnerable survivor who is constantly on the verge of becoming part of the zombie horde.

Like the hero narrative, the zombie narrative is set in a world shaken up by a crisis, usually against an apocalyptic or post-apocalyptic setting. The world as we know it, its social and political institutions and structures, have collapsed. As in most post-apocalyptic stories, the narrative is focalised through one or more of the few remaining survivors, who now struggle to navigate this new world and fight for their survival. These characters are often cast as 'last wo/men'. Eva Horn describes the figure of the last wo/man as 'the figure of an ultimate truth about humankind, which is only revealed to this last specimen'.[31] This last truth often concerns the question of what it means to be human in general, but especially in times of crisis.[32] Horn explains that humans lose all humanness under the pressure of a crisis or catastrophe. The last wo/man is no longer characterised by Enlightenment ideals of empathy, friendship and rationality. Stripped of the comforts of civilisation, exposed to a life-threatening situation, the last wo/man becomes selfish, fearful and brutal.[33] What is more, the last wo/man is no longer understood 'as a creature of God but as a natural living being'.[34] As such, the last wo/man is represented as an ultra-vulnerable mortal body rather than an intellectual mind. This notion of the human as a mortal body is even strengthened in the zombie-apocalypse, as the last wo/men are constantly on the verge of becoming one with or being consumed by the undead horde. As Sarah Juliet Lauro and Karen Embry point out in their essay on zombies, '[t]he zombie poses a twofold terror: There is the primary fear of being devoured by a zombie, a threat posed mainly to the physical body, and the secondary fear that one will, in losing one's consciousness, become part of the monstrous horde'.[35]

The notion of always being on the verge of becoming a zombie is particularly highlighted in *The Walking Dead*, in which all human survivors already carry the zombie-virus within themselves. They no longer need to be bitten by a zombie to turn into one, but, regardless of their cause of death, they will eventually become part of the horde. In so doing the series casts the human body as already dead, but not yet dead,[36] to paraphrase Lauro and Embry. It emphasises the notion that we are always already dragging our corpse with us. Accordingly, the (still) human protagonists of zombie narratives are frequently presented as vulnerable bodies rather than rational agents. The opening scene of *28 Days Later* shows Jim waking up in a hospital, as yet unaware of the apocalyptic state of the world. He is naked, strapped to a hospital bed, with various tubes entering and leaving his body. Jim is shot from the bird's eye perspective so that he is fully exposed to the viewer's gaze.[37] This draws an image of Jim's body as being vulnerable, porous and exposed. Likewise, in *The Walking Dead* viewers often see survivors being torn apart – for instance, in the *TWD* episode 'Sorry Brother' we see Dale's abdomen being torn apart by a zombie while Dale is still alive[38] – or we see the survivor's body being dismembered – in 'No Way Out' Carl loses his eye,[39] and in 'Vatos' Merle saws off his own hand as he was cuffed to a roof and attacked by zombies.[40] Representations of the wounded, bleeding and dismembered body of the survivor highlight the impression that, just as the zombie's body, the living body is material, vulnerable and mortal. Hence, as Laura and Embry observe, such images suggest that we are all 'already zombies (but not yet zombies)'; both the zombie and the last wo/man enhance their viewer's sense of our frailty, the limits of our consciousness and our personal agency.[41] The materiality of the last wo/man's body is further highlighted as it is not only threatened with death but also of being devoured by the zombie. Hence, the last wo/man's body is portrayed as meat and as potential food for someone else. In being consumed as food the borders of our bodies dissolve in the body of the other. Representations of the zombie's body extrapolate the notion of the corporeal and vulnerable materiality of the human, but before turning to the zombie I want to consider the last wo/man in a little more detail.

The vulnerability of the last wo/man not only manifests in representations of its mortal and material body, but also in the architecture of the stories that are told about them. Unlike stories about the hero, stories about the last wo/man do not reassure us of our resolve and immortality but rather highlight human vulnerabilities and weaknesses. As pointed out earlier, one defining moment of the hero narrative is the climb into the abyss, where the hero faces his trauma, dies and is reborn more powerful than before – sometimes this rebirth occurs as a resurrection of the same character, sometimes as a passing-on of the heroic identity that is placed onto another character. In contrast, last wo/men find themselves in a constant, endless struggle for survival. Stories about last wo/men in the zombie narrative are often anti-cathartic; they do not offer resolution. Unlike the hero, the last wo/man does not emerge from their traumatic story stronger and glorious. Instead, many last wo/men find themselves stuck in a continuous loop of traumata. Whenever the last wo/man manages to climb out of the abyss, they are immediately thrown into the next one. For instance, Rick Grimes, the protagonist of television series *The Walking Dead*, drags himself from one traumatic event to the other throughout the entire series, never finding any resolution or catharsis: first, he is forced to kill his best friend, then he loses his wife in childbirth, he later loses his son to a zombie bite, as well as losing various friends and allies and finding himself in life-threatening situations time and again. Other characters from the series follow a similar plot line.[42]

Like the narrative architecture of the last wo/man's story, representations of the zombie's body deconstruct the idea of rebirth after trauma. In its portrayal of the hero dying in the abyss and then being reborn triumphant and strong, the hero monomyth takes up on the resurrection myth that has gained prominence in Western culture through Christianity. Vervaeke, Mastropietro and Miscevic observe that the zombie constitutes a perversion of Christian and other resurrection myths.[43] Like the hero, the zombie is resurrected from the dead. Unlike the hero, however, the zombie does not return as an improved and stronger version. Instead, the zombie returns as a rotting corpse; a body that is divorced from its mental capacities and rational agency (hence, all qualities that we believe make us human), and reduced to one primal instinct, which is to consume the bodies of others. In so doing, the zombie reminds us that there is, in fact, no returning from the dead, as our being is tied to our mortal bodies. As Lauro and Embry write, '[t]he lumbering, decaying spectre of the zombie also affirms the inherent disability of human embodiment – our mortality'.[44]

The idea of the human body being a material, potentially rotting body with porous borders is particularly played out in filmic representations visualising the materiality and vulnerability of the human body. Zombie films from the twenty-first century frequently show zombies vomiting highly contagious blood[45] or oozing such blood from their noses, mouths and eyes. The zombie's body is sometimes bloated[46] and its skin is often greyish, peeling off and rotting from the body, and its body is featured as disintegrating and fragmented.[47] Such representations of the zombie play on the idea of the abject. Julia Kristeva's term 'abject' describes an emotional response to being confronted with the corporeal reality of the human body; a response to when we see (bodily and other) boundaries dissolving, systems of order collapsing and established social, cultural and conceptual rules being ignored.[48] Kristeva explains that a feeling of abjection arises when we see bodily fluids that we excrete. These fluids include blood, saliva, excrement and vomit. They evoke a feeling of abjection because, as we excrete them, they are both part of our body and not part of it.[49] They are alive in our body one moment and dead matter the next. Therefore, they unsettle the idea of bodily integrity as they move beyond the borders of our body. A feeling of abjection also manifests in relation to corpses. Kristeva observes that as we see corpses disintegrate, we experience the human body as borderless and material.[50] Accordingly, visual depictions of the abject body of the zombie remind us that to be human is to be a vulnerable, porous and material body.

Even though Kristeva's text focuses on representations of bodies, she suggests that feelings of abjection can also arise when we see other (than bodily) borders dissolve.[51] Hence, the zombie imagination often portrays a post-apocalyptic world in which most, if not all, social, cultural and political institutions and structures have collapsed. This is why, in most zombie films, there are no more national governments with institutions that ensure security. The zombie imagery is highly metaphorical of the perceived ineffectiveness of borders and institutions of order. Zombies shaking, tearing down and, ultimately, breaching fences are a recurring visual trope;[52] in the episode 'Seed' from *The Walking Dead* we see zombies in protective suits, wearing helmets with glass visors, gloves and shields. When Rick takes the helmet off one zombie, we see that beneath it is a rotting, disintegrating corpse.[53] Such images highlight the idea that there is no real protection from the viral threat and that the barriers we create to protect ourselves are ineffective. Indeed, *The Walking Dead* takes this idea a step further by imagining the zombie-virus to be innate to all human bodies already.

Conclusion: The Zombie in Times of Human-Made Crises

Through the COVID-19 pandemic we have once more been confronted with the corporality of the human, the human body's vulnerability and the limits of human agency and power. To re-contain such anxieties, we have sought and created pandemic-heroes, which re-establish a sense of human power and control over the non-human world of viruses and pathogens; hero-narratives render the human, and the human body in particular, invulnerable, immortal even. In contrast, the zombie-imagination of the past twenty-one years has nurtured such fears by visualising the horror of our materiality; by revealing that the human body is already a walking corpse; by showing us that we are enslaved by our corporality; and by suggesting that our real and conceptual (social, cultural and bodily) borders often prove ineffective.

In times of crisis, the hero re-assures humans of their bodies and social structures' resilience and invulnerability. In so doing, it perpetuates a deeply anthropocentric worldview that, as ecocritics including Lynn White, Serpil Oppermann and Serenella Iovino, Ursula Le Guin and Donna Haraway, among others, have argued, is at the root of most of the recent human-made crises.[54] We have been granting humankind a privileged position in the order of the world; we have assumed that the human is divine, exceptional and powerful. This understanding of the world – and our place in it – has not only been used to justify our oppression, exploitation and destruction of the non-human world, it also ignores that we are an integral part of the non-human world, it disregards the co-constitution of the human and the non-human and ignores the fact that the survival of humankind depends on the human-friendly conditions of our non-human environment.

This is also valid for the emergence and spread of pathogens and diseases. As Hinchliffe and his co-authors stress, a disease does not only emerge from microbes but from the interplay of various other conditions. These include relations between people, animals, microbes, infrastructures and ways of governing disease.[55] Instead of acknowledging the human-non-human entanglements that contribute to the emergence and spread of diseases, in the face of a crisis, we seem to favour symbols and narratives that uphold the idea of the nature/culture dichotomy (for instance, the speculation that the COVID-19 coronavirus emerged from animals from the Wuhan rainforest) that uphold the idea of human power, agency and invulnerability (e.g., the hero-narrative) and reinstate notions of containability.[56]

Whereas heroes maintain such ideas, zombies in the twenty-first century remind us that humans are, in fact, material bodies that are vulnerable and co-inhabited by many small life forms; bodies, whose survival depends on the conditions of their environments. If we become aware of our vulnerabilities and mortalities, both as individuals and as a species, and if we become more aware of the fragility of the ways in which we structure the social world, we can also acknowledge the need to change the ways in which we live in and interact with the world.

Notes

1. Lars Schmeink, *Biopunk Dystopias: Genetic Engineering, Society, and Science Fiction* (Liverpool: University Press, 2016), p. 7.
2. Mark Honigsbaum, *The Pandemic Century: One Hundred Years of Panic, Hysteria and Hubris* (London: Hurst and Company, 2019), p. xviii.
3. Dahlia Schweitzer, *Going Viral: Zombies, Viruses, and the End of the World* (New Brunswick NJ: Lehmanns, 2018), p. vii.
4. Peter Schuck, *Viele untote Körper: Über Zombies der Literatur und des Kinos* (Bielefeld: Transcript, 2018), p. 402.
5. Schuck, *Viele untote Körper*, p. 418.
6. Such conceptualisations of the human body usually refer to able bodies. People with disabilities may experience their embodiedness in their own particular ways.

7. Alessandra Boller, *Rethinking the Human in Dytopian Times: Modified Bodies and the Re-/deconstruction of Human Exceptionalism in Margaret Atwood's* Madd-Addam *Trilogy and Kazuo Ishiguro's* Never Let Me Go (Trier: WVT, 2018), p. 5.
8. Boller, *Rethinking the Human in Dystopian Times*, p. 5
9. Schweitzer, *Going Viral*, pp. 3–4.
10. Steve Hinchliffe *et al.*, *Pathological Lives: Disease, Space, and Biopolitics* (Hoboken NJ: Wiley Blackwell, 2017), p. 6.
11. Hinchliffe *et al.*, *Pathological Lives*, p. 6.
12. 'Pandemic Heroes' Portraits to be Pasted up in Bridgewater', *BBC News*, *www.bbc.com/news/uk-england-somerset-57788657* (last accessed 25 July 2021).
13. 'Thank You Day: Community Events to Thank COVID Heroes', *BBC News*, *www.bbc.com/news/uk-england-57713004* (last accessed 25 July 2021).
14. Charlotte Ball, 'Coronavirus: Norwich Comic Book Artist MJ Hiblen Draws NHS "Heroes"', *BBC News*, *www.bbc.com/news/uk-england-norfolk-52506324* (last accessed 25 July 2021).
15. '*Australia Post* Pays Tribute to Frontline Heroes with Five New Stamps', *Nine-News*, *www.9news.com.au/national/australia-post-five-new-stamps-featuring-frontline-heroes-during-COVID19-pandemic/35e4d23e-7ae2-4c1f-a160-744febde5c9c* (last accessed 25 July 2021).
16. Jeffrey A. Brown, *The Modern Superhero in Film and Television: Popular Genre and American Culture* (New York: Routledge, 2017), p. 1.
17. Brown, *The Modern Superhero*, p. 64.
18. Sidney Hook, *The Hero in History: A Study in Limitation and Possibility* (London: Martin Seeker and Warbug, 1943); *https://en.wikisource.org/wiki/The_Hero_in_History* (last accessed 24 May 2022), p. 16.
19. Joseph Campbell, *Hero with a Thousand Faces* (Princeton NJ: University Press, 2008), p. 288.
20. Campbell, *Hero with a Thousand Faces*, p. 3.
21. Umberto Eco, 'The Myth of Superman', *Diacritics*, 2/1 (1972), 14–22, *www.jstor.org/stable/464920?seq* (last accessed 24 May 2022).
22. Eco, 'The Myth of Superman', 15.
23. Campbell, *Hero with a Thousand Faces*, p. 12.
24. Campbell, *Hero with a Thousand Faces*, p. 84.
25. Campbell, *Hero with a Thousand Faces*, p. 85.
26. Campbell, *Hero with a Thousand Faces*, p. 18.
27. Campbell, *Hero with a Thousand Faces*, p. 311.
28. Yen-Lian Liu, 'The Masculine Masquerade of Superheroes in Watchmen', *Gender Forum*, 62 (2017), 39.
29. Liu, 'The Masculine Masquerade of Superheroes', 40.

30. Liu, 'The Masculine Masquerade of Superheroes', 40.
31. Eva Horn, *The Future as Catastrophe: Imagining Disaster in the Modern Age* (New York: Columbia University Press, 2018), p. 25.
32. Horn, *The Future as Catastrophe*, p. 26.
33. Horn, *The Future as Catastrophe*, p. 34–5.
34. Horn, *The Future as Catastrophe*, p. 26.
35. Sarah Juliet Lauro and Karen Embry, 'A Zombie Manifesto: The Nonhuman Condition in the Era of Advanced Capitalism', *boundary 2*, 35/1 (2008), 85–108, *www.thing.net/~rdom/ucsd/Zombies/ZombieManifesto.pdf* (accessed 22 May 2022).
36. Lauro and Embry, 'A Zombie Manifesto', 90.
37. Danny Boyle (dir.), *28 Days Later* (DNA Films, 2002), 0:05:40.
38. 'Sorry Brother', in *The Walking Dead*, directed by Greg Nicotero (AMC Networks and Fix Broadcasting Company, 2012), 0:37:31–38:31.
39. 'No Way Out', in *The Walking Dead*, directed by Greg Nicotero (AMC Networks and Fox Broadcasting Company, 2016), 0:21:39.
40. 'Vatos', in *The Walking Dead*, directed by Johan Renck (AMC Networks and Fox Broadcasting Company, 2010), 0:04:20.
41. Lauro and Embry, 'A Zombie Manifesto', 90.
42. As *The Walking Dead* has not concluded yet, it remains to be seen whether the series continues its anti-cathartic narrative construction or whether there will be resolution for some characters in the series in the end.
43. John Vervaeke, Christopher Mastropietro and Filip Miscevic, *Zombies in Western Culture: A Twenty-First Century Crisis* (Cambridge: Open Book Publishers, 2017), p. 5.
44. Lauro and Embry, 'A Zombie Manifesto', 90.
45. *28 Days Later*, 0:04:30.
46. Zack Snyder and Marc Abraham (dirs), *Dawn of the Dead* (2004), 0:49:32.
47. 'Days Gone Bye', in *The Walking Dead*, directed by Frank Darabont (AMC Networks and Fox Broadcasting Company, 2010), 0:14:49.
48. Kristeva, Julia, *Powers of Horror: An Essay on Abjection* (New York: Columbia University Press, 1982), p. 4, *http://users.clas.ufl.edu/burt/touchyfeelingsmaliciousobjects/Kristevapowersofhorrorabjection.pdf* (last accessed 22 May 2022).
49. Kristeva, *Powers of Horror*, p. 3.
50. Kristeva, *Powers of Horror*, p. 3.
51. Kristeva, *Powers of Horror*, p. 4.
52. cf. for example, 'Seed', in *The Walking Dead*, directed by Ernest Dickerson (AMC Networks and Fix Broadcasting Company, 2012), 0:22:12; and *Dawn of the Dead*, 1:01:34.

53. 'Seed', 0:21:45–22:39.
54. cf. for example, Lynn White, 'The Historical Roots of Our Ecological Crisis', in Ken Hiltner (ed.), *Ecocriticism: The Essential Reader* (London: Routledge, 2015), p. 41; and Donna Haraway, *Staying with the Trouble: Making Kin in the Chthulucene* (Durham NC: Duke University Press, 2016), p. 35.
55. Hinchliffe *et al.*, *Pathological Lives*, p. 6.
56. Hinchliffe *et al.*, *Pathological Lives*, p. 13.

11

Human Individuals versus Zombie Masses

Dystopia or (Hyper-)Individualistic Utopia?

Hossein Mohammadzade

THE ZOMBIE GENRE is increasingly popular, and post-apocalyptic narratives have often been associated with various contemporary economic, social or cultural crises, which at least partially account for the popularity of post-apocalyptic settings.[1] Despite the various challenges that a society might face, economic competition is a value in capitalist societies. Without competition, the improvement of living conditions and a higher quality of life are considered to be unattainable. Neoliberalism puts competition at the centre of human relations.[2] Fighting for survival has been mixed with competition under capitalism.[3] However, it is naive to think that the competition remains confined to corporations offering better products and does not affect any other aspect of production. For instance, it leads to competition among job applicants. While corporations benefit from an abundance of people in the workforce – which usually means lower wages due to the supply-and-demand principle of the market – the workers, obviously, do not appreciate the competition. In almost every competition, having fewer participants usually means a better chance of winning. Therefore, while overpopulation serves corporations in the form of labour and the consumer market, it does not please middle-class or working-class individuals.[4] In such conditions, individuals might find escape in fantasising about a world in which billions of other people have turned into useless zombies, because it would make them feel special and not so expendable. In certain forms of capitalism, competition is like a social war, justifying social Darwinism that leads to some individuals turning into disposable losers.[5] Stratton has argued that people who have been deprived of certain rights or privileges and are not protected by the state (such as displaced asylum seekers) resemble zombies in that it is as if they are not completely – that is, legally and socially – alive or living a full life.[6] Moreover, Bishop has said that for him, the primary characteristic of a zombie is a lack of complete consciousness and choice, and obviously, those compared to zombies by Stratton cannot really have (fully conscious or independent) choices.[7] Stratton also pointed out that under a neoliberalist state, even members of a modern Western state are not immune to zombification, and might be zombified if they lose the protection of the state under certain economic circumstances.[8] Therefore, if a society only gives increasing privileges to fewer and fewer members while a growing number of people struggle with a declining quality of life, then 'masses' resembling zombies could appear. Interestingly, the zombies in the television series *The Walking Dead* also resemble the masses and have some behavioural features in common with them, which will be discussed later. In *Fallout 4*, the feral ghouls are not really alive either and are very similar to zombies. While zombies infect others with a bite, feral ghouls could poison people by radiation, especially the Glowing Ones. One of the loading screen tips in *Fallout 4* says, 'while they can easily be mistaken for zombies, Feral Ghouls are actually horribly irradiated humans whose brains have rotted away, causing madness'. However, whether feral ghouls are referred to as 'ghouls' or 'zombies' does not diminish their zombie status based on the definitions presented so far.

Bethesda's *Fallout 4* is an open-world action role-playing video game in which the player-character – the Sole Survivor – comes out of a nuclear vault and aims to find his kidnapped son in a post-apocalyptic irradiated wasteland filled with dangerous creatures, 210 years after a nuclear war. AMC's *The Walking Dead* is a post-apocalyptic zombie television series in which the few human survivors struggle to find shelter and resources and to survive and protect themselves and their loved ones.

Almost all post-apocalyptic zombie worlds have an essential element in common: a few individual survivors. In fictional worlds and simulational gameworlds, these survivors allow the post-apocalyptic story to develop. While these universes and their zombies have various significations, the few survivors can also embody certain ideologies. Further, the contrast between the zombie masses and the individualism of the survivors seems to help the audience empathise with the main characters, and it could be one of the features that have made the zombie genre popular. However, it is important to understand whether these post-apocalyptic universes are dystopias or (hyper-)individualistic utopias – that is, if the characters or the audience would mourn and contemplate the loss of a society that nurtured them, or if they would celebrate the destruction of various obstacles (including the government and society itself), wasting their potential. Since zombies are often used to promote various political agendas,[9] through examining *The Walking Dead* and *Fallout 4*, this study also tries to see whether the protagonists in both universes embody an individualism that is considered necessary to the well-being of both the individual and society, and prevents the individual from being forced to conform to outdated illogical norms, or if they represent the socio-economic values of a hyper-individualistic ideology – often encouraged by capitalism – that romanticises the independence of the individual and can endanger any community by creating such a fetish. This study also tries to find out whether these works challenge and blur the distinction between the individual and the antagonistic masses or if they reinforce it.

Individualism and Hyper-Individualism

Before examining the video game and the television series, a distinction between individualism and hyper-individualism must be made. For an individualist, a zombie apocalypse would be both a utopia and a dystopia simultaneously. Individuals who regard society or community as that which lets them survive and grow, would not like to lose it all, but also, they would be happy to trade all the obstacles they face for the opportunities presented in a post-apocalyptic universe. For instance, in the United States where people have felt that the institutions have failed them,[10] this can be the case. Consider how they feel when they can watch old money burn in the series or when, in the game, they can just scrap it or hear their companion calls it junk. Moreover, in a zombie apocalypse, individuals can simply kill the zombie herds and just own the mall. For an individual who was losing more and more during the Great Recession, that would be the dream – taking everything they need or want for free. For a hyper-individualist, however, it would be survival of the fittest, which could let them own most of the resources – very similar to the social Darwinism in a cut-throat capitalism that hyper-individualists prefer. Arguably, these utopian images could be one of the reasons why such universes have become so popular. Platts has also asked if the audience of zombie stories might see the apocalyptic fall of a society as a need for 'rugged individualism' and seeing the government as the problem.[11]

Hyper-individualism could be defined as a tendency to consider individuals to be mainly distinct and separate beings instead of members of a group.[12] It exists when values such as autonomy and freedom are not tamed and become destructive.[13] As an ideology, it is deeply related to neoliberalism.[14] It is narcissistic and goes against social protections, leading to a criminalisation of those suffering in a society following a natural-selection logic.[15] Therefore, hyper-individualistic tendencies are common under the current economic system because, as Rego has pointed out, capitalism has also been compared to natural selection.[16]

Nevertheless, some thinkers promote it. Friedman has suggested that responsible individuals should not behave like children by looking for a paternal government. He explained that progress is accomplished by individuals not by government imperatives, and when governments show signs of paternalism and intervene to create welfare and equality, they halt the community's progress.[17] It is clear here that to defend such logic, neoliberalism must talks about the ideal individual who overcomes every obstacle or unfair situation while discussing labour conditions.[18] Friedman has also argued that equality of outcome where everyone should have equal levels of living or income is against liberty, and even when children have parents from different walks of life, thus resulting in an unfair difference in property inheritance, it is like when children inherit different levels of talent in mathematics, and there is no ethical difference between the two situations.[19] The first part of his argument is ideological, because, why should outcome be understood as income, and not, say, the intellectual product or social rank or position of the person?

Why would someone not want to give everyone equal access to housing, education and health care to begin with, or to help them focus on more serious objectives in life than to worry about bills, which in turn, could make individuals prostitute their skills for a roof over their heads? Determinism is obviously the big flaw in the logic of the second part of his argument. How can freedom and individuality be discussed when there is almost no social protection, and even a baby is doomed from birth? Buchanan has said that people are not equal but are only treated neutrally or equally by the law.[20] However, does this mean that if some individuals are simply 'not talented' – that is, if we can even reach a common definition for talent – in financial issues, they should not receive health care, housing and education? Should we leave such a, let us say, cancer patient, unattended simply because they have not been 'fit' enough to overcome their historical, social and economic limitations or boundaries? He has also argued that social life is for achieving individual aims, not a common utopian ideal.[21] Von Mises has said that there is only individual action; the collective does not act. It is the individual that does the action. The collective has no life without the individual.[22] Nevertheless, what is usually claimed to be unique individual behaviour is actually a product of social values and influence. Agency exists in a social construct, and an alienated one does not lead to freedom.[23] Even human experiences and feelings tend to be social and historical.[24]

Hayek has argued that every form of collectivism is totalitarian because they want to direct the whole society into a single direction, which is vague at best. He explained that individualists are free, not selfish. They should be free within limits, but their actions should not be imposed by others.[25] However, despite talking about limits, there is usually an illusion that defending freedom needs to exclude non-libertarian ways of thinking including social democracy, let alone socialist tendencies.[26] Moreover, welfare is not totalitarian. Being anti-welfare is totalitarian, because it keeps people's hands tied like slaves. It is better when an educated, healthy society helps all individuals grow; only a hyper-individualist would not be able to see this. Interestingly, two years before *The Walking Dead* aired, Stringham proposed the abolition of all government.[27] Anderson and Hill have even suggested that anarcho-capitalism was fine in the American West.[28] Such propositions clearly prove the existence of hyper-individualistic tendencies.

Zombie Masses

Zombies are associated with the so-called 'masses'. For instance, in discussions of George Romero's *Dawn of the Dead*,[29] they are considered to represent consumerist American society.[30] The film shows the United States as a nation that consumes but does not produce.[31] In addition, when basic services such as proper education or free health care are still not accessible to everyone and, at least in some cases, many people do not seem to even have the time to think or grow intellectually, it is not very difficult to perceive people as homogenous zombified masses. Harman has pointed out that currently the world is not exactly stable and the situation is worsening. A billion people are hungry, and the numbers are going up.[32] While the hunger in zombie films represents consumerism, it can also refer to the actual hunger of the masses, which are deemed unpleasant disposable beings that the middle class or upper middle class do not even want to look at.

Moreover, the zombies in *The Walking Dead* are drawn to sound and light, much like people in an increasingly audio-visual culture. In one scene, groups of zombies walk into trailers following moving lights and music at night. They often appear in masses or herds and move together following a sound clearly without thinking. They consume endlessly, as do undereducated masses around the world under a consumer capitalist culture. They consume without producing anything, just like at least a part of the living human population. Even many of the names assigned to them probably remind the audience not only of zombies but also living people, such as walkers, eaters, roamers or maybe even lame-brains.

A commercial poster in the game shows the words 'radio' and 'television' coming closer and closer and forming the word 'radiation', which could tell us about one of the possible significations of radiation or radiation poisoning in the game, and make us think of constant exposure to mass media.[33] Therefore, here, we could say that the zombie-like feral ghouls in *Fallout 4* also have one major thing in common with the masses: high levels of exposure to radiation in this sense. Interestingly, the Institute – which is an elite, technocratic organisation working from an underground base that has been sealed off from the dangers of the irradiated world on the surface thanks to their invention of a means for teleportation – used to look for people who have not been affected by radiation and have a 'pure DNA', which can also be read as a metaphor for an elite group's search for people who have not been affected by 'radiation' in the sense that the aforementioned poster has defined the term. Moreover, the feral ghouls' looks and their seemingly indefinitely increased lifespan could also remind us of the old ideologies that haunt the under-educated masses deprived of a chance to think, either working non-stop or being exposed to mass media even in their so-called 'free time', which they are given arguably only to recover for the next day's work, like when the player-character gets the ghoulish perk and then radiation restores their lost health. Feral ghouls are also often found in hordes, but much smaller than the herds of walkers seen in the series. Interestingly, in the game, churches are often infested with feral ghouls, which again is another metaphorical example of old ideologies ending in mental degeneration.

Individualist Survivors

The survivors in these universes are a few outnumbered individuals who win the viewer's empathy and must get rid of the zombie masses. Mentally healthy people are very difficult to find. Every kind of professional or expert is scarce. Therefore, the importance of the few survivors increases. One cannot help but contemplate the changes in population in an apocalypse. These individuals no longer feel expendable the way they did before, when they could be stressed by an increasingly competitive jobs market as a result of excessive population growth. Therefore, the workforce would probably welcome a reduction in population and consequently the competition, especially when they are not the ones who have to feel guilty for what is generally regarded as a dystopia, and for being drawn to it.

Further, Raymen has pointed out that dystopia has ideological roots in capitalism. The aggressive individualism and structural violence inherent in capitalism becomes manifest in a dystopia. For instance, *The Waking Dead* both includes and denies the values of such a system.[34] Romanticisation of the autonomy of the individual in the universe of *The Walking Dead* becomes clear, particularly with the glorification of Daryl. He is a skilled tracker and hunter, often quiet, and he usually seems to need more private space than others. He is regularly shown alone, sometimes makes decisions alone and occasionally insists that he is better on his own, as does Glenn when he goes scavenging. Even when their community grows after defeating the Saviours, Daryl feels nostalgic about their old small group. He is often more relaxed while living alone in the wild. Such adventures romanticise the individual's freedom, independence and ability to survive, live and enjoy life alone. It can remind the audience of films like *Into the Wild*.[35] The characters in such works pretend to be tired of civilisation, but every now and then they return to it to get medicine or scavenge tools. Daryl, too, is shown to be in grave danger and in need of help after being injured while on his own in the woods. Such moments defy the romanticised individual and indicate that they would fail to survive alone.

Moreover, what Tulloch has said about *Bioshock* could also be correct about *Fallout 4*. He has argued that Rapture, the dystopian city in the game, was actually a limitless *laissez-faire* utopia for individualists that went out of control.[36] The nuclear war in *Fallout 4* can be considered a consequence of such a system. Moreover, choice and player agency have been an increasingly important feature of games.[37] Therefore, it is clear that the individuality and autonomy or 'freedom' of the player-character is also a significant part of *Fallout 4*'s appeal as they have various freedoms in the game – from creating their own character and designing their settlements or buildings to choosing among different factions – and can see the impact of their choices on how the story progresses.

One of the things that these two works have in common is that the protagonist is a post-apocalyptic cowboy, with the difference that in *Fallout 4* the players can choose to be male or female. Post-apocalyptic stories tend to have cowboys as protagonists.[38] In the second episode of the show, Rick actually resembles a cowboy that represents certain ideologies.[39] *Fallout 4*'s protagonist could also be categorised as a post-apocalyptic cowboy.[40] Zombie stories also feature the self-determinism traditionally associated with the Western genre.[41]

Individuals and Communities

It is clear that part of the gratification of a post-apocalyptic universe is its opportunities. For instance, in *The Walking Dead* Carol and Daryl got a chance to start over and grow due to the zombie apocalypse.[42] Kidder has argued that a bike messenger's job that was once simple and only a phase or a stepping stone in a character's life in Hollywood, became an independent and proper job, depicted almost as heroic with epic challenges, creating an illusion of individual efficacy.[43] *The Walking Dead* does this to a pizza delivery guy. The zombie pandemic has given new meaning to Glenn's pizza delivery experience and skills. He feels important and becomes important. Also, he would probably not have even dreamed of living in such a house in Alexandria before the apocalypse. In this sense, the player-character in *Fallout 4* can be seen as the 'Glenn' of the gameworld in terms of the various opportunities that they are given. Another example of post-apocalyptic opportunity in the series would be the Governor, who moves from being a bored employee to being the leader of a community, and probably the ultimate hyper-individualist, using the community only as human shields, providers and soldiers, very much like Negan.

In the series, there are other hyper-individualists, such as Spencer who steals after lecturing everyone on not storming the storage, but then says if everybody stops taking stuff except him then nothing would go wrong. There are also others like Dale who seems worried that at some point it would be the needs of the few versus the needs of the many. The cheese maker, Eastman, who insists that by saving others, people actually save themselves, or Benjamin who says those who hurt others, hurt themselves, might remind us of the Great Recession when the situation hurt not only working-class families but beyond. O'Flynn has pointed out that neoliberal policies did not change when only ordinary working people faced the consequences, but only after it turned into a financial crisis that endangered opportunities for profitable investment. Representatives of the neoliberal individualistic free market ideology did not really ask for a reduction of government interference altogether, only the kind that would create obstacles for big firms.[44] Therefore, it can be argued that if there are obstacles for everyone except for big businesses, such an economic system would probably take people back to the feudalist system that was replaced because it did not give everyone freedom to grow. Individuals needed to break out of their formerly fixed social status and escape historical determinism, at least to some extent. However, such a government would merely replace lords with big corporate personalities, and aristocrats with rich oligarchs. It obviously contradicts capitalism's promise of progress and freedom for everyone, which is constantly advertised.

Virtually every form of state is portrayed as corrupt, such as Woodbury, the Commonwealth or the Saviours. This seems to be the case even when protagonists such as Rick or Maggie are in charge. Almost everybody shines as an individual but makes stupid decisions as a leader. In *The Walking Dead*, government has failed and continues to fail, which can reflect how contemporary Americans have stopped believing in the government's ability to solve their problems; even medicine has turned to individual care in the series.[45] The Saviours in particular, with their exploitation of the weak, resemble a capitalist government in economic crisis. This is reinforced when the character Spencer compares Alexandria's payment to Negan, the Saviours' leader, to paying tax. When Gabriel asks Negan about the workers, Negan says that it is an economy; some people lose, some people win. The Saviours have nothing to offer their subordinates except a mostly false sense of protection or safety, as do many governments whose people suffer every day. Even when the workers ask why they are surrounded by zombies and not protected as promised, Simon says that workers are supposed to stay on the ground level. However, the series gradually moves from a world that is all about the raw survival instinct of an individual to a form of civilisation that both provides and requires the control of human urges and instincts, and shows that people are the most important resource. People seem to need communities to survive. They seem to have almost nothing without other people.

Fallout 4's universe also moves in the same direction; however, the inclusion of automation complicates things and presents a difference in some cases. In building settlement defence, finding a companion, providing provisions or services such as food or medical help, the robots are there. The Institute even creates its own robots called synths, therefore making humans redundant, at least to some extent, thus making the player-character feel more independent individually. Further, the community that the player creates is not primarily a social community but a resource that provides employees for the player.[46] *Fallout 4* does not use a system of karma, which seemed to operate as a universal standard in the previous games in the *Fallout* series; instead, the judgement is done by individual companions.[47] The player-character can choose how honourable they want to be in the gameworld; for instance, they can decide whether they want to help others, and in the Nuka-World expansion of the game, they can even choose to help raiders and raid their own settlements in the Commonwealth, which is where the main game is set.

Players in *Fallout 4* will most probably feel special. The game's intro says things like, 'following total atomic annihilation, the rebuilding of this great nation of ours may fall to you', or asks, 'do you know what makes you special?' then talks about the 'seven defining attributes that make you special!' Although SPECIAL is an acronym standing for the player-character's main statistics – strength, perception, endurance, charisma, intelligence, agility and luck – it does still carry its common meaning. The player character has been 'selected' for their family's services, to enter Vault 111. They are the 'Sole Survivor'. They are asked to do great things such as becoming the General of the Minutemen, or replacing Father, the director of the Institute. However, no matter what faction they help, many people will still die, and the player-character will not feel special then. The upgradable health bar also has two sides. It gives the player a strong feeling of individual power that no one else could really challenge, not even a deathclaw – arguably the most dangerous predator in the game, with deadly claws, as its name suggests – after a while, but it also tells the player that they would not actually be able to eat the bullets left and right the way they do in the gameworld, and makes them contemplate the impossibility of an individual accomplishing so much in physical reality. The save-and-load mechanism also disillusions the individual player, reminding them how they can do what they do. In addition, when with the ghoulish perk, radiation heals the player-character, and hostile feral ghouls sometimes become friendly, and with the cannibal perk, the player-character can feed on a corpse to regain health, the game makes the player-character further resemble a zombie, thus fading the line between them.

Conclusion

An analysis of *The Walking Dead* and *Fallout 4* has shown that both present a hyper-individualistic utopia and challenge its underlying ideologies at the same time. Although there is sometimes a sharp contrast between zombies and the survivors, and between various communities identified as 'Others' and the protagonists, the line between them is blurred at times. Nevertheless, having discussed the various aspects or forms of individualism in these two universes, it has become clear that at least in certain moments in the game and the series it is shown that a healthy relationship between individuals and society is beneficial to both, but hyper-individualistic attitudes promoted in late capitalism and neoliberalism help neither the individual nor the community. Moreover, alienation of individuals – even members of modern Western societies – and hyper-individualistic ideologies, eventually lead only to a zombie apocalypse fetish.

Notes

1. See, for instance, Laura Hubner, Marcus Leaning and Paul Manning, 'Introduction', in L. Hubner, M. Leaning and P. Manning (eds), *The Zombie Renaissance in Popular Culture* (New York: Palgrave Macmillan, 2015), pp. 3–14; Gerry Canavan, '"We Are the Walking Dead": Race, Time, and Survival in Zombie Narrative', *Extrapolation*, 51/3 (2010), 431–53; Melissa Lavin and Brian Lowe, 'Cops and Zombies: Hierarchy and Social Location in *The Walking Dead*', in B. Gurr (ed.), *Race, Gender, and Sexuality in Post-Apocalyptic TV and Film* (New York: Palgrave Macmillan, 2015), pp. 113–24.

2. George Monbiot, 'Neoliberalism – The Ideology at the Root of All Our Problems', *The Guardian* (15 April 2016), *www.theguardian.com/books/2016/apr/15/neoliberalism-ideology-problem-george-monbiot* (last accessed 28 February 2025).
3. Fredric Jameson, *Archaeologies of the Future: The Desire Called Utopia and Other Science Fictions* (London and New York: Verso, 2005), p. 185.
4. Hossein Mohammadzade, 'Resource Wars: From Gameworlds to Physical Reality [Conference Presentation]', FROG – Future and Reality of Gaming (22 November 2020).
5. Henry Giroux, *Zombie Politics and Culture in the Age of Casino Capitalism* (New York: Peter Lang, 2011), p. 2.
6. Jon Stratton, 'Zombie Trouble: Zombie Texts, Bare Life and Displaced People', *European Journal of Cultural Studies*, 14/3 (2011), 265–81.
7. Kyle William Bishop, *How Zombies Conquered Popular Culture: The Multifarious Walking Dead in the 21st Century* (Jefferson NC: McFarland, 2015), p. 145.
8. Stratton, 'Zombie Trouble', 265–81.
9. Daniel W. Drezner, 'Metaphor of the Living Dead: Or, the Effect of the Zombie Apocalypse on Public Policy Discourse', *Social Research*, 81/4 (2014), 825–49.
10. Paul A. Cantor, *Pop Culture and the Dark Side of the American Dream: Con Men, Gangsters, Drug Lords, and Zombies* (Lexington KY: University Press of Kentucky, 2019), ch. 5.
11. Todd K. Platts, 'Locating Zombies in the Sociology of Popular Culture', *Sociology Compass*, 7/7 (2013), 547–60.
12. Zachary Casey, 'Chapter 37: Hyperindividualism', in Z. A. Casey (ed.), *Encyclopedia of Critical Whiteness Studies in Education* (Leiden: Brill, 2020), pp. 279–85.
13. Peter Callero, *The Myth of Individualism: How Social Forces Shape Our Lives*, 2nd edn (Lanham MD: Rowman & Littlefield Publishers, 2013), p. 16.
14. Mary Wrenn, 'Agency and Neoliberalism', *Cambridge Journal of Economics*, 39/5 (2014), 1231–43.
15. Henry Giroux, 'The Politics of Disimagination and the Pathologies of Power', *Truthout* (27 February 2013).
16. Paul Rego, *American Ideal: Theodore Roosevelt's Search for American Individualism* (Lanham MD: Rowman & Littlefield Publishers, 2008), p. 2.
17. Milton Friedman, *Capitalism and Freedom*, 40th anniversary edn (Chicago IL and London: 2002), p. 4.
18. Jeffrey Di Leo and Uppinder Mehan, 'Introduction: The Wrath of Capital', in J. R. Di Leo and U. Mehan (eds), *Capital at the Brink: Overcoming the*

Destructive Legacies of Neoliberalism (Ann Arbor MI: Open Humanities Press, 2014), pp. 11–28.

19. Milton Friedman and Rose Friedman, *Free to Choose: A Personal Statement* (New York and London: Harcourt Brace Jovanovich, 1980), p. 136.
20. James Buchanan, *The Collected Works of James M. Buchanan, Volume 7 (The Limits of Liberty: Between Anarchy and Leviathan)* (Indianapolis IN: Liberty Fund, 2000), pp. 15–16.
21. Buchanan, *The Collected Works of James M. Buchanan*, p. 3.
22. Ludwig von Mises, *Human Action: A Treatise on Economics* (San Francisco CA: Fox & Wilkes, 1996), p. 42.
23. Carl Ratner, 'Agency and Culture', *Journal for the Theory of Social Behaviour*, 30/4 (2000), 413–34.
24. Julie Wilson, *Neoliberalism* (New York and London: Routledge, 2018).
25. Friedrich Hayek, *The Road to Serfdom* (London and New York: Routledge, 1944), pp. 14–16.
26. Steven Lukes, *Individualism* (Colchester: ECPR Press, 2006), p. 9.
27. Edward Stringham, 'Introduction', in E. P. Stringham (ed.), *Anarchy and the Law: The Political Economy of Choice* (New Brunswick NJ and London: Transaction Publishers, 2007), pp. 1–17.
28. Terry Anderson and P. J. Hill, 'American Experiment in Anarcho-Capitalism: The Not So Wild, Wild West', *Journal of Libertarian Studies*, 3/1 (1979), 9–29.
29. George Romero (dir.), *Dawn of the Dead* (Laurel Group, 1978).
30. Kyle Bishop (with Hogle, J. E.), *American Zombie Gothic: The Rise and Fall (and Rise) of the Walking Dead in Popular Culture* (Jefferson NC and London: McFarland, 2010).
31. Shannon Mader, 'Reviving the Dead in Southwestern PA Zombie Capitalism: The Non-Class and the Decline of the US Steel Industry', in H. Wu (ed.), *Axes to Grind: Re-imagining the Horrific in Visual Media and Culture*, Special Issue of *Spectator* 22/2, (Los Angeles CA: University of Southern California, 2002), pp. 69–77.
32. Chris Harman, *Zombie Capitalism Global Crisis and the Relevance of Marx* (Chicago IL: Haymarket Books, 2009).
33. Hossein Mohammadzade, 'Cultural Values, Ideology and Narrative Form in Fallout 4: A Cultural-Studies Perspective' (master's thesis, University of Guilan, 2019), p. 40.
34. Thomas Raymen, 'Living in the End Times Through Popular Culture: An Ultra-Realist Analysis of *The Walking Dead* as Popular Criminology', *Crime, Media, Culture*, 14/3 (2018), 429–47.

35. Sean Penn (dir.), *Into the Wild* (Paramount Vantage, 2007).
36. Rowan Tulloch, 'Ludic Dystopias: Power, Politics and Play', in M. Ryan (ed.), *Proceedings of the Sixth Australasian Conference on Interactive Entertainment* (Sydney: University of New South Wales, 2009), article no. 13.
37. Daniel Muriel and Garry Crawford, 'Video Games and Agency in Contemporary Society', *Games and Culture*, 15/2 (2020), 138–57.
38. Barbara Gurr, 'Introduction: After the World Ends, Again', in B. Gurr (ed.), *Race, Gender, and Sexuality in Post-Apocalyptic TV and Film* (New York: Palgrave Macmillan, 2015), pp. 1–13.
39. Katherine Sugg, '*The Walking Dead*: Late Liberalism and Masculine Subjection in Apocalypse Fictions', *Journal of American Studies*, 49/4 (2015), 793–811.
40. Óliver Pérez-Latorre, 'Post-apocalyptic Games, Heroism and the Great Recession', *Game Studies*, 19/3 (2019).
41. Jeffrey A. Sartain, 'Days Gone Bye: Robert Kirkman's Reenvisioned Western *The Walking Dead*', in C. J. Miller and A. B. Van Riper (eds), *Undead in the West II: They Just Keep Coming* (Lanham MD: The Scarecrow Press, 2013), pp. 249–68.
42. Clay Routledge, 'Finding Your Purpose in the Zombie Apocalypse', in T. Langley (ed.), *The Walking Dead Psychology: Psych of the Living Dead* (New York: Sterling, 2015), ch. 19.
43. Jeffrey Kidder, 'Hollywood, Bike Messengers, and the New Economy', *Critical Sociology*, 42/2 (2014), 307–22.
44. Michael O'Flynn, *Profitable Ideas: The Ideology of the Individual in Capitalist Development* (Leiden: Brill, 2009).
45. Joshua Ambrosius and Joseph Valenzano III, '"People in Hell Want Slurpees": The Redefinition of the Zombie Genre through the Salvific Portrayal of Family on AMC's *The Walking Dead*', *Communication Monographs*, 83/1 (2016), 69–93.
46. Óliver Pérez-Latorre, Víctor Navarro-Remesal, Antonio Planells de la Maza and Cristina Sánchez-Serradilla, 'Recessionary Games: Video Games and the Social Imaginary of the Great Recession (2009–2015)', *Convergence*, 25/5–6 (2019), 884–900.
47. Joan Casas-Roma and Joan Arnedo-Moreno, 'Categorizing Morality Systems Through the Lens of Fallout', Proceedings of the 2019 DiGRA International Conference: Game, Play and the Emerging Ludo-Mix (2019).

PART THREE

ZOMBIE POLITICS

12

Decomposition and Excavation of War Memories and Massacres in Na Hong-jin's *The Wailing*

Grace Jung

IN 2016, SOUTH KOREAN filmmaker Na Hong-jin's third feature film *The Wailing* made its international premiere at the Cannes Film Festival. *IndieWire*'s David Ehrlich describes it as 'demented occult non-sense'.[1] On *RogerEbert.com*, Simon Abrams uses words like 'cacophonous', 'ambiguous', 'implausible' and 'ludicrous' to describe the film's plot twists and ending.[2] Maggie Lee's *Variety* review declares that *The Wailing* 'makes no logical sense whatsoever', while gesturing to parts of modern Korean history as insight to open an avenue for analysing the film:

> Weighed down by a bloody history of Japanese colonialism, civil war and partition, the scars of the Korean psyche find their way into Na's film, whether it's the horror of people being murdered by their own families or the exorcism that serves as its dramatic centerpiece – a likely metaphor for the need to purge ghosts of the past.[3]

These ghosts in Na's psychological thriller appear in physical form as both strangers (the Other) and kin (family and neighbours), and what the critics collectively call confusion is actually a national frustration at the limits to recovering evidence of war crimes and injustices against Korean civilians committed by their government, patriarchal heads and foreign military. The confusion that stems from *The Wailing*'s elaborate structure and density is a deliberate theme that allegorises the tumult and fog of modern Korean history in the national memory. *The Wailing* is a colonial, postcolonial and cold war hermeneutic of the Korean peninsula's traumas, specifically evoking the nation's scars of mass rape and massacres caused by foreign as well as domestic forces. In fact, all of Na's films up until this point can be read from the access point of mass death and collective suffering.

By 'cold war', I am not referring to the global north's history of a tenuous but generally peaceful period post-Second World War; I am concentrating on Korea's political violence endured during its postcolonial phase. Even the term 'postcolonial' is questionable; as Steven Hugh Lee establishes, Korea was occupied by the United States twice in its history – in 1945 and 1955 – and a US military presence continues to persist in South Korea. Historical anthropologist Heonik Kwon challenges Western-centric concepts of the cold war as the 'long peace', which 'conflicts with the dominant image of the cold war as a single encompassing geopolitical order'.[4] Kwon suggests that historians refer to the latter phase of the cold war as a 'decomposing process' and not 'a given chronological reality', for this reality was not shared by every country equally.[5] While North America and Western Europe did not have activated firepower on their lands during the cold war, there was a great deal of death and destruction from guns, bombs, raids, invasions and rape in Korea during that shared period due to the political tension stemming from the United States and the Soviet Union over the alleged threat of communism, and America's logic in necessarily 'containing' said threat. Korea's decomposition of cold war trauma visually manifests as zombie-like beings who represent the slow decay of memory as well as the breakdown of the mind and body through an incomprehensible psychic haunting. Kwon argues: '[T]he "decomposition" of the cold war is the unsettling situation in which the lived reality is not really free from the immediate past and has not reintegrated the past into the time present as a past history.'[6] My analysis of *The Wailing* draws heavily on Kwon's concept of 'decomposition', particularly with regard to the literal and figurative decay of national memory (trauma) of the massacres in Korea, which were never properly mourned due to laws in the Republic of Korea (ROK) that enforced 'guilt by association', rendering anyone remotely related to a named communist guilty of treason. Kwon alerts us to the range of perceptions and lived experiences of the cold war's closure at a local level. Maggie Lee's premise that *The Wailing* is 'a metaphor for the need to purge ghosts of the past' carries a Western-centric assumption that the cold war has indeed passed. As per Kwon's argument, however, in the case with the ROK, there has never been a clear break from past traumas, only a continuation. *The Wailing*, therefore, requires a shift in vantage point for it to make sense. Through Na Hong-jin's commentary via filmmaker interviews, necropolitics theory and modern Korea's history of sexual subjugation to foreign powers, I offer a framework for this analysis and observe how *The Wailing* discursively excavates decomposing national traumas figuratively through the zombie.

Nationalising the Western Occult and Constructing a Metanarrative

Na claims that he referred to 'textbook' Hollywood horror classics such as *Rosemary's Baby* (1968), *The Exorcist* (1973), *The Omen* (1976) and *The Shining* (1980) to make *The Wailing*.[7] Beyond American occult films, *The Wailing* also harkens to Edgar Allen Poe's literature, with the sound design of a cat thumping and screeching through the ceiling, and a scene of a shaman breaking open a clay pot to reveal a dead crow soaking inside. In one darkly comedic scene, when the townsmen show up at the Japanese stranger's (Kunimura Jun) home with the intention of murdering him, they come across a dead man named Park Choon-bae (Kil Chang-gyoo), who's been brought back to 'life' through a shamanistic ritual. The townsmen who have never encountered a zombie before, don't know how to confront it. The men initially beat the zombie out of fright then try reasoning with it through dialogue as if it were still their old friend Choon-bae, before succumbing to its wrath as a consequence of their rural ignorance.

As a concept, the zombie has no origins in Korean folklore or history. In recent years, however, zombie films and TV shows have become a popular fad in Korea, making it appear as though it had always been there.[8] The same year that *The Wailing* hit cinemas, Yeon Sang-ho's commercial film *Train to Busan* starring Gong Yoo, Jung Yu-mi and Ma Dong-seok was also released. As a result of *Train to Busan*'s popularity, Ma transitioned to Hollywood's Marvel universe after adopting an English name 'Don Lee' and playing Gilgamesh in *Eternals* (2021), directed by Oscar-winner Chloé Zhao. In 2016, Yeon also released an animated zombie film titled *Seoul Station*, which was not met with as much international acclaim as his live-action sequel. *Train to Busan* is not in the least bit ambivalent about being a zombie-genre movie compared to *The Wailing*, it and contains the typical tropes of a zombie film where people get bitten and turned into zombies while trapped on a moving train headed to Busan. Both of Yeon's zombie films are sharp critiques of capitalistic greed, classism and corruption in modern Korean society. The zombie genre is commonly read as a critique of capitalism; Jaecheol Kim specifically analyses *Train to Busan* as a dystopic vision that may result from neoliberal economics.[9] Fred Botting sees parallels between zombie narratives and debt theory.[10] As Sung-ae Lee notes, there's a common tendency to analyse zombie apocalypse films to Korea's economic struggle with 'global crisis, disorder and fear' due to foreign economic intervention/invasion like the IMF bailout in 1997.[11] The characters who lose their sense of subjectivity and consciousness while succumbing to the zombie transformation represent subjects suffering the 'destructive effects' of their short-term neoliberal capitalistic pursuits.[12] Discussions of the slow decay of memory and trauma around casualties of the Korean War and its immediate aftermath, as well as what the zombie is in the context of Korean indigeneity, however, are missing in this discourse. How do zombies unearth long-buried memories and unresolved damages from massacres suffered at the hands of foreign military, as well as their own, in the chaos of war? In what way do zombies in Korean screen texts process the inexplicable horrors that were witnessed by lived individuals who were forced into silence for generations?

The clumsy zombie scene with Choon-bae in *The Wailing* signifies Korea's anxieties, conjuring the loss of national autonomy via annexation by Japan and the United States, but its subtexts complicate the narrative. *The Wailing*, in part, deals with questions of the self versus the whole in a national context, reflecting David Boyns and Robert Wonser's reading of the zombie genre representing a loss of self that results in panic, 'express[ing] cultural anxieties about … threats of de-individualization'.[13] What *The Wailing* presents, however, is Korea's confusion at the very notion of zombies, as the nation lacks the language and information to make sense of this foreign phenomenon; if the traumatised subject has no awareness of their trauma or how to process it, how could anything they say be understood? The characters' wailing or the infected characters' growling, moaning and screeching replace a sensible use of words and tone to effectively describe their suffering. Characters in *The Wailing* signify the under-processed state of the trauma wounds that the people of Korea live with and the fact that they have nowhere to turn to get the right answers about how to heal from this pain. In the film, no matter where the protagonist turns – to religion, law or medicine – there is no clear answer as to what is destroying his town and family. *The Wailing* reflects Korea's first encounter with this strange disease; the characters who encounter the sight become infected by fear that eventually leads to a physical and mental decay. The disease in *The Wailing* is not necessarily a physical epidemic but rather a psychic one; it is the spread of fear and suspicion rather than infection from skin-to-skin contact. Similarly to the days when those suspected of communism were ruthlessly imprisoned, beaten or killed, the people of Goksŏng in *The Wailing* latch onto rumours or strange encounters and allow their fear to fester in their subconscious until they eventually lose themselves.

While shows like *Kingdom* on Netflix are very clearly marketed as zombie content with a great deal of expository scenes of the characters' pointed attempts to understand the infection, the filmic metadata and plot in *The Wailing* does not include 'zombie' at all for it is not marketed as a zombie film but rather a generic horror picture. There's no mention of zombies in *The Wailing*, although the physical movements, sound effects and make-up of the film's infected characters are identical to those found in *Train to Busan*, *Kingdom* and *All of Us Are Dead*. The comical scene with the ignorant townsfolk confronting dead man Choon-bae in *The Wailing* is a jab at Korea's maladroit (indigenous) handling of foreign monsters (zombies, vampires and Satan) – going so far as to misunderstanding the Westernised concept of the zombie by trying to reason with it or help it rather than run away from it. On the same note, Na appropriates Christ's image and applies it to the Devil, thereby eliminating the good/evil binary that typically leads to a climactic face-off at the end of occult classics such as *The Exorcist* (1973). The Japanese stranger, who the narrative portrays as both a shaman and the Devil, possesses the Christ-like power to raise the dead like Christ did with Lazarus; in *The Wailing*, the Japanese stranger raises a dead man – Park Choon-bae – and makes him walk like a zombie.

According to Chungmoo Choi, 'Colonization of consciousness … [is] the imposition by the dominant power of its own world view, its own cultural norms and values, on the (colonized) people so that they are compelled to adopt this alien system of thought as their own and therefore disregard or disparage indigenous culture and identity', which 'perpetuates cultural dependency and colonial subjectivity'.[14] Through the scenes with the zombie and the Devil, *The Wailing* twists our Hollywood (imperialised) and Ameri-Christian (colonised) understanding of the occult, thereby subverting viewers' expectations against Hollywood tropes of Western texts. In this regard, it's possible to even argue that *The Wailing* is not a zombie film at all. The film could even go so far as claiming that Korea has no zombies – just a confused idea of what it might be and ultimately constructed in the imaginary out of fear of the Other/the coloniser and their foreignness.

Na states that of all the films that he's made up until now, *The Wailing* is packed with 'the most commercial elements' (i.e., Western) because of Korea's 'great diversity of spectators'.[15] Na is describing his awareness of the international audience (the Western gaze) that Korean cinema now has, as well as the domestic audience that acquired an appreciation for Hollywood's horror canon. Na tells *Screen Daily* that he wanted to 'put an Eastern and Korean twist on the [Western] canon' by including shamanism in his film.[16] Na repeats this comment in a *ScreenAnarchy* interview and says that the purpose of the shamanic scenes is 'simply because I am a Korean and this is a Korean film', thereby nationalising the text by appropriating Western tropes but blending them with Korean signifiers.[17] Na constructed a text to appeal to those who have an understanding for Hollywood horror classics, but also one that speaks directly to Korea's national past and its collective political (un)consciousness. Na's inclusion of a ritualistic Korean practice is subversive, as the film not only contains a criticism of domestic and foreign powers but also an attempt to nationalise the Western horror canon with a Korean mark:

> Dissenters need their own language, through which they both stigmatize the establishment as lacking legitimate power and cultural nationalism and legitimize their own counterculture. Shamanism is a source of language because of its power to invoke and dramatize. Through this, violence and resistance become sacred, and people construct their own space for a popular reappropriation of their history in which national unification, cultural identity, and popular democracy are accommodated. Through the magic power of shamanism, a history becomes history, the muted are given voice, and a private space becomes the public space.[18]

With that said, Na skirts any specific political issues when commenting on his film and claims that casting Japanese actor Jun Kunimura had 'nothing to do with' xenophobia.[19] Given the two nations' contentious history, however, it is difficult to ignore the connotations of a Japanese antagonist in a Korean movie, just as it is difficult to overlook Japan and Korea's tensions in *Kingdom*. In 1905, Japan forcefully declared Korea its protectorate prior to its official annexation as a colony in 1910. When the United States bombed Japan in 1945, Korea was officially liberated but immediately swept into political tensions between the United States and the Soviet Union, which resulted in its national division.[20] Considering the nation's painful experience in loss of autonomy to foreign powers, the fear of foreign invasion is a constant presence in *The Wailing*, and this fear eats away at the characters' subconsciousness.

Na takes viewers on an introspective ride by planting fear in the audience who get entangled in the diegetic discombobulation with several suspicious characters who might all be in on the plot to destroy the protagonist – Jong-gu (Kwak Do-won); in the same way, Jong-gu, who initially suspects just one character is led down a labyrinthine tension between faith and doubt in the quest to save his daughter Hyo-jin (Kim Hwan-hee). The audience's viewing experience is thus meta, as Jong-gu and the other townsfolk, like the young priest, undergo the same process: a seed of suspicion, fear or doubt gets placed inside their consciousness and their own presumptions become the haunting itself. Depending on who the viewer decides is the antagonist, the storyline and ending shift. *The Wailing* is Na's choose-your-own-adventure film: 'Whatever ideas come to you while you watch the film, they're yours. I want this film to be your own.'[21] In this way, *The Wailing* is also deliberately cacophonous due to its multivalent nature. This cacophony gestures towards the disordered nature of Korea's political history, such as the government killing its own people or the confusion and terror erupting between townsfolk who were once close, leading to massacres influenced by America's McCarthyist agenda against communism.

Bricolage Horror Figure and Female Victimhood

According to Na, *The Wailing*'s narrative is about victimhood, so the main plot is built not around the motive of evil but around the victim's search for the reason behind his victimhood.[22] Na claims that there isn't any real reason for the protagonist to be victimised except for the fact that he is a victim, and therein lies the existential disturbance.[23] Who are the victims that Na turns the viewers' gaze towards?

In the rural town of Goksŏng in Chŏlla Province, a cop named Jong-gu – a family man who lives with his mother, wife (Jang So-yeon) and daughter – gets called in at the crack of dawn to a crime scene on a rainy day. The camera pans in slowly and uneasily from Jong-gu's view onto the disturbing sight of a murderer sitting in front of a house with his hands cuffed, skin covered in boils and blood, eyes glazed over in white film and staring off into space. Inside the house are two dead bodies – a married couple – piled on top of each other. The cops declare the incident a crime of passion then link the psychosis to a bad reaction to mushrooms, which the media picks up and circulates. On a late night at the station, Jong-gu's partner – officer Oh Seong-bok (Son Kang-guk) – tells him a spooky story that he has heard going around town, about a mysterious Japanese man who lives deep in the woods. The man was found eating raw deer carcass wearing nothing but a loincloth, crouched down like Golem with red eyes and mouth dripping with blood. More rumours around the Japanese stranger collects inside Jong-gu's mind when his local friend – a butcher (Choi Gwi-hwa) – tells him that the latest murder was committed because the woman who did it was raped by the Japanese man who lives in the mountains. Ever since, she has been found at bath houses covered in boils, mouthing gibberish to herself and running around town naked in the middle of the night. Jong-gu encounters a young woman in a white dress, sporting a green military jacket – Mu-myŏng (Chun Woo-hee) – who tells Jong-gu that she'd seen the mad woman murder her entire family first hand. *Mu-myŏng* literally means 'no name', suggesting no identity; it's further suggested that she may be a ghost. Once she has Jong-gu's attention, Mu-myŏng says, 'The old woman said that the Jap is a ghost. The Jap wanted to suck the Missus' blood dry … Be careful. The old woman said that if you keep seeing him, it's a sign that he's after you'.[24]

'The Jap' – who is consistently referred to as *waenom* and translates literally into 'Japanese bastard' thereby reaffirming his waif status – is a bricolage embodiment of all the spooky things found in non-Korean Gothic literature and movies; he is not only a demonic ghost who can stalk and possess, but also a vampire who is after a family bloodline to suck it dry. The Japanese stranger manifests in Jong-gu's dreams, crouching down like a beast while feasting on animal carcass. The Japanese man's identity is purposefully elusive since, as Na mentions, the plot is centred not on the victimiser but the victim's experience. Nevertheless, the stranger is associated with the disease spreading throughout the town, just like the rumours, and the symptoms have a pattern of turning victims into zombies who develop a skin rash, become psychotic, then ruthlessly murder their own kin before succumbing to a catatonic state. The Japanese stranger – just like Mu-myŏng – has no name. It's the townspeople's ignorance as well as the language barrier that make it easy for them to scapegoat the Japanese stranger for all the bizarre tragedies that unfold around town. In this regard, the Japanese stranger is also a victim to a misunderstanding and miscommunication as a result of Korea's traumatic memory around the loss of sovereignty to Japanese imperialism. Towards the climax of the second act, Jong-gu and four other townsmen decide to take matters into their own hands and kill the Japanese stranger, although no one has evidence that he is the one causing this outbreak. At the end of the chase sequence, the Japanese stranger is forced to jump off a cliff, injuring his leg. The camera closes in on his face as he tries to suppress his screams from pain. He weeps while trying to hide from his pursuers who search avidly for him from the cliff above – a pitiful sight that humanises the character who keeps getting chased down as the villain.

Whereas the zombie genre has a firm place in sociological discourse as a metaphor of the public's anxiety of the spread of disease and debt, literary and filmic criticism of Dracula suits the Japanese character better.[25] Na's narrative repeatedly positions 'the Jap' as a strange, mysterious, unknowable or unidentifiable being (ghost, creature, vampire, the Devil, etc.), which parallels Dracula's textual presence per Leland Monk: 'Dracula's foreignness … taps into anxieties about a dangerous immigrant population coming to the United States not to assimilate into but to subvert and destroy the American way of life.'[26] Bram Stoker's *Dracula* has also been interpreted as Britain's fear of 'reverse colonization' during the Victorian era by 'primitive forces'.[27] In addition, Monk cites Francis Ford Coppola's *Dracula* (1992) as a representation of the global AIDS crisis of the early 1990s and how it spreads: 'The vampire's bite, with its erotic appeal, has deep affinities with a wasting disease transmitted via the exchange of bodily fluids, especially blood, often through high-risk penetrative sexual acts with an infected body.'[28] Such are the qualities of this bloodsucking outsider in *The Wailing*, who allegedly caused the rape victim to develop a skin disease and lose her mind through the defilement; the town's unexplainable occurrences are then blamed on the stranger – the non-Korean – whose identity no one knows and is therefore a threat to the community. Just as Dracula represents the threat of the Other, 'the Jap' poses a similar problem to Jong-gu's family as Mu-myŏng declares, 'That Jap is waiting for your return. To end your family bloodline'.[29] Shaka McGlotten writes, 'Zombies are especially useful in thinking through the vectors and politics of reproductive socialities', because contagion and contact are at the centre of the narrative's drive and infection spreads across families.[30] In the context of postcolonial Korea, sexuality is an anxiety-inducing threat. The visual of a Japanese man raping a Korean woman taps a particular nerve in Korea's collective consciousness – the sexual enslavement of Korean girls through 'comfort' stations for Japanese soldiers during the Second World War. Bruce Cumings writes that 'millions of foreign soldiers' have raped Korean girls and women since the turn of the twentieth century.[31] Foreign entry into the Korean peninsula represents the threat of ethnic miscegenation and 'impurity' through the rape of female Korean bodies, especially to a rural village's patriarchal clan mentality that emphasises bloodline due to nationalism fuelled by colonial peril.[32]

The Japanese stranger's anthropomorphic range as a ghost and the Devil – both with the ability to possess – is metaphoric of foreign invasion in a quaint rural town and the bodily violation of an innocent girl. The patriarchal contradiction expressed by Korean men outraged over the sexual enslavement of Korean female bodies is that more than 200,000 Korean men were recruited to serve the Japanese imperial army during the Second World War and many of them took advantage of these comfort stations themselves.[33] Furthermore, the Korean girls who were forced into these stations were given up by Korean men such as 'civilian brokers, colonial stooges, lying pimps, or businessmen claiming to have good factory jobs'; these men would coax the girls with promises for work then 'initiate' the virgins by raping them before selling them to sexual enslavement for the Japanese military; rural areas also participated in the sex trafficking of Korean girls through the power dictates of village patriarchy: '[A] dominant clan in a Korean village would tell a Japanese official and a Korean policeman where to find a pretty young girl among the residents of the subordinate clan households.'[34] Such harrowing historical realities are part of the patriarchal Korean psyche, plagued by guilt, shame, contradiction and confusion – themes that are present in Na's oeuvre.

Massacres, Unappeasable Rage and Excavating Repressed Memory

At the end of his rope, Jong-gu desperately asks the hired shaman Il-gwang (Hwang Jung-min), 'Why me?' Jong-gu wants to know why this disaster befell his daughter. Na's philosophy is that victimhood occurs randomly and with no explanation just like life and death. One of the symptoms of the disease that spreads throughout Goksŏng is that once psychosis sets in, the infected person kills everyone in their closest proximity including their own family and neighbours. The 'why me?' question that Jong-gu asks Il-gwang has no real answer, just as the question, 'why is my family killing my family?' has no answer. The idea alone is absurd; as modern Korean history shows, villages were tightly knit communities that functioned like a large family unit. During the Korean civil war, however, the South Korean army kidnapped women from the North and forced them into sex slavery just like their colonial oppressors had done. In *The Wailing*, the infected beings wind up murdering their family and neighbours just as it was a historical reality during and shortly after the Korean War:

> the violence of civil war seeped deeply into traditional communities, resulting in vicious reciprocal violence carried out by people from neighbouring villages, between sections within a residential community, and even between competing kin groups within the same line of descent … the war was centrally about the struggle for survival by unarmed civilians against the generalized, indiscriminate violence perpetrated by the armed political forces on all sides.[35]

These war crimes committed against their own are catching up to them in *The Wailing*.

Towards the midpoint of act one, Jong-gu hears Hyo-jin screaming in the middle of the night. When he goes to comfort her, she tells him that a man is banging on the door, trying to enter, suggesting a break in and rape. One afternoon, Jong-gu confronts his daughter about her relationship to 'the Jap', aggressively pressing her for details out of anxiety and concern. Hyo-jin responds to her father's interrogation with screams until her face turns red with rage, causing Jong-gu to sit back in dumbstruck terror. Later that night, Jong-gu sneaks into Hyo-jin's room and flips through her notebook to find scribbled profanity, drawings of women's bodies shedding blood from between their legs, and the Devil's face, suggesting sexual violation. Jong-gu then examines his sleeping daughter's body for traces of the zombie rash, which he finds on her legs. This awakens Hyo-jin who defensively confronts her father for looking at her legs with another vicious tantrum. Through Hyo-jin's body, *The Wailing* channels Korean girls' and women's – living and dead – unappeasable rage at the history of unjust rape, torture and murder of their bodies committed not just by foreign soldiers but also their own family members, neighbours, police and military. The deranged woman rumoured to have been raped by the Japanese stranger and little Hyo-jin both show evidence of Korean war crimes decomposing on their bodies and in their psyche as they lose themselves to the anguish of Korean women's trauma from the early to mid-twentieth century. Steve Jones argues that the zombie is a figure that threatens the establishment, system and order, and argues that the female zombie is particular a threat in the form of female empowerment; Jones claims that 'the reorganization of the flesh embodies a specifically sociopolitical reordering, gore linking the violence of social injustice to the substance of the body'.[36]

For Na, *The Wailing* is a slight departure from his earlier two films, which contain an unhealthy sexual preoccupation with the abject female body that gets repeatedly objectified by his male protagonists. In *The Chaser* (2008), female characters are locked in a system of prostitution that leads them to a violent death by a psychopathic killer; in *Yellow Sea* (2010) the deviant positions of female bodies plague the male characters' egos with a cuckold's wrath. None of the female characters in Na's films have autonomy over their own bodies. Even in *The Wailing*, Hyo-jin's body is a vessel to a demonic possession. All three of Na's films are in dialogue with one another around themes of sexual violation, irrepressible anger and unfathomable rage with no outlet or comfort, conveying his persistent cynicism that has become his filmic auteur signature. In *The Wailing*, however, there is greater ire seeking peace.

The Truth and Reconciliation Commission (TRC) was established in South Korea in 2005. South Korea's TRC, modelled after South Africa's TRC, has a mission to excavate a silenced past during the early part of the Korean War when millions of civilians died in terror and chaos. North and South Koreas' ideological motives were coerced by US McCarthyism and the Soviet Union's communism, which led to them committing acts of 'preemptive violence' against one another by suspecting anyone to be sympathisers of the other side – 'hypothetical collaborators' – without any concrete evidence.[37] The zombies in *The Wailing* are not unlike the ones in other Korean zombie content in that they attack whoever's in front of them for no apparent reason other than just being there. This, too, answers Jong-gu's question: 'Why me?' The answer is that it was never personal. It's just circumstantial, and there's no real logic to the chaos of war and its aftermath.

Na uses the Sino-Korean 哭聲 for the title – 곡성 – which is homonymous with 谷城 in Korean, although they differ drastically in meaning; whereas the former is the title of the film playing on the homonym of *goksŏng*, which means 'sorrowful wailing', the latter is the actual name of the county and the film's setting, which means 'village in the high hills'. Goksŏng County is located in Chŏlla Province – the southwestern part of the peninsula, far from the demilitarised zone. In November 1946, however, just a year after Korea was liberated from Japan and reoccupied with US forces, there were more than fifty peasant uprisings in Chŏlla Province alone that led to bloody clashes with the local police, US troops and right-wing terrorists against unarmed civilians, resulting in massacres. Cumings writes: '[T]hese distant events remain an unknown moment of history along the dusty roads and "parched hills" of Chŏlla … except to those who witnessed them, or those who died … What happened to the families of the dead – how do they commemorate a battle that no one ever heard of?'[38] *The Wailing*'s homage to the peasant wars is visible in the shot of the townsmen throwing pitchforks, animal bones, a concrete block, an umbrella and other farm tools into the pickup truck on their way to confront the Japanese stranger. In another scene, when Jong-gu, Seong-bok and the young priest break into the Japanese man's home, Seong-bok finds a room filled with candles and dozens of photographs and personal belongings of the town's victims – a compilation of the dead and their memorabilia. Towards the end of the film, the boot of Il-gwang's car is full of photographs of the dead. What do these items – particularly shoes of the dead – signify? Are they evidence of a crime? Is the mound of shoes that once belonged to the living a memorial, as those bodies decompose in the ground while the memories of the dead decompose within the living? There is a myth about how taking a photograph of a person steals their soul. In what ways have photographs of the living and the dead in Korea during and after the war led to the chipping away of the civilians' souls and the nation's spirit? Whose gaze falls on these photographs, and what are the politics of such viewings?

Na set his film in Goksŏng because it was a haven to North Korean Catholics who sought refuge while escaping religious persecution, but once they were found they were eventually martyred.[39] Goksŏng is an hour's distance from Kwangju City, where, in 1980, South Korean state troops massacred more than a hundred activists, mostly college students, who demonstrated against Chun Doo-hwan's martial law. The Korean zombie's significance is rooted in a shameful history of necropolitical choices enacted by their own government and patriarchal heads who killed those suspected of being a communist or a national traitor, and gave up or exploited girls, sending them to their deaths in order to survive the ideological warfare between foreign powers before and during the so-called 'cold war'. South Koreans who lived with the horrifying memories of these pasts were not allowed to speak on them; they had no one to turn to for help or find justice for the very people responsible for justice were the perpetrators. The South Korean state authorities (i.e., police), committed pre-emptive violence against small villages and communities, killing anyone suspected of being a communist – cops like Jong-gu; in *The Wailing*, Jong-gu's occupation as a police officer makes him face a karmic consequence of state offences against civilians who were killed and buried in mass graves – left nameless and forgotten. Kwon writes that although these communities and families witnessed the deaths of their families and neighbours, and were forced into silence, the stories of the war persisted 'in whispered conversations' among elders and trusted relatives, or 'in the furious self-expression of some forgotten ancestral spirits who intruded into shamanic rites to express the terror of summary killings and the agony of an afterlife in a mass grave'.[40]

Another complicating factor to *The Wailing*'s narrative is the protagonist's occupation as a cop. The Korean police have a long history of corruption by consorting with oppressive forces; for example, the imperial government, US military and the ROK's authoritarian regimes. This is partially the reason why so many contemporary Korean films portray the police as incompetent and untrustworthy, and it is particularly true in all three of Na's films, although *The Wailing* is the first to have a cop at the centre of the plot. In 1956, villagers on Cheju island built a tombstone to commemorate the dead who were killed then buried in a nameless mass grave. Bodies were exhumed and pieced together to make them appear like a complete human form before being offered a proper burial.[41] The police, who were working for an authoritarian state at the time, destroyed the tombstone, stating that such a commemoration was a threat to national security. This destruction corresponds to the shaman's hex ritual scene that Jong-gu rudely disrupts despite Il-gwang's warning, which prevents a complete spiritual healing in Hyo-jin and results in the death of Jong-gu's wife and mother at her hands.

In 1948, when Syngman Rhee tried to exercise the ROK's power over Cheju island, civilians responded through guerilla insurgency to claim local autonomy and preserve peace on their land. Right-wing extremists like the Northwest Youth Corps (NWY) harassed, tortured, raped and murdered thousands of civilians on the grounds that they were 'commies', while American forces stood by and watched complacently; the NWY technically represented democratic freedom, and were therefore protected by the auspices of the United States. The Cheju massacres estimate more than 80,000 civilian deaths during the US occupation of the island between 1945–8:

> The documented violence was so extreme, so gratuitous, as to suggest a peculiar pathology [of the] unremittingly vicious conflicts that have wracked divided Korea … This pathology, perhaps, has something to do with the self-hatred of individuals who did Japanese bidding, now operating on behalf of another foreign power, and with extremes of misogyny in Korea's patriarchal society.[42]

Such pathology is quite evident in Na's films, which frequently dwell on shots of dead bodies piled on top of one another. In *Yellow Sea*, there are multiple images of excessive blood and violence resulting from large groups of gang men killing one another due to orders given by their superiors. In *The Chaser*, the serial killer takes the lives of multiple people – primarily female sex workers – and buries them in a yard. In the penultimate scene of the film, the camera dollies on the ground from left to right capturing the muddied bodies being unearthed in the pouring rain by police officers. The camera slowly pans over the crime scene as the dead are exhumed, some of which are simply body parts, to be documented and traced back to their identities – a process that is currently taking place through the TRC at mass graves in the ROK where body parts are being excavated for documentation, historicisation and proper commemoration. Shots with piles of nameless dead bodies in Na's films evoke the cold treatment of human bodies as nameless/faceless objects for easy slaughter, as well as the horrors of mass graves where innocent civilians were killed then thrown into, left to be forgotten – travesties that were silenced by the government for decades until recent years. This recent acknowledgement as well as the efforts of the TRC are examples of cold war decomposition that Korea is currently dealing with; this slow decomposition is reflected in horror films such as *The Wailing* where the dead are either zombies who've been brought back to life from the stillness of death, or living beings that slowly decompose into a zombie-like state before murdering their own parents, spouse, grandparents, children, etc. These zombies are embodiments of

Korea's decomposing process containing an inexpressible haunting, sorrow, confusion and anger at the history of blind and demented violence incited by foreign ideologies; *The Wailing* captures a grand disturbance of peace that still echoes out from the grave and in the living generations' minds as they live in the beautifully lush rural county of Chŏlla Province, just as imperialism and war have done to the entire peninsula of Korea, the land of morning calm.

At *The Wailing*'s Cannes press conference, a French moderator sarcastically asks Na why he likes to confuse his audience.[43] But is Na's film necessarily inscrutable and therefore to be disregarded? Or does it just require the viewer to shift their vantage point? Is Korean history necessarily inscrutable and therefore irrelevant, or is it perceived that way because the dominant historical discourse stemming from hegemonic powers mystifies so-called subaltern vantage points? Or would the said powers rather not see its role in the mass death of millions of innocent people? And who is to mourn the unnamed and unidentifiable dead? *The Wailing* contains numerous shots of sacred rite offerings with food, incense, candles and animals to honour the dead; these offerings are also made to appease dead souls that harbour resentment, sadness and rage.

Contradictions, absurdity, illogical scenarios, cacophony and chaos are all iterations of modern Korean traumas that Na synthesises in *The Wailing*. Na's film dwindles the importance of specifying any particular villain by focusing the narrative around the victim's experience with confused helplessness while slowly revealing that the face of the antagonist is no different from that of the protagonist's own daughter, parent, neighbour or self. As colonial and postcolonial Korean history indicates, the face of the enemy isn't always a foreigner's. Na narrates Korea's history of victimhood through *The Wailing*, speaking directly to national memory, loss and the desire to recoup what was lost in a non-linear manner, seeing as an organised recitation is impossible due to the lack of documentation that was either lost or deliberately erased by those in power at the time; the masses of buried bodies and their disconnected parts are still being uncovered with attempts at identification through science but also through oral histories retrieved from decaying memories like Kwon's ethnographic work illustrates.

Although the female body wails out of anger as Hyo-jin's does, the male body also wails, and it contains the heartbreak of a father left powerless in the face of a problem that he is unfit to resolve for it is far too big for him to comprehend, much like the men who were subject to their local community's patriarchal and colonial influence. The men who fought for imperial causes are left haunted by their actions stemming from ideological confusion, which led to the injury and death of countless members of their own country and family – a history and psychological conundrum that Na's oeuvre summons and confronts.

Notes

1. David Ehrlich, 'Cannes Review: "The Wailing" is an Epic Korean Horror Movie too Crazy for its own Good', *IndieWire*, 23 May 2016, *www.indiewire.com/2016/05/cannes-review-the-wailing-is-an-epic-korean-horror-movie-too-crazy-for-its-own-good-288923/* (last accessed 14 January 2017).
2. Simon Abrams, 'The Wailing', *RogerEbert.com*, 3 June 2016, *www.rogerebert.com/reviews/the-wailing-2016* (last accessed 14 January 2017).
3. Maggie Lee, 'Cannes Film Review: "The Wailing"', *Variety*, 19 May 2016, *http://variety.com/2016/film/reviews/the-wailing-review-goksung-cannes-1201776287/* (last accessed 30 January 2017).
4. Heonik Kwon, *The Other Cold War* (New York: Columbia University Press, 2010), p. 6.
5. Kwon, *The Other Cold War*, p. 8.
6. Kwon, *The Other Cold War*, pp. 33–4.
7. Jean Noh, 'Cannes Q&A: Na Hong-jin, "The Wailing"', *Screen Daily*, 18 May 2016, *www.screendaily.com/festivals/cannes/cannes-qa-na-hong-jin-the-wailing/5104060.article* (last accessed 5 March 2017).
8. For an extended filmography of South Korean zombie films, see Sung-Ae Lee, 'The New Zombie Apocalypse and Social Crisis in South Korean Cinema', *Observatori: Centre d'Estudis Australians i Transnacionals/Observatory: Australian and Transnational Studies Centre* (Universitat de Barcelona, Coolabah, Nr 27, 2019).
9. Jaecheol Kim, 'Biocalyptic Imaginations in Japanese and Korean films: Undead Nation-States in *I Am a Hero* and *Train to Busan*', *Inter-Asia Cultural Studies*, 20/3 (2019), 437–51.
10. Fred Botting, 'Undead-Ends: Zombie Debt/Zombie Theory', *Postmodern Culture*, 23/3 (May 2013).
11. Sung-Ae Lee, 'The New Zombie Apocalypse', p. 151.
12. Sung-Ae Lee, 'The New Zombie Apocalypse', p. 162.
13. David Boyns and Robert Wonser, 'Between the Living and Undead: How Zombie Cinema Reflects the Social Construction of Risk, the Anxious Self, and Disease Pandemic', *The Sociology Quarterly*, 57 (2016), 628–53.

14. Chungmoo Choi, 'Decolonization and Popular Memory: South Korea', *Positions: Asia Critique*, 1/1 (1993), 79.
15. Na Hong-jin, interview, Pierce Conran, 'NA Hong-jin and KWAK Do-won chat about *The Wailing* after Cannes Premiere', *Kobiz*, 24 May 2016, *www.koreanfilm.or.kr/jsp/news/interview.jsp?blbdComCd=601019&seq=221&mode=INTERVIEW_VIEW* (last accessed 13 February 2017).
16. Noh, 'Cannes Q&A: Na Hong-jin'.
17. Pierce Conran, 'Interview: The Wailing's Na Hong-jin, Questions for a Mastermind of Evil', *ScreenAnarchy*, *https://screenanarchy.com/2016/06/interview-the-wailings-na-hong-jin-questions-for-a-mastermind-of-evil.html* (last accessed 2 March 2025).
18. Kim Kwang-ok, 'Rituals of Resistance: The Manipulation of Shamanism in Contemporary Korea', in Charles F. Keyes, Laurel Kendall and Helen Hardacre (eds), *Asian Visions of Authority: Religion and the Modern States of East and Southeast Asia* (Honolulu: University of Hawaii Press, 1994), p. 219.
19. Conrad, 'Interview: The Wailing's Na Hong-jin'.
20. See Immanuel Wallerstein, 'War in Asia? An Interpretative Essay', in Zheng Yangwen, Hong Liu and Michael Szonyi (eds), *The Cold War in Asia: The Battle for Hearts and Minds* (Boston MA: Brill, 2010), pp. 15–24; Bruce Cumings, 'Korea's Centrality to the Cold War', *Asia Review*, 5/2, issue 10 (2016), 185–210; Dong-choon Kim, *The Unending Korean War: A Social History*, (Durham NC: Duke University Press, 2009).
21. Nikola Grozdanovic, 'Interview: "The Wailing" Director Na Hong-jin On Death, Genre, Religion & Comedy', *The Playlist*, 27 June 2016, *http://theplaylist.net/interview-wailing-director-na-hong-jin-20160627/* (last accessed 11 February 2017).
22. Cymovie, '(kangnyŏksŭp'ojuŭi) 160510 "koksŏng" kwan'gaekkwaŭi taehwa/megat'ok'ŭ megabaksŭ tongdaemun (kangnyŏksŭp'ojuŭi)', *YouTube*, 11 May 2016, *www.youtube.com/watch?v=NGWyxLqslIo* (last accessed 11 February 2017).
23. Cymovie, '(kangnyŏksŭp'ojuŭi) 160510'.
24. Na Hong-jin (dir.), *The Wailing* (Twentieth Century Fox, 2016), translation by author.
25. See Daniel W. Drezner, 'Metaphor of the Living Dead: Or, the Effect of the Zombie Apocalypse on Public Policy Discourse', *Social Research: An International Quarterly*, 81/4 (winter 2014), 825–49; Wonser and Boyns, 'Between the Living and the Undead'.
26. Leland Monk, 'Undead Images, Images of the Undead: *Dracula* on Film', in John Paul Riquelme (ed.), *Dracula: Bram Stoker*, 2nd edn (Boston MA: Bedford/St Martin's, 2016), p. 499.

27. Stephen D. Arata, 'The Occidental Tourist: "Dracula" and the Anxiety of Reverse Colonization', *Victorian Studies*, 33/4 (1990), 621–45.
28. Monk, 'Undead Images, Images of the Undead', p. 500.
29. Na Hong-jin, *The Wailing*.
30. Shaka McGlotten, 'Zombie Porn: Necropolitics, Sex, and Queer Socialities', *Porn Studies*, 1/4, (2014), 364.
31. Bruce Cumings, *The Korean War* (New York: Random House, 2010), p. 122.
32. Gi-wook Shin, *Ethnic Nationalism in Korea: Genealogy, Politics, and Legacy* (Stanford CA: Stanford University Press, 2006), Location 303.
33. Cumings, *The Korean War*, p. 42.
34. Cumings, *The Korean War*, p. 43.
35. Heonik Kwon, 'Korean War Mass Graves', in Richard Wilson, Antonius C. G. M. Robben and Francisco Ferrándiz, *Necropolitics: Mass Graves and Exhumations in the Age of Human Rights* (Philadelphia PA: University of Pennsylvania Press, 2015), pp. 76–91, 78.
36. Steve Jones, 'Porn of the Dead: Necrophilia, Feminism, and Gendering the Undead', in Cory Rushton and Christopher Moreman (eds), *Zombies Are Us: Essays on the Humanity of the Walking Dead* (Jefferson NC: McFarland, 2011), pp. 40–60, 43.
37. Francisco Ferrandiz and Antonius C. G. M. Robben, 'The Ethnography of Exhumations', in Francisco Ferrandiz and Antonius C. G. M. Robben (eds), *Necropolitics* (Philadelphia PA: University of Pennsylvania Press, 2015), p. 18.
38. Cumings, *The Korean War*, p. 117.
39. Noh, 'Cannes Q&A: Na Hong-jin'.
40. Kwon, 'Korean War Mass Graves', p. 79.
41. Kwon, 'Korean War Mass Graves', p. 79.
42. Cumings, *The Korean War*, p. 124.
43. 'GOKSUNG – Press Conference – EV – Cannes 2016', Festival de Cannes (Official), *YouTube*, 18 May 2016, *www.youtube.com/watch?v=26dbkoukAUU* (last accessed 13 March 2017).

13

The Symbolic Zombification and the Capitalist Modes of Production

Rodrigo Gonsalves

THE INTERSECTION OF ZOMBIE narratives and capitalism has been a subject of increasing scholarly interest, reflecting a broader cultural engagement with themes of consumerism, alienation and the commodification of human life. In this vein, recent research has delved into how zombie films and literature not only serve as metaphors for societal decay and the dehumanisation inherent in capitalist systems but also critique the pervasive influence of consumer culture on individual and collective identities.[1] Works by scholars such as Harman and others have laid the groundwork by examining the evolution of the zombie from a figure of folkloric horror into a symbol of capitalist consumption, highlighting the zombie apocalypse as a narrative framework through which the excesses and failures of capitalism are explored and critiqued.[2] Capitalism creates zombies.[3] An affirmation such as this does not necessarily strike as either bold or absurd today. Zombies, ghouls and the living dead are culturally popular in TV shows and films, their popularity only increasing.[4] Recently, the approximation of zombies and capitalism has grown popular in theoretical thinking[5] – zombies do indeed return to the spotlight from time to time. Nonetheless, zombies play a deeper role in our imagination, symbolising something of our traumatic fear of death and the angst of having no alternative against our own finitude. Beyond the aesthetic representation of such figures and subjective sensibilities that they allow us to investigate, monstrous figurations have a certain effect on us, their meaning more impactful because of their specific association with capitalism's effect on labourers. Nonetheless, this is a classic approximation that deserves better appreciation. In the same way that capitalism transforms and reinvents itself over time, forcing societies structured by these economic foundations to transform themselves along with it, such changes will produce specific individualities and subjective sensibilities that will reflect such conditions and the needs of those in power.

One way of explaining this is to look at symptoms from a psychoanalytical perspective. When you have a fever and treat it with pills, you are dealing with the symptom of *something*, not its cause. Metaphorically, this point can be applied to think about the social-economic structure of capitalist societies and its individuals, who are forged as symptoms of the economic conditions that cause them. Understanding capitalism as an economic system based on profit and that it now globally scaled, we begin to notice how the labour supporting it fulfils its conditions of existence and that the majority of the individuals providing the labour pay the price. The reference to zombies and economics is not necessarily new, it has been attempted many times before, but the specificity of examining how it expresses a certain aesthetic that portrays a symptom of our material reality is something that can be found in this chapter. Nonetheless, the scope required aims at a Marxist approach. Not only because Marxism develops a formidable critique to the exploitative conditions of capitalism, but because it invites a more monstrous dialectical perspective to do so.

Karl Marx's classic gravedigger thesis from *The Communist Manifesto* (2004 [1848]) revolves around particular dialectics of the working class and its struggle.[6] Although this argument is not rescued by Marx in his later works, it sets the precedent for a particularly *monstrous metaphor* or *monstrous terminology* that is pertinent to discussing the 'inevitability' of a revolution against capitalist domination. This theory is usually used to criticise Marx for an improper or inadequate prognosis or is approached poorly by orthodox Marxists who persist in sustaining a teleological approach.[7] This chapter seeks to defend that this theory, instead of simply 'disappearing' in Marx's subsequent work, was actually further *developed* towards more monstrous dialectical figures. In other words, how Marx took on the gravedigger theory in a more monstrous way – certainly not for the sake of being more aesthetically pleasing, but actually, to be more *dialectically precise* in his materialist revolutionary thesis. The symbolic zombification of modes of production investigated here, concerns the *excesses* and *remainders* of capital that are not fully subsumed into the symbolic fabric of our reality, thus always finding new ways to re-emerge.

For a Marxist Monstrous Metaphor

Marx used monstrosity as a metaphor to investigate capital's language (Gonsalves, 2021), transposing the previous motif of the gravediggers.[8] Based on objective factors, instead of persisting with a crude metaphor to translate his idea of a class struggle against capitalism (e.g., gravediggers), Marx chose to translate his dialectical movement against capitalism with a much more nuanced and monstrous approach.[9] In other words, the investigation of Marx's 'monsters' – werewolves, vampires, the living dead – reveals a derivation of this dialectical motif in a more precise terminology towards its particular revolutionary *topos*.[10] There have been many discussions within studies of Marxism to delineate the role of the living dead in Marx's critique of capitalism, but there seems to be no clear consensus about its proper role – this chapter aims to add to the debate. Throughout the pages of *Capital*, one can easily find direct references to vampires, werewolves, living-dead approximations and other 'monstrous' terminology.[11] One of Marx's most famous passages on this subject concerns the capitalist's vampire-like hunger for the blood of the working class:

> Capital is dead labour which, vampire-like, lives only by sucking living labour, and lives the more, the more labour it sucks. The time during which the worker works is the time during which the capitalist consumes the labour-power he has bought from him. If the worker consumes his disposable time for himself, he robs the capitalist.[12]

Neocleous's mapping of the different interpretations of Marx's approach to monsters can be separated into four key areas: first, those who defend such usage as historical, literary and philosophical allusions (which is the case made by Robert Paul Wolff); second, those who defend this as Marx's approach to 'modernism' (as Marshal Berman does); third, those who alongside Stanley Hyman argue that 'we get closer to the essential nature of *Capital* if we deal with it, not as science, social science, or exhortation, but as imagination literature'; and finally, those like Wylie Sypher and Andrew

Smith, who interpret Marx's use of the living dead as 'merely one of his "occult tropes", used because he recognized "how crucial it was to give an imaginative account of things"' – a point that Neocleous himself supports, referring to 'Marx's metaphor in the wider context of nineteenth-century gothic'.[13] This last line of interpretation seems to be the most well accepted today, between scholars concerning Marx's use of vampires, werewolves and the living dead, resonating with the developments of a certain Gothic materialism. Although the Gothic appreciation provides Marx's monstrous discussion with dignity, it is still captured by a metaphorical rhetoric discussion lacking a more dialectical materialist approach.

Creating a radically different way of thinking requires us to commit to developing alternatives to capitalism's problems. However, to do this effectively, we must first understand capitalism's own complex and problematic language structure.[14] Of course, this does not mean that zombies are *literally* out there, or vampires or werewolves for that matter, but it does mean that while analysing Marx's gravediggers in terms of the living dead, to consider it as a strictly as metaphorical embellishment seems to overlook the full philosophical depth. Marx's materialist perspective regarding his critique of capitalism seems to approach from a different angle, which seems to refine a teleological approach towards a more *indeterminate* perspective within his materialistic view. Nonetheless, one argument becomes clear, to adequately critique capital, one can do so accurately only in its most monstrous terms.[15] Marx himself dignifies such monstrous metaphor. Thus, it's only by understanding its implications that a proper critique of capitalism can be formulated. To put it bluntly, Marx's living-dead discussions – with their most monstrous capabilities – translate a fundamental philosophical dimension of dialectics that has long fallen on deaf ears, a fact that has perhaps contributed to the persistence of late capitalism in its most neo-imperialist mode, since it evades the depths of a proper *dialectical* materialist framework.

Fredric Jameson's notion of *figuration* provides a crucial operator for this argument. *Figuration* was coined by Jameson in *Representing Capital: A Commentary on Volume One*, where he defends Marx's concern with the theorisation of the *entirety* of the capitalist system and not finding quick fixes for its contradictions.[16] Thus, forcefully disagreeing with the suggestion that these monstrous elements are there for no good reason or simply as embellishments, what Jameson's notion of figuration allows is a different understanding of the 'interplay of the dialectics of the One and the Many, of subject and object, of the circumference whose center is everywhere and the *ens causa sui*'.[17] In other words, Jameson's figuration deepens the understanding of the symbolic fabric of reality itself within capitalism, translating the intricacies of the dialectical operations within a materialist perspective.[18] This also allows for a radical approach to the zombie-like conditions, scenarios and situations solidified in late capitalism. Through Jameson's figuration late capitalist zombification has a symbolic dimension that cannot be ignored, introducing a refinement to the false dialectical twists that reproduce capitalism in its persistence. Instead of assuming strictly imaginary zombies in Marx's work (which Gothic metaphorical interpretation already does), Jameson's figuration permits a refined localisation of the *embodiments* of symbolic contradictions within (symbolic-imaginary) reality. Wherever we see signs of capitalism's problems – whether they appear as mindless conformity (zombie-like), exploitative relationships (vampiric), persistent historical patterns that won't go away (ghostly) or fundamental transformations of human nature through work (werewolf-like) – we are witnessing capitalism's deep contradictions at work. Only monstrous metaphor seems to capture the realm of *negativity* dialectically present in late capitalism.[19]

Marx Returned to Hegel? From the Gravediggers to the Monstrous Dimension of Capital

In *Hegel, Haiti and Universal History* Susan Buck-Morss explains how, prior to Marx, Hegel had already built a bridge between monstrosity and capitalism.[20] As Buck-Morss explains, in Hegel's *Jena Systementwürfe I* (1803) the German philosopher debates Adam Smith's *The Wealth of Nations* (1776), criticising capitalism as an:

> uncontrolled and 'blind' interdependence of laborers in the global economy, the 'bürgerliche Gesellschaft' (civil society) of market exchanges that forms a 'monstrous system' (*ungeheueres System*) of mutual 'dependency' (*Abhangigkeit*) and that 'like a wild beast needs to be tamed'.[21]

Hegel's interpretation of Adam Smith's metaphor of the 'invisible hand' of the liberal markets in capitalism is that of a monstrous system; that is, the *monstrous self-regulating functioning* of *capital* was actually already present in Hegel's philosophical investigations.[22] Despite Marx being a ferocious critic of Hegel's philosophy, there is an astonishing point of convergence (although from opposite approaches) between the two thinkers. Perhaps both realised the inherent contradiction within private property and the monstrous dimension of capital's self-regulating operations. It is no secret that Marx was an avid reader and critic of Hegel's idealism, but, perhaps, here lies a shared *concern* between both.

Certainly, in order to settle firmly on this 'common ground' between Hegel and Marx, or to attempt to draw accurate or direct influence, would require a biographical work retracing Marx's steps, something that this chapter does not even pretend to do. Nonetheless, assuming a more speculative approach permits a productive investigation of such common ground, perhaps something of this clear, shared perplexity over Smith's theories could serve as a valuable hint to substantiate Marx's shift from the gravediggers theory to his more monstrous perspectives. This shift in critical operators – the tools Marx used to examine capitalism (e.g., the monstrous vampires, zombies and werewolves) – towards a more monstrous metaphor of capital, understood as more fitting notions necessary to grasp capital's parasitic foreignness, was certainly a task that Marx assumed for himself. More than a straightforward teleological approach of simple opposites, like the position defended by orthodox Marxists who misguidedly argue that capitalists would *eventually* produce their own downfall (i.e., the gravediggers' theory), it is shifted by Marx towards monstrous characters, revealing a much more complex dialectical depth that recoils to examine its possible predicaments. One thing is certain, there is nothing teleological when we are dealing with living-dead productions in a monstrous system, there is no clarity towards an end game or acknowledgement that there is a preconceived ending to all this. Although highly speculative, Marx's shift in a more monstrous direction, very much along the lines of Hegel's criticism towards Smith's formulations, seems to fulfil two key points: first, it 'speaks' directly the monstrous language of capital; and second, it imposes a more refined dialectical consideration against crude materialism, since this monstrous metaphor or terminology circumscribes a *position* of contradiction embodied in a particular situation. Investigating the monster metaphors in Marx's analysis of capitalism reveals an important but often neglected dimension of his work. This approach prevents both crude materialist interpretations and misunderstandings of Hegelian philosophy. Marx's use of monstrous imagery challenges teleological readings that view history as automatically marching forward through class struggle alone.[23]

Three Moments in Zombie Films, Three Marxist Monstrous Moments

Theodor Adorno and Max Horkheimer's *Dialectic of Enlightenment* anticipates cultural productions as reflections of the capitalist system in strategies of mass deception: 'Culture today is infecting everything with sameness. Film, radio and magazine form a system. Each branch of culture is unanimous within itself and all are unanimous together. Even the aesthetic manifestation of political opposites proclaim the same inflexible rhythm.'[24] In a way, zombie films seem to accurately capture the monstrous opposites of capital's contradictions, which are prepared to be calmly and interpassively enjoyed.[25] This section introduces three different zombie films that corroborate with this speculative development of capital's monstrous dimension, how they seem to translate capital as it shifts in order to persist in its parasitic activity over social reality. Basically, these zombie films translate three different ideological moments of exploitative relations of production and expropriation by capital. I won't further examine the subjective dimension of workers that zombies certainly permit us to explore, but I will seek a broader examination of capitalism and its effects through popular culture.

The three films denote three moments that can be approached within a certain movement (almost like a peculiar Hegelian triad) in zombie filmography. Approaching the representation of zombies in these three moments shows how, first, zombies were controlled, and obeyed their masters; second, the zombies became mindless roamers; and third, more recently, zombies became accelerated figurations of bursting rage, running down their victims to sate their hunger. To better illustrate these three zombie moments in cultural productions, let us invoke three paradigmatic films that exemplify this shift: first, Victor Halperin's *White Zombie* (1932), which is known to be the first film about zombies and was based on William Seabrook's book *The Magic Island* (1929), a collection of tales of zombies from Haiti. The second is captured by George A. Romero's trilogy (1968–85), which re-introduced zombies, now freed from their master's command and roaming everywhere. Finally, the third is illustrated by Danny Boyle's *28 Days Later* (2002), where zombies stop being 'interpassive' creatures to become completely aggressive and violent in fulfilling their need to feed off the living.[26]

Although the time between these three films (around seventy years) seems brief, the films appear to have been perfected in terms of *refining negativity* through three different zombie *figurations*, and in sustaining an interesting figuration of capital's transformation in terms of production techniques across this period. Exploring these three different zombies in film production can certainly spark many discussions leading in many directions. I aim to (re)approach the Marxist critique of capitalism via the living dead to investigate the monstrous dimension of capital portrayed by these cultural products; that is, products calmly consumed by us, retroactively generating more profit for this very system and thus perfecting our dystopian predicament.[27]

After laying out these elements, it now makes sense to return to the three zombie paradigmatic references: *White Zombie*; Romero's zombie trilogy; and *28 Days Later*. Looking at these zombies as *figurations* (i.e., more than a rhetorical element or an aesthetic embellishment within Marx's critique of capitalism) invites the necessity of (re)approaching them as circumscribing a contradiction of capitalism itself (which any cultural production always is). In a way, this helps explain how zombies are philosophical speculative figurations beyond the usual imaginary rhetorical fabulations. In other words, zombies capture and translate (only to be consumed and thus *normalised*) the worker's *position* in the class struggle against the capitalist. But, even deeper, its monstrous metaphor reveals the zombification of workers in capital's current world domination. It reveals its position to capital's mode of production at a particular moment through perfecting the manoeuvres of exploitation.

White Zombie revolves around a young couple in love (Madeleine and Neil) who are invited by Monsieur Beaumont to get married at his Haitian plantation. The actual reason that Beaumont has lured the couple to his home is that he wanted to break them up and convince Madeleine to be with him instead. To fulfil his plan, Beaumont turns to 'Murder' Legendre, a dreadful plantation master who uses witchcraft to fabricate a zombie potion that controls other people. Beaumont uses this potion on Madeleine, who becomes a zombie. He regrets depriving Madeleine of her being and confronts 'Murder' Legendre to return her to normal, but Legendre has no intention of decreasing his zombie collection. Meanwhile, Neil is convinced that Madeleine is still trapped in her zombified body and tries to revert the spell – but to do so he must quash Legendre's control over his zombies.

Through a renewed Marxist lens, one can see how this film portrays Haitian slaves who cannot find peace with their master even after they are dead. The devilish power of 'Murder' Legendre has nothing *magical* about it (at least not in *fantastic* terms), what 'Murder' *figurates* is the level of the *mystics* of capital. Hidden in plain sight, 'Murder' enacts a radical fetishist commodification of people in its more brutal sense, the most cruel objectification of turning people into commodities for his own capitalist profit denotes Legendre as a slave owner, but much more brutal than that, his monstrous twist lies in his control once his victims' lives are ended: he controls the impossibility of symbolising their *deaths*. This film illustrates Haitian slaves figurated by zombies that are always under the master's spell, preventing the symbolisation of their passing. The opposing forces struggling is clear between the master and the zombies but in radical, asymmetric dispute: the zombies are under the master's control.

Many interpretations could be inspired by this film, one is how such tension depicted by the zombies reveals the massive non-symbolised backbone of capital: slavery. In short, colonisation and slavery were fundamental operations used to increase the power of nations and states, but what actually benefited was capital itself, which could now spread across the world and slowly place itself as the prevailing mode of power over reality through commodification.[28] This film illustrates how slaves were radically exploited beyond their own lives and deaths, finding no escape even after death. This predicament generated by capital's commodification of reality, illustrated in the film's monstrous depiction, brings light to capital's hidden operation, an invisible practice that permitted massive accumulation for wealthy nations. Marx's primitive accumulation argument against Smith's naive approach prevents the mistake of examining capitalism as a world system to be examined apart from these brutal historical massacres. Thus, Marx localises the monstrous perspective, capitalist primitive accumulation that occurred in its monstrous dimension through colonisation and slavery. Therefore, slavery was a condition that enabled the establishment of global capitalism – colonialism is still in capital's DNA and zombies are an excellent reminder of this. Although zombies 'transform', they still retain this internal logic: the symbolic zombification of reality between life and death. Capital's exploitative objectification of bodies and languages has no limits in its exploitative hold and the first zombie film illustrates this clearly.

The idea that liberal capitalism 'freed' the world from slavery is fallacy. Capitalism symbolically perfected and perpetuated slavery, and zombies can help us make this point. Just consider the shift from the zombies in *White Zombie* to Romero's undead trilogy. Taking a closer look at Romero's zombies, you can see precisely how capitalism has been pervasively *embedded into each and every one of us* as 'normality' (e.g., zombies heading to the mall from 'muscle memory') – this is a brutal blow by capitalists against workers, demobilising class struggle through small crumbs of comfort, an invisible practice that improves capitalist domination. Romero's zombie trilogy can be approached as a critical figuration against the implications of the welfare state and Reagan economics (Reaganomics).[29] This could explain the key transformation of the logic behind zombies no longer needing a master, or how capitalism is now an integral part of all our lives. It illustrates the impasse of a growing middle class at the beginning of late capitalism, where liberal ideology falsely implies that you can be the master of your labour, when, in reality, you are merely zombifying yourself further. Nonetheless, this ideological mentality is now transmissible: if you get bitten by a zombie, you will become a zombie; if you die, you automatically become a zombie. The (capitalist) spell took over the world, the invisible monstrous spell, has infiltrated everywhere. The domination of capital over reality is a fundamental element of Romero's trilogy, his zombies are a renewed rendition of the exploited and murdered bodies from the colonial past that are buried beneath the wealth of the centre of the world (Europe and the United States). Nonetheless, Romero's genius figuration of the roaming mindless zombie in all its numbness against reality, brilliantly translates the neocolonial advances of capital over the (semi) peripheries and peripheries of the world – a new growing middle class enjoys the benefits of capitalism, while the vast majority of the riff-raff spread to the peripheries of the world.[30]

After the 1980s, global capitalism took over, subsuming symbolic (and imaginary) reality – there was no longer any alternative narrative in place. Sustaining the logic of our monstrous investigation on zombies figurating the contradiction of the workers under capitalism, this could explain another quintessential transformation to in the lure of zombies in popular culture. Danny Boyle's *28 Days Later*, a dystopian film, introduces zombies that instead of roaming around now run and chase their targets; Boyle's zombies are *accelerated*, relentless and ferocious monsters that will not stop until they consume their victims. The zombies from *28 Days Later* must be actively stopped by their prey. The film depicts a new zombie figuration that illustrates the effects of capitalism after the advance of the internet and the virtualisation of finance.

In *28 Days Later* zombies may be anywhere, but they are inherently driven by an unstoppable force towards consuming the living, producing more zombies. Isn't this also another crucial feature of capitalism? To either find or tear another inch of our shared social reality to exploit. The digital financial regime after the 2000s added a further twist in capital's already total operations over reality. Étienne Balibar describes this shift within capitalism as the transformation from generalised surplus value to total subsumption.[31] Balibar (provisionally) calls this 'absolute capitalism', translating the capitalist current creation of 'fictitious commodities' in order to sustain the process of accumulation. The biological, intellectual and symbolic are nothing but means incorporated to sustain this reproduction necessary to persist the credit and debt functions that now dictate human activity.[32] The zombies from this film seem to fully illustrate the return of the repressed, the remainder of slavery and colonialism that sustained capitalist accumulation and the wealth of rich nations and that was not fully symbolically subsumed and now returns in its accelerated form against its own citizens (meaning that the neocolonialism of peripheral countries will only intensify to balance this calculation). These zombies are not figurations of a passive contradiction of our reality under capitalism, but are an active predatory driving force against everyone, against every living thing and each and every hidden secret of life itself, in the name of additional surplus value.[33] In a way, Boyle's zombies translate the intensification of our zombified symbolic-imaginary, after conquering the world capitalism must repeat its formulas of perpetual contradiction to continue to exist.

What these films illustrate is that zombies are crucial figurations when thinking about our predicament in capitalist societies. As *undead* figures, zombies cannot speak but are spoken of. They are the figuration of the capitalist's ideal worker. Placing the undead in a philosophical scope means to understand how it manages to formulate crucial questions about capital's hold on us and how it permits us to read the implications of our (in)humanity.[34] Following Žižek's argument in *Parallax View* to affirm a non-predicate, means to be able to understand how we can logically conceive that something neither alive nor dead; but, more than that, it also permits us to think of a societal position that is always radically neglected and attempted to be laid to rest by the capitalist.[35] The importance of refining our terminology towards such a monstrous domain means to be able to recognise the position of those who are brutally neglected and radically *unrecognised*. Thus, to engage in class struggle today means to comprehend it in its more monstrous capabilities – as a proper materialist dimension – in order to understand the position of those who are radically without a place in our society as a result of capital's monstrous operations. If the terminology of capitalism is monstrous and if capitalism operates in a 'self-reinforcing feedback loop', then it makes perfect sense how capitalism can only produce undead monstrous economics in order to sustain itself.[36] Nonetheless, it coextensively generates zombified monstrous modes of symbolic production along its way and, we, as its battery, are inherently traversed by such zombified operations in our everyday lives. Another good example for the need of undead investigations to conceive Capital, comes from Benjamin Noys:

> Capitalism is more alive than us, in its formation as a social form making over the world, accumulating dead labour in the mad dance of speculative accumulation, as the 'life drive' that absorbs and condenses life into surplus-value. Capitalism is also less than dead, not only in its dependence on our life. But also in its indifference to life and death, its violent remaking that works 'blindly' to no teleology except repeating the production of surplus-value.[37]

Zombies are a symbolic reminder of the rationality that operates within capital, zombies are its monstrous metaphor. If our argument holds, zombies are an accurate monstrous figuration of capitalist exploitation against workers, introducing the necessity towards a dialectical materialist approach that can understand its nuance.

Conclusion

When Marx formalises his critique of capitalism in *Capital*, instead of persisting or adapting the gravediggers' thesis from *The Communist Manifesto*, he moves towards the monstrous terminology of the *undead*. Instead of approaching this as an aesthetical manoeuvre or a linguistic metaphorisation, Jameson's notion of *figuration* provides a dialectical materialist insight that offers dignity to Marx's monsters (zombies, vampires, werewolves) under a different scope. The undead are present in Marx's critique of capitalism, suggesting elements of subjectivisation and alienation, but also as key elements to consider the impasse of class struggle under capitalism. Zombies are a quintessential monster through which to examine the impasse of capitalism in its more monstrous terms. What the filmic renderings of zombies examined by this chapter have demonstrated, is how these undead creatures figurate three different moments of capitalism perfecting its operations of exploitation. Thus, zombies are a pertinent embodiment to think of capital's strategies of intensifying its exploitative mechanisms.

Notes

1. Johannes Fehrle, '"Zombies Don't Recognize Borders": Capitalism, Ecology, and Mobility in the Zombie Outbreak Narrative', *Amerikastudien/American Studies* (2016), 527–44.
2. Chris Harman, *Zombie Capitalism: Global Crisis and the Relevance of Marx* (Toronto: Haymarket Books, 2010); David R. Castillo, David Schmid, David A. Reilly and John Edgar Browning, *Zombie Talk: Culture, History, Politics* (London: Palgrave Pivot, 2016), pp. 39–62.
3. Fehrle, 'Zombies Don't Recognize Borders'.
4. James F. Thompson, 'The Rise of the Zombie in Popular Culture', in Amy L. Thompson and Antonio S. Thompson (eds), *...But if a Zombie Apocalpse Did Occur* (Lanham MD: McFarland, 2015), pp. 11–25.
5. See the edited collection, Laura Hubner, Marcus Leaning and Paul Manning (eds), *The Zombie Renaissance in Popular Culture* (Basingstoke: Palgrave Macmillan, 2014).
6. Karl Marx and Friedrich Engels, *The Manifesto of the Communist Party*, *www.marxists.org/archive/marx/works/1848/communist-manifesto/index.html* (last accessed 1 March 2025).
7. Slavoj Žižek (ed.), *Mapping Ideology* (London: Verso, 1994).
8. Rodrigo Gonsalves, 'Groundwork for Monstrous Materialism: (In)humanity and the Uncanniness of Our Everyday Life (unpublished PhD, Universidade de São Paulo, 2021).
9. Marx and Engels, *The Manifesto of the Communist Party*, p. 353.
10. Gonsalves, 'Groundwork for Monstrous Materialism', pp. 111–16.
11. Karl Marx, *Capital* (London: New Left Review and Penguin Books, 1982 [1867]), pp. 342–416.
12. Marx, *Capital*, p. 342.
13. Mark Neocleous, 'The Political Economy of the Dead Marx's Vampires', *History of Political Thought*, 24/4 (2003), 672–5.
14. Ian Wright, 'Prolegomena to a Demonology of Capitals' (2020), *https://ianwrightsite.wordpress.com/2020/03/05/prologomena-to-a-demonology-of-capitalism/* (last accessed 1 March 2025); Ian Wright, 'What is Abstract Labour and Who Does the Abstracting? (2020), *https://ianwrightsite.wordpress.com/2020/06/13/what-is-abstract-labour-and-who-does-the-abstracting/* (last accessed 1 March 2025).
15. Mark Fisher, *Capitalist Realism: Is There No Alternative?* (Winchester: Zero Books, 2009).

16. Fredric Jameson, *Representing Capital: A Commentary on Volume One* (London: Verso Books, 2014), p. 13.
17. Jameson, *Representing Capital*, p. 19.
18. As Jameson explains: 'figuration, as we have seen, is capable of arresting the effects of nomination and reappropriating them for a new moment of dialectical awareness. For another, the very structure of binary oppositions which would seem to condemn thought to a perpetual repetition of stereotypical dualisms contains mechanisms which can be turned against its own traditional ideological dynamic to short-circuit it and produce a more complex and historical awareness in its place.' (Jameson, *Representing Capital*, p. 15)
19. Gonsalves, 'Groundwork for Monstrous Materialism'.
20. Susan Buck-Morss, *Hegel, Haiti, and Universal History* (Pittsburgh PA: University of Pittsburgh Press, 2009), pp. 52–5.
21. Buck-Morss, *Hegel, Haiti, and Universal History*, p. 35.
22. Buck-Morss, *Hegel, Haiti, and Universal History*, p. 35.
23. Simone Weil, *Oppression et liberté* (Paris: Gallimard), translated as *Oppression and Liberty*, Arthur Wills and John Petrie (trans.) (London: Routledge & Kegan Paul, 1958), p. 43.
24. T. Adorno and M. Horkheimer, *Dialectics of Enlightenment: Philosophical Fragments* (Stanford CA: Stanford University Press, 1987), pp. 90–4.
25. Robert Pfaller, *Interpassivity: The Aesthetics of Delegated Enjoyment* (London: Edinburgh University Press, 2017).
26. George A. Romero's trilogy: *The Night of the Living Dead* (1968), *Dawn of the Dead* (1978) and *Day of the Dead* (1985).
27. This line of argument corroborates Fisher's capitalist realism endeavour on *Wall-E* and *Avatar*, which instead of subjectivising people towards the social political causes that they portray, simply produce its opposite reaction: de-mobilising the people and their struggles. Of course, the arts can surely mobilise new symbolic positions against capitalist domination, but there are also cultural productions that simply, critically help, if problematised as ideological portrayals. Alain Badiou, *Being and Event* (London: Continuum, 2005), pp. 14–18.
28. Kojin Karatani, *The Structure of World History* (London: Duke University Press, 2014), pp. 279–80.
29. See more in John Quiggin, *Zombie Economics: How Dead Ideas Still Walk Among Us* (Princeton NJ, United States: Princeton University Press, 2010).
30. Karatani, *The Structure of World History*, pp. 279.
31. Étienne Balibar, 'Towards a New Critique of Political Economy: From Generalized Surplus Value to Total Subsumption', in Peter Osborne, Éric Alliez and

Eric-John Russell (eds), *Capitalism: Concept, Idea, Image – Aspects of Marx's 'Capital' Today* (Kingston: CRMEP Books, 2017), pp. 36–57.

32. Balibar, 'Towards a New Critique of Political Economy', p. 52.
33. As Emma Tonkin has pointed out, in a sense they are a *reductio ad absurdum* of the concept of society eating itself, or perhaps the survival-of-the-fittest refinement. Indeed, they are great points to be considered here.
34. Alenka Zupančič, *What is Sex?* (Cambridge MA: MIT Press, 2017), pp. 1–20.
35. Slavoj Žižek, *The Parallax View* (Cambridge MA: MIT Press, 2009), p. 21.
36. Wright, 'Prolegomena to a Demonology of Capitalism'.
37. Benjamin Noys, 'Between Two Vampires' (unpublished conference paper), *www.academia.edu/30913519/Between_Two_Vampires* (last accessed 1 March 2025).

14

Race, Class and the Goal of the Dead

Marginalised Identities in French Zombie Cinema

Reece Goodall

SINCE THE TURN of the twenty-first century, France has seen a considerable upsurge in the production of horror media, a surprising development given a historical national disinterest in the genre on the production level.[1] Over the past twenty-five years, filmmakers have increasingly drawn on the grammar of horror, making films ranging from brutal art cinema to distinct genre products, thus generating a noticeable (if still small) cycle of funding and creative opportunities within the genre. France has become an important site for the horror genre, making a number of significant contemporary texts (such as *Haute tension* [Alexandre Aja, 2003] and *Grave* [Julia Ducournau, 2016]) and producing figures associated with the genre on both a national and international level. There are far from enough texts to clearly delineate dominant sub-genres, but an analysis of the corpus since the turn of the millennium is instructive: it suggests that, despite no formal organisation, French horror filmmakers have tended towards the zombie and its associated imagery.[2] Of the approximately 100 horror films in this corpus, there are nine explicit zombie films and many more that employ zombie imagery,[3] amounting to around one-third of the entire output in this period.[4] Indeed, one of these films, Michel Hazanavicius' *Coupez!* (2022), used the filming of a zombie movie as its narrative drive for a meta horror-comedy, attracting great critical reception in the process. The presence of the zombie is a surprising development, and one that warrants analysis, because it indicates that the monster has clear pertinence to contemporary France.

That the zombie is a body onto which sociocultural concerns can be projected and read is far from a new observation;[5] indeed, as Peter Dendle notes in his work on zombie cinema, the zombie often functions as a 'barometer of cultural anxiety'.[6] Scholarship has typically focused on the US zombie film, most notably in relation to the works of George A. Romero, the so-called 'Father of the Zombie Film': his canonical *Night of the Living Dead* (United States, 1968) has been discussed in terms of sociocultural changes in the United States during the 1960s, particularly given the casting of African-American actor Duane Jones in the lead role, while there is much work on the ways that the shopping mall-set *Dawn of the Dead* (United States/Italy, 1978) satirically reflects consumer culture. Romero's work has proven a fertile ground for scholars to read the zombie in terms of race and class, readings I discuss further later in this chapter; indeed, the film considered the first in the zombie subgenre, Victor Halperin's *White Zombie* (United States, 1932), evokes the notion of race in its title. That much of the writing and case studies on zombie cinema are US-centric is unsurprising, given the predominance of American film and criticism, but this is not to say that there is no work dealing with zombies in other national contexts, including Italy, Japan and Cuba. The idea of zombie pandemics has also taken on an increased global significance during the COVID-19 pandemic and associated health measures to contain it.[7]

Although there exist examples of scholarship specifically concerned with individual zombie films in the contemporary period in France,[8] there has not thus far been a reading of French zombie cinema that attempts to connect the creature with wider societal concerns in the nation. Therefore, through a close reading of the film *Goal of the Dead* (Thierry Poiraud/Benjamin Rocher, 2014), this chapter will build on Dendle's description of the zombie to bring out some of the collective anxieties surrounding identity in France, and explore the ways that the zombie in this film can be read as their articulation. I will analyse the narrative trajectories of three of the main characters, and some of the villainous characters, with a view to their wider ideological potentials, and consider how the film's narrative eschews simple binaries of self/other and city/rural to present a space in which contemporary discourse about race and class is troubled. I contend that the resolution of French zombie narratives may also provide a form of catharsis for a national audience, by presenting a space in which sociocultural concerns about marginal identities are articulated, acknowledged and (to a certain extent) addressed.

In *Goal of the Dead*, the Parisian football team is on tour and heads to the small town of Caplongue to play a friendly game. One of the team's star players, Sam Lorit (Alban Lenoir), is from the town, and he receives a hostile welcome from its inhabitants for his perceived betrayal in transferring to a major team years ago. His misery is compounded by one of his teammates, rising star Idriss Diago (Ahmed Sylla), trying to steal the limelight and the appearance of a young woman, Cléo (Tiphaine Daviot), who claims to be his daughter. His former teammate and one of the local players, Jeannot (Sebastien Vandenberghe), is injected with infected steroids before the match, sending him on a violent rampage as he heads to the stadium to confront Lorit. When he arrives, the virus quickly spreads to both players and spectators, and the few uninfected humans work together to survive.

The film touches on questions of immigration and assimilation on the bus on the way to Caplongue, the team's coach Coubert (Patrick Ligardes) expresses annoyance that his three Asian players haven't yet learned French, meaning he is unable to communicate with them. One of them is left behind on a pit stop and killed by the zombie Jeannot but, despite the coach's repeated references to the value of teamwork and coming together as one throughout the film, he actually doesn't realise that he is missing a player until they reach the stadium. Although the sequence is played for comedy, it also works to highlight concerns over integration – the Asian players are unable to communicate in French and are therefore not regarded by the coach as truly part of the team. Similarly, all of the of the players are named Park and played by deliberately visually similar actors, comedically conforming to a conservative view of immigrants as 'all the same' (a view only espoused by Coubert, who is regarded as old-fashioned by several of the other characters). The symbolism of football as a site of integration and as a representation of the nation is much discussed in both scholarship and the French media, particularly after France's national team won the 1998 World Cup with a culturally and racially diverse team, seemingly heralding 'une nouvelle ère de fraternité "black-blanc-beur"' ('a new era of "black-white-beur" brotherhood'). The team's success was, as Vinay Swamy writes, 'the perfect mediator [for] bridging the widening gap between mainstream French society and those who found themselves – politically, economically, socially, culturally, and even spatially – in its margins',[9] although the extent to which this is an accurate reflection has been questioned after the 2002 electoral success of Jean-Marie Le Pen and the *banlieue* riots of 2005.[10] Coubert expresses annoyance that the three Parks do not speak French nor understand the rules he sets out for the team (by putting on their studded boots on the coach, for example), but this annoyance never becomes outright hostility. It is never implied that he dislikes the Parks because of their racial difference, and it should be underlined that Idriss is a major part of his team: the implied reading of Coubert's attitude is less racial resentment than the need for integration and, by stressing the values of teamwork, cooperation and unity.

Although there are references to Idriss's racial and national identity in the film, he is respected by members of his team as a football player and idolised by several of the Caplongue residents, indicating that we should not read his racial difference as threatening. His rivalry with Lorit is in fact centred on age and physical prowess rather than race. Frequently, his character is played for laughs, such as in sequence where he distracts Béné (Joana Person), a female zombie (who was formerly a living fan) with an elaborate dance. His panicked whimpers, jerky body language and high-pitched scream all indicate that Idriss should be read as comedic and particularly unthreatening, with his use as a distraction a contrast to his action-focused companion Michel (Benoît Moret). This scene, although not narratively racially charged, does however seem to evoke the character of the minstrel and suggests that Idriss's value is in his ability to perform for a white audience (in the football match, for the zombified Béné and Michel and, ultimately, for the audience). Similarly, in the film's climactic battle with the zombies, Idriss's exaggerated screams about being left behind by Lorit are used to introduce some comedic relief into the scene. However, his actions reinforce a dynamic identified by Donald Bogle: discussing interracial buddy pairs in popular Hollywood cinema, he notes that 'such movie friendships have usually held to one dictum: namely, that interracial buddies can be such only when the white buddy is in charge'.[14] Idriss is not coded as threatening to the viewer because in all his partnerships, he is distinctly powerless: his agent Marco (Bruno Salomone) controls his wealth; Michel knows the stadium and the area; Lorit is the protagonist and he has a family, as opposed to Idriss's single life. A conversation between Caplongue residents towards the film's opening, although also played for comedy, indicates that any potential threat embodied by Idriss is not because of his race or ethnic identity, but rather a more geographically French difference. Idriss's character does evoke certain aspects of power relations between races and the construction of black identity within media, but *Goal of the Dead* explicitly states that it is his Parisian identity that renders him problematic for the Caplonguians, and I suggest that this is a more useful place to explore the ideological underpinnings inherent in this film.

The Caplongue fans run through a potential chant for the match: 'Paris, ville capitale/Paris, que de banale/Paris, ville le lumière/Paris, que de misère' ('Paris, capital city/Paris, such banality/Paris, city of light/Paris, such misery'). The fans all enjoy these lyrics and are impressed at the writing craft, but it is the subsequent one that causes them some consternation, specifically the line 'vous sauriez á rien sans l'ivoirien' ('you wouldn't know anything without the Ivorian'). The fans have a discussion about whether referring to Idriss's nationality is racist, and whether he should be denounced as an Ivorian or as Senegalese in the chant. In the end, there is broad agreement not to use a slur for two reasons: the fans don't want to provide negative press to Caplongue by falling in with a stereotype that the small town is racist and, importantly, because Idriss's nationality is not ultimately that relevant to them. They dislike Idriss 'parce qu'il est Parisien, pas parce qu'il est Sengelin' ('because he's Parisian, not because he's Senegalese'). The issue is not that Idriss represents racial difference, but rather than he embodies Paris and the connotations of the big city. The group's chant is later played on the stadium's speaker system at the film's climax, as is an announcement that Caplongue is to play, causing the zombies to assemble at the stadium and appearing to pacify them to an extent, meaning they do not immediately attack the living characters. The zombies are only inhabitants of Caplongue (the Parisians are all killed rather than zombified), and the pacifying effect of acknowledging their town indicates that the threat of the undead here could also be read in terms of violently asserting regional identity. Thus, despite references to ethnic identity in *Goal of the Dead*, the film's major focus is clearly identifiable in another oppositional relationship: that of Paris and Caplongue, which can be read as a divide between the big city and a small rural town or, in more ideological terms, between progress and seeming stagnation.[12] *Goal of the Dead* is a comedy-horror, and it shares this thematic concern with other contemporary comedies, including *Bienvenue chez les ch'tis* (Dany Boon, France, 2008) and *La famille Bélier* (Eric Lartigau, France/Belgium, 2014).[13] On the former film, Raphaëlle Moine writes that 'the alterity portrayed in *Bienvenue chez les Ch'tis* is a regional alterity within a strictly national framework'.[14] Such an observation is pertinent to my analysis of French horror: rather than comedically juxtaposing two different ideas of French identity, the films elicit horror by asking about the conflicts between regional identities, and whether the overarching identity of being French can and does encompass all its citizens when these differences exist within French borders.

This narrative of belonging (in particular, to the small town) is evoked twice in *Goal of the Dead*: in Lorit's choice to leave Caplongue for the opportunities offered by the Parisian team and his subsequent reflection on this decision during the zombie outbreak, and in the suggestion that Michel must pass an initiation ritual in which he disavows Paris (the place of his birth) to prove himself a true Caplonguian. The contrast between the two areas is highlighted in their respective introductions. Lorit first appears on the Parisian coach, which is vibrant, fitted with technology and full of bright reds and blues as travels down a sunny road, whereas Michel is on a decrepit-looking car, surrounded by litter and the blocky grey stadium. There is a fence outside the stadium that bisects the shot, suggestive of both a hostility to the outside (something the residents clearly show to the Parisian team) but also containment and segregation: the issues of Caplongue, or of the rural town, are confined to these locations. This is a stark contrast to the flawless road that bisects shots of the Parisian coach, implying movement (linked to opportunity) and connecting infrastructure to the city. The scene is cloudy, the colour scheme is grey and muted: a title on screen identifies this scene as Caplongue, the second time despite the fact we have already watched several scenes set there, and it suggests that this deprivation is how Poiraud and Rocher seek to define the rural. Thus, the contrast between the two sets of shot composition and *mise-en-scène* accentuates the disparity between the rural and the city, a disparity that is implicitly linked (through Lorit) to the transfer of talent and money: this is implied further by the construction of the two bisected frames, with the Parisian coach on the top half and the Caplongue car on the bottom, indicating a power dynamic in which Paris and the rural are different: the threat of the zombie emerges from a place that is clearly defined as 'left behind', evoking the French word *revenant*. However, the fact that Michel is only Parisian on a technicality (his mother, a Caplonguian, went into labour while in Paris) and his protestations about whether he should be considered as such seem to suggest a certain fickleness to fixed regional identifications, and force the audience to ask whether there is a significant difference between the city and the rural. *Goal of the Dead* uses this sequence to highlight the disparity between the city and the rural, while stressing that the distinction is one of reputation and characterisation rather than any significant different in value systems.

Carol J. Clover has discussed the relationship between the rural (country) and the city in US horror, finding that a transition from the (sub)urban environment to the country, likening it a fairy-tale trope of a character leaving their village and finding danger in the 'deep, dark forest'. She writes that, in horror, the rural 'is a place where the rules of civilization do not obtain. People from the city are people like us. People from the country (… the threatening rural Other) are people not like us'.[15] She then identifies numerous signifiers that separate the rural villains from the urban heroes: the rural Other is mostly characterised by groups of men, an emphasis on its own social rules and, importantly, they are obviously poor (particularly in relation to the main characters). They live in squalor, drive old cars and they work in menial jobs or not at all. Clover's analysis here calls this opening sequence of *Goal of the Dead* to mind, as the wealth and status of the Parisians is contrasted with the deprivation of Caplongue and the gang that contains Michel as a member. As Lorit has moved from his hometown to Paris, it evokes a major implication for the city/country split: that the poverty and destruction of the rural has been caused by the comforts of the city, as talent and resources are attracted away. Social class is an important subtext of what Clover terms the 'urbanoia' film, and there is potential for horror because, when the city enters the domain of the rural, it is possible that the rural will subvert the city-rural relationship by taking over the role of exploiter. Economic guilt linked to inequality and a class exploitation drives these films, and one way for the city to reduce its sense of culpability is to portray the rural residents as literal monsters.[16] Of course, this horror construction relies on a fundamental assumption: that the viewer is of a background more akin to that of the urban character, and thus they will identify with them in face of the horror of the rural. In the case of monstrous hillbillies and redneck rapists that appear in Clover's corpus, this is a fair assumption, but I argue that *Goal of the Dead* eschews such simplistic characterisation.

The film's opening shots, intercut with the title cards, are a flash-forward from the midpoint of the narrative, as the first zombie attack begins. We see a number of figures standing on a football pitch, and we can hear muffled cries and loud banging in the background. The figures are shadowy and, although we can infer that they are football players, there is no indication as to their team (or whether they are all teammates at all). The opening shot, then, is one of a group in its most basic form, allowing the viewer no point of identification with a single figure. We follow with a shot of a riot on the pitch: the figures are running, and the viewer can hear screaming and swearing. There is a shot of people screaming as a figure attacks, able to vomit at them despite them being separated by a wire fence. A hulking figure walks, his back to the camera, and then there is a cut to a street, which is covered with destroyed and abandoned cars (evoking, once again, imagery of real-life riots). The final shot in the opening sequence sees (although they are not yet identified) Lorit and his daughter Cléo hiding in a bar and commenting on the events, describing it as an '*emeute*' and '*pas normale*' ('riot', 'not normal'), before Lorit cracks a joke linking it to football riots. Through stylistic techniques and evocation of real-life events, this sequence works to create an idea of the group as threatening, linking it with violence and destruction (and, through Lorit's joke, football), but it also gives no indication of who the group actually is within the world of the film. Thus, *Goal of the Dead*'s opening seems to operate on two levels. By using imagery of *banlieue* riots and jokingly equating the group threat with the football hooligan, it suggests that the film will conform to a conservative reading of the group threat as a race and/or class allegory. However, the deliberate choice to not identify the group or any of the human characters forces the viewer to consciously question any immediate identification: if we understand the group as representing racial diversity or those in lower classes, seeing them as threatening because of their lack of identity and representation in this sequence makes us complicit in the processes of Othering. This opening plays on assumptions, constructing the premise of a group threat before using the film to challenge our preconceptions and relations to the Other.

Goal of the Dead works to align the Caplongue residents with the zombies even before Jeannot reaches the stadium and begins the epidemic. As the fans sing their Caplongue football chant, it is cross-cut with shots of the zombified Jeannot running through a forest, implying a link between the zombies and the assertion of Caplongue's identity (and as a force to challenge Paris). The opening sequence has encouraged the viewer to be wary of threatening groups, and the first such example we see of a group is when the Parisian team arrives at Caplongue. As the team disembarks from the coach, the Caplonguians jeer at them: a majority of the supporters are wearing identical red and white make-up, thus encouraging us to read the crowds in terms of shared purpose rather than individuality. This is not a collection of individuals at this point, but rather a mass of people that define themselves solely through their location and regional identity. However, *Goal of the Dead* then works to humanise this crowd, as the journalist Solène (Charlie Bruneau) speaks to a number of them, asking about the town, the football game and their reactions to Lorit's return.

These shots are framed as news interviews, an important stylistic choice for a number of reasons: the framing separates individuals from the group, thereby decreasing the threat that the group initially appeared to pose and challenging the viewer's assumptions that such a group would be a source of concern. Although we do not learn the names of these characters, the viewer can recognise some of them as they are attacked and zombified in Jeannot's attacks on the stadium, meaning the coding of the threat cannot be read simply in terms of urbanoia. By providing us with these interviews as well as introducing us to Cléo and Michel's gang earlier on, *Goal of the Dead* presents sympathetic and negative characters on both sides of the city/rural divide, indicating that its ideological concerns cannot be read simply in terms of how the two sides are characterised (something implied further by Lorit's and Michel's conflicted statuses as both Parisian and Caplonguian), but rather in how they react to events in the narrative. Importantly, too, news framing implies authenticity and documentation, suggesting that these shots indicate a more genuine picture of Caplongue (and, consequently, the rural town), one that is defined more by good-natured individuals of all ages rather than threatening mobs. The viewer's prejudices are contrasted with a framing that is construed as 'true' or 'real', challenging an urbanoia assumption that rural implies bad or deficient by presenting the residents of Caplongue as people just like us.

The film's sympathy towards Caplongue is indicated in the narrative arc of Lorit. His conflict is that of living a city life while confronting his rural upbringing, bringing him into conflict with his estranged daughter and father. However, rather than asserting his new Parisian status, Lorit is able to survive and defeat the zombies by acknowledging and reasserting his rural nature. In confrontation with the zombified Jeannot, seemingly the leader of the horde (suggesting that football can be an indicator of regional as well as national identity), Lorit tells him that Paris is a terrible place and that Caplongue is their home: gentle piano music indicates that this is a moment of emotional importance and serves to simplify Lorit's statement to its most basic. This recourse to only the piano, the only time in the film that such basic instrumentation is used, is markedly different from the rest of the score, which is characterised by lots of bass notes and low instrumentation, contributing to a sinister atmosphere and exacerbating the threat of the undead. The zombies have been identified by low, aggressive music and, by removing this from the soundscape as Lorit makes amends with Jeannot, it implies to the viewer that the zombie threat is negated by this act of recognition. There is no need for the soundtrack to represent the zombies when Lorit finally does so. Although Idriss uses the moment to stab Jeannot in the back and kill him, it is not violence that succeeds so much as it is acknowledgement of the factors driving Jeannot to anger. Jeannot was a threat to Lorit because he represented a past and a location that he tried to forget and ignore, and a friendship that was broken because Lorit spurned him to go to Paris. As the Caplongue fans praise Jeannot as their best player and a symbol of the town, it is clear that he should be read as an embodiment of the town: his narrative is concluded not by killing Lorit (and, symbolically, the city in Paris), but through being recognised. It is through his acceptance of his rural identity that Lorit is able to pacify the threat posed by Jeannot and the Caplonguians. If we read the zombie threat as symbolising the 'left behind' in French society, the ending makes clear that the best way to contend with this societal divide is implicitly to acknowledge and address their concerns.

At this point, it would be instructive to deconstruct the supposed villain role played by Dr Belvaux (Philippe du Janerand), Jeannot's father and the man who begins the zombie outbreak by injecting his son with a contaminated drug. As this drug is delivered to Belvaux's house, the delivery man drops two parcels and confuses them. It is heavily implied that the parcel Belvaux receives is by mistake, and that he intended to inject his son with steroids. Jeannot states that he wants to win the game, and is told by Dr Belvaux that the game should in fact be about revenge (for his abandonment by Lorit or, in a wider sense, for Lorit's move to Paris and the detrimental impact it had on Caplongue): although the footballer indicates that beating Paris will be sufficient for him and for the town to ease the collective trauma represented by Lorit's departure, it is Belvaux's actions that ultimately spur the narrative. It is not enough to defeat Paris – rather, Caplongue must succeed at the cost of Paris and, specifically, at the cost of Lorit for having chosen the city over Caplongue. Belvaux is a villain because of his zero-sum mentality, believing that Caplongue's success must necessarily come with the fall of Paris, rather than concurring with his son's belief that strengthening Caplongue's reputation is a more sensible approach to resolving this historical opposition. *Goal of the Dead* uses Lorit as a tool to suggest the fallibility of a system that transfers talent and money to cities at the cost of rural towns – in Dr Belvaux, we see a condemnation of a mentality that would protect the rural at the cost of the city. By criticising both these extremes, the film implies its true political stance: that the best outcome for France is one in which city and rural are both successful, and part of a wider French cultural fabric.

Lorit and Michel's narrative arcs are contrasted in part with that of Idriss, who is the Parisian team's star player, and his agent Marco. The agent is one of the film's least sympathetic characters: he wears a suit (differentiating him from any of the other characters); he has an oppositional relationship with the comedic, and thus sympathetic, Coubert and openly expresses distaste for the coach's ethos of teamwork and unity; his facial expressions are continually smirks and winces; and he is a narrative coward, leaving characters to die on several occasions in order to save his own life. Marco first appears in the locker room, as Coubert briefs his team before the Paris-Caplongue football game, with news for Idriss that he will soon be able to transfer to London. Introducing him in this way brings him into conflict with the coach, who is stressing the value of teamwork and unity, implying that the transfer of talent in this way can prove detrimental to the team (and, as we have seen, teams take on the symbolic value of locations too). Importantly, we later learn that Idriss himself is a symbol of this movement from rural to city: as Michel and Idriss are passing through the underside of the stadium, Idriss mentions that he is from the Val d'Oise, not Paris. It is implied that Idriss's success in Paris enables Marco to demand a €35 million transfer fee for him, essentially stripping away his identity to focus on his economic value. In the locker room discussion, Marco is annoyed that Coubert will play Idriss as a striker because it risks lowering Idriss's financial value; Coubert, on the other hand, sees Idriss in terms of his collective value to the team. Similarly, after Coubert takes Marco into a gym to hide from the undead hordes, the coach's frustration grows until he demands a fight: he gives Marco a chance to fight on even terms, citing good sporting values and fair play, and Marco responds by punching him in the face. *Goal of the Dead* is fundamentally a film about belonging and relationships in opposition to the transfer of talent and money, and Marco represents the negative half of this opposition. He has only two major character relations in the film – Coubert, who he clearly does not respect and whose values he derides, and Idriss, who is useful and valued only as long as he has monetary value to Marco. Although Idriss (prior to renouncing his Parisian identity) is on friendly terms with his agent, Marco is ultimately happy to sacrifice him simply because his playing career only has a few years left. Marco is the embodiment of a system that moves money and resources from poorer and underdeveloped areas to larger, more financially successful cities, and this is one of the issues that necessitates the outcry represented by the zombie outbreak. *Goal of the Dead* does not cast the Caplonguians or the Parisians as outright villains, meaning we cannot impugn either side for the conditions in which they live. However, by making Marco a representative of a system of economic mobility and ensuring that his character is so unpleasant, the film instead vilifies a mentality that prizes economic success above all else, ignoring large swathes of France because they are under-resourced and thus contributing to a worsening situation. As we have seen, the zombies have been coded as sympathetic and their motives understandable, but great care is taken to render Marco unsympathetic: the zombies are merely the symptoms of a socio-economic problem, a problem represented by Marco. The moment when he is eventually consumed by the zombies is consequently a cathartic experience for the viewer.

Goal of the Dead ends with the survivors in the back of a truck, being driven away from Caplongue as the army arrive. Idriss jokingly asks Cléo whether she has seen the Eiffel Tower, to which she fails to respond. Michel talks about how he'd like to see it, and starts to describe the sophistication of its construction – Idriss, in exasperation, asks whether he ever stops talking, at which point the film ends. Concluding with such a blunt dismissal, as the conversation is on the subject of a building that instantly suggests Paris to an audience, is indicative of the film's stance towards the city: there is the implication that Cléo should head to Paris because of its culture, a suggestion that is immediately dismissed (both within the world of the film, and then by the film itself). The Parisian team is all dead, and the only three survivors linked to this side of the narrative – Lorit, Idriss and Solène – have all been disassociated with the city. The death of Marco implies an end to Idriss's transfer to London, and it is implied (and, in the mid-credit scenes, made explicit) that Lorit and Solène will remain in Caplongue, forming a family unit with Cléo. These mid-credit scenes are interesting in that they seem to consolidate the film's ideological stance on the transfer of wealth: we see that Lorit has returned to Caplongue and taken over the local bar. His return has enabled the creation of new jobs, which are held by local people. Although they are still zombies, it is clear that Lorit's return (and a renewed interest in the area, indicated by the news interview framing) has pacified their anger, further cementing the reading that the undead outbreak in this film represents a demand for recognition. Returning to the rural town has established a return to traditional values, as we hear that Lorit is in a partnership with Solène, looking after Cléo and is back on good terms with his (zombified) father. In the first half of the film, we see that Lorit is sleeping around and even mistakes his daughter for a potential sexual partner, and Lenoir's sunken expression indicates that this has not brought the footballer much happiness or satisfaction in his life – this is a marked contrast to Lorit's casual conversational style in these scenes. *Goal of the Dead* implies that, in moving to the city for economic success, Lorit had to sacrifice his cultural and social happiness. The single-minded pursuit of money (as embodied by Marco) is shown to encourage selfishness and devalue human relationships: by casting the city as a place in which wealth exclusively is focused, the film implies the loss of a wider cultural fabric in France. Lorit's narrative arc is resolved by the unification of his success and his rural identity – he is not solely Parisian or Caplonguian, but rather an embodiment of the best elements of both places, united under a single identity. Lorit succeeds in surviving the undead threat and finding happiness not through opposition of identities, but rather through their reconciliation and unification. To be recognised is, ultimately, the goal of the dead.

Discourse built around class concerns and rural/city binaries has only expanded in France since the release of *Goal of the Dead*, and was employed to significant effect by Marine Le Pen in her two presidential runs in 2017 and 2022. The Front National in 2017 ran an anti-globalisation platform and positioned itself as the party of protest against existing and harmful governing structures,[17] appealing to what has been identified as a 'peripheral' France[18] who existed in '*territoires oubliés*' ('forgotten territories').[19] Polls conducted after the first round of the 2017 presidential election showed that Le Pen came first in both the rural communes and among workers.[20] Her vote share among these contemporary figures I read as associated with *revenants* only increased in 2022 to 60 per cent of the rural vote margin after a campaign focused on cost-of-living issues and addressing lack of representation,[21] indicating how resonant this message is to a significant portion of the electorate and demonstrating the increased relevance of the anxieties present in *Goal of the Dead*.

Although I have employed *Goal of the Dead* as an emblematic case study, it is far from unique in its exploration of marginal concerns. The action-horror *La Horde* (Yannick Dahan/Benjamin Rocher, France, 2009) is set in a *banlieue* and clearly engages with similar racial, class and gendered questions to this film, while French horror also offers us a number of more pensive examples of the genre in the form of *Les Revenants* (Robin Campillo, France, 2004) and *La Nuit a dévoré le monde* (Dominique Rocher, France, 2018), which largely eschew violence in favour of exploring the ways that the zombie troubles distinctions (of dead/alive, of self/other) and thus provokes wider questions about the boundaries that form and reinforce identities. French zombie cinema, in all its varying forms, poses questions about personal identities and national contexts, and it is partially through confronting and resolving these questions that the characters are able to survive: the implication is that, in contending with the zombies, the audience is able to undergo a process of recognition of the identities and sociocultural issues that the monster represents. If, as Dendle states, the zombie is a barometer of cultural anxiety, its sheer prevalence in French cinema and the myriad ways that the zombie reflects marginal identities and the left-behind – the *revenants* within its own borders – is indicative of a nation plagued with anxieties about itself.

Notes

1. M. Bey-Rozet, 'Cycles of Death and Rebirth in Twenty-First Century French Horror', *French Screen Studies*, 21/3 (2021), 191–203.
2. I count here traits of the zombie: the eating of flesh, particularly brains; the appearance of a shuffling and bloody communal threat; fears of being consumed by or assimilated into the mob; silence; characters driven solely by consumption. Certain characteristics, framed in certain ways by filmmakers, evoke the zombie even if it is not present in the text.
3. I acknowledge here the difficulties in definitive generic classification as to exactly what constitutes a 'horror' film, particularly in a French context where the label is less freely employed than countries such as the United States.
4. For a full list of the corpus, see R. Goodall, 'Defining Twenty-First-Century French Horror in a Global Media Economy' (PhD thesis, University of Warwick, 2023).
5. See Kyle William Bishop, *American Zombie Gothic: The Rise and Fall (and Rise) of the Walking Dead in Popular Culture* (Jefferson NC: McFarland & Co., 2010); J. J. Cohen, 'Undead (A Zombie Oriented Ontology)', *Journal of the Fantastic in the Arts*, 23/3 (2012), 397–412.
6. P. Dendle, 'The Zombie as Barometer of Cultural Anxiety', in Niall Scott (ed.), *Monsters and the Monstrous* (New York: Rodopi Press, 2007), p. 46.
7. L. Reis Filho, 'No Safe Space: Zombie Film Tropes during the COVID-19 Pandemic', *Space and Culture*, 23/3 (2020), 253–8.
8. To provide some examples: on *Les Revenants,* see D. Pettersen, '*Les Revenants*: Horror in France and the Tradition of the Fantastic', *French Screen Studies,* 21/3 (2021), 239–57; on *La Meute* (Franck Richard, 2010), see Alexandra West, *Films of the New French Extremity: Visceral Horror and National Identity* (Jefferson NC: McFarland & Co., 2016); and on *La Nuit a dévoré le monde,*

see T. Palmer, 'Frontier Poetry: New Adventures in Contemporary French Horror Cinema', *Modern & Contemporary France*, 30/1 (2022), 1–17.

9. Vinay Swamy, *Interpreting the Republic: Marginalization and Belonging in Contemporary French Novels and Films* (Lanham MD: Lexington Books, 2011), p. xv.
10. See P. Ndiaye, 'Pap Ndiaye: "N'attendons pas de la victoire qu'elle change la société"', *Le Monde* (2018), *www.lemonde.fr/idees/article/2018/07/13/pap-ndiaye-n-attendons-pas-de-la-victoire-qu-elle-change-la-societe_5330728_3232.html* (last accessed 2 March 2025).
11. Donald Bogle, *Toms, Coons, Mulattoes, Mammies, & Bucks: An Interpretive History of Blacks in American Films*, 4th edn (New York; London: Continuum, 2003), pp. 271–2.
12. For more on the issues raised by contemporary working classes and the myriad difficulties faced when attempting to define class structures in contemporary France, see Yasmine Siblot, Marie Cartier, Isabelle Coutant, Olivier Masclet and Nicolas Renahy, *Sociologies des classes populaires contemporaines* (Paris: Armand Colin, 2015).
13. The films see a southerner transferred to a northern French post office where she confronts her own prejudices and preconceived ideas, and the only hearing member of a deaf family torn between life on the rural family farm and moving to Paris respectively. Much like *Goal of the Dead*, the tension in these films is linked to clashes between rural and city life.
14. R. Moine, 'Stereotypes of Class, Ethnicity and Gender in Contemporary French Popular Comedy: From *Bienvenue chez les Ch'tis* (2008) and *Intouchables* (2011) to *Qu'est-ce qu'on a fait au Bon Dieu?* (2014)', *Studies in French Cinema*, 18/1 (2018), 38.
15. Carol J. Clover, *Men, Women, and Chain Saws* (Princeton NJ: Princeton University Press, 1992), p. 124.
16. Clover, Men, *Women, and Chain Saws*, pp. 124–37.
17. N. Hewlett, 'The Phantom Revolution: The Presidential and Parliamentary elections of 2017', *Modern and Contemporary France*, 25/4 (2017), 387.
18. Christophe Guilluy, *La France Périphérique* (Paris: Flammarion, 2014).
19. L'Obs, 'Le Pen défend la 'ruralité' face aux banlieues et aux étrangers', *L'Obs* (2017), *www.nouvelobs.com/politique/20170413.AFP1365/le-pen-defend-la-ruralite-face-aux-banlieues-et-aux-etrangers.html* (last accessed 2 March 2025).
20. Y. Surel, 'How to Stay Populist? The Front National and the Changing Party System', *West European Politics*, 42/6 (2019), 1230–57.
21. A. Parsons, 'Why Did Le Pen Reap Record Numbers of Rural Votes?', *Arc2020* (2022), *www.arc2020.eu/france-why-did-le-pen-reap-record-numbers-of-rural-votes/* (last accessed 2 March 2025).

Select Bibliography

Articles

Ambrosius, J. D., and J. M. Valenzano III, '"People in Hell Want Slurpees": The Redefinition of the Zombie Genre through the Salvific Portrayal of Family on AMC's *The Walking Dead*', *Communication Monographs*, 83/1 (2016), 69–93.

Anderson, T. L., and P. J. Hill, 'American Experiment in Anarcho-Capitalism: The Not So Wild, Wild West', *Journal of Libertarian Studies*, 3/1 (1979), 9–29.

Arata, Stephen D., 'The Occidental Tourist: *Dracula* and the Anxiety of Reverse Colonization', *Victorian Studies*, 33/4 (1990), 621–45.

Babaee, Ruzbeh, Sue Yen Lee and Siamak Babaee, 'Ecocritical Survival through Psychological Defense Mechanisms in MR Carey's *The Girl with All the Gifts*', *Journal of Science Fiction*, 1/2 (2016), 47–55.

Baić, V., O. Lajić and Z. Ivanović, 'Sexual Fantasies of the Rapists', *Trames: A Journal of the Humanities and Social Sciences*, 23/4 (2019), 439–54.

Bering, Jesse, 'Perv: The Sexual Deviant in All of Us', *Scientific American*, 66/12 (2013), 155.

Bey-Rozet, M., 'Cycles of Death and Rebirth in Twenty-First Century French Horror', *French Screen Studies*, 21/3 (2021), 191–203.

Botting, Fred, 'Undead-Ends: Zombie Debt/Zombie Theory', *Postmodern Culture*, 23/3 (2013).

Boyns, David, and Robert Wonser, 'Between the Living and Undead: How Zombie Cinema Reflects the Social Construction of Risk, the Anxious Self, and Disease Pandemic', *The Sociological Quarterly*, 57 (2016), 628–53.

Canavan, Gerry, '"We Are the Walking Dead": Race, Time, and Survival in Zombie Narrative', *Extrapolation*, 51/3 (2010), 431–53.

Chandler, A., 'Masculinities and Suicide: Unsettling "Talk" as a Response to Suicide in Men', *Critical Public Health*, 32/4 (2022), 499–508.

Choi, Chungmoo, 'Decolonization and Popular Memory: South Korea', *Positions: Asia Critique*, 1/1 (1993), 79.

Christensen, Kyle, 'The Reparative Bite of the Zombie Mouth', *The Velvet Light Trap*, 85 (2020), 4–15.

Cohen, J. J., 'Undead (A Zombie Oriented Ontology)', *Journal of the Fantastic in the Arts*, 23/3 (2012), 397–412.

Connell, R. W., and J. W. Messerschmidt, 'Hegemonic Masculinity: Rethinking the Concept', *Gender & Society*, 19/6 (2005), 829–59.

Cox-George, C., and, S. Bewley, 'I, Sex Robot: The Health Implications of the Sex Robot Industry', *BMJ Sexual & Reproductive Health*, 44/3 (2018), 161–4.

Davies, Thom, Arshad Isakjee and Surindar Dhesi, 'Violent Inaction: The Necropolitical Experience of Refugees in Europe', *Antipode*, 49/5 (2017), 1247.

Demetriou, D. Z., 'Connell's Concept of Hegemonic Masculinity: A Critique', *Theory and Society*, 30/3 (2001), 337–61.

Drezner, Daniel W., 'Metaphor of the Living Dead: Or, the Effect of the Zombie Apocalypse on Public Policy Discourse', *Social Research*, 81/4 (2014), 825–49.

Eco, Umberto, 'The Myth of Superman', *Diacritics*, 2/1 (1972), 14–22.

Fehrle, Johannes, '"Zombies Don't Recognize Borders": Capitalism, Ecology, and Mobility in the Zombie Outbreak Narrative', *Amerikastudien/American Studies*, 61/4 (2016), 527–44.

Harvey, Lauren J., Caroline Hunt and Fiona A. White, 'Dialectical Behaviour Therapy for Emotion Regulation Difficulties: A Systematic Review', *Behaviour Change*, 36/3 (2019), 143–64.

Hewlett, N., 'The Phantom Revolution: The Presidential and Parliamentary Elections of 2017', *Modern and Contemporary France*, 25/4 (2017), 387.

Jenzen, Olu, 'The Queer Uncanny', *Gender: Power and Authority*, 9 (2007), 9.

Jones, Steve, 'Gender Monstrosity Deadgirl and the Sexual Politics of Zombie-Rape', *Feminist Media Studies*, 6/2 (2012), 1–15.

Jones, Steve, 'Porn of the Dead: Necrophilia, Feminism, and Gendering the Undead', *Feminist Media Studies*, 6/2 (2012), 1–15.

Kabalek, Kobi, 'Ghosts, Vampires, Zombies', *Handbuch Sozialwissenschaftliche Gedächtnisforschung* (2022), 13–19.

Kim, Jaecheol, 'Biocalyptic Imaginations in Japanese and Korean films: Undead Nation-States in *I Am a Hero* and *Train to Busan*', *Inter-Asia Cultural Studies*, 20/3 (2019), 437–51.

Kirshner, Lewis. A., 'Rethinking Desire: The *Objet Petit A* in Lacanian Theory', *Journal of the American Psychoanalytic Association*, 53/1 (2005), 83–102.

Kwon, Heonik, 'Korean War Mass Graves', *Necropolitics: Mass Graves and Exhumations in the Age of Human Rights* (2015), 76–91.

Laue, Cheyenne, 'Familiar and Strange: Gender, Sex, and Love in the Uncanny Valley', *Multimodal Technol: Interact*, 1/1 (2017), 2.

Lee, Sung-ae, 'The New Zombie Apocalypse and Social Crisis in South Korean Cinema', *Coolabah*, 27 (2019).

Liu, Yen-Lian, 'The Masculine Masquerade of Superheroes in Watchmen', *Gender Forum*, 62 (2017), 39–65.

McGlotten, Shaka, 'Zombie porn: Necropolitics, Sex, and Queer Socialities', *Porn Studies*, 1/4 (2014), 364.

McNeillie, Natalie, and John Rose, 'Vicarious Trauma in Therapists: A Meta-Ethnographic Review', *Behavioural and Cognitive Psychotherapy*, 49/4 (202), 426–40.

Meszaros, J., 'American Men and Romance Tourism: Searching for Traditional Trophy Wives as Status Symbols of Masculinity', *Women's Studies Quarterly* (2017), 225–42.

Moine, R., 'Stereotypes of Class, Ethnicity and Gender in Contemporary French Popular Comedy: From *Bienvenue chez les Ch'tis* (2008) and *Intouchables* (2011) to *Qu'est-ce qu'on a fait au Bon Dieu?* (2014)', *Studies in French Cinema*, 18/1 (2018), 38.

Muriel, Daniel, and Garry Crawford, 'Video Games and Agency in Contemporary Society', *Games and Culture*, 15/2 (2020), 138–57.

Palmer, T., 'Frontier Poetry: New Adventures in Contemporary French Horror Cinema', *Modern & Contemporary France*, 30/1 (2022), 1–17.

Patton, Michael. S., 'Masturbation from Judaism to Victorianism', *Journal of Religion and Health*, 24 (1985), 133–46.

Pérez-Latorre, Óliver, 'Post-Apocalyptic Games, Heroism and the Great Recession', *Game Studies*, 19/3 (2019).

Pérez-Latorre, Óliver, *et al.*, 'Recessionary Games: Video Games and the Social Imaginary of the Great Recession (2009–2015)', *Convergence*, 25/5–6 (2019), 884–900.

Pettersen, D., '*Les Revenants*: Horror in France and the Tradition of the Fantastic', *French Screen Studies*, 21/3 (2021), 239–57.

Platts, Todd K., 'Locating Zombies in the Sociology of Popular Culture', *Sociology Compass*, 7/7 (2013), 547–60.

Ratner, Carl, 'Agency and Culture', *Journal for the Theory of Social Behaviour*, 30/4 (2000), 413–34.

Raymen, Thomas, 'Living in the End Times Through Popular Culture: An Ultra-Realist Analysis of *The Walking Dead* as Popular Criminology', *Crime, Media, Culture*, 14/3 (2018), 429–47.

Reis Filho, L., 'No Safe Space: Zombie Film Tropes during the COVID-19 Pandemic', *Space and Culture*, 23/3 (2020), 253–8.

Renner, R. J., 'Zombie Desire, Queerness, and Race in The Girl with All the Gifts', *Revenant Journal*, 55/3 (2021), 165–89.

Rosman, J. P., and J. P. Resnick, 'Sexual Attraction to Corpses: A Psychiatric Review of Necrophilia', *Journal of the American Academy of Psychiatry and the Law Online*, 17/2 (1989), 153–63.

Seligowski, A. V. *et al.*, 'Autonomic Responses to Fear Conditioning Among Women with PTSD and Dissociation', *Depression and Anxiety*, 36/7 (2019), 625–34.

Stratton, Jon, 'Zombie Trouble: Zombie Texts, Bare Life and Displaced People', *European Journal of Cultural Studies*, 14/3 (2011), 265–81.

Sugg, K., '*The Walking Dead*: Late Liberalism and Masculine Subjection in Apocalypse Fictions', *Journal of American Studies*, 49/4 (2015), 793–811.

Surel, Y., 'How to Stay Populist? The Front National and the Changing Party System', *West European Politics*, 42/6 (2019), 1230–57.

Walton, J. L., *et al.*, 'Sometimes Less is More: Establishing the Core Symptoms of PTSD', *Journal of Traumatic Stress*, 30/3 (2017), 254–8.

Wiedmann, T., *et al.*, 'Scientists' Warning on Affluence', *Nature Communications* 11 (2020), 1–10.

Wrenn, M. V., 'Agency and Neoliberalism', *Cambridge Journal of Economics*, 39/5 (2014), 1231–43.

Books (Monographs)

Adorno, T., and Horkheimer, M., *Dialectics of Enlightenment: Philosophical Fragments* (Stanford CA: Stanford University Press, 1987).

Badiou, Alain, *Being and Event* (London: Continuum, 2005).

Bishop, Kyle William, *American Zombie Gothic: The Rise and Fall (And Rise) of the Walking Dead in Popular Culture* (Jefferson NC: McFarland, 2010).

Bogle, Donald, *Toms, Coons, Mulattoes, Mammies, & Bucks: An Interpretive History of Blacks in American films*, 4th edn (New York; London: Continuum, 2003).

Buck-Morss, Susan, *Hegel, Haiti, and Universal History* (Pittsburgh PA: University of Pittsburgh Press, 2009).

Callero, Peter, *The Myth of Individualism: How Social Forces Shape Our Lives*, 2nd edn (Lanham MD: Rowman & Littlefield Publishers, 2013).

Clover, Carol J., *Men, Women, and Chain Saws* (Princeton NJ: Princeton University Press, 1992).

Day, Allison, *Feminism and Pornography after the Sex Wars: Diversifying Pornography* (Berkeley CA: University of California, 2009).

Fisher, Mark, *Capitalist Realism: Is There No Alternative?* (Winchester: Zero Books, 2009).

Friedman, Milton, *Capitalism and Freedom*, 40th anniversary edn (Chicago IL and London: 2002).

Friedman, Milton, and Rose Friedman, *Free to Choose: A Personal Statement* (New York and London: Harcourt Brace Jovanovich, 1980).

Giroux, Henry, *Zombie Politics and Culture in the Age of Casino Capitalism* (New York: Peter Lang, 2011).

Gonsalves, Rodrigo, 'Groundwork for Monstrous Materialism: (In)humanity and the Uncanniness of our Everyday Life' (unpublished PhD, Universidade de São Paulo, 2021).

Guilluy, Christophe, *La France Périphérique* (Paris: Flammarion, 2014).

Haraway, Donna, *Staying with the Trouble: Making Kin in the Chthulucene* (Durham NC: Duke University Press, 2016).

Harman, Chris, *Zombie Capitalism: Global Crisis and the Relevance of Marx* (Toronto: Haymarket Books, 2010).

Hayek, Friedrich, *The Road to Serfdom* (London and New York: Routledge, 1944).

hooks, bell, *Feminism is for Everybody: Passionate Politics* (London: Pluto Press, 2000).

Jameson, Fredric, *Archaeologies of the Future: The Desire Called Utopia and Other Science Fictions* (London and New York: Verso, 2005).

Jameson, Fredric, *Representing Capital: A Commentary of Volume One* (London: Verso Books, 2014).

Karatani, Kojin, *The Structure of World History* (London: Duke University Press, 2014).

Kee, Chera, *Not your Average Zombie: Rehumanizing the Undead from Voodoo to Zombie Walks* (Austin TX: University of Texas Press, 2017).

Kellogg, John Harvey, *Plain Facts for Old and Young* (Battle Creek MI: Battle Creek Sanatorium, 1888).

Kim, Dong-choon, *The Unending Korean War: A Social History* (Durham NC: Duke University Press, 2009).

Kirk, Robert, *Zombies and Consciousness* (Hounslow: Clarendon Press, 2005).

Kristeva, Julia, *Powers of Horror: An Essay on Abjection* (New York: Columbia University Press, 1982).

Kwon, Heonik, *The Other Cold War* (New York: Columbia University Press, 2010).

Marx, Karl, *Capital* (London: New Left Review and Penguin Books [1867], 1982).

Marx, Karl, and Friedrich Engels, *The Manifesto of the Communist Party*, *www.marxists.org/archive/marx/works/1848/communist-manifesto/index.html* (last accessed 1 March 2025).

Pfaller, Robert, *Interpassivity: The Aesthetics of Delegated Enjoyment* (London: Edinburgh University Press, 2017).

Quiggin, John, *Zombie Economics: How Dead Ideas Still Walk Among Us* (Princeton NJ: Princeton University Press, 2010).

Shin, Gi-wook, *Ethnic Nationalism in Korea: Genealogy, Politics, and Legacy* (Stanford CA: Stanford University Press, 2006).

Swamy, Vinay, *Interpreting the Republic: Marginalization and Belonging in Contemporary French Novels and Films* (Lanham MD: Lexington Books, 2011).

Tissot, Samuel. A., *Diseases Caused by Masturbation: Onanism* (New York: Gottfried & Fritz, 2015).

von Mises, Ludwig, *Human Action: A Treatise on Economics* (San Francisco CA: Fox & Wilkes, 1996).

Weil, Simone, *Oppression et liberté* (Paris: Gallimard, 1958).

West, Alexandra, *Films of the New French Extremity: Visceral Horror and National Identity* (Jefferson NC: McFarland, 2016).

Wilson, Julie, *Neoliberalism* (New York and London: Routledge, 2018).

Zupančič, Alenka, *What is Sex?* (Cambridge MA: MIT Press, 2017).

Book Chapters and Edited Collections

Balibar, Étienne, 'Towards a New Critique of Political Economy: From Generalized Surplus Value to Total Subsumption', in Peter Osborne, Éric Alliez and, Eric-John Russell (eds) *Capitalism: Concept, Idea, Image: Aspects of Marx's 'Capital' Today* (Kingston: CRMEP Books, 2017), pp. 36–57.

Casey, Zachary, 'Hyperindividualism', in Z. A. Casey (ed.), *Encyclopedia of Critical Whiteness Studies in Education* (Leiden: Brill, 2020), pp. 279–85.

Castillo, David R., David Schmid, David A. Reilly, John Edgar Browning and David R. Castillo, *Zombie Talk: Culture, History, Politics* (London: Palgrave Pivot, 2016), 39–62.

Dendle, P., 'The Zombie as Barometer of Cultural Anxiety', in Niall Scott (ed.), *Monsters and the Monstrous* (New York: Rodopi Press, 2007).

Ferrandiz, Francisco, and Antonius C. G. M. Robben, 'The Ethnography of Exhumations', in Francisco Ferrandiz and Antonius C. G. M. Robben (eds), *Necropolitics* (Philadelphia PA: University of Pennsylvania Press, 2015), 1–38.

Hubner, Laura, Marcus Leaning and Paul Manning, 'Introduction', in L. Hubner, M. Leaning and P. Manning (eds), *The Zombie Renaissance in Popular Culture* (New York: Palgrave Macmillan, 2015), pp. 3–14.

Jones, Steve, 'Porn of the Dead: Necrophilia, Feminism, and Gendering the Undead', in Cory Rushton and Christopher Moreman (eds), *Zombies Are Us: Essays on the Humanity of the Walking Dead* (Jefferson NC: McFarland, 2011), pp. 40–60.

Kim Kwang-ok, 'Rituals of Resistance: The Manipulation of Shamanism in Contemporary Korea', in Charles F. Keyes, Laurel Kendall and Helen Hardacre (eds), *Asian Visions of Authority: Religion and the Modern States of East and Southeast Asia* (Honolulu: University of Hawaii Press, 1994), pp. 195–219.

Lavin, Melissa F., and Brian M. Lowe, 'Cops and Zombies: Hierarchy and Social Location in *The Walking Dead*', in B. Gurr (ed.), *Race, Gender, and Sexuality in Post-Apocalyptic TV and Film* (New York: Palgrave Macmillan, 2015), pp. 113–24.

Monk, Leland, 'Undead Images, Images of the Undead: *Dracula* on Film', in John Paul Riquelme (ed.), *Dracula: Bram Stoker*, 2nd edn (Boston MA: Bedford/St Martin's, 2016), pp. 496–516.

Wallerstein, Immanuel, 'War in Asia? An Interpretative Essay', in Zheng Yangwen, Hong Liu, Michael Szonyi (eds), *The Cold War in Asia: The Battle for Hearts and Minds* (Boston MA: Brill, 2010), pp. 15–24.

White, Lynn, 'The Historical Roots of Our Ecological Crisis', in Ken Hiltner (ed.), *Ecocriticism: The Essential Reader* (London: Routledge, 2015), pp. 39–46.

Zambaco, D., 'Onanism and Nervous Disorders in Two Little Girls', in G. Rubin (ed.) *Deviations* (London: Routledge, 2011).

Index

also in series

Vera Dika, *Games of Terror: Halloween,* Friday the 13th a*nd the Films of the Stalker Cycle* (2025)

Barbara Chamberlin, Kom Kunyosying and Julia Round (eds), *Horror and Comics* (2025)

Edmund P. Cueva, *Horror in Classical Literature: ' On a Profound and Elementary Principle'* (2024)

Heather O. Petrocelli, *Queer for Fear: Horror Film and the Queer Spectator* (2023)

Jamil Mustafa, *The Blaxploitation Horror Film: Adaptation, Appropriation and the Gothic* (2023)

Agnieszka Kotwasińska, *House of Horrors: Familial Intimacies in Contemporary American Horror Fiction* (2023)

Dawn Keetley and Ruth Heholt (eds), *Folk Horror: New Global Pathways* (2023)

Miranda Corcoran, *Witchcraft and Adolescence in American Popular Culture: Teen Witches* (2022)

Todd K. Platts, Victoria McCollum and Mathias Clasen (eds), *Blumhouse Productions: The New House of Horror* (2022)

Scott Hamilton and Conor Heffernan (eds), *Theorising the Contemporary Zombie: Contextual Pasts, Presents, and Futures* (2022)

Meredith Conti and Kevin J. Wetmore, Jr. (eds), *Theatre and the Macabre* (2022)

Sandra Becker, Megen de Bruin-Molé and Sara Polak (eds), *Embodying Contagion: The Viropolitics of Horror and Desire in Contemporary Discourse* (2021)

Lindsey Decker, *Transnationalism and Genre Hybridity in New British Horror Cinema* (2021)

Stacey Abbott and Lorna Jowett (eds), *Global TV Horror* (2021)

Michael J. Blouin, *Stephen King and American Politics* (2021)

Eddie Falvey, Joe Hickinbottom and Jonathan Wroot (eds), *New Blood: Critical Approaches to Contemporary Horror* (2020)

Darren Elliott-Smith and John Edgar Browning (eds), *New Queer Horror Film and Television* (2020)

Jonathan Newell, *A Century of Weird Fiction, 1832–1937* (2020)

Alexandra Heller-Nicholas, *Masks in Horror Cinema: Eyes Without Faces* (2019)

Eleanor Beal and Jonathan Greenaway (eds), *Horror and Religion: New literary approaches to Theology, Race and Sexuality* (2019)

Dawn Stobbart, *Videogames and Horror: From Amnesia to Zombies, Run!* (2019)

David Annwn Jones, *Re-envisaging the First Age of Cinematic Horror, 1896–1934: Quanta of Fear* (2018)